# The Vilokan Asylum of the Magically and Mentally Deranged (Books 4-6)

ISBN: 9781804675830
Perfect Bound

First published in 2023 by bookvault Publishing, Peterborough, United Kingdom

An Environmentally friendly book printed and bound in England by bookvault, powered by printondemand-worldwide

# THEOPHILUS MONROE

# CHAPTER ONE

I GLANCED UP FROM my book—a collection of Shakespeare's plays—to see Rutherford looking back at me, a pair of my socks dangling from her pinched fingers.

"Why are you holding my socks?"

"Why were they on the floor, Cain?"

I narrowed my eyes. "Because I took them off and left them there."

"It didn't occur to you to put them in a laundry basket?"

I scratched my head. "Honestly, no. I've been wearing socks for centuries. I didn't have a laundry basket until three weeks ago, when I moved in with you."

"What did you do with your socks before, when you lived alone?"

I shrugged. "I took them off and tossed them right in the wash bucket."

Rutherford looked at me with wide eyes, as though I'd just said the stupidest thing she'd ever heard. "Wash bucket? Who the hell has a wash bucket anymore, Cain?"

I smiled. "Washing machines creep me out. I've been washing my clothes in a bucket and drying them on a line for centuries. Why change, now?"

"Because washing machines are a hell of a lot easier, Cain."

"I'm six thousand years old, Rutherford. I don't easily latch on to fads. My ways work for me. Why change just because some newfangled appliance that costs a lot more than a bucket and a washboard is supposed to do the same job I could do by hand?"

Rutherford stared at me blankly for what felt like ten seconds before she started speaking. "It's simple, Cain. Literally, all you do is collect your clothes in a basket. You separate whites from colors. You throw them in the washing machine, add detergent, and push a button."

"My method is just as simple. I throw my clothes in a bucket with soap. Scrub them on a washboard, and hang them on a line. It's not that hard, Rutherford."

"You still aren't explaining why you felt the need to leave your stinky socks sitting on the carpet in the middle of the room."

I smiled. "I get it. This was your apartment first. You think I'm marking my territory?"

Rutherford raised an eyebrow. "Well, you are a dog, Cain."

I smiled. "I'm a werewolf. There's a difference."

"Are you saying that werewolves *don't* mark their territory?"

I scratched my head. Sometimes we did mark our territory. During the full moon, we had a tendency to raise our legs on trees, rocks, or whatever we saw just to let other werewolves know we were there. Still, I would not give Rutherford this one so easily.

"If I were going to mark my territory, it wouldn't be by leaving my socks around. I'd be happy to piss on all my things, though, if that's what it takes for you to recognize what's mine."

Rutherford rolled her eyes, leaned over, and kissed me on the cheek. "Just do me a favor, dear, and try to pick up after yourself. I'm not your mother."

"Good. After last night, I'd sure hope you weren't my mother."

Rutherford shrugged. "The way many people read the Bible, there was Adam, Eve, Cain, Able, and eventually Seth. Somehow y'all had to reproduce. Wouldn't that mean you were all mother fuckers?"

I winced. "First, I hate that word. You know this, Rutherford. Second, that's untrue! What you read in the Bible is the story of one, peculiar, group of people. It's the history of the relationship between the Divine and those who became the Hebrew people. My parents were originally a priest and priestess, living in a temple garden, representing all of humanity before the Almighty. They were not the only people who existed."

Rutherford giggled. "It's cute, you know, when you get defensive. You realize, Cain, you've explained that to me several times before."

I scratched my head. "Sorry. The F-word triggers me."

"It's just a word, Cain. And it's not like it's always existed. It came from a Dutch word, meaning 'to thrust,' and was adapted into English in the early sixteenth century."

I snorted. "I never took you for a linguist, Rutherford."

"I'm not. But I was curious once. I did a Google search for 'the history of the F-word.'"

I laughed. "I suppose I'm a bit old-fashioned."

"You think? Mister 'I do my laundry with a bucket and scrub board' is old-fashioned? I'm shocked!"

I shook my head. "Well, you keep me on my toes. That's a part of what I love about you."

Rutherford smirked. "I didn't realize we were using the L-word now."

"Well, why shouldn't we? We already do the F-word. Shouldn't we be using the L-word? Again, maybe I'm old-fashioned, but I still believe L-wording should come before F-wording. That's the proper order of things."

A little rouge appeared on Rutherford's cheeks. "I feel the same. Since that's the case, out of love, would you mind picking up your socks in the future and tossing them in the basket?"

I nodded. "I think I can manage that."

Rutherford turned to return to whatever she was working on in the kitchen. Then she pivoted and looked back at me over her shoulder. "And while we're at it, please lower the toilet seat when you're done. I sat down on the rim today, and it wasn't clean."

I bit the inside of my cheek. "Ah, yes. Sorry about that, Rutherford."

Rutherford chuckled. "I always aim to please, Cain. All I'm asking is that you'd aim too, please."

I grinned. "It's been a while since I've lived with a woman. Bear with me. I'll adjust soon enough. I promise."

"I'm sure you will. Now, you'd best get up and get yourself dressed. You have a full schedule today, including a new patient at the asylum."

"A new patient, you say? I didn't see that on my schedule."

"He wasn't on your schedule. I just received a text from Annabelle."

I rolled my eyes. Annabelle was the Voodoo Queen. A young and talented mambo. I didn't have a cellular phone so, if she ever needed to reach me, she usually texted Rutherford. "Did she give you any details?"

"A few. She said it's a vampire."

"Another youngling looking to tame his newfound cravings?"

Rutherford shook her head. "Not this time. He came to New Orleans seeking you out specifically. According to Annabelle, he claims to know you."

I bit my lip. I'd met my fair share of vampires through the years. Vampires and Werewolves rarely interacted. Vamps avoided us like the plague. A werewolf's bite can turn a human into one of us. When we bite vampires, though, the wound festers for nearly a hundred years. I'm told it's quite painful. Enough to drive some vampires mad.

"Do you have a name?" I asked.

"Ruthven," Rutherford said. "That's all I know."

My jaw nearly hit the floor. "Lord Ruthven?"

"Well, Annabelle didn't say he was a lord. I suppose that might be the case. He's several centuries old."

I sighed and sat down on my newly purchased La-Z-Boy recliner. Rutherford hated the chair, but it was a necessity. She referred to it as my "man throne," whatever that meant. I didn't know why. I didn't rule anyone. It was a thinking chair. I couldn't recall the last time Lord Ruthven had crossed my mind. It didn't take long to recall those events.

"Why don't you sit down?" I asked. "This is going to take a while to explain."

Rutherford sat down on the couch beside my recliner and crossed her legs. I took a deep breath. If there was one vampire I'd ever met during my existence that I hoped I'd never encounter again, it was Lord Ruthven.

# CHAPTER TWO

**Four Hundred Years Ago**

Over the course of the centuries, I'd never once visited a Scottish castle. Not until that day. It was a modest structure, so far as castles go. The walls were tall, but hardly towering. A moat surrounded the castle, which featured a long but rickety drawbridge. Most castles had long windows, or arrow-slits, but this facility had very few openings at all. Their biggest fear wasn't outsiders, not usually; it was sunlight. It was, perhaps, the only castle I'd ever seen where the greater threat came to those who dared to breach its walls than those who attempted to attack its defenses. The vampires who lived there welcomed ignorant intruders. Convenient meals.

The drawbridge shook as I stepped across it. These vampires knew I was coming. They also knew better than to try and kill me. If they did, well, they'd inherit the seven-fold curse. No one really knew what would happen if a vampire transgressed the Mark of Cain. Would they become werewolves in the same way that a human might? Would they still be vampires at all, or would they turn into a hybrid of the two? Such a monstrosity was difficult to imagine.

The safety of both our kinds—werewolves and vampires—depended on secrecy. The vampires understood as much. They wouldn't dare harm me. If any of them inherited my curse, well, there was no way to predict how such a beast would behave. Anything that threatened the anonymity of the vampire, as much as the werewolf, was a danger to both our kinds.

Lord Ruthven sent for me to exact a truce with a local pack of werewolves. Far be it from me to compromise with vampires. Werewolves didn't need to consume humans to survive. Vampires did. Werewolves were only a threat once every lunar cycle. Vampires were a constant terror to the human race. I had no love lost for vampires. Wolves could be tamed. Vampires, though? Not likely.

I'd never met Ruthven. I didn't know the local pack, nor its alpha—a gentleman who went by the name of William. I wasn't likely to empathize with the vampire's cause, but it was he, not William, who sought my help. I'd promised to hear him out. It was, after all, to the advantage of werewolves and vampires alike that their skirmish be quelled sooner rather than later. More than the wolves and vampires were a threat to one another, an ongoing war between our races threatened to expose both our kinds to the humans.

I entered a dark corridor on the opposite side of the bridge. Someone must've seen me. A cacophony of squeaks and creaks, plus the dimming beam of sunlight that barely illuminated the stone tunnel I was inside, signaled that someone had raised the drawbridge behind me.

"Welcome, Son of Adam," a deep but gravelly voice said from somewhere in the darkness. "Follow my voice. We have much to discuss."

I stepped forward, my feet sticking a little with each step as I moved forward along the damp stone path. "Lord Ruthven?"

No sooner did I speak, and several torches lining the corridor burst into flames. I didn't know the age of this vampire lord. He was apparently ancient enough to gain an ability aligned with fire magic. Over the centuries, after thousands of feedings, vampires could tap into the power latent in human souls.

I saw the vampire, his eyes ablaze, at the end of the hall. I approached him. The flames in his eyes faded. Still, his irises remained red and alluring.

I extended my hand. "It's a privilege."

The vampire did not shake my hand. Instead, he nodded. "Likewise. Forgive my caution. Your Mark is legendary and I would prefer to avoid any contact that might trigger your curse."

"A handshake will pose no threat to you," I said.

The vampire nodded. His hair was long, wavy, and reddish-blond. He had a long beard to match. "Take no offense, Cain. I have not survived so long by taking unnecessary risks."

"I'm not easily offended, Ruthven. Still, I understand and respect your trepidation."

Ruthven nodded. "Follow me. Excuse my brethren. It has been some time since we welcomed an outsider into our fortress."

I followed the vampire through the corridor into an open room. In the middle was a large stone sarcophagus. Ruthven rested his hand on it. Several other vampires, their eyes also red, surrounded us.

I looked around and did my best to nod at each of them. They did not nod back. They fixed their eyes on me.

"Who lies in the sarcophagus?" I asked.

Ruthven narrowed his eyes. "Not all vampires, contrary to what you might have heard, are descended from Niccolo the Damned. Here lies the Baobhan Sith."

I raised an eyebrow. "The Baobhan Sith? I've never heard of such a creature."

"It has been our sacred duty to ensure her slumber for better than a century. Niccolo the Damned aided us in the suppression of her kind and helped us secure her in this very tomb. Before we intervened, the Baobhan Sith would rise from her grave once a year to terrorize the countryside. This sepulcher helps us prevent her return."

"Let me get this straight. To prevent the resurrection of a single vampire, Niccolo commissioned an entire coven of vampires here instead? How does that make the village safer?"

"I know how it sounds. Is one vampire a greater threat than all of us combined? This one most certainly is. The Baobhan Sith has much in common with our kind. She, too, is averse to sunlight. She feeds from human blood, drawing it through her claws, rather than fangs. She can shape-shift into virtually any animal form. But her lusts know no limits. She can manipulate the mind of an immortal—even of our kind. Any man she feeds upon will die. Any woman upon whom she feeds will turn into one like her. But this one, the first of the Baobhan Sith, was never human. She is a corrupted fae. No one knows her true origins. Many believe she is the product of a devil's machinations."

"So she can turn others? Are there none of her progeny who still dwell in these lands?"

Ruthven shook his head. "We eliminated the lot of them. They can only be staked with iron. Wooden stakes are not sufficient. Though, this one, the original, has no heart to stake. The iron only puts her into a temporary slumber. She must remain imprisoned here. Each year, when she attempts to rise, it is our duty to ensure she's staked quickly."

I pressed my lips together. "What does this have to do with me?"

Ruthven raised the left leg of his trousers, revealing a festering wound. "Nothing directly, though a pack of wolves has set their sights on our coven. I am not the only one whom they've bitten. Should they continue and weaken our coven further, I cannot say we will be strong enough to hold the Baobhan Sith forever. She can manipulate our minds if we are not well-focused and well-fed."

"So you want me to encourage these wolves to leave you be?"

Ruthven nodded. "More than that. They must leave our lands. When the Baobhan Sith rises each year, it corresponds with a full moon. With a shriek, she called upon these wolves and manipulated them, drawing them here, to our castle. The wolves are not to blame. Though she still slumbers, they remain under her influence. Each full moon they return here, again, to attempt to free her. If another year passes, and we suffer more assaults, I cannot say we are likely to thwart their efforts again."

"So this Baobhan Sith can control werewolf minds?" I asked.

Ruthven sighed. "We don't know the limits of her power. But yes, for one reason or another, werewolves are more susceptible to her power than vampires. We believe that whatever she's done only affects them when they are shifted. None of the wolves have attempted to assault our fortress at any time other than during the full moon. We're simply asking you, Cain, to use your influence over the pack to encourage them to leave our lands and find another home."

I scratched my head. "I can sniff them out. I will find them and do what I can."

"That is all we can ask. It is essential you succeed. Trust me, Cain. The only reason we could subdue the Baobhan Sith before was because she and her progeny did not yet know what we were. I cannot say, if they reemerge, we will be able to stop them a second time."

# CHAPTER THREE

**Present Day**

RUTHERFORD CROSSED HER LEGS and sipped on her cup of coffee as I told her the story. Convincing the pack to back off was easier than I'd expected. Doing what needed to be done was more challenging. They simply weren't aware of how the Baobhan Sith had been manipulating them during their shift. It was heartbreaking. We didn't know how powerful the Baobhan Sith's influence was. There was only one option. We had to break up the pack. With each wolf under the influence of a new alpha, we hoped we could thwart whatever compulsions the Baobhan Sith exacted upon their minds.

I hadn't heard from Lord Ruthven since. Our effort was successful. Now, though, Ruthven had checked himself into the Vilokan Asylum; I could only fear the worst.

"Is there any reason Ruthven wanted my help?"

Rutherford shook her head. "According to Annabelle, he is only willing to speak to you about his situation."

I sighed and tried to kick down the leg-rest on my recliner. It wouldn't click into place. I tried again. It bounced out again. "Damn it."

Rutherford laughed. "Use the handle on the side."

I grunted, reached down, and pulled on the handle as I pushed the leg-rest back into place. It clicked. I stood up, went to my bedroom, and got dressed. "I have a bad feeling about this."

"It could be nothing at all, Cain. Lord Ruthven may simply be suffering from a common case of depression. It's quite common in older vampires, weary of their never-ending existence."

I nodded. "You might be right. Still, the way he described the Baobhan Sith was enough to send chills down even my wolf-shifted spine. She's some kind of vampiric faerie who hunted men; turned women; had mind control *and* shape-shifting capabilities. It's not even fair."

Rutherford smiled. "Well, suppose that she's been awakened. She's been stopped before."

I nodded. "True. Though, in those days, Lord Ruthven had the help of Niccolo the Damned."

"Fair enough," Rutherford said. "But again, Cain, there's no reason to worry until there's reason to worry."

I headed out the door and Rutherford locked the dead-bolt on her apartment door behind us. We climbed into my truck and headed to Vilokan.

Jessie was managing the front desk. She was a junior nurse. A Black girl, with long, straightened hair, and a kind smile that featured a set of perfectly straight teeth. She'd grown up in Vilokan and recently graduated from the Voodoo Academy. She had the aspect of Ogoun, the Loa of War. That meant, like Annabelle Mulledy, she possessed an ethereal weapon. Hers corresponded with the element of earth. She had a strength that far eclipsed what one would expect. Especially considering her dainty frame. I hadn't seen her in action, but, according to Annabelle, if we ever needed someone to join us in a fight, she could hold her own.

I didn't hire Jessie. Annabelle did. After a slew of incidents at the Vilokan Asylum, the Voodoo Queen thought it was important to add a little "muscle" to the crew. I didn't object. It was a smart move.

"I hear we have a new patient," I said, approaching the desk.

"We do," Jessie said, glancing past me at Rutherford. "Will you be taking over the desk?"

"You can handle it," Rutherford said. "I'll do rounds while Cain interviews the new patient."

Jessie nodded. "That's fine. I already finished the rounds, though."

I cocked my head. "How'd you manage that?"

Jessie shrugged. "I'm efficient. And I'm driven. Get used to it, doctor. I'm here for the long-haul and I intend to make an impression."

I grinned. "That's good to hear."

"I've also enrolled in a counseling program on-line."

I raised an eyebrow. "Oh, really? I'm intrigued. We'll have to chat more. It would be nice to have another counselor on staff who understands the unique demands of our patient population."

"That's what I thought," Jessie said. "That's why I signed up!"

Rutherford snorted. "Well, how about that? I have some patient files piling up I need to sort. I suppose I'll work on those."

"The files that were stacked in the bin on the desk?" Jessie asked. "If so, I filed them in the cabinet."

Rutherford scratched her head. "Yes. Those were the files. I usually take care of that. I have a system."

I laughed. "Well, Rutherford, you've been hoping to work more directly with the patients. It looks like Jessie has cleared your schedule so you can."

Rutherford pressed her lips together. Jessie buzzed us in through the security doors. Rutherford moved briskly through the hall, past my office. I raised an eyebrow and looked back at Jessie.

"Is she okay?" Jessie asked.

I nodded. "She will be. Good work, Jessie. She's just used to handling all of those tasks."

"I'm sorry! Did I overstep? I didn't mean..."

"You're doing marvelously," I said, smiling at the young nurse. "Keep it up. Rutherford needs the help and I'm sure she'll appreciate it in time. Sometimes, though, letting go of responsibilities can be difficult."

"I'm sorry, Doctor Cain. I didn't mean to upset her."

"Like I said, Jessie, keep doing what you're doing. You'll go far. I meant what I said before. If you have the skill and dedication, I could use another counselor. If that's your passion, I intend to encourage you and nurture your talents. Send me some information about your new program. Printed copies, if possible. I know most things are online nowadays, but I still work with paper."

Jessie smiled. "I already did. It's on your desk next to Ruthven's patient file."

I laughed. "Alright. I'll take a look at it soon. Is the patient in my office?"

Jessie nodded. "He is! He's very nice for a vampire, I should say."

I raised an eyebrow. "Nice, you say?"

"Very! And he speaks highly of you, Doctor Cain."

I chuckled. "Well, I should hope he does. He and I have a history. Let's hope all goes well."

I headed down the hallway to my office and stepped inside. Ruthven was waiting on my chaise longue, his legs crossed. His hair was still long and wavy, but now his beard was trimmed to a stubble.

"Hello, Lord Ruthven," I said, stepping into my office, pulling my chair out from behind my desk, and sitting down in front of him.

"Doctor Cain! You look as virile as ever!"

I laughed. "As do you, Ruthven. It's been a long time."

"Indeed, it has."

"So, what brings you to me? Is all well with the Baobhan Sith?"

Ruthven sighed. "Yes, and no."

I waited a moment to give Ruthven a chance to explain further. "Would you care to elaborate?"

"I'm not here for her, Doctor Cain. Not exactly. Only in a round-about way. It's funny, you know. Calling you a doctor. It seems you've changed as much over the last few centuries as I have."

"The entire world has changed, Ruthven. More in the last half-century than in all the millennia I've experienced before."

"Call me Patrick," Ruthven said. "As you said, the world has evolved. Formalities no longer carry the weight they once did."

I grinned. "Very well, Patrick. I trust you're well fed?"

Patrick nodded. "I am. I shouldn't require a feed for several weeks."

"Then would you care to explain what brings you here? To leave behind your castle, and the Baobhan Sith, isn't something I'd imagine you'd do lightly."

"Well, I haven't left her behind, Cain. She's here."

I almost swallowed my tongue. "Excuse me?"

"Aye. I relocated, along with my coven."

"Why wouldn't you just send for me as you did once before if you needed my help?"

"That's the thing, Doctor Cain. Scotland isn't the safe haven for our kind it once was. The seat of power for the Vampire Council no longer resides in Europe, but here, in New Orleans. I came here on my sister's suggestion."

"You have a sister?" I asked.

Patrick laughed. "Well, not by blood. Well, not by our human blood, at least. We share a common sire, Doctor Cain."

"You speak of Mercy Brown?" I asked, raising an eyebrow.

"Indeed. She was my sire's favored progeny. I do not begrudge her that. She's proven herself, well."

"And I suppose she's the one who referred you to me here?"

"Aye, she did."

"And the Baobhan Sith is here, in New Orleans?"

"At the place Mercy calls Casa do Diabo."

I sighed. "Well, that certainly raises several concerns, Ruthven."

"Patrick."

"Of course. My apologies. You realize, Patrick, that there are many werewolves here in New Orleans? If the Baobhan Sith can still manipulate werewolves, this is hardly the best place to bring her."

"I already thought of that," Patrick said. "Again, my sister has proved her worth. She is a witch, besides being a vampire, you know."

"I'm well aware."

"And she lives with another powerful witch. A young vampire."

I nodded. "Yes, Hailey is quite accomplished."

"Well, the witches have a connection with the Phantom Queen. The Goddess, the Morrigan."

"They did, once. I cannot say that they still hold the Morrigan's favor."

"Still, the Baobhan Sith was a cursed creature born in the lands where the Morrigan once reigned freely. No witch has successfully garnered the Morrigan's favor more recently than Mercy and her fellow vampire-witches."

I shook my head. "You realize this is quite the risk, Patrick."

Patrick stood up from the chaise longue and paced. "Over the years, Cain, the Baobhan Sith has gained strength at a rate that has exceeded the maturation of my coven. We are strong, yes. But her power grows. I hear her voice, I believe, even now."

"The Baobhan Sith now speaks to you?"

"That is why Mercy believed I should see you, Doctor Cain. She said she once faced a similar predicament."

I shook my head. "When I treated Mercy, the spirit of her deceased brother possessed her. That was an entirely different matter. You're talking about the influence of a spirit who has exhibited the ability to warp the minds of werewolves in the past. Are you certain that she is not also manipulating you now?"

"I'm sure of nothing," Patrick said. "But I can say that if we persisted with our routine, subduing the Baobhan Sith each year, whether it be this year or next, it would only be a matter of time before she overwhelms us. There are werewolves here, this is true. But if we can stop her before she rises, if the vampires and witches can evoke the aid of the Morrigan, I have to believe we can end the Baobhan Sith once and for all."

I scratched my head. "If you're wrong, Patrick, you might unleash a real terror on the world. You're also risking the wellbeing of my werewolves."

Patrick shrugged. "Only if she rises before we can end her, Doctor Cain. Only then will she be able to call out to them and rally the wolves to her aid."

"How much time do we have before the Baobhan Sith will attempt to return?"

"She will rise on Samhain, in October."

I stared at Patrick blankly. "That's only two months away, Patrick."

Patrick nodded. "I should have come sooner, I regret. But you must understand, relocating a coven of vampires takes... convincing."

I bit my lip. "Tell me, Patrick. When the Baobhan Sith speaks to you, what does she say?"

"Nonsense, mostly. The ravings of a lunatic. What you'd expect, I suppose, for a creature who's been subdued and imprisoned for several centuries."

"But what does she say, specifically, Patrick?"

Patrick bit his lip. "She wants me to kill myself."

"Have you considered it? Staking yourself, I mean?"

Patrick sighed. "No vampire who has lived as long as I have hasn't considered it, Doctor Cain. But I would never do it. I've been staked before, Doctor Cain. I have no desire to return to vampire hell. Should my heart be burned, I fear I might be trapped there forever. This existence can be insufferable. It's nothing compared to the torment I'd experience if I ended my life."

"Are you certain that it's the Baobhan Sith who is speaking? Have you considered the possibility that having spent so much of your existence suppressing her existence that your own subconscious mind might manifest in her voice?"

"I've considered it, Doctor Cain. Either way, the solution is the same. The Baobhan Sith must die. If she's the one who wants me to end my life, and she's worked her way into my mind, I cannot allow her influence to persist. If it is truly my angst, my subconscious mind, that is considering suicide, well, then it is for no other reason than that my whole life has been consumed with a single task for longer than anyone's should be. Doctor, I am tired. I may be a vampire, but so long as the Baobhan Sith exists, I have no choice but to guard her sepulcher. I crave liberty, Doctor Cain. This has been a prison. If I must shoulder the weight of this responsibility for even another decade, it will crush my sanity. I may be ancient. I might be strong, so far as vampires are concerned. But at my age, madness is a growing threat. Mercy was right to send me here."

# CHAPTER FOUR

THE BEST TIME TO track down Mercy Brown was during the day. At night there was no telling where she might be, what kind of vampiric shenanigans she might be up to, or if I might find her fangs-deep in her next meal. Don't get me wrong, Mercy was one of the good ones so far as vampires were concerned. Her heart was in the right place a good eighty percent of the time. If I needed her help, she'd answer. She was no villain. Yes, she had an inner-darkness that she entertained more often than most of us. She was a vampire, after all. But if she indulged in anything unsavory, it was never the take-over-the-world, dominate humanity and destroy everything decent, sort of way. With the big things, she was as trustworthy as anyone else I'd ever worked with in the supernatural community. Since she'd sent Patrick Ruthven to me and undoubtedly knew about my history with him, she surely expected my visit sooner rather than later.

Jessie had the front desk well in hand. Rutherford was busy checking on patients. I didn't bother her on my way out. As I looked down the hallway, I saw her moving with an extra vigor in her gait around the nursing station at the central hub of the asylum. I knew that walk. When she moved that way, I knew better than to intervene. She felt like

Jessie had come in and over-stepped. I didn't need to ask Rutherford why she was upset. It was obvious. She'd adjust. Eventually.

I made my way past the reception desk. I smiled and nodded at Jessie. She was arms-deep in the file cabinets.

"Hi, Doctor Cain!" Jessie said. "I'm reorganizing the patient files. You wouldn't believe how disorganized everything is."

I smiled. "That's fantastic, Jessie. You might want to run your ideas past Rutherford though. She's kept those files for years."

Jessie bit the inside of her cheek and tucked a strand of hair behind her ear. "Do you think she hates me?"

I shook my head. "Not at all. But would you care to listen to a word from the wise?"

"Of course!"

"I appreciate what you're doing. Your initiative is impressive. You'll do a lot better, though, if you talk to Rutherford about your ideas, first."

"I'm really just trying to make a good impression."

I grinned. "You already have. I'm beyond impressed with you, Jessie."

Jessie looked away, then looked back up at me with wide eyes. She smiled at me and placed her hand on mine. "Thank you. That means a lot."

I pulled my hand away. "Of course, Jessie. You just need a little patience when you're encroaching on someone else's territory. You need to move slowly. Eventually, she may be willing to give you what's hers. But for now, this is still her domain."

Jessie cocked her head. "I get it. I'm used to taking what I want. I'm competitive like that."

"Rutherford is not your competition," I said, smiling back at Jessie. "You are special in your own right. I'm sure you'll find a place here where you can thrive. You've said it before, your ambitions are higher than working the reception desk and sorting files. Focus on what you really want and try not to step on too many toes on the way."

Jessie bit her lip and tilted her head. "I think I know what you mean. Did you look at my paperwork yet?"

"Not yet, Jessie. But I'd be happy to go over the program with you later this evening, after my afternoon sessions."

"I'll put it on your schedule," Jessie said, returning to her desk, sitting down and crossing her legs. "I'll really look forward to it."

I smiled and nodded. "Me too, Jessie. I'll see you soon. If anyone asks, I'm going to pay a quick visit to Mercy Brown. Please push this morning's sessions to this afternoon or tomorrow. Wherever there are openings."

"I'll handle it, Doctor Cain. And thank you for the advice. I'll be sure to take it to heart."

I stepped through the door and into the front room. I glanced back at Jessie and grinned. She smiled back. I had a lot of hope for the girl. She was young, excited, and more than competent. As long as she followed my advice and watched her step with Rutherford, she'd fit in well. I'd hired several nurses in the past who lacked initiative. Her enthusiasm, while excessive, was a different challenge. It's easier to tame a tiger, though, than it is to turn a pussy cat into one. This girl was eager. It was both her greatest fault and her most valuable asset.

I got in my truck and drove to Casa do Diabo. It was only ten in the morning. When I stepped out of my truck, the sound of bagpipes immediately struck me, echoing from somewhere inside Mercy's mansion.

I knew better than to knock. Mercy never opened the door when the sun was out. Instead, I pressed the little white circle beneath the small camera on her video doorbell.

A few seconds later, the bagpipes went silent. "Come in," Mercy said, her voice coming from the small speaker on her doorbell.

I opened the door and stepped inside. I locked the door behind me.

Mercy appeared in the foyer wearing high-heels and not much else. Something black, lacy, and revealing dangled from her body. A half-second later, a red-eyed vampire, wearing nothing but a kilt, stepped up behind her.

"I'm sorry. I didn't mean to interrupt... whatever this is..."

Mercy giggled. "We're just having fun, Cain. No worries. I expected you'd stop by today at some point."

I briefly made eye contact with the Scottish vampire. I didn't recognize him. That didn't mean he wasn't a part of Patrick Ruthven's clan. Those vampires, the last I'd seen them, all donned long beards. This one was clean shaven. It was also dark in that castle when I'd met them before.

"Good to see you again, Cain," the vampire said.

I nodded. "My apologies, I do not remember you."

The vampire shrugged. "I didn't expect you would. It was a long time ago, and we never spoke. Still, I couldn't forget meeting you. You're rather famous, you know. An encounter with the legendary Cain isn't something one is likely to forget."

I nodded. "I'm well aware."

"I suppose you're here to check in on the Baobhan Sith?" Mercy asked.

I cocked my head. "She's here?"

Mercy nodded. "In the basement."

"Seriously? Mercy, this thing is dangerous."

"Trust me," the male vampire said. "We've got it under control. More now than ever."

"I'm sorry. I didn't catch your name."

The bare-chested vampire shrugged. "That's because I didn't tell you. I'm Brendan."

I sighed. "Well, Brendan, would you give Mercy and me a moment to talk alone?"

"Certainly," Brendan said. "We'll be downstairs. We can resume our fun after Cain is gone."

"I can't wait," Mercy said, winking at Brendan as he headed back down the stairs toward the basement.

I sighed. "What is going on here, Mercy?"

Mercy chuckled. "Does it matter, Cain?"

"Not at all. You're consenting adults. It's none of my business, but..."

"Yes, Cain," Mercy said, interrupting me. "All the adults here have fully consented to the dance that the Scottish vampires are teaching us."

"You're dancing in heels?" I asked, raising an eyebrow.

"Well, I'm trying to. What did you think we were doing?"

I shook my head. "I'd rather not say."

"I have this situation in hand, Cain. I realize this creature is frightening, even for me. That's exactly why I demanded that Patrick bring it here."

"Excuse me? This was *your* idea?"

"Have you spoken with Patrick?"

I nodded. "I have."

"He's exhausted, Cain. The last time I saw that look in a vampire's eyes, it was shortly before Nico planned to end his existence. He needs your help. All I need from you is to help him get his mind right. I intend to relieve him of much of his burden. But I'm not sure that will be enough."

I shook my head. "He said you intend to evoke the Morrigan again."

Mercy nodded. "With Hailey and Julie together, we can call upon her again."

I snorted. "You really think she can kill the Baobhan Sith?"

Mercy shook her head. "Kill her? Maybe. I don't think she will. At the very least, perhaps she can alter the creature's cycle so that she doesn't emerge on a full moon."

"So that she can't manipulate werewolves?"

Mercy nodded. "Then, I'll see to it that another vampire can relieve Patrick of his responsibilities in time. Like I said, Cain, I have this matter under control."

"Mercy, bringing the Baobhan Sith to New Orleans, where so many werewolves live, is reckless."

"We have time, Cain. If we fail, we will move her out of the region again before the full moon. I'm not an idiot, you know."

"I never said you were, Mercy. But I've dealt with this issue before. You realize, the last time I was called upon to aid with the suppression of the Baobhan Sith, I had to break up a pack. That might not sound like a big deal to you, but for werewolves, separating a pack is every bit as painful as it would be to separate a whole family from each other. With the rougarou here, including Julie, not to mention Abel and his pack, it would be nothing short of devastating."

"I understand that, Cain. When have I ever let you down? Trust me."

I grunted. "I trust you, Mercy. I wish you'd spoken to me before you did this."

"Would you have agreed to it, Cain?"

I scratched the back of my head. "Probably not."

"Exactly. If I didn't intervene, Cain, the Baobhan Sith would likely break free the next time she rises. The vampire community here in New Orleans is much better equipped to manage this issue now that Patrick Ruthven's coven is alone."

"Understood," I turned to the door to leave. "Please, just keep me apprised of the situation. If anything at all goes awry and I need to move the werewolves, the more notice I have, the better."

"Cain!" Another familiar voice said, running upstairs and into the Foyer.

"Mel! You look well!"

"My cravings are all under control!" Mel exclaimed. Mel was Mercy's most recent progeny. Mercy turned her out of compassion. Mel had suffered from a condition that made it painful to walk. She'd spent her last years, while still a human, bound to a wheelchair. After Mercy turned her, Mel spent a brief time at the Vilokan Asylum to work on her cravings. Things didn't pan out as well as planned under my care. I was glad to see that back under the wing of her sire, she was thriving.

Before I knew it, Mel wrapped her arms around me. I wasn't big on hugs. Still, I hugged her back. As awkward as hugs from former patients could be, standing there like a board and refusing to hug back at all only made it worse.

"What are you wearing?" I asked.

Mel shrugged. "It's a leotard. Don't you like it?"

"Sure," I smiled. "I'm sure dancing is quite a thrill for you. Especially considering, you know, that you couldn't dance before you were turned."

Mel cocked her head. "Dancing? Who told you we're dancing?"

I turned and glared at Mercy. She shrugged and giggled. "Goodbye, Cain."

# CHAPTER FIVE

THEY WERE MESSING WITH me. They *had* to be messing with me. Vampires don't do lewd things like that. You know, the O-word. I don't even like to say it because it sounds so dirty. Vampires just aren't into physical, carnal pleasures. Not like that. Mercy had told me before that vampires establish intimacy by *feeding* together. Not by, you know, doing the sort of thing my wolfish companions only do on the Discovery Channel.

My stomach twisted as I went to my car. Surely not. I didn't see any blood dripping from their lips. Visions of human victims, swarmed over by vampires, flooded my mind.

I sighed. The one thing I knew about Mercy Brown was that she rarely killed. She knew how to feed in moderation. It wasn't so much because she was opposed to killing as that she didn't like the attention it brought upon her, and other vampires, when too many bodies turned up devoid of blood. That sort of thing drew the attention of hunters.

Then again, perhaps these Scottish vampires were a bad influence. It was the kilts. It had to be the kilts. Can you ever, really, trust a man who wears a kilt? Or, perhaps it was the bagpipes. The high-pitched sound of the instrument was especially grating to my super-sensitive ears.

Usually, the enhanced senses I had, even in human form because of being a werewolf, were an advantage. There were exceptions. Nails on a chalkboard. The sound of crunching styrofoam. Any film featuring Gilbert Gottfried. Those were the only sounds I could think of that might have been more intolerable to my werewolf ears than bagpipes.

I didn't know how old that tradition was. Perhaps that was how the Scots kept werewolves out of their lands. That's how they'd avoided the Baobhan Sith's manipulation of werewolves. Sure, it was a longshot of a theory. But it made sense. At least to me.

I made my way back to the asylum. I needed to check in on the satellite location where the werewolves were housed, but that would have to wait. My schedule at the original site was already full. Besides, the wolves were doing well. Abel had grown into his role as alpha and, mostly, all his wolves had resumed their daily lives. They wouldn't return to the asylum until the next full moon. Only a few of them—Ryan, Cassidy, and Julie—stayed there permanently. Still, we had nightly group sessions. I insisted that all the wolves attend at least three sessions a week. Most of them exceeded the minimum. When you're at risk of becoming a homicidal monster without sufficient therapy, it motivates folks to put in the necessary work. Between my patients at the original asylum and my promise to meet with Jessie later in the evening, then my group session with the wolves, I wouldn't have a lot of time at home with Rutherford before I had to hit the sack and get ready to embrace the next day's unpredictable set of adventures.

I walked through the door of the asylum. Rutherford was back at the front desk.

"Oh, thank God, Cain. You're back."

I raised an eyebrow. "Is something wrong? Where's Jessie?"

Rutherford shook her head and buzzed me through the security door. "Come in. I need to show you the monitors."

I stepped through the door. Rutherford tilted her computer monitor toward me. Patrick was in the common room, standing on a table.

Jessie was there, standing between the vampire and a crowd of other patients.

Patrick snarled. He dove at Jessie. With some kind of weapon in her hand, something like a giant club or baton aglow with green magic, she smacked the vampire across his face. Then she pointed at him and started yelling something. I could have asked Rutherford to turn up the volume, but this wasn't entertainment.

I turned and ran down the hall.

"Cain, wait!" Rutherford shouted.

I didn't stop. Whatever she had to tell me could wait. I wasn't about to let an out-of-control vampire make a meal out of my patients. Yes, Jessie had the aspect of Ogoun. She was a skilled fighter. That's why Annabelle hired her. Did she really stand a chance against an angry, ancient vampire? I wasn't about to find out.

A crowd of patients ran past me, fleeing to their rooms as I made my way around the nurses' hub at the center of the asylum. I took off down the hall leading to the common room.

"Bring me Cain!" Patrick shouted, his voice echoing through the halls.

"You need to calm down," Jessie screamed back. "Or I'll shove this club so far up your..."

"Wait," I said. "I'm here, Patrick. There's no need for this."

"Cain," Patrick said, snarling, as he stared at me. "You did this to me!"

"What did I do to you, Patrick?"

Patrick laughed. "You don't know what you're dealing with. Free me, Cain!"

"Patrick, you're here of your own accord. You wanted my help and I intend to give it to you. Please, come with me to my office so we can talk through this."

"Cain, I don't think that's a good idea," Jessie said. "He's not himself."

I raised my hand. "I've got this, Jessie."

Patrick laughed. "Look, it's the mighty Cain! Always in control! Defy him, and it will be the death of you, child! Heed my warning!"

I scratched my head. "Patrick, this isn't you. You need to snap out of it. I'm your friend, Patrick. I'm here to help."

"Step aside, girl!" Patrick shouted. "He's mine."

Jessie shook her head and stepped between Patrick and me. "You can't do this, Patrick. If you want to fight me, go for it. But you know what will happen if you try to attack Cain."

Patrick shrieked in glee. "Yes, I do!"

Patrick dove toward me. Jessie took her weapon, glowing in green energies, and struck the vampire in the gut.

Then, Patrick looked at me and grinned, flashing his fangs. "All it takes is an attempt, does it not?"

"Jessie. You need to leave. Get everyone out of here."

"Cain, I can't. I'm here to…"

"I said leave, Jessie! Get everyone to safety!"

Patrick's body expanded. His red eyes doubled in size as his head elongated, forming a snout.

"Holy crap," Jessie said. "The seven-fold curse…"

"Jessie, do as I said! He won't stop until he's turned seven more wolves…"

Jessie nodded and took off running down the hall. Alarms sounded throughout the facility.

I clenched my fist and stared at Patrick. Anyone who attempted to kill me assumed a seven-fold curse. They became a werewolf. They wouldn't shift back, no matter the state of the moon, until they'd turned seven more in kind. The only way to stop him was to kill him. I didn't have any silver. We had syringes loaded with colloidal silver at the nurse's station, intended for situations exactly like this.

I took off running. I couldn't exert control over him. Not now. He'd triggered the Mark of Cain. Only once he turned seven more wolves might I dominate him as an alpha. I couldn't allow that to happen. Patrick was my patient. I'd do anything to save a patient. The cost of saving Patrick was too great. I couldn't sacrifice others, allow them to get bitten and turned, for his sake or anyone else's.

I dove over the desk at the nurse's station and grabbed a syringe.

Patrick blasted past me and through the hall toward the exit. I'd never seen a wolf move so fast. He'd already tried to kill me. He didn't need to finish the job. I wasn't his target at all. He'd said he thought he heard the voice of the Baobhan Sith. Had she gained control over his mind? If that was the case, attempting to kill me was all he needed. He was trying to escape.

I took off after Patrick, a syringe in my hand. He plowed through the security door as if it were made of paper.

Then, he left the asylum and fled into the streets of Vilokan.

"Rutherford!" I shouted. "Alert Annabelle! Wolf on the loose!"

"Already done!"

I shook my head. He wasn't going to bother with Vilokan. At least, I didn't think that was his goal. He didn't care if he turned more wolves or didn't. He had one goal. He was heading to Casa do Diabo. He was going to free the Baobhan Sith.

# CHAPTER SIX

"Rutherford, call Mercy. She needs to know he's on the way. Tell her what happened. It will take every vampire in that place to fend him off."

"I can help!" Jessie said. "Let me fight him."

I shook my head. "You did well, Jessie. As a vampire, you might have stood a chance against him. Now, though, there's only one way to stop him."

"Then we can stop him together!" Jessie pleaded. "That's why I'm here, Cain. Annabelle said to protect you at all costs. She taught me how to kill a wolf if it came to that."

I nodded. "I understand that. This is not a run-of-the-mill werewolf. It's a vampire, and now he bears my curse. We don't know how strong he might be or what it could take to stop him. The usual methods might not be enough."

"I'll check in on the patients and make sure no one was harmed," Rutherford said. "You two, go. Stop him before he can hurt anyone else."

I nodded. Jessie twirled her baton in her hand.

"That won't be of much use against a werewolf," I said.

"It won't kill him," Jessie said. "But it will hurt. I have earthen strength."

"Alright. Well, if we can corner him, all I need is a distraction. Give me an opening to inject him with silver. Hopefully, we can catch him before he leaves Vilokan."

"I saw how fast he moves. It won't be easy."

"You're right," I said. "But we have to try."

I could have really used Julie Brown at the moment. Her flambeau used to wield infernal power. Now, we'd "converted" what used to be the Witch of Endor's flambeau to a celestial relic. Even now, her flambeau could force me to shift into a wolf in an instant. It was better than shifting under a full moon. The celestial power that empowered a werewolf's shift gave us clarity of mind, a control that we never experienced during a natural, lunar shift. Julie was at the Vilokan Asylum extension site. I couldn't get to her in time. If I could, I might be fast enough to stand in a paw-race with Patrick to the French Quarter above Vilokan and, from there, to Casa do Diabo.

We had two advantages. First, I knew Vilokan a lot better than Patrick did. Sure, he'd been brought to the Asylum and probably had some recollection of the direction he had to take to the world above, but the voodoo underworld was a complex labyrinth of closely arranged buildings. I could only hope that the time it would take him to find the stairway out of Vilokan would compensate for the advantage he had as a wolf, enhanced by vampiric speed.

Second, new werewolves tend to be loud. Patrick was no exception. The blue firmament aglow above Vilokan was every bit as enthralling to a werewolf as a full moon. He howled as he made his way across the city. There were screams, too. Could Patrick avoid biting someone? If he was possessed or, at least, influenced by the Baobhan Sith, would she recognize she could turn at least six more wolves, expanding her pack, before turning the seventh and returning to human form? If I were going to take on a coven of vampires, including the likes of Mercy Brown, I'd do it with a pack.

I could only hope that Rutherford had gotten word to Annabelle. She could focus on rallying her most adept mambos and hougans to protect the citizens of Vilokan. I had to focus on ensuring that Patrick didn't escape.

Jessie and I made it to the stairway out of Vilokan while Patrick's howls still echoed throughout Vilokan. In an underground world, with a magical dome over all of it, sounds bounce around. It's hard to tell the direction a sound is coming from. Still, the howls were getting louder.

"Remember, Jessie. I just need a distraction. A half-second to jab him with the syringe."

Jessie winked at me. "No problem."

I widened my stance, ready to move the second I had a chance, as Patrick bounded towards us on all fours.

Jessie charged him, her club in hand, and with a swipe caught the wolf across the snout. He tumbled over to the side. I had to admit, her ability was impressive. She was like a much cuter version of the Hulk, and she didn't need to get angry in order to bring out her strength.

It didn't do much. No sooner did Patrick hit the pavement, sliding into the side of a building, and he was back on his paws. Now, he had his sights set on Jessie. She taunted him, waving her club through the air.

This was my chance. I ran as hard as I could, the syringe in my right hand, and thrust it into the wolf's back. He shrieked.

Patrick buckled over and coughed. He vomited blood on the pavement. It wasn't his blood. He was a vampire, after all. It was the remnants of his last meal. Whoever he'd fed from before he arrived at the asylum.

Then he turned, stared at me, his eyes red like a vampire's; charged over me and through the stairway that led out of Vilokan.

"Did you get him?" Jessie asked, helping me back to my feet.

I nodded. "I did. But when he looked at me, when I saw his eyes... Silver can kill a wolf, but he isn't only a wolf, Jessie. He's also a vampire. The silver hurt him, but I don't think it's enough to kill him."

"Come on," Jessie said. "We need to catch up to him."

Jessie and I took off up the stairs. I skipped two steps at a time. My legs and butt burned. These stairs were steep. There were too many to count. Still, I couldn't let the pain dissuade me.

I pushed through it, but it slowed me down. Jessie took off in front of me. The vigor of her relative youth had its advantages. What I'd give to be twenty again... well... to feel twenty again. Once you turn six-thousand, you're bound to experience a few more aches and pains than you'd had before.

I heard the wolf cry ahead of us. When I reached the top, Jessie stood there staring into the alley.

"Where did he go? I thought I heard the wolf a second ago."

Jessie nodded. "You did. But he didn't like the sunlight."

I nodded. "He's a vampire and a werewolf. His vampirism might have helped him survive silver; it also makes him vulnerable to sunlight."

"Will it kill him?"

I sighed. "I don't think so. As a werewolf, he'll be more resilient to the effects of the sunlight than a vampire. It'll hurt like hell though, I imagine."

"So, let me get this straight. Ruthven has both the strengths and weaknesses of vampires *and* werewolves?"

"I'm afraid that might be the case. We won't be able to stake him, either. At least not with a wooden stake."

"But if we forged a silver stake..."

I smiled. "Great minds think alike. That's exactly the idea I was considering."

"Where do you think he went? He ran off so fast I couldn't even tell which direction he went."

I shook my head. "I can't say. What I know, though, is that I'd fully expect he'll be heading to Casa do Diabo after nightfall. For now, weakened by the sunlight, my guess is he'll try to avoid confronting the vampires head-on."

# CHAPTER SEVEN

UNTIL WE RECEIVED REPORTS of a beast attacking people in the city, the priority was to defend Casa do Diabo.

All I could figure was that over the centuries the Baobhan Sith had worked her way into Patrick's mind, gradually influencing him a little more each year's Samhain, to such a degree he didn't even notice it—until her influence was too pervasive to ignore.

When Patrick arrived at the asylum, he said we had two months until the Baobhan Sith rose again. Now, it seemed, we had about ten hours. Would she rise if Patrick got to her? Not likely. From what I understood, she only rose one night a year as did all of her kindred.

"Nice truck," Jessie said, climbing into the side of my F-150.

"Are you being sarcastic?" I asked, raising an eyebrow. "I love the truck, don't get me wrong, but it's a decade old."

Jessie shrugged. "I think trucks are sexy."

I raised an eyebrow. "I've never had the hots for any vehicle. I prefer animated entities."

Jessie giggled. "You know what I mean. When I say tight jeans are hot, I'm not talking about the jeans. I'm talking about the man wearing them."

I almost said something when it dawned on me what she was saying. I gripped my steering wheel, bit my tongue, and ignored her comment. Was my junior nurse coming on to me? Inappropriate! Not that I didn't find her attractive. She was beautiful. But I was in love with Rutherford. I understood what was happening. I was in a position of authority. Some people find authority alluring.

"We're going to Casa do Diabo to check on the vampires. After that, we need to head to the extension site and rally the wolves. They're meeting there shortly before sundown. We'll have to hurry, but we'll need them to track Patrick and defend the Baobhan Sith."

Jessie sighed. "Technically, you're not my boss. Annabelle hired me. It's not inappropriate."

I bit my lip. "I will not entertain those thoughts, Jessie."

"Why not? Don't you find me attractive?"

"No," I said. "I mean, I do. Or, no. Not really in any way that matters. That's not the point, Jessie. I'm with Rutherford and you're too young for me."

Jessie rolled her eyes. "Everyone is too young for you, Cain. Think about it. With my strength, and yours... you wouldn't have to worry about breaking me. You wouldn't have to hold back like you do with her."

I snorted. "I told you, Jessie. I'm not talking about this with you. It's off the table."

"On the table, off the table. I'm not picky about location."

"Jessie, I..." Jessie kicked her bare feet onto my dash, wiggling her red-painted toes. Not only did the gesture leave me tongue-tied, it caught my glance for a half-second.

"Do you like them? I just had them done."

"Please put them down. You're blocking my view of the road. And it's not safe to put them up like that. If we had an accident..."

Jessie giggled and put her feet back down where they belonged. "Well, you didn't answer my question. Did you like them?"

"They're fine. They're toes, Jessie. I will not entertain these flirtations. It's not appropriate."

"What do you mean? Because we work together?"

"Exactly," I said. "Whether I'm technically your boss..."

"Didn't you work with Rutherford? That didn't stop you before."

"That's different."

"Is it?"

I was speechless. Jessie had a point. That we worked together wasn't the real problem. She was right. Rutherford and I had been on-again, off-again for years.

"Look, Jessie. You're a beautiful girl. But I'm *with* Rutherford."

"Does she make you happy?"

"We love each other."

"That's not what I asked. Does she make you happy? Does she really satisfy you?"

I snorted. "I'm happy. The point is, Jessie, that I'm not interested. You need to accept that if we're going to work together."

Jessie sighed. "Well, just know that the offer stands. If you ever get bored, you know, and want someone who can match your... vigor..."

"Understood. I'm quite flattered, Jessie. But like I said, it's not happening."

"I get it. I'm sorry if I was too forward. I'm just a girl who knows what she wants and will do anything to get it."

"Sometimes it's best to know when to give up, Jessie. I'm not what you want. You have bigger aspirations for your life than pursuing old, washed up men like me."

Jessie sighed. "You're right. I do."

"Then it would be best if you set aside whatever crush this is you think you have on me. I'm happy to help you advance in your career.

If this flirtation continues, though, you'll force my hand. I might not be your boss, strictly speaking, but don't think for a minute Annabelle won't let you go if I ask."

"Got it. Message received. Your loss."

"I'm glad we have that clear. Now, if it's all the same to you, I'm going to act like this conversation never happened. I'm going to give you another chance. You were already making a good impression, before. You don't need to flirt with me to earn my favor."

Jessie scratched her head and folded her arms. Then she sniffed. "I'm sorry."

I sighed. "Jessie. Have other men in your life had... that kind of expectation of you?"

Jessie snorted. "Everyone has expectations."

"That's not what I mean. Have other men taken advantage of you, men who had authority in your life?"

"You're not my therapist. I don't want to talk about it."

I pressed my lips together. She was right. I wasn't her therapist. Even if I wasn't her boss, I was her supervisor. I knew how to read between the lines. Her silence was deafening. It revealed all I needed to know. "I will just say this, Jessie, and then we'll let it be. You are incredible and talented. To see that, I need nothing more from you than giving your best and pouring your passion into your work. You're worth more to me than you think. You're an asset and you're valued. If you're interested in becoming a therapist, I want to help you achieve that. I expect nothing in return. Seeing you succeed and realize your dreams is all the reward I require."

Jessie wiped a tear from her eyes. "Oh, my God. I'm so embarrassed."

"You don't need to be," I pulled up next to Casa do Diabo. "I've lived a long time. I get it. We all have our wounds. Whatever yours are, you've survived. You will overcome it. Just know that you're worth more than you realize. You deserve a man who can love you for all that you are, who respects you for your talents."

"Thank you, Doctor Cain. Were you serious before? When you said you'd forget about all this?"

I nodded. "None of this happened. We're good."

# CHAPTER EIGHT

THIS WAS GOING TO be a challenge. I knew better than to think that Jessie's misplaced feelings would immediately fade. Showing her I cared could backfire. I'd studied under Freud, after all. It wasn't just the reproductive urge that was involved in her feelings, it was her need for acceptance and belonging. I'd counseled thousands of people before I ever worked with supernaturals. She wasn't the first person I'd engaged, though most were clients rather than coworkers, who'd mistaken my care and concern for romantic interest.

The key was boundaries. Now that I knew what was happening, I could be more deliberate about setting up those boundaries. It would take time for Jessie to come around. The truth was, she had no reason to be insecure. She'd been conditioned, probably by men she'd respected in the past, to believe she could only earn a man's favor in a certain way. It was tragic, but it didn't mean she couldn't be helped. I just couldn't be her therapist. When the time was right, perhaps I could refer her to another therapist. It would certainly help maintain our working relationship. She had issues that needed to be addressed. I just couldn't be the one to help her through whatever she was dealing with. Not anymore. At the same time, I couldn't cut her off entirely.

She needed to realize that she had assets beyond the physical that were valuable and respectable.

"I suppose this is your first time at Casa do Diabo?" I asked.

Jessie nodded. "I've met my share of vampires, but I've never been, you know, in their domain."

"Be prepared for anything. When I came here earlier, they were doing... weird things."

"Weird things?" Jessie asked, stepping out of my truck. "What does that mean, exactly? Weirdness is relative. Are we talking asylum-level weird or..."

I chuckled. "I'm not sure exactly what was happening. I have a few guesses, but I'd rather not make assumptions. Just remember that vampires have different urges than you or I. Being human, with no kind of mark to deter them from craving you, I cannot say that they might not show you undesirable attention."

Jessie chuckled. "Undesirable attention? You have a thing for euphemisms, don't you? I know vampires drink human blood, Doctor Cain. They're as likely to see me as a potential meal as they are an ally. I get it."

"Right," I said. "Just be on your guard."

Jessie grinned. "If any of them try anything, I'll make sure they learn their lesson."

"Just let me do the talking. I know Mercy well. She can come off rough around the edges but I can handle her. As for the other vampires here, I know many of them as well. I can't say much for the Scottish vampires. They're less predictable."

"Understood," Jessie said with a quick nod.

We approached the door. No bagpipes this time. I was grateful for that. I pressed the doorbell and waited.

"You can't come in," Mercy said through the speaker.

"There's been an incident. We must speak of it in private."

"I know, Cain. Rutherford called already and filled me in. We've set up wards that will prevent the entry of any werewolves. We should be set, for now."

"For now?" I asked.

"We still need Julie's help before we can evoke the Morrigan. The first time we evoked her, she was one of the three who engaged the three personas of the triple-goddess."

"Julie will be at the extension site in an hour or so. Can you and Hailey meet us there? You can do whatever ritual you need to do to evoke the goddess there."

There was a pause for a moment. "I know she's there. We'll come when we can but I'm not sure it's a good idea right now, Cain."

"Why not?" I asked.

"There won't be anyone left, apart from Mel and Sarah, to guard the Baobhan Sith. That won't be enough, even with these wards."

"What about the Scottish vampires?"

There was another long pause. "They've been compromised."

"What do you mean by 'compromised,' Mercy?"

"It seems their minds might have been affected by the Baobhan Sith as well as Patrick's. Before Rutherford called, they took off all at once into the sunlight."

"Right into the sun? Did they die?"

"I don't think so," Mercy said. "They're all old enough they could survive in the sun for a few hours. It'll hurt like hell and will leave some scars. If what Rutherford said is true, if Patrick has incurred the seven-fold curse..."

"Then they joined Patrick. They've formed a pack of vampire wolves."

"Right. These wards are only as strong as the house is itself. They can't get past the wards, but they might be able to tear down the house brick-by-brick. When they do that, the wards will fail."

"Even if they're turned, they're weakened under the sunlight. They'll be back come nightfall."

"I agree," Mercy said. "Hailey wants to move the Baobhan Sith. The problem is, we can't exactly leave right now, either."

I sighed. "I'll gather the wolves. We'll transport her to the extension site. Can you come after the sun sets and set up a similar ward there to stop them?"

"We can, Cain. But it will also prevent you from entering."

I bit my lip. "Alright. Around the backside of the extension facility, the old Mulledy plantation, there's another small building."

"The old slave quarters?"

"Yes. I think it's our best option. Set up the wards there. Do your ritual just outside to summon the Morrigan. We'll do what we can to protect the Baobhan Sith's sarcophagus at all costs."

# CHAPTER NINE

THIS WAS JESSIE'S FIRST time to visit the extension site. We were going to need nurses there sooner rather than later, so introducing her to the rougarou was an inevitability. Chances were better than not, she'd end up working there at some point. Annabelle hired her largely to handle any werewolf problems that might arise in the asylum. Since most of the wolves were treated at the extension site now, once she got her feet wet, I expected she'd spend most of her time there. She was still new. I'd hoped she'd have more time to shadow Rutherford. It also meant, given that I had more inpatient responsibilities at the original location, she and I wouldn't interact as frequently. Given the situation, it was probably best. Of course, we needed more nurses at both locations. There was a nationwide nursing shortage. It was worse in the domain of mental health. Add to that the remote specialty of working with magical persons and supernatural creatures, and new nurses were exceedingly difficult to come by. We had to recruit nurses from the Voodoo Academy. By the time they graduated, and also finished their necessary secular nursing training, it was a multi-year process. Resolving our nursing shortage wasn't something we could do overnight. For now, we had to get by with those we had.

I'd be remiss to admit that cutting Jessie loose because she'd flirted with me a little probably wouldn't fly with the Voodoo Queen. I was telling Jessie the truth when I said I didn't want to get her fired. The fact was, I wasn't entirely sure that what she'd done so far was enough to convince Annabelle it was necessary even if I thought it so. Annabelle would likely tell me to do my "mind-shrinking mojo" and figure it out. For all her virtues, Annabelle didn't understand that therapy isn't magic. Mental health isn't achieved by waving a wand through the air. It's a process, a journey. It requires hard work and patience. All the more reason to set up the necessary boundaries to ensure that Jessie didn't develop any additional feelings for me.

So far, so good. No more pretty red toes on my dashboard. No more awkward, flirty comments. She was all business. "So, let me get this straight. There are two packs, right?"

I nodded. "That's right. Donald is the alpha of the rougarou. The original pack dwelled in Manchac Swamp for nearly two centuries. They have a few new members, though, who are still adjusting to the wolf."

"And your brother leads the other pack?"

"He does. It's a long story how all that came about, but yes."

"I know the story. Annabelle filled me in on most of the details when she offered me the job."

"Then you know that all of Abel's pack, including Abel himself, are relatively new wolves. Abel is learning what he can about leading a pack from Donald, but he *was* dead for the better part of the last six thousand years. He's still learning how to navigate the world, not to mention how to lead a group of werewolves who've only recently had their lives overturned on account of his bite."

"Because he also incurred the seven-fold curse? That's what Annabelle said."

I sighed. "Yes."

Jessie cleared her throat. "That must be awkward. You killed him. He tried to kill you. That's not something you just get over."

I laughed. "When you're a werewolf, you have to learn how to deal with resentments in short order. Otherwise, when you shift, the worst of whatever hatred or anger you're harboring will be amplified a hundredfold."

Jessie scratched her head. "That's terrifying."

"It can be. But that's why we have almost nightly group sessions and the wolves attend as many as they can make."

"That's not what I mean. I was talking about the new vampire wolves. If the wolf brings out the worst of their nature... we're talking about *vampires*, Doctor Cain."

I took a deep breath. "You aren't wrong. It's a concern. We're at something of a crossroads, here, and I have a decision to make."

"What kind of decision?"

"Well, now that Patrick's pack is almost complete, if he bit one more person, be it a vampire or a human, he'd shift back."

"So you could save seven vampires and it would only cost one more person getting bitten to do it?"

I nodded. "That's the thing. I still can't in good conscience sacrifice one good person to the wolves in order to save seven others, Patrick and the six vampires he turned."

Jessie bit her lip. "Well, why not?"

"Because the ends don't justify the means, Jessie."

"But saving seven people is surely a greater good than sacrificing one, who wouldn't die anyway but would just be turned into a wolf, not doing so would be immoral."

"If you subscribe to utilitarianism, perhaps. I'm more of a deontological ethicist."

"I know you're smart, Cain. You don't have to use big words to prove it."

I laughed. "All that means is I don't focus on the result of an action when judging if it's right or wrong. I judge the action based on whether the deed itself is universally right or wrong, regardless of circumstances."

Jessie laughed. "You actually read Immanuel Kant and stayed awake long enough to agree with him?"

I raised an eyebrow. "You knew I was referring to Kantian ethics?"

Jessie giggled. "I'm more than a pretty face, Doctor Cain. Annabelle didn't hire me just because I'm a badass with Ogoun's aspect, either. I'm also well read and I study hard."

"In that case, I shouldn't have to explain the flaws of a worldview that judges right or wrong based purely on the results, on what produces the so-called greatest good for the greatest number."

"Humor me, Doctor Cain. Given the situation we're facing, I'm not sure I agree with that conclusion."

I bit my lip. "Harming innocent people is never justified. Say, though, that there's a single child in a village with a deadly virus that could spread and kill the whole village. What if someone suggested we simply kill the child to save the rest? Would that be acceptable?"

"No," Jessie said. "It would be wrong. But face it, if the child had a deadly virus, he'd die eventually, anyway."

"Would you volunteer to kill the child?"

"Of course not!"

"Well, why not? If you could justify it, why wouldn't you just eliminate the kid and end the crisis?"

Jessie sighed. "Killing is never right. Especially when it comes to innocent people."

"That's my point, Jessie. Forget the big words I used before, which, apparently, you understood anyway. Ethics aren't that hard. But tell me, how do you know that killing innocent people is wrong?"

Jessie shrugged. "I don't know. I mean, it's sort of obvious."

"Would you know that if no one ever taught you that killing was wrong?"

"Of course I would. I wouldn't want to be killed, so how could I think it was right to kill innocent people?"

I sighed. "Some people believe that what's right or wrong is because of some kind of law prescribed by God."

"Well, I don't think you have to be a Jew or a Christian to agree with 'thou shall not kill.'"

"I knew it was wrong when I killed my brother, even though God didn't give Moses the Ten Commandments until centuries later. When I was cursed and God placed the mark on me, a mark meant to protect me from those who might kill me, I couldn't feign ignorance over what was right or wrong. I knew it in my heart. What's right or wrong is generally something we know by nature. Call it natural law, if you must. Certainly, we can go to great lengths as rational beings to justify wrong actions, but at the end of the day, when one lays in bed at night in the quiet, there's no denying the truth."

"So, you're saying that even if it might force the Scottish vampires to become, well, vampires again, that we shouldn't let Patrick claim his seventh?"

I nodded. "In this case, Jessie, we definitely shouldn't, no matter what ethical theory you might embrace. Yes, it's wrong to subject any innocent person to the werewolf curse without consent. However, consider what the greatest good might be for the greatest number of people. These aren't common werewolves. As we already discussed, the wolf will bring out the worst of their natures."

"But these vampires haven't been especially evil so far as vampires go. They were trying to prevent a greater evil, in fact, from emerging in the world. These vampires didn't choose to become wolves. Not if it was that monster in the tomb that manipulated them to do it. They are victims, too."

"That's true."

"But you still think we have to kill them?"

I scratched my head with my free hand while the other steered the wheel of my truck. "I'm not saying it's right or justified. But if someone has to live with the burden of being a murderer, I'm well practiced."

Jessie turned and stared at me. "Respectfully, that's bullshit."

I shrugged. "I'm not sure what choice we have. Unlike you, I will go on living for centuries more. I'll have time to atone for my misdeeds."

"Bullshit doesn't stop smelling just because you pile more on top of it, Doctor Cain. Tell me, when Abel incurred the seven-fold curse, how did you stop him, then?"

"I didn't. Julie sacrificed herself to become the seventh of his pack."

"And you think that what you're doing, by killing them, is a sacrifice, too? Like you're the martyr who will incur the burden of killing innocent vampires, so no one else has to?"

I pressed my lips together and gripped my steering wheel tightly. "That's not what I'm saying."

"Yes, it is. I haven't met Julie yet. But from what I understand, she didn't commit some kind of atrocity to save your brother and his pack. She sacrificed herself. She accepted the werewolf curse. No offense. But her sacrifice and what you're suggesting here aren't the same."

"You're right. I'm sorry, Jessie. You'll find when working with the magically and mentally deranged that situations often present themselves that don't have a clear, virtuous resolution."

"Well, I think we should still try to find a better solution. Thankfully, there aren't a lot of silver stakes lying around and I don't think there's enough time before now and nightfall to make some."

I nodded. "That's a fair and practical point. I suppose, for now, the question is moot. Regardless, we're going to have to deal with them one way or another. Let's hope relocating the sarcophagus to the asylum extension will buy us a night. New wolves aren't great at tracking. Hopefully, the same holds true for vampire wolves."

# CHAPTER TEN

MOST OF THE WOLVES were already waiting at the extension site, hanging out on the porch, when we pulled up on the circle drive. I parked behind Donald's truck. He had an F-350. I only had an F-150. Yes, I admit it. I suffered from a minor case of truck envy. We men fixate on size. We measure our virility by the size of our trucks, and other things. Of course, it's the size of one's heart that really matters. In that respect, Donald was probably the best man I'd known in a century or more. He was alpha for a reason. While he had the size advantage over the other rougarou, and also drove the biggest truck, it was his compassion that had earned him the loyalty of the other wolves. Not his gigantic truck.

There are a couple of different ways that an alpha can gain dominance over a pack of werewolves. Many do it through intimidation and fear. That approach has its problems. Leading through fear is exhausting. I used to operate that way. Those who lead like that, though, have deeper fears and insecurities themselves than those they impose upon the rest. It was certainly the case for me. That approach never ended well. It's only a matter of time before packs run that way, turn to rage. After all, anger is a close cousin to fear. I have enough horror stories in my past to prove the point. Leading by compassion, though, engenders genuine loyalty. There's nothing that Donald wouldn't do for his fellow wolves and there's nothing the rougarou wouldn't do for him.

Jessie and I stepped out of my truck.

Abel jogged down the marble steps in front of the old plantation home toward us. "Brother!"

Before I could respond, he wrapped his arms around me and lifted me about an inch off the ground.

"Abel, this is my new junior nurse, Jessie."

Jessie extended her hand. "Pleased to meet you."

Abel smiled at Jessie kindly as he released me from his bear hug. "We were just talking about you. It's nice to meet you, too."

"You were talking about me?"

Abel nodded. "Rutherford called over about an hour ago."

Jessie winced. "What did she say about me?"

"Only that you were a very talented nurse, and she expected us to treat you well."

"Well, that's a relief!"

I grinned. "Did you think she'd throw you under the bus, Jessie?"

Jessie shrugged. "I wasn't sure, honestly!"

I laughed. "Jessie reorganized Rutherford's files earlier today."

"Sounds like a rookie mistake," Abel snickered.

"Trust me," Jessie shook her head. "I've learned my lesson."

"Did Rutherford fill you in on the situation?" I asked.

Abel nodded. "She spoke to Donald about it. A vampire werewolf? Is that really a thing?"

"It is now. He's also turned six more."

"Did you say he's turned more?" Donald asked, approaching us while the other wolves continued chatting on the porch.

"That's right. So far, we've learned that silver won't kill them outright. We're guessing a silver stake to the heart might be the magic combination."

Donald tugged at his beard. "Silver stakes? I take it you don't have too many of those on hand."

"We don't. Tonight, though, the hope is we can avoid them. They can endure the sunlight to a point, but it hurts them. We believe they're taking cover until dark. We have to move fast. Did Rutherford tell you about the Baobhan Sith?"

"She did. Sounds like a nightmare."

"We need to relocate her sarcophagus here before sunset. I'm not sure my truck bed is big enough. We'll need to use yours."

"Of course," Donald said. "We'd better get going."

"Is Julie here? We may need her flambeau to fend off the vampire wolves if they track us here."

"She's out back with Cassidy, Ryan, and a few of Abel's wolves. She said something about gathering some sticks from the woods to build something that Mercy and Hailey needed for a spell."

"They're constructing a wicker man. They intend to call the Morrigan."

"Who is the Morrigan?" Abel asked.

"She's a goddess. Mercy believes she might be helpful for dealing with the Baobhan Sith."

Abel scratched his head. "A goddess? I don't know how I feel about that, Cain."

"I get it, brother. Remember that Mercy and Hailey are witches. They revere the old, pagan deities."

Abel sighed. "That's just it. Are you sure that's wise? Can we really trust such deities?"

"I think it would behoove us to maintain an open mind, brother. Our parents taught us to believe in a single God who works through other agents, those we call angels, who are extensions of his will. Perhaps it would be easier if you thought of the Morrigan as one such agent."

Abel scratched his head. "Cain, I don't know..."

I smiled. "Abel, I've learned through the centuries that the Divine Spirit is grander and more infinite than our minds might comprehend. I know little more of this Morrigan than you do. I have to believe, though, that Mercy and Hailey would not willfully evoke a malevolent spirit."

Abel nodded. "You've been alive as long as I've been dead. Who am I to deny that the same Divine love might manifest in as many diverse ways across the world as the people who dwell in it? If you trust Mercy and Hailey, I'll do the same. Not because I understand or accept their views, but because I trust your judgment."

"I appreciate that, brother. I've had my fair share of encounters with witches through the centuries. Some were vile and evil, as you might suspect, but the great majority were kind and honored the same earth our parents were once charged to care for and protect. Dare I say that we are closer in spirit to them than those who claim to use the same terms that our parents did when they taught us of our Maker, but exploit nature for selfish gain and cast judgment upon others devoid of compassion? With some, we might share a common language or knowledge regarding our beliefs, but we share with others a reflection of the same Divine heart. It is the latter, rather than the former, with whom I'd argue we hold the closest kinship."

Abel grinned. "I suppose that's why you have no problem working with a Voodoo Queen and serving an entire underground community populated by hougans and mambos."

I laughed. "Even the Voodoo Queen believes herself to be both a mambo and a Catholic. The same was true of her predecessor, Marie

Laveau. The vodouisants honored and followed her. She also received the Eucharist weekly at St. Louis Cathedral."

"The truck is ready," Donald said. "Ready to go?"

"Certainly." I turned to Jessie. "How would you like to lead the group session with the other wolves while we retrieve the sarcophagus?"

Jessie grinned. "I'd like that. But really, Doctor Cain. I don't know what to say or how to start."

I laughed. "Therapy is ninety percent listening. If you say something wrong, well, so long as you've listened well and given everyone a chance to share, you've still earned an A-minus."

Jessie chuckled. "My mom always told me to take the cotton balls out of my ears and stuff them in my mouth."

"That's good advice. Keep in mind, though, that there is a difference between listening and hearing. We all hear. Hearing is easy. We can't help but hear. Listening is a skill. Consider this an opportunity to practice. The best therapists don't have golden tongues. They have well-turned ears."

# CHAPTER ELEVEN

DONALD'S TRUCK WASN'T JUST bigger than mine. It was louder, too. Short of adding a set of chrome testicles to the hitch, I don't think his truck could have been any more manly than it was. We rumbled down the highway towards the French Quarter.

"How are things going at home?" I asked. "Is Carol's pregnancy progressing well?"

"Huh?" Donald asked. "Can't hear you. My engine is too loud."

I chuckled. So much for small talk. As werewolves, we had acute hearing. For humans, their hearing declines with age. For werewolves, it's just the opposite. I could hear Donald better than he could hear me. Given his age, though, that he couldn't make out my words testified to the ridiculousness of the situation. There were plenty of large trucks out there, fully capable of towing most anything from point A to point B, that weren't half as loud.

I raised my voice. "Why is this truck so damn loud? Is it really necessary?"

Donald laughed. He heard me that time. "I love it. I can feel the power. It's the closest thing to being a wolf when it isn't a full moon."

I grinned. Donald, like the rest of the rougarou, were werewolves constantly for most of their existence. Along with Julie, who was the spirit-guardian of the Witch of Endor's flambeau, they were the pro-tectors of the infernal relic. With most of the wolves I counseled, the challenge was convincing them to embrace the wolf, to accept their new reality, while dealing with whatever human emotions they might have that would be amplified during the shift. When I first started counseling the rougarou, they had experienced no human emotions for years.

As much as the world had changed while they were still wolves, my biggest challenge was helping them learn to be human again. Reinte-grating into the human world meant developing new emotions, both positive and negative, that they'd never had to deal with before. It was quite the shock the first time they shifted back into wolf form again. For months, I'd had to accompany them on their shifts, overruling Donald's position as alpha, to prevent them from losing control. There were advantages to the process, though, from a therapy perspective. Since the wolf amplified their human emotions, after a shift, it was often easier to identify their feelings than before.

Now, the rougarou were so accustomed to self-reflection and used to talking through their emotions in therapy, that it was rare for anything to slip through the cracks. They dealt with their issues before the full moon. For the newer wolves, including Abel and his pack, it was still a work in progress.

So long as Abel was of sound mind, and the two packs ran together, the risk of anything going awry was low. Abel dealt with his primary resentment---me---already. Since then, though, he'd forged very few connections with anyone who wasn't a werewolf. I had to monitor him. For now, he was fine. What would happen if he got a job, or started a family, or signed up for the Bookface or whatever social media platform was currently in vogue though? Eventually, he'd have to deal with other emotions and we'd have to work through them before his problems affected his pack.

We couldn't go into Casa do Diabo on account of the anti-were-wolf security wards that Mercy and Hailey had set up. I wasn't sure how we were going to get the sarcophagus into the back of Donald's truck. If I'd anticipated the problem, I would have insisted Jessie come along. Even then, the best I could remember, the sarcophagus was big. Enhanced strength is one thing. Getting your arms around something like that without help and trying to carry it upstairs, out of a basement, and out the door into the truck wasn't something one person could handle.

"Get back in the truck," Mercy said, speaking through her doorbell speaker. "We've got this."

"It's still light out. I don't know..."

"I said we're handling it, Cain."

Donald and I exchanged glances, shrugged, and returned to the truck. I watched as the door opened and the Baobhan Sith's sarcophagus floated through it. Yes, I said *floated*.

A dim light, barely visible from where we sat, explained it. One of them, Hailey most likely, was moving the thing with some kind of levitation spell.

Donald watched with concern. "No, a little further. No... no... don't scratch my truck!"

I grinned. His concern wasn't out of place. Hailey was an accomplished witch. Still, moving something of that size and setting it perfectly into the truck bed from such a distance must've been difficult.

Beads of sweat formed on Donald's brow as he held his breath, watching the sarcophagus descend slowly until it rested in the back of his truck without incident.

Donald exhaled. "Damn, that witch is good."

I grinned. "You don't know the half of it. I could count on one hand the number of witches or sorcerers I'd met through the centuries who might rival her abilities. What's even more impressive, she's mostly self-taught. Hailey is what most practitioners call a hedge witch."

Donald shook his head. "I know little about witchery and magic. Are you saying she figured out how to do all this with no help at all?"

"Oh, she's had help. She's consulted with grimoires and worked with different witches from time to time. She's eclectic. Hailey picks up a few things here, a few things there."

"So she's a Jack of all trades?"

I laughed. "She might prefer you call her a Jill of all trades, but yes. Only, in her case, she doesn't suffer from the same syndrome that such Jacks or Jills might. Most who dabble in all trades master none of them. She's proficient in every magic I've ever seen her attempt to wield. She's even developed a number of abilities, probably on account of also being a vampire and having access to the power latent in human blood, that I'm not sure any other witch has experienced."

"Isn't Mercy a witch, too?"

I nodded. "She is. But, she's always seen herself as a vampire, first. A witch, second. For Hailey, it's the opposite. As inferior as Hailey is to Mercy with respect to her vampirism, Mercy is to Hailey with the craft . Mercy is a respectable witch in her own right. But she's not quite in Hailey's league."

"How does such a young witch ever learn so much on her own?"

"Some of it is natural talent, I suppose. She's also fearless. Most witches work in covens. The wisdom of the coven protects them from anything that might go wrong when they attempt a spell. Hailey experiments with no trepidation."

"Isn't that dangerous?" Donald asked.

I nodded. "It is. But again, I think that's where her natural talents play a role. I won't say she has made no blunders at all though, if she has, no one told me about it. So far, though, any mistakes she might have made, she's corrected."

Donald stepped out of the truck and closed the tailgate. The last thing we needed was for the Baobhan Sith to fall out of the truck and end up awakening on the Interstate.

I glanced at the horizon as Donald climbed back into the driver's seat. "We'd better hurry. We only have an hour or so until sunset and we need to get moving before any of the vampire wolves see what we're up to. They could be anywhere, watching."

Donald sniffed at the air. "I don't smell any vampires, apart from the girls inside the mansion."

I shook my head. "That's the other thing that was strange, Donald. When Patrick shifted, back in Vilokan, he didn't smell much like a werewolf at all. He smelled more like a vampire. I thought I'd be able to track him. Once he hit the sunlight, though, the odor was gone. Or, perhaps, it was changed, baked, and now I can't pick it up. Either way, I can't track these vampire wolves."

"So you're telling me that if they find us, if they're following us, we won't know?"

I shook my head. "Probably not. That's why we need to prepare as if they'll attack tonight."

"Even so, Cain. We might be ready for an attack, but when we can smell vampires or other werewolves, we know exactly when they're about to arrive."

"That's true. What we have, though, is better numbers. And we have witches. Will it be enough? I can't say. These monsters moved fast. Faster than common wolves. Even faster, I dare say, than most vampires."

"But if silver alone can't kill these vampire wolves, or even a common stake, how are we going to stop them?"

I shook my head. "I don't know. We don't have enough silver to melt down into stakes. We wouldn't have the time to do it if we did. Not before sunset. All I can say is that I have no reason to believe that they have any silver either. We might be more vulnerable than they are, but with no silver on either side, it should be a fair fight."

"Except for the whole speed thing. And whatever enhanced abilities they might have as vampires."

"Right. Given our numbers, though, I still like our chances. Even if we can't kill them, we just have to hold them off until sunrise. We can't allow them to take the Baobhan Sith."

# CHAPTER TWELVE

DONALD OFF-ROADED IT BACK to the old slave quarters and we unloaded the sarcophagus together. The other wolves saw us and joined us just as we were getting it into place.

"How'd the session go?" I asked as Jessie jogged toward us, ahead of the rest.

"Great! It's really cool, you know. To hear people open up like that. There aren't a lot of places you can go in this world, it seems, where you can really be yourself."

I chuckled. "Trust me. If anyone knows that, it's me."

Jessie winced. "Yeah, I guess you don't have the best reputation throughout the world. You know, because of that whole Genesis debacle."

I laughed. "Before anyone could judge me, they'd have to believe I am who I am."

"No sign of the vampire wolves at least," Jessie said, glancing over toward the tree line. Julie, Cassidy and Ryan were still working on assembling their wicker man.

"Were they in therapy?"

Jessie shook her head. "They said they had too much work to do."

I nodded and walked over to the strange figure they were assembling. "What does this do, exactly?"

"It's a proxy sacrifice," Julie explained. "When Mercy and Hailey get here, we'll set it aflame and say a few prayers. If the Morrigan is willing to help, she'll come."

I hadn't even noticed the sun pass beyond the horizon. "Well, we're here."

I turned. Mercy and Hailey stood there looking as extravagant as ever. Mercy was in a long black dress and boots. Hailey was wearing a plaid skirt and a red sweater. She was twirling her wand between her fingers.

"How did you get here so fast? The sun barely set!"

"Vampire speed," Mercy shrugged.

Hailey giggled. "And I know a spell. Call it vampire speed times two."

I cocked my head. "Will it work on werewolves?"

"Perhaps. But I don't believe it will if you're using the flambeau to shift. The spell coheres in your blood. The flambeau also triggers the shift at the blood-level. The only way this spell might work would be during a normal shift, during the full moon."

I bit my lip. "Well, it was worth asking. Still, I'm glad you're here. We set the sarcophagus inside the slave quarters. Can you ward the place to prevent the wolves from entering?"

"We're on it," Mercy said as she and Hailey walked past me and into the slave quarters.

It wasn't going to be a perfect plan. As well as Patrick and the vampire wolves could have torn down Casa do Diabo to get to the sarcophagus, they could demolish the slave quarters. At least here, though, we could keep the fight out of the busy streets of New Orleans.

A twig snapped in the woods. I turned, looking past the wicker man, and saw a shadow move between the trees. Then another one.

"Quick! Julie! We need the flambeau!"

Julie nodded, extended her hand, and the flambeau, now blazing with a blue celestial flame, formed in her hand.

I started to shift. Before I changed completely, while my mouth could still form human words, I turned to Jessie. "Get into the slave quarters. The ward should offer you some protection."

I didn't see if she obeyed my order or not. This part of the shift was always the hardest. The other wolves were shifting, too, including Julie. Donald howled once he completed the change and the rest of the rougarou, along with Cassidy and Ryan rallied behind him. Abel and his wolves surrounded the slave quarters. I took off through the trees.

The vampire wolves were out there. It had to be them. They were playing their strategy carefully.

*No matter what happens,* I told Abel, using the psychic connection we communicated with while shifted, *protect the sarcophagus. They mustn't get to the Baobhan Sith.*

*We'll defend it with our lives, brother.*

My eyesight was more acute now that I was shifted. I caught one of the vampire wolves scurrying through some brush about twenty yards ahead. I bounded toward him.

He was already gone.

*They're moving too fast!* Donald said.

*I'm having the same problem. So long as we can keep this up, though, and they don't get closer to the slave quarters, it's a win. Just so long as we can hold them off until morning.*

I wasn't sure I even believed it when I said it. Patrick knew we had them outnumbered. It didn't take long to figure out his strategy. *Donald! Stay together! They're trying to split us up!*

*If we stay together, they'll get around us.*

*If they split us up, they'll gang up on us when they have the advantage. They might not have silver, but I cannot say they're not strong enough to rip us apart.*

No sooner did I say it and Patrick appeared right in front of me. I recognized him from before, when he'd shifted in Vilokan. Only now, wounds oozed with some kind of pus all over his body. Dried blood and mud were caked in his fur. All the result of half a day in sunlight.

I roared at him. He roared back.

Donald and the rougarou, meanwhile, were pursuing another one of his wolves, moving the opposite direction.

I dove at Patrick. He threw himself back at me. Our bodies collided, but with his vampiric strength, he ended up on top. As he snapped at me I saw his teeth. His canines were twice the length of mine. Blood dripped from his jaws. From the smell, I knew it was human blood. They'd fed during the day. It must've helped them keep their strength under the sunlight.

Patrick opened his jaws wide and reared his head back to go for the bite.

Then something blasted through Patrick's chest. It was long like a javelin. It was silver but aglow with green energy.

Patrick collapsed beside me.

I turned. Jessie was standing there holding the silver instrument she'd used to kill him.

*Donald. It's done. Patrick is dead. The seven-fold curse was broken.*

A few seconds later, Donald and the rougarou came running in my direction, howling as they approached. One of the Scottish vampires was chasing them, nipping at their tails.

Julie was running right beside him, holding her flambeau in her jaws. The blue flame was impossible to miss.

*You can extinguish the flambeau,* I told her. When she did, we shifted back into human form.

I scurried back to all fours, and eventually on my two legs as my body shifted back. I looked around. Five more bodies, now back in human form, lay naked in the brush, shivering. The vampire wolf who was following Donald and the rougarou was somewhere in the brush.

I recognized one of the vampire wolves near me. It was Brendan, the vampire I'd met at Casa do Diabo before.

I stood up and dusted off my body.

"Well this is awkward," Jessie said, still holding her silver javelin in her right hand. "I've never been surrounded by so many naked people. I feel a bit left out."

"Jessie, I don't know what to say..."

"You could put on some pants. Or not. I mean, I don't mind the view. But you know, as you said before, it's probably not appropriate."

"But how did you..."

Jessie smiled. "My soul weapon coheres with the elements of the earth, Doctor Cain. Silver is one of those elements. Haven't you ever seen a periodic table?"

"Why didn't you tell me that before?"

Jessie shrugged. "I thought you might try to stop me. That whole lecture you gave me about not killing people and all. But you know, I figured since Patrick was the one who was cursed, I only needed to kill him."

I sighed. "You still took a life, Jessie."

"Patrick was prepared to die," Brendan said, his red eyes catching the light radiating off of Jessie's javelin. "The girl saved us all."

"We might still have time," Julie said. "Let me get Hailey and Mercy. If we can evoke the Morrigan, enough of the night remains that we may be able to seal the Baobhan Sith."

"It's no use," Brendan said.

"You don't think the Morrigan can do that?" Julie asked.

"It's not that," Brendan said. "Patrick wanted to be sure that we could trust Mercy and the vampires here to guard the sarcophagus."

"What are you saying, Brendan?" I asked.

"The Baobhan Sith is not in that sarcophagus, Cain. It is a replica. Patrick had it made that he might first test the New Orleans vampires to ensure they were up to the task."

"Then where is the real one?"

"That's just the thing," Brendan said. "Patrick is the only one who knew where it was."

"Wait," Jessie said. "How do we know that the Baobhan Sith isn't also influencing you now? You were guarding her as long as they were, right?"

Brendan shook his head. Patrick's body had returned to its normal human-like form. He brushed a strand of hair out of Patrick's face. "Rest in peace, brother."

Then Brendan rolled Patrick over. Four long scars ran along the length of his back.

"What happened to him?"

"During one of her risings, a few years back, the Baobhan Sith scratched him. It didn't kill him. But that was when the voices began. You can examine each of us. We stand here exposed in front of all of you. He is the only of us who was wounded. He is the only one who she manipulated."

"Bullshit!" Mercy said, stepping up behind us. "You left us and joined him before!"

Brendan sighed. "We knew that the sarcophagus there did not truly hold the Baobhan Sith, Mercy. I apologize, on Patrick's behalf, for the deception. He believed it was necessary. We only left in what proved to be a futile attempt to save him. We had no choice. Somehow we had to find out where he'd hidden the real Baobhan Sith."

"If that's the case, why did he lead you all here to fight us tonight?"

Brendan shook his head. "It didnae matter that you had the fake sarcophagus. He knew where she was the whole time. Even under her influence, though, he couldnae awaken her until the time arrived. He led us here to kill you. He believed, warped though his mind was, as was ours while under the curse and his control, that if you survived, if any of you lived, that you posed a threat to the Baobhan Sith."

I scratched my head. "Did he indicate exactly how the Baobhan Sith thought we might kill her?"

Brendan chuckled. "Not at all. Though, I admit, that would have been convenient."

"Let's go inside and talk more. The bugs are biting my butt. I think we can probably find some clothes for you all to get by."

"We don't need much," Brendan said. "Just a good cloth to cover the jangly bits."

I chuckled. "Well, hopefully, sweats will do. We're fresh out on kilts."

"Aye," Brendan said. "I suspected as much. It's a pity, you know."

I snorted. "That we don't have kilts?"

Brendan nodded. "As the great William Wallace once said, albeit through the mouthpiece of Mel Gibson, ye can take our lives, but ye can never take our freedom."

I bit my lip. "I've seen that movie. I don't think he was talking about freeing your... you know... jangly parts."

"If yer balls aren't free, Cain, ye don't know what true freedom is."

# CHAPTER THIRTEEN

IT DIDN'T TAKE LONG to get dressed. Brendan and the other Scottish vampires kept tugging their crotches. They clearly weren't accustomed to the prison otherwise known as pants. We gathered around the large table that we had set up in what used to be Annabelle Mulledy's living room. Now, it was where we conducted our group sessions. We barely had enough seats for all the wolves. With Brendan and five more Scottish vampires, along with Mercy and Hailey, we were beyond max capacity. Abel and his pack volunteered to stand around the perimeter of the room.

Based on the gurgling sound coming from the kitchen and Jessie's absence, combined with the savory odor that was already spreading through the house, coffee was coming soon. Thank God for that. This wasn't the first time I'd worked with vampires to quell a supernatural threat. It meant that my days and nights got reversed. Since most of those in the room had recently shifted to wolf form and back again, we were bound to crash sooner rather than later. Something about every cell in your body changing, your entire skeleton expanding along with your organs, takes a toll.

Jessie set a mug in front of me even while the coffee continued to brew. Usually I'm a gentleman. When I have guests, I let them go first. With my coffee, though, I would not wait for anyone. I *needed* it.

"Can you just summon the Morrigan, anyway?" I asked, looking across the table at Mercy. "If she's a goddess, maybe she can do what she has to do, you know, on a long distance basis. The God I know works that way almost exclusively."

Mercy, Hailey, and Julie all exchanged glances. "There's something we need to tell you, Cain. I'm sorry I didn't before. I didn't mean to involve you in any of this."

I shrugged. "What's done is done, Mercy. What is it?"

"We weren't calling the Morrigan to seal the Baobhan Sith. We were calling her to free her."

I stared at Mercy blankly. "Why the hell would you do that?"

"The Morrigan is also known as the Phantom Queen," Hailey said. "She's most associated with foretelling doom or death. She can also incite warriors to battle and help ensure they achieve victory."

"Patrick didn't bring the Baobhan Sith here so we could watch over her," Mercy said. "He knew it was only a matter of time before her influence would take hold. He only hoped he could kill her before it happened. Sadly, that wasn't how it worked out."

"So you intend to evoke the Morrigan so she can kill the Baobhan Sith?"

"She doesn't kill. Not directly. When we evoke her, she'll invest each of us three witches with one of her three personas: Macha, Babd, and Anand. Working together we can handle the Baobhan Sith."

I scratched my head. "She's the original. I thought she couldn't be killed."

"But she can be sent to the void. That's as good as death."

I sighed. I'd been to Eden before. Abel and I both went there. It's on a plane of existence distinct from that of the earth. When my parents ate the fruit and were banned from the garden, it was severed from this world. From what I'd learned, earth operates on a single fabric of space and time. Eden's fabric of space and time is distinct. If you go to Eden, unless there's some kind of portal connecting the two worlds that remains constant, you could end up in Eden at any time at all. Come back through a different portal than the one you took to get there and you could end up on earth at any time past, present, or future. Since no soul can ever exist in the same place and time twice, if you end up going to either realm and you're already there, you end up dumped into the void. The nothingness that separates the worlds. Mercy's plan, as I understood it, was to create a portal that forced the Baobhan Sith into the void. Presumably, by sending her through a portal to a place she already was.

"You're certain that the Morrigan can create portals like that?"

"The Baobhan Sith only emerges one night a year," Hailey said. "We revere that day as Samhain. It corresponds with what people call Halloween. It's the time when the veil between the worlds is the thinnest. We believe that the Baobhan Sith doesn't exist on earth at all. She's not dormant in that sarcophagus. The place you call Eden, or Guinee, or Annwn, has another side to it. A darker side. Some call it Samhuinn, or Samhain. There, it's always the day of the dead. It is the opposite of Eden's garden groves, a place of life."

"The Morrigan," Mercy said, "is called the Phantom Queen for a reason. She has eminent authority over that side of the divide."

"Then she knows the Baobhan Sith and has authority over her?"

Hailey nodded. "She does. In that domain. But if we were to bring the Morrigan here, we think we can control her. If we try to send the Baobhan Sith back to her realm through a different portal, not through the sarcophagus which maintains a connection to the dark side of Eden, she won't be able to enter that place because she's already there."

"So the portal will send her into the void."

"And if we can awaken her early, draw her into this world at a different time, the portal won't likely hold. The veil between worlds won't be thin enough. She'll have no way to flee back through her sarcophagus until we send her back ourselves."

I pinched my chin. "The plan is sound. There's only one problem. We don't know where Patrick hid her. If we can't find her before Samhain, what are the chances your plan would work if you cast her through a portal when she rises at the time she normally would."

Mercy sighed. "We believe that any portal we form at that time would send her to the same time and place where the portal that forms in her sarcophagus connects."

"Would that be the end of the world? If that happened, couldn't we just wait another day and then carry out your plan to end her forever?"

"That's just it, isn't it, Cain? There are a lot of wolves here."

"And now that we've been bitten," Brendan said, "we'll shift when you do."

I sighed. "Of course. That poses a problem or six."

"More than that," Hailey added. "She could manipulate all of you. Your shifts would never be the same. If she gets a chance to infect the minds of all of you, we don't know if that influence will leave after she's gone."

"The way she got to Patrick wasn't through possession or anything of the sort." Brendan tucked his long hair behind his ears. "She plants seeds in the mind that later sprout. It's impossible to know after she's touched your mind what thoughts are your own and which she's given you from the start. That we're here, Cain, in New Orleans, suggests that she's well aware of you."

"You're saying that the reason you all came here to begin with was because the Baobhan Sith intended for Patrick to seek me out? She wanted him to inherit the seven-fold curse?"

Brendan sighed and leaned against the wall. "We cannot know for certain. But I believe that's the case. Patrick insisted before we left Scotland that only six of us come along. The rest were to remain at Castle Ruthven to keep our affairs in order. We didnae question it, but now it makes sense why he wanted six of us. No more. No less."

I pinched my chin. "Yes. Because of the sevenfold curse. All of this tracks. I fear you might be right. There's still a problem, though. Julie is a werewolf, too. You need her to revive the Morrigan, do you not?"

"We do," Mercy said. "She's one of the three with whom the Morrigan has already aligned."

"She's also a werewolf. If the Baobhan Sith can manipulate her mind with as much ease as she might the rest of us, would she also be able to influence a third of the Morrigan?"

"We don't know," Julie said. "It is a risk, I admit. We hope if we evoke the Morrigan soon enough, she can tell us how much of a risk it might be."

# CHAPTER FOURTEEN

ACCORDING TO BRENDAN, PATRICK arrived in the country before the rest. Traveling overseas with a sarcophagus containing a supernatural killer isn't easy. I haven't ever tried, but I'm pretty sure that the TSA would confiscate vampiric monsters at the gate. That, along with your opened containers the of baby formula and shampoo.

Patrick came with the sarcophagus across the Atlantic in a shipping container on a barge. The plan was to touch base with the other vampires so they could come after he'd arrived. He refused to allow any members of his coven to accompany him. Now we know why, even if he didn't realize it at the time. Not all the ideas Patrick thought were his own were, in fact, his own.

There was something haunting about that realization. Patrick didn't realize how deep the Baobhan Sith's influence was when I met with him in my office. He experienced whatever seeds she'd planted in his mind as if they were his own. So far as we knew, she had infected none of the other Scottish vampires. But could we really know for certain? Not even they would realize it if that were the case.

I couldn't imagine what Brendan and the rest were going through. Losing Patrick was jarring. He'd led their coven for centuries. While Brendan believed that Baobahn Sith's influence over Patrick began when he was scratched, there was no way to know for certain that was when or how it happened. If that couldn't be determined, and there was a possibility she was influencing others even now, not only was it hard to trust anyone else, Brendan couldn't even trust himself. None of them could. Anyone who'd ever had contact with the Baobahn Sith was susceptible.

"We're going to stay and work on the wicker man," Mercy said. "We need to make use of the night so that it's ready when we need it."

Hailey snorted. "The wicker person."

I raised an eyebrow. "Excuse me?"

Hailey chuckled. "We don't know his, her, or their preferred pronouns."

"That's ridiculous, Hailey. The wicker man isn't real. He doesn't have any preferred pronouns."

Hailey grinned. "They do not have any preferred pronouns."

Julie cocked her head. "I'm confused."

I could tell by the look on Hailey's face that she was screwing with the others. I also related to Mercy's and Julie's confusion. When you come from another era, keeping up with the sensitivities of the day can be a challenge. It feels like the world is always leaving you behind.

Mercy huffed. "Fine. We'll be working on the wicker person."

Hailey giggled. "Actually, I think it might be wicker man on second thought. I mean, he's constantly showing us his wood."

Mercy face-palmed. "Cain, you see what I'm dealing with here?"

I grinned. "If I recall, when you and Nyx were in the asylum, it was you who insisted I call her Nicky, was it not?"

"Of course. I also remember you were reluctant to do so."

I nodded. "As I explained at the time, it was only because she needed to be the one to embrace and advocate for her own truth. I've met her a few times since, and she's Nicky to me now."

"It doesn't matter," Hailey said. "I was just screwing around. Sort of. Though, the point I want to make has nothing to do with the wicker dude."

"It's a wicker dude, now?" Mercy raised an eyebrow.

Hailey smiled. "We know that the Baobhan Sith only turns females. She usually kills and consumes men. Her progeny will do the same."

"It's not the same with vampires," Brendan paced behind us. "She can't turn or consume us. We are already vampires and it is strictly human blood she craves."

"You're right in line with my train of thought. When the Baobhan Sith is awakened, you will need a human male and female both to lure her out. One to feed from, the other to turn."

"Aye," Brendan said. "It makes sense. For centuries, we've deprived her of either pleasure. If we give her that opportunity, it may be enough to lure her through the portal even before Samhain."

Jessie raised her hand. "I volunteer."

"I don't know, Jessie."

"Think about it, Doctor Cain. I'm the only human female here. I can also defend myself. Iron kills her, right? Well, I can form my ethereal weapon out of iron as easily as I could form silver."

"Your nurse has a point," Mercy said. "You'll still need a human male."

"I might be able to help with that." Brendan reached down to his ankle and pulled a phone out of an elastic band that he'd used to secure it there while shifted. It was a clever move, I suppose. It also speaks to how addicted people are—even ancient vampires—to their damned phones. He couldn't even go a night as a vampire-wolf without the thing.

I tilted my head. "You use a cell phone?"

"Aye. I might be old, Cain. But I'm not dead. Patrick used to say if you're not changing with the times, the times will leave ye behind."

I narrowed my eyes. "I suppose there's *some* truth to that."

"Most of the people left behind by time are in graveyards," Mercy said.

I snorted. "Thanks for that. I'm very much alive."

Mercy grinned. "I wasn't implying that you're dead, Cain. I wasn't talking about you at all, although you still insist on using land-lines only."

Jessie furrowed her brow. "You talk on corded phones?"

"I do. They're easier to use."

"No, they aren't. You have to remember phone numbers. I haven't memorized a phone number since I was a kid. Hell, I don't think I even remember what my own number is right now."

I sighed. "I have my little black book. It works for me."

Brendan grinned. "I believe I can access Patrick's e-mail account."

"You know Patrick's password?" Mercy asked.

Brendan smiled. "Guessed it a while back. It was 'blood.' Might as well have made his password 'password.' Until now, I didnae have much reason to use it other than to use his Netflix account."

I shook my head. "Well, on the bright side, you don't have to worry about him finding out you know his password."

Brendan sighed.

I winced. "Apologies. He just died. That was insensitive."

Brendan chuckled. "That's not it. You said 'on the bright side.' For vampires, that means precisely the opposite of what it does for humans."

I tilted my head. "I suppose that makes sense!"

"As I said before, Cain. Patrick had wished for the ultimate death for several years now. His loss is substantial. He would not wish for us to mourn. His only desire would be that we finish what we came here to do."

I nodded. "To kill the Baobhan Sith."

Brendan set his phone down in front of me. "This must help us fulfill my sire's last wish."

"What am I looking at?" I asked. I was afraid to touch the screen. Not that I thought it would shock me or anything like that. I just thought if I touched it I might close the screen, or delete whatever it was he was showing me.

"It's the shipping order for the sarcophagus," Brendan said. "Patrick couldn't move it alone. He must've had help. If you want to find it, I'd suggest tracking down whoever helped him. If I were to place a bet on it, I'd wager it was likely a human male."

Jessie huffed. "Why do you say that? I'm a girl. I could lift that thing, no problem."

"No offense intended," Brendan said. "But you take that whole girl power thing to a different level."

"She's got beauty and brawn," Abel said, pulling up a chair next to me and examining the phone. I glanced at my brother even as Jessie chuckled at his subtle attempt at a compliment. "There are initials on the order. What does that mean?"

"Probably someone who works in the shipping yard and received the shipment," I said. "If we can figure out who has the initials O.R.C. it might lead us to some answers."

Hailey shook her head. "Orc? Seriously? This guy is an orc?"

"Not a literal orc," I said, laughing. "So far as I know, orcs aren't real. Ogres, sure. But orcs? Only in the movies."

Jessie giggled. "I don't know. I think a few of my ex boyfriends might qualify as orcs."

"Tell me about it," Hailey said. "I mean, I've made some bad choices through the years. I don't think any of them compare to the choice of guys I used to date before I was a vampire. I was beginning to wonder if something was wrong with me. Did I have some kind of thing for losers or something? Every guy I dated ended up being one."

"How much did you really date?" I asked. "You were, what, sixteen or seventeen when you were turned?"

Hailey grinned. "I'm not saying we had the best dates in the world back then. It was always dinner and a movie. Every now and then a guy would get creative and take me to miniature golf or a theme park."

"Not just dinner and a movie," Jessie added. "It's always Applebees and a movie."

"I know, right!" Hailey exclaimed. "What's with High School dates and Applebees?"

Jessie shook her head. "It was the same with the guys at the Voodoo Academy. Applebees was usually considered a score. Anything above fast food usually meant that the boy wanted to see you more than once."

I cleared my throat. "I'm glad you girls are all bonding, but we have things to do. Considering the fact that we're working with vampires, we only have so many hours of darkness at our disposal."

Mercy nodded. "I agree with Cain. We don't know how soon we'll need the Morrigan's aid. We best get to work on the wicker man. Even with vampire speed, I don't know that we'll get it all done by the end of the night."

Julie shrugged. "I can finish it tomorrow, so long as we get the main skeleton of it all lashed together tonight."

I pulled my truck keys out of my pocket. "Alright, ladies. Well, I'd best go orc hunting."

"I'm coming along," Jessie said.

"I will, too," Abel spoke up. I bit my lip. The eagerness with which he volunteered only a half-second after Jessie did suggested that the trip to the freight yard wasn't the real draw. Abel wasn't much older than Jessie when he died. His voice, though, was aged. His thoughts were refined. His body might not be much older than Jessie's, but his soul certainly was. I'm not sure where to draw the line in terms of the appropriateness of age disparity, but, in this case, if they kindled a spark, it could be positive. At least it would likely help dismiss any worries I had about Jessie's crush on me.

"Alright. Well, I wasn't planning on retrieving the sarcophagus. Not until we know for sure that it's there. I don't need that much help."

Jessie snorted. "No offense, Cain. But this shipping order is on a phone. Brendan, can you text it to me from Patrick's phone?

"I can send you a screen shot," Brendan said.

"Perfect. See, Cain? You need me."

"She's right, you know, brother."

I smirked. "Then why are you so eager to come along, Abel?"

Abel shrugged. "Perhaps I'd like a change of scenery."

"A change of scenery?" I raised an eyebrow, then glanced toward Jessie. She was already climbing into the passenger side of my truck and didn't notice.

Abel followed her with his eyes. "Yes, I appreciate the scenery."

# Chapter Fifteen

Jessie took the back seat so Abel could sit up front. The back seat of a truck is like the front row at church. You can sit there, but no one ever does. Not unless there isn't any other option.

It wasn't a long drive. I didn't have a middle console in the front. Jessie could have squeezed between us. After our last car ride together, though, I figured she was trying to set her own boundaries.

"So, Abel. What's it like to be dead?"

"Jessie! That's not an appropriate question."

Abel raised his hand and laughed. "It's okay, brother. It's not an irrational question. I suppose most people have a curiosity about the other side. To answer your question, Jessie, it's peaceful."

"What kind of peaceful?"

"I'm not sure I understand the question."

Jessie snorted. "Well, is it 'drinking a cocktail on a beach' peaceful, or 'laying down in bed in a dark room after the hardest day ever' peaceful?"

I glanced at Jessie in the rearview mirror. "What's the difference, Jessie?"

"I get what she's asking, brother. Sometimes we surround ourselves with things we like and enjoy to find peace. At other times, we try to remove everything and anything from our minds and discover peace through absence, through nothingness."

"Exactly!" Jessie said. "Is being dead more like a trip to paradise or like floating through the abyss of nonexistence?"

"More like paradise, I suppose," Abel scratched the back of his head. "But not like you'd think. It's certainly not a beach."

"Right," Jessie chuckled. "Life's a beach, and then you die."

I laughed. "I don't think that's exactly how the saying goes."

"But it is à propos," Abel smiled. "I've never had a cocktail on the beach. It sounds nice. But it also sounds like a vacation, an escape. In the afterlife, call it heaven, you have no desire to escape anything. Not that you do not want to live again. It's more like the thought of returning to your life never occurs at all. It's simple contentment."

"If it's so great, why'd you come back?"

I gripped the steering wheel and bit my tongue.

"I didn't return by choice. I was resurrected. Twice, in fact."

"That sucks."

Abel grinned. "I thought so at first. But then I discovered, as I lived again, forging a new relationship with my brother and developing a bond with my pack, that I didn't want to die. I had something to live for. Simple contentment. Only this time, I wasn't in heaven. I was here on earth."

My eyes welled up with tears. I choked it back. Abel hadn't really talked about death before. After he came back the first time, he forgave me. He said he could die in peace knowing we'd reconciled. Then, the next time he was resurrected, we bonded. Not just him and me. The entire pack bonded.

I know this might come as a surprise, but our family life growing up wasn't exactly wholesome. My parents had serious guilt issues—you know, over the whole plunging the entire universe into sin thing—and they tried way too hard to compensate for it. They had rules for everything. You'd think, you know, since they couldn't keep only one rule—don't eat from that stupid tree—they'd know better than to load us up an entire, detailed code of conduct. They didn't.

They expected perfection. When my sacrifice wasn't accepted, all that pressure, all that rage, came out at once. My brother paid the price. But that was a long time ago. A few thousand years processing my rage, letting it loose as a literal monster once every lunar cycle, helped me get past that. Therapy helped, too. Abel's forgiveness allowed me to put those issues behind me (mostly).

It hadn't occurred to me until now that my brother had issues stemming from our upbringing, too. He'd found a new family, one united by a bond created by a curse.

My map of New Orleans was in my glove box. I reached in, grabbed it, and tossed it to Jessie. I figured maps might not be a thing Abel had figured out yet.

"What the hell is this?" Jessie asked.

"I need you to look up the address on the shipping order."

Jessie smiled so wide I thought her head might split in half. "You *seriously* use maps, Cain?"

I raised an eyebrow. "I know New Orleans fairly well, but I don't know where everything is. It's a big city. Don't tell me you don't know how to use a map."

Jessie bit her lip. "I think I learned a little about maps from *Dora the Explorer* when I was five. You know, *I'm the map, I'm the map, I'm the map...*"

I narrowed my eyes. "Fascinating. I am the map. That's a pretty profound existential insight. I could use that. If you're trying to find where you want to go in life, look inside. You *are* the map!"

"It's a cartoon, not philosophy, Doctor Cain."

"Right. Whatever. Just look up the address so I know where to go."

Jessie chuckled and tossed the map onto the seat next to her. She opened her phone, presumably to get the address.

"It helps if you unfold the map," I said.

Jessie rolled her eyes. Then, after a few seconds, a woman with a kind voice spoke from her phone. "In three and a half miles, take exit 9B onto Gen di Gaulle Drive."

"With whom am I speaking?" I asked. "Do you work at the shipyard?"

Jessie giggled. Even Abel laughed a little.

"Hello? Are you there?"

"She's not real," Abel said. "She's a computerized voice. Jessie programmed the address into her GPS."

I cocked my head. "She did? How did you know that, Abel?"

Abel laughed. "I wasn't born yesterday, brother. I've lived in the twenty-first century long enough to know about smartphones and global positioning satellites. That's pretty much week-one material."

I sighed. "Well, I never saw a reason to spend a thousand dollars on a device like that just so it could do what a map I got for less than a dollar can do just as well."

"You have plenty of money, brother."

I nodded. "I do. It's not that I can't afford a smartphone. It's the principle. There was an article in the International Journal of Psychoanalysis about how attachment to electronic devices becomes a crutch to fill the void we all experience when separated from our mothers wombs."

Abel turned and looked at me. I didn't turn back. I was still looking for exit 9B and didn't want to miss it. "That sounds like bullshit. No offense, brother."

"No, Abel. It makes sense. Think about it. In the womb, we receive everything from our mothers. We're literally plugged in. We receive our nutrients. The womb protects us as we grow and develop. Then, in an instant, all of that is stripped away and we find ourselves in a world we've never known. We take that first breath and cry. Why do we cry? It's not just because we're babies. It's because we're terrified. It's the initial trauma that sticks with us forever. We turn to devices like phones and obsess over them because we imagine they satisfy our needs, too. They might not feed us directly, but they provide knowledge. They approximate social needs. They also give us a sense of safety. We think if we have a phone on us, if we have an accident, we'll be okay because we can call for help."

Jessie giggled. "That sounds like an excuse from someone who really doesn't want to be embarrassed trying to learn how to use a smart-phone."

"I'm telling you! It was in a peer-reviewed journal. I'm not making this up!"

*In half a mile, exit right.*

"Oh crap," I said. "I almost missed the exit. I was talking too much."

Jessie shook her head. "See, Doctor Cain. The phone is *helpful.*"

I grunted. "If it wasn't for phones, I wouldn't have been distracted talking about the infantile origins of a person's technology addictions."

From my peripheral vision, I could see Abel shaking his head. I chose to ignore it as I flipped on my turn signal, merged into the exit lane, and followed the strange digital voices' subsequent instruction to turn "right" at the end of the exit ramp.

Then, she started barking out orders like one of my former wives used to, only after we'd been married for twenty years. "She's really pushy, isn't she?"

Jessie laughed. "It's nothing personal, Doctor Cain. The program is just trying to help you get to the shipping yard."

I sighed. "She's saying so many things. I'm confused."

Jessie handed her phone to Abel. "Show it to him."

Abel held it out. A little cartoon version of a car was moving across what looked like a map.

"Who is that? I'm in a truck. That looks like a little blue car."

"It's us," Jessie said.

"So much for smart phones being smart. It doesn't even have my truck right. How am I supposed to trust that it knows where it's taking us?"

Abel gasped. "Maybe it's finally happened. Technology is taking over. It's trying to kill us. It's going to make you turn right into Lake Pontchartrain. It's going to kill us, Cain!"

I narrowed my eyes. "I might be naïve, Abel. I'm not gullible."

Jessie giggled. "Just follow the highlighted route. She'll tell you where to go, too. We're only a couple of minutes away."

I grinned. "It's a good thing you're wrong, Abel. I wonder, if technology really tried to kill me, would it trigger the mark and inherit the seven-fold curse?"

"Cyborgian werewolves!" Jessie exclaimed. "It's official. That's how the apocalypse begins!"

# Chapter Sixteen

The shipping yard was surrounded by a security fence. There was a guard in a booth at the entrance. We were still a good hour or two before sunrise but, apparently, the shipping industry never sleeps. That didn't mean their security guards didn't.

I reached through my window and tapped on the security booth window. The man almost jumped through the roof of his miniature booth, his eyes wide and his hair a mess.

He looked out the window at me and sighed in relief. I wasn't his boss.

"Can I help you, sir?"

"I'm here to follow up on a shipment that came through the last month or so."

The guard snorted. "I'm going to need more details than that. We move a lot of cargo."

Jessie handed me her phone. I held it through the window up to the glass.

He leaned toward the window. He looked at the phone. His eyes went wide when he looked at it. He knew something.

I glanced at his nametag. The guard's name was Oscar. If his middle name happened to begin with an R, and his surname with a C, he was exactly the person we hoped might have the information we needed.

" I'm sorry," Oscar said. "We can't give anyone except the name on the order any information about the cargo in question."

I bit my lip. "My name is Patrick Ruthven. Please, I need to know if the shipment is still on the property."

"You're not... I mean... do you have a legal ID to prove otherwise?"

I bit my lip, turned, and whispered. "He knows I'm not Patrick. That might mean he remembers him."

"He definitely knows something," Abel whispered back. "Someone doesn't look at a shipping order in shock, especially if you work in a shipping yard, unless there's something fishy about it."

"Sorry," I said. "Forgive me. I come as a representative of Patrick Ruthven. He died last night, you see, and it's essential we acquire the package on this order."

Oscar cocked his head. "He died? Well, in that case, I'd need something proving you're next of kin, which, given his pale complexion compared to yours, I find unlikely."

"How do you know we weren't adopted brothers?" I asked.

Oscar sighed. "Look, no offense, I need documentation to verify what you're claiming. We can't just give anyone who tells us a sob story about someone, who may or may not have died, access to said person's cargo."

"But the cargo *is* here," I said.

Oscar shrugged. "No ID, no answers."

"Let me talk to him," Jessie said.

"Jessie, I don't know..."

"Just unlock the door, Cain."

I sighed and unlocked the door. Jessie was a beautiful girl. Still, I didn't think the whole "I'm going to flirt my way past security" routine was going to work. That sort of thing only happens in the movies. In the real world, people have jobs and families to support. They will not be as easily swayed by a pretty face as one might assume.

Jessie took her phone back and stepped out of the truck. She tapped on the security guard's window again.

"I already told you.."

"Just look at this a little closer," Jessie said. "I think you'll find that we have permission to access the cargo."

The guard sighed and leaned in toward the glass.

"I don't see..."

Before Oscar could finish speaking, Jessie punched her fist straight through the glass. Some of her green magic coursed through her arm and her skin looked thick, almost like tree bark. She grabbed Oscar by the scruff of his shirt and pulled him against the window.

"How the hell. This shit is double-paned..."

"This is what's going to happen, Oscar. Or should I call you Orc? Those are your initials, aren't they?"

"I guess. I mean, yes. What do you want?"

"You're going to let us through. You're going to show us to the cargo and you're going to tell us what you know. If you don't, people will die."

"Jessie..."

Jessie raised her free hand to silence me. "What will it be, Oscar? Are you going to cooperate or am I going to have to jump through this window and force you to let us in?"

Oscar's face was plastered against the glass. "I need to reach the button to..."

"Tsk, Tsk, Tsk," Jessie said. "How do I know that's not the button for an alarm?"

"It isn't! Look at it. It fucking says 'gate' on the button, you crazy bitch!"

Jessie smirked and pulled the man harder into the glass. "What did you call me?"

"Sorry! I didn't mean..."

"Yeah, you did. You meant it. Maybe you're right. Say I am a crazy bitch. If that's the case, you don't know what I might do if you don't comply."

"I can't reach the fucking button like this!'

"Sure you can," Jessie said. "It's just a button. You can hit it with your foot."

"I'm not that flexible!"

"Then you'd better loosen up real fast."

Oscar stretched as best he could and bumped the button with his boot. With a buzz, the security bar raised. "Now let me go!"

"I will," Jessie said. "After you tell us what you know about the shipment."

"I know nothing!"

"You're a poor liar, Oscar. That look on your face when you saw the shipping order told me everything I needed to know. As you said before, a lot of cargo passes through here. You wouldn't recognize one particular container unless there was good reason to remember it."

"He said he'd kill me if I told a soul!"

"The vampire who told you that is dead, Oscar. I killed him."

Oscar gulped. "Seriously?"

"What? Don't you think I can stake a vampire?"

"It's not that... I didn't realize..."

"Like I said, Oscar. We're dealing with things, here, way above your paygrade. You'd best play ball."

"Yes, of course. Drive through. I'll meet you outside. Oh God, if he finds out..."

"He won't find out," Jessie said. "I was telling you the truth. So was my colleague, here. Patrick Ruthven is dead. If we don't get his shipment soon, people will get hurt."

Jessie released Oscar. He stepped out of the booth and approached my truck after I pulled past the gates.

Before he made it all the way around, Jessie turned, looked at me, and smiled. "I've got this one, Doctor Cain."

I bit my lip. "Jessie, I don't know…"

Abel grabbed my arm. "She got us this far, Cain. I say we let her see it through."

I nodded. "Alright, Jessie. You take point."

Jessie smiled. She turned and caught Oscar as he approached. "What exactly do you know about this shipment, Oscar?"

Oscar shook his head. "All I know is that we were to keep it secure. We aren't a storage facility, but… sort of like you… that Ruthven guy was persuasive."

"I'm sure he was," Jessie said. "When I said people were going to die if we didn't get access to the shipment, I wasn't threatening you. It's what's inside that container that is the threat, Oscar. We're the good guys, I promise."

Oscar shook his head. "Look, this whole shipment has been more trouble that it's worth. I don't want Ruthven's money. I mean, I do. But it's not worth it."

"Our truck might not be big enough to handle it. If we give you an address, could you have it delivered?"

Oscar nodded. "I can make that happen."

"First," I said, "we need to see the merchandise."

"Let me get my cart," Oscar said. "You can follow me. I'll take you to it."

Oscar climbed into a small golf cart and started it. Jessie hopped into the bed of the truck.

The freight yard had rows upon rows of forty-foot shipping containers. Some of them were stacked four or five tall. I could only hope that Patrick's container wasn't sandwiched in between others. Given the unorthodox way we'd gained access to the yard, I didn't want to spend any more time there than necessary. I didn't have any reason to suspect Oscar had contacted the authorities. Still, something about threatening a man and breaking and entering (I think this qualified) had me uneasy. Through the years, I'd learned that the best way to stay hidden and keep supernatural secrets is to avoid breaking laws or making scenes. Still, I couldn't deny that Jessie's method was effective.

We followed Oscar to a single container that sat alone at the end of a row. Given Patrick's needs, and the contents of the container, I suspected he'd directed Oscar to ensure it was easily accessible.

Oscar unhooked a set of keys from his pocket. It was larger than the gaudy key chain I usually carried around at the asylum. I parked the truck. Abel and I stepped out. Jessie hopped out of the bed, landing on both feet.

Oscar unlocked a padlock on the front of the container. He lifted a couple of levers and turned them, opening the large, metal door.

"It's all yours," Oscar said.

"You two go in and check," Jessie said. "I don't think it wise that we all go inside and leave him out here."

I nodded. "Good thinking."

Abel and I stepped inside the container. The sarcophagus—at least a package shaped the same size as the replica that was stored in Mercy's basement before—was covered in tarps and secured to the side with ropes.

I pulled back enough of the tarp to confirm what it was. I turned back to Jessie and nodded.

Abel and I stepped out.

"This is it. If you don't mind, we'll have it delivered. I'll cover the costs. You can also invoice me for the window."

Oscar nodded. "In that case, follow me to the office. If you'll pay for it, you'll get no problems from me. I'm just glad to put this nightmare in my rearview mirror."

# Chapter Seventeen

It was morning by the time we made it back to the Vilokan Asylum extension site. Hailey and Mercy were gone. Brendan and his coven left when they did for the same reason—it was daytime. I imagined they were all sheltering back at Casa do Diabo.

The wicker man was significantly larger than when we left. They'd made a lot of progress. Julie was still working on it. Apparently, they weren't done. She believed she'd be able to have it ready by nightfall.

Oscar, aka ORC, was eager to get the container to us as soon as possible. I didn't know what Ruthven had said to him. Whatever it was, had Oscar on edge. Jessie's approach, while it grated against my better instincts, was undeniably effective. Oscar said he'd have it sent over before noon.

Most of the other wolves were gone. They had day jobs and lives.

Oscar delivered the container himself. Jessie helped me move the sarcophagus into the slave quarters. We'd dropped the wards there when we realized protecting the fake one was pointless. The replica was still there. The building was big enough. We'd also recently completed renovations on the place. We divided it into different rooms. We kept the sarcophagi together.

Oscar charged me two thousand dollars for the window. It was high-way robbery but, you know, if he wanted to, he could probably have charges pressed against us. I paid it on top of the additional thousand dollar delivery fee.

I took a nap. I couldn't rest too long, though. There were appointments at the original Vilokan Asylum. Jessie reminded me of that. So did Rutherford. She called the land-line at the extension site first thing in the morning. She wanted to know what happened since I'd never come home. She also wasn't exactly thrilled that she had to stay up wondering, not knowing if I was coming home or not.

Relationships are tricky. This was the first genuine relationship I'd had in the technological era. I don't know why people say that technology is liberating. My experience has been quite the opposite. It was like a leash. As a werewolf, I wasn't easily collared. Still, Rutherford got uneasy if it was going to be an all-nighter and I didn't call. You'd think after surviving for centuries, not to mention being protected by a mark I've borne for the better part of that time, she wouldn't worry so much. I suppose, though, it was just in her nature.

I could only wonder how bad it would be if I had a smartphone. Come to think of it, the telephone was a rather rude device. It rings and, suddenly, whoever's on the other end demands your attention no matter what else you're doing. You can ignore the phone, of course. But you still have to listen to it. And in my experience with those contraptions—I'm still talking about the corded type of phone, mind you, not smartphones—having one ring puts you on alert. It makes you feel obligated, no matter what, to respond. I know answering machines were supposed to solve that. These days, people had what they called voicemail. Or they sent texts. It all confused the snot out of me. The point was this. Life was simpler when people couldn't get ahold of you whenever the hell they wanted. People learned not to worry because, well, they didn't expect to touch-base repeatedly during a single night, or even over a weekend.

If I didn't come home at night, my former wives all knew there was a reason. Maybe I was out hunting, or had to take part in a skirmish somewhere. If it was over a full moon, they all knew why I didn't come home. Still, my former wives didn't worry half as much as Rutherford did now. It was nonsensical. You'd think being *able* to contact each other periodically would ease her mind. Then again, she was conditioned to the immediacy of cellphones. I barely adjusted to the rotary phone before the push-button ones came out. Now, I'd finally grown accustomed to using those. Smartphones were off the table. In another decade, well, maybe I'd get a flip phone.

After I napped at the extension site, I returned to the original site for my day's sessions. Jessie came with me. She wasn't nearly so tired as I was. She and Rutherford were on top of things. I just had to sit in my office and take one patient after the next and do my best to listen.

The day flew by and before I knew it we were back at the extension site along with Mercy, Hailey, Julie, a handful of the other wolves like Cassidy and Ryan, and of course, the Scottish vampires. Jessie and Abel were there, of course, too.

Julie apparently finished the wicker man during the day. I wasn't sure what she'd done that kept her so busy. It didn't look *that* different from the night before. It was basically several hundred limbs, sticks, branches, and twigs, gathered from the nearby forests, all lashed together with ropes into a shape that only vaguely resembled the human frame. It was ugly. I knew better than to point it out. A lot of work went into it and I didn't want to be rude.

Hailey pointed her wand at the wicker man. She muttered a few words under her breath before blasting the effigy with a torrent of fire.

Hailey smiled widely. "Alright, ladies. Let's join hands and do this."

Julie and Mercy each took one of Hailey's hands, then each other's, forming a circle. Then they spoke. The girls were reciting some kind of verse together in unison.

"We call upon thee, O Great Morrigan,
Threefold Goddess of Power
From the depths of Lir, from the world of man,
From the reaches of Uindimagos
Do we call on thee
To descend upon our bodies
Thy servants and priestesses
And lend us your energies this day
As we walk in the human world
Ever seeking balance."

The wicker man continued to burn. Its flames grew as the tinder they'd stuffed between the branches that formed the body of the thing caught flame.

The wicker man burned in silence as we stood there waiting.

"Is she coming?" I asked.

Hailey shrugged. "The Morrigan is a busy goddess. Sometimes you have to wait your turn. It's sort of like trying to call customer service somewhere, without the crappy music blasting in your ear the whole time."

I sighed. "At least listening to the instrumental version of songs that were bad already lets you know that you're still on the line. How do you know she heard your little poem at all?"

"It's an incantation, technically an evocation." Mercy rolled her eyes. "Not a poem."

"Anyone have any marshmallows?" Jessie asked. "Might as well make the most of the fire."

Hailey narrowed her eyes. "It *will* work. We must be patient. Deities are not beholden to our requests. She'll respond to it out of good will. I doubt she will if we desecrate the effigy by making s'mores."

Jessie shrugged. "Or make s'mores and maybe she'll come running. Have you ever had s'mores? They're fantastic!"

Mercy narrowed her eyes. "We're not making s'mores on an effigy. We're summoning a goddess, not camping with the scouts."

"Chill," Jessie said. "I'm just joking with you."

Mercy nodded. "Apologies. I'm on edge at the moment, which usually means someone's head is going to roll. I'm the one who accepted this responsibility. If this doesn't work, I'm not sure what to do next."

"Where are the Scottish vampires, anyway?" I asked. "I figured they'd be here."

Mercy grinned. "They're feeding, Cain. If the Baobhan Sith raises, we need to ensure we're all well-fed and full of strength. Even with the Morrigan's aid, there could be a struggle."

I gulped. "Well, I trust these vampires understand the proper protocols? The last thing we need right now are reports of vampire attacks in the French Quarter."

"Wouldn't be the first time," Mercy shrugged. "I've found through the years that reports of weirdness in the French Quarter are immune to the scrutiny they'd receive if they pertained to any other location. People expect strange things to happen there. Or, at least, they are accustomed to people making odd claims."

I checked my watch and glanced back at the burning wicker man. "How much longer is this going to take?"

"It shouldn't be much longer," Hailey said. "Hold on to your horses, Cain."

I snorted. "I don't have any horses. I haven't owned a horse in almost a century."

We watched the entire effigy burn to the ground. So far, nothing happened. I did my best to bite my tongue.

"I don't understand," Mercy bit her nails. "Did she reject our proxy sacrifice?"

Hailey shook her head and pointed her wand through the woods. "Look there!"

A black raven perched itself on the branch of a tree just behind where the wicker man stood before.

"It's a bird," Jessie said.

Mercy shook her head. "That's more than a bird. It is the Morrigan."

"What does this mean?" I asked. "I thought she was going to possess the three of you. Didn't you say that's what happened before?"

"It wasn't a possession," Mercy said. "It was a communion. Perhaps we need to be clearer about our purpose."

Hailey tucked her wand behind her ear. She extended her arm. The raven spread its wings and floated toward Hailey before perching itself on the young vampire witch's forearm.

Hailey and the raven made eye-contact. Then Hailey moved into the slave quarters. We followed.

"What's going on?" I asked.

Mercy raised her hand to silence me. "Watch and wait."

The raven, apparently some kind of embodiment of the Morrigan, cawed as Hailey approached the sarcophagus. Then Hailey opened it.

It was empty.

"I don't understand."

"Shh." Hailey snapped. She waved her wand across the sarcophagus. A swirl of red energies appeared before a figure appeared frozen in place. Her body was covered with white fur. Her eyes, wide open, were red as any vampire's. She looked almost like a werewolf. Her snout was long. Her paws had such long claws they more closely resembled talons. She stared straight up, her mouth agape, flashing her longer-than-average fangs.

She must've inherited the seven-fold curse. When she commanded Patrick to kill me. Like a magistrate who orders an executioner to kill. It is the magistrate, not the executioner, who is responsible for justice. But then, if that was the case, why did Patrick change? Why did he become a werewolf? He wasn't responsible. Not if he was merely acting on command.

The Baobhan Sith opened her jaws and shrieked. She leaped out of the sarcophagus and a white cloud formed around her. A white raven emerged from the cloud and flew out of the slave quarters. She and the black raven, presumably the Morrigan, flew around each other, cawing back and forth. Then, the Baobhan Sith shifted again. This time, into a larger creature. I'd seen nothing quite like it. She resembled a wolf, but with wings and long, sharp talons. She howled and took off through the skies.

The Morrigan spread her wings, gliding in a circle around us. Mercy, Hailey, and Julie stood behind me. The Morrigan shrieked before three beams of golden light formed from her body, striking Mercy, Hailey, and Julie each in the chest. The raven was gone. She was inside the girls.

"Son of Adam," the girls said together in unison. "We have much to discuss."

# CHAPTER EIGHTEEN

MERCY STARED AT ME. "Come, let us discuss the matter at hand."

Her voice was changed—devoid of snark, smoother in tone with a strange cadence. "You are the Morrigan, I presume?"

"Your friends are here with me," the Morrigan said. "They are well. I will return their volition when we've finished speaking."

The three girls turned and walked in step, almost like they were members of a marching band, and walked toward the Vilokan Asylum extension, the old Mulledy mansion.

Cassidy and Ryan moved to the perimeter of the living room, staring at them with wide eyes, and the three girls, now possessed by the Morrigan, sat down at the table.

"Coffee?" I asked.

"I will have a cup. Sisters?" The voice speaking through Mercy's mouth asked before turning to Julie and Hailey, respectively. They each raised a hand and declined.

Cassidy and Ryan got the hint and stepped into the kitchen to retrieve a cup. They knew me well. They didn't need to ask. Cassidy set a cup in front of me. Ryan set a cup in front of Mercy.

"I am Babd," the voice of the Morrigan within Mercy said. "These are my sisters, Macha and Anand."

"Pleased to meet you."

"We were not always as we are, Doctor Cain. Though, you walked the world even when I and my sisters were human still. It is not often I have occasion to speak with one older than I."

I took a sip of my coffee. It was warm but not hot. "I know the feeling. I'd love to spend more time getting to know one another, reflecting on the good ole days, but we have something of a crisis on our hands."

"Indeed, we do," Babd said, taking the cup of coffee into Mercy's right hand and lifting it to her lips. She cocked her head. "An interesting beverage. I relish in new experiences. I cannot say this one is altogether pleasurable."

I grinned. "It's an acquired taste."

"The Baobhan Sith is not as vile a creature as you might believe. She is a part of the balance that maintains all things, that guards the divide between life and death. She represents creatures immortal. Vampires, for certain. It was an inevitability that she would eventually seek you."

"She triggered my mark on purpose? She wanted the seven-fold curse?"

"It was necessary, Adam's son. In Annwn, or what you might call Eden or Guinee, the balance of life and death is maintained. The divide between the garden groves of Eden and the blighted lands of Samhuinn is one through which most all will pass in time. Yes, even vampires and werewolves, like you, will one day meet their end."

I shrugged. "Well, six thousand years and counting, no end is yet in sight."

"It is an inevitability. You are capable of death, are you not?"

"I suppose. Enough silver, I suppose, could do it."

"Do you not imagine that even you might one day lose the resolve to live?"

I shook my head. "I can't imagine that."

"Eternity is an awful long time. You cannot say that you will never grow weary of this existence. When you do, you will be glad that the Baobhan Sith has forged a path for you through the divide of life and death."

I cocked my head. "But why now? If she wanted my curse, why has she waited this long?"

"She has not. What is time, Cain? In our realm, the fabric of time flows separate from yours. Have you not considered why she had an acute influence over wolves?"

I shrugged. "I figured it was something unique to her abilities."

"This is only because in her timeline, Cain, this is the first time she's engaged you. From a time more ancient in Annwn, in Eden, she has been called forth here today. She inherited your mark in your presence. When she was first entombed by the vampires, Ruthven, and the others, from her perspective, it was only after this occurred. This is why she seems both vampire and wolf. She keeps traits of both. At least she shall. Once she returns."

I snorted. "You're saying we can't cast her into the void?"

"The young witches' plan is ignorant. It was not ill-conceived. Still, you are correct. She cannot be sent to the void. If she does, the boundary between life and death will fail. If such occurs in Annwn, in Eden, then there will no longer be such a divide for you, or for the vampires."

"What are you saying? Spell it out for me."

"If you do not return the Baobhan Sith to Eden, to Annwn, to Samhuinn, you will die. All werewolves. All vampires."

"Can you do that?" I asked.

"Together, we three sisters, within your friends, can forge the portal required. However, not until the curse has run its course."

I snorted. "You're saying that she must replicate. She will turn more of her kind."

"She will. But fear not, Son of Adam. They shall only rise once a year with their mother."

"If the Baobhan Sith is native to your realm, can't you simply command her to return? Forge the portal, tell her to leave before she turns anyone else. She's already inherited my curse."

"The curse did not affect her until she arrived here, in this realm. This was her intention all along. However, until the mark has run its course, I cannot control her any better than you might."

"This is not wholly true," Julie said—her voice higher-pitched than usual and reflecting the same cadence as Babd's.

"Speak, Macha. What do you know?"

"This witch is not the same as she was before."

I nodded. "She's also a werewolf."

"More than that," Macha said. "The power she wields. It is no longer infernal."

"The flambeau is now vested with celestial power, the power of heaven."

Mercy's head nodded. "Yes, this vampire confirms that what you say is true."

Hailey's head tilted to her right shoulder. "There may be a chance for you to shed your mark, Son of Adam."

I shook my head. "My mark was a gift. It was meant to protect me so that any who might kill me would be dissuaded by the curse."

Anand, the aspect of the Morrigan within Hailey, stared at me with unblinking eyes. "The curse will remain. You will still be a wolf. Only the mark should be removed. Has not your situation changed? Are there many who still wish to see Cain killed?"

I shrugged. "You might be surprised."

"It is your choice. If we remove the mark, together, with your influence over the wolf within the Baobhan Sith and my influence over her as my child, as a creature of Samhuinn, we may be able to force her to return to the otherworld."

I pinched my chin. They had a point. As of late, more people had manipulated my mark than had been dissuaded by it. The werewolf had power, albeit the sort of power that usually left bodies in its wake. "How do I do this?"

"The mark upon you is seven-fold. Within it coheres the spirit of seven. You must confront each of the seven and overcome them."

I shook my head. "Even if I were to be a wolf myself, how could I defeat seven more? The numbers are not in my favor."

"You may confront the wolves how you wish," Babd said, still speaking through Mercy. "Know, however, that your greatest power may be in your humblest form."

"The celestial flambeau is ready," Julie said. "Macha will connect the power to each of her sisters and the Morrigan will initiate our confrontation with your pack when you're ready."

I snorted. "My pack? Are you speaking of the rougarou?"

Macha shook Julie's head. "The pack I speak of is the one within you. It is a seven-fold pack. A spirit of seven bound to you for nearly six thousand years."

"You're telling me that there are seven wolves inside of me?

"Of a sort. Shall we begin?"

I shook my head. "Not yet. Not until I speak with Rutherford. She'd never forgive me if I never returned and hadn't bothered to say goodbye."

"Make it fast," Babd said. "The Baobhan Sith is free. I dare say we might not have the time for you to make it to Vilokan, or even your apartment, wherever Rutherford is, and back again."

I sighed. "Jessie. Can I borrow your phone?"

"Seriously?" Jessie asked.

"I have to admit it. You're right. These things are damned convenient."

# CHAPTER NINETEEN

JESSIE GAVE ME HER phone. She had Rutherford's contact screen up already and told me to push the green "call" button. I didn't see a button. All I saw was a circle on a screen. I suppose it represented a button. Sort of. It didn't click when I tapped it. The screen changed. The word "calling" appeared on the screen.

"Sorcery," I said, shaking my head. "That's the only explanation."

I put the phone up to my ear.

"Hello? Jessie?"

"It's me," I said, elevating my voice. "It's Cain."

"You're on Jessie's phone?"

"I am," I shouted back.

"You can speak normally, Cain. I can hear you just fine."

I sighed. "Alright, I'm here. I wanted to call you because... I'm afraid."

My admission hung in the air for a few seconds. "Why are you afraid?"

"The Baobhan Sith is free. She's inherited my curse. The only way to defeat her, it seems, is to get rid of my mark. To do that, I have to confront the spirits of seven wolves."

"Your mark includes these spirits?"

I nodded even though I knew she couldn't see me. It was instinct. "Apparently, so."

"If that's the case, Cain, they've been with you for nearly all of your life."

"I don't know what to do with that, Rutherford. If that's the case, they might know me a lot better than I do them."

"That's not necessarily the case, Cain. If these wolves, these spirits, have been with you all this time, perhaps they're simply a part of you. You've overcome a lot in your life. Sin. Guilt. Worry. Whatever the case, these wolves represent nothing you've never faced before. So long as one of them isn't the spirit-wolf of leaving dirty socks on the floor, you'll be fine."

I chuckled. "Heaven forbid. If that's the case, I'm sorry, dear. I'm done for. I'll see you on the other side."

Rutherford sighed. "This is what you do, Cain. It's what you've always done. You confront things no one else will. You help anyone who comes to you see the light and escape their darkness. You can do this because you've been through the darkness already. You've passed through the dark night of your soul and now you see."

"I still don't know what I'm facing. Not exactly."

"I'll see you home for dinner, Cain. I'm making spaghetti right now."

Something like a shriek echoed in the background of the call.

"You're at the apartment? What was that sound?"

"Of course I am. I couldn't get a signal if I was still at work. I'm sure it was just some animal outside. Ah yes, there's a white bird perched outside the kitchen window."

"Do not engage it. Do not even look it in the eye, Rutherford. She's looking for human females to turn."

"Are you saying..."

"Yes, Rutherford. That is the Baobhan Sith."

"Then you'd better hurry, Cain. Do what you have to do. If she really is as powerful as you say, I'm not sure our double-paned windows will keep her out forever."

# CHAPTER TWENTY

"WE HAVE TO DO this now! The Baobhan Sith is coming for Rutherford!"

Mercy nodded and joined hands with Hailey and Julie. Their eyes went dark then wide welcoming the Morrigan into her person. Julie's flambeau formed in the middle of the room, a blue flame dancing at its apex. I didn't shift. Neither did Cassidy, Ryan, or Julie. Some kind of veil, like a magical canopy, red in hue, enveloped the three.

"Step inside the circle," Mercy said, the tone of her voice suggesting that once again it was Babd speaking through her.

Hailey and Mercy each raised their joined arms. I ducked and walked between them. When I did, my body changed. The celestial flames blasting from the flambeau expanded and enveloped my expanding frame.

The blue flames blinded me. When I saw again, I was standing in green grass, fully shifted into wolf form. Only now, my fur was white rather than its usual black. Seven shadows, dark wolf-shaped bodies, circled around me.

The flambeau was the only thing from before that remained.

"These seven represent your protection," the voice said. I couldn't tell exactly if it was the Morrigan or someone else, something else.

Could it have been God? The one who gave me the Mark in the beginning? Perhaps.

"Touch the flame and resume your natural form."

I reached out with my paw and placed it into the blue flame atop the flambeau. In an instant, without so much as the crack of a single bone, I stood in my human shape, naked, in the very garden my parents once frolicked through adorning a comparable lack of attire.

"I don't understand. These seven spirits sealed the mark?"

"I gave you the mark after you appealed to me out of fear, Cain, that men might wish you dead on account of what you did to your brother."

"I remember."

"It is out of fear that these spirits were born. Tell me, son, are you still afraid?"

"I don't know. Not for my life. For my friends, I am. For Rutherford, I'm terrified."

"Fear alone is neither virtue nor vice. It is the source of your fear that dictates whether it corresponds with darkness or light."

I tilted my head. "Fear is a primal, foundational emotion."

"These are all children of fear. Have you tamed your fear, Cain?"

"I fear for Rutherford."

"You love her. In her case, love, not fear, is the foundation of your emotion. Fear built upon itself is devastating. Fear built upon love is natural. It is the fear a parent has for a child in danger. It is the fear that drives one to cling to his beloved, cherishing each moment, knowing that one day they will be separated by death. You know this fear, Cain, because you know love."

"How can I defeat these wolves?"

"To conquer your fear is not to defeat it. It is to redirect it, repurpose it, to a holy and noble purpose. You must allow these wolves to consume you. If your foundation is true, if love is truly at the center of your soul rather than fear, then they will be one with you and your mark will fade."

"What about the Baobhan Sith?"

"You need only touch her and the seven wolves within you, should you survive, will fulfill the curse and bind her again to her place in the otherworld."

I looked around. I counted the shadows. "Why do I only see six?"

"The final one now belongs with the Baobhan Sith. If you endure these six, you must confront her directly."

"What if I fail?"

"Fail with any of the seven and you will die. Fail with the final of the seven, and you will be consumed by the Baobhan Sith. You will live only as the wolf within her."

"But if I prevail?"

"Then she will serve as you were assured, as the paragon of balance, the one who guards the barrier between life and death for vampire and werewolf alike."

# CHAPTER
# TWENTY-ONE

WHEN THE VOICE STOPPED speaking I found myself standing alone, the tall uncut grasses of Eden's garden groves tickling my bare shins. Seven black wolf specters encircled me as predators preparing to devour their prey.

I sat down and crossed my legs. I took a deep breath. I'd like to say I had no fear at all. That wasn't true. I wasn't sure if the voice that spoke to me was the God of my youth or the Morrigan. Perhaps it was both of them or neither of them. All I knew was that whoever spoke had a wisdom and power greater than my own. If the deity was right, it wasn't fearlessness that was necessary. Fear is not a character defect if relegated to its proper place. It couldn't be my foundation. Love was my foundation, which, I suppose, was why I was more terrified at the moment for Rutherford.

I had to face these wolves, if for no other reason than to save her. If I couldn't, I'd die. And worse, she'd become the first of the Baobhan Sith's progeny.

One wolf broke rank with the rest and dove upon me. Its form struck my body and enveloped me completely. Anger. Rage. That was what this wolf represented. A second wolf charged me at the same time. Jealousy. Envy. The two wolves struck a combination I'd known early on. Envy led to rage when God accepted Abel's sacrifice but rejected mine. The seeds of envy had started much earlier. That's just when everything boiled over and my jealousy turned to anger.

I clenched my fists as another wolf dove into my body. An overwhelming sadness flooded over me when he struck me. The pain of loss. All my former wives, my children, my friends. Over six thousand years, I'd lost hundreds of people I'd loved.

Another wolf bounded toward me and blasted itself into my chest. This time, desire. Lust. Most recently, Jessie tempted me. I resisted. I wasn't always so strong. In the past, I'd often indulged in the pleasures of the flesh. I don't know what I was looking for, but it never gave me the satisfaction of happiness I thought it would.

The fifth wolf came with a surge of power. I once ruled over a city in the land of Nod. I'd terrorized the people, as a wolf, until they granted me a crown. It was one of the first and most frequent temptations I'd faced during my time. It wasn't just about ruling peoples or kingdoms. It was about control. The more I thought I could control, the less I had to fear. But there are some things beyond our control. Over time, I'd accepted that. I'd discovered serenity when I was given the wisdom to discern the difference between the things I could or couldn't change.

When the sixth wolf hit me, I felt nothing at all. Emptiness. Depression. The previous five wolves inevitably led here. When rage, envy, or lust didn't satisfy, it left me with nothingness. When the pursuit of power or control left me feeling more powerless and out of control than ever before, I descended into depression.

This was the first time in more than a century I'd felt that kind of despair. I'd dealt with so many of my flaws, my defects, my resentments, that it didn't overwhelm me like it used to.

The final wolf encircled me until it met me face-to-face. I tilted my head.

"Who are you?" I asked.

"I am you."

"I don't understand."

"What do you wish me to be? I am the foundation. I am your identity. Who are you? I am you. But you are who?"

I scratched my head. "I'm not sure."

"I am whoever you choose me to be. Shall I withstand the rest? Will I emerge as the alpha? Can I control the other wolves who seek to overwhelm you? Or will I falter and fail? The choice is yours. Choose wisely."

I pressed my lips together. I thought about the episode with my brother. We'd resolved our differences since. He forgave me. I had so many memories. Good times I'd experienced with those I loved and lost. Could the pain of loss really be greater than the joy of the times shared? Even my failings, the lusts I'd sometimes given into in the past, taught me something about myself. I've made mistakes. Still, I couldn't say I had regrets. I learned from those mistakes. I grew. I changed. Even when I sought power and authority over others, I've learned that true power comes not in ruling or domineering but in love and service. True power raises others up rather than forcing them into subjugation.

"Gratitude," I said. "You are gratitude."

The wolf nodded. "A wise choice. I am the one who shall remain with you. I am the wolf who will emerge when you change."

"What of the others?" I asked.

"You may still have fear. You might suffer loss or experience lust. You will be tempted by power. You may even feel empty at times. When gratitude, however, prevails, none of the others can stand. I am alpha. I am your future, your foundation."

"So what of my mark?" I asked.

"If you wish it gone, it is gone. But know this: it will no longer protect you. The threat of the seven-fold curse will no longer dissuade those who wish you dead."

I nodded. "I'm not afraid."

"Then you must leave. Your beloved needs you. Go to her now."

The final wolf dove into my body. An explosion of light blasted out of my body. The other wolves swirled around me, no longer dark shadows but blazing like fire. As each one dove back into my chest, a warmth spread throughout my body as I shifted into wolf form.

All those emotions—anger, envy, sadness, lust, the need for control, and emptiness. They were all defense mechanisms. My mark was never meant to offer complete security. Still, these seeds of emotion had forced me to learn and evolve. Now, I was grateful. Not just for the good things. I was grateful for the difficult times, the losses, the pain I'd experienced that forced me to grow.

I wasn't perfect. I still had flaws. I'd still have anger, lust, sadness, and the rest. But if I maintained the right foundation, these emotions wouldn't become alpha. They wouldn't dominate my life. They'd remain in their proper place. Those other wolves, they weren't gone. But they didn't rule over me. Gratitude was now the alpha of the pack of emotions that formed my soul.

Back in wolf form, I stood on my hind quarters watching the blue celestial flame of the flambeau reform in front of me. Was all of this real or was it a hallucination, a dream, or a vision? Did it come from the Divine, from the Morrigan, or from somewhere in the recesses of my subconscious mind? I could make a case for any or all of the above. Who is to say that dreams aren't real? Manifestations of the subconscious mind are not artificial. Such things are real for what they are. Considering as much, I could even argue that what I'd witnessed might be more meaningful if it were a product of my mind than if I'd experienced it in the actual Eden. Whatever the case, what I experienced shifted my mindset. It elevated to my conscious mind the realization that I'd been blessed. Despite all my flaws, I'd been given much more than I ever took from the world or the people I loved. I stole my brother's life and was given hundreds of lifetimes to live. I've lost more loved ones to death than anyone who has ever lived, but I've also had more opportunities to love than anyone else, too.

Now, my heart was Rutherford's. She wasn't getting my ex wives' sloppy seconds, or thirds, or forty-fifths. I wasn't the same person in any of my previous relationships that I was now. Love changes us. Loss changes us. We grow. We learn. We evolve. The heart that I gave to Rutherford was a heart that could only be grown through many lifetimes of experience. I had an old heart. An ancient one. At the same time, I had the heart of a child.

I stuck my snout into the blue flame of the flambeau. It didn't burn my fur. It felt oddly cool to the touch even as a warmth welled up from within me on contact.

The light blinded me for a second.

I blinked. When I opened my eyes, I was in Rutherford's apartment—*our* apartment. The Baobhan Sith was there, frozen in mid-air, still resembling some kind of hybrid between a white wolf and a hawk or a raven. The claws on her talons were extended toward Rutherford, who still held her phone in her hand.

Was she still on the phone with me? I know smartphones are supposed to do some pretty incredible things, but I was reasonably certain that teleporting one person into an alternate dimension, out of that dimension into the location of the person on the opposite end of the line, all the while freezing time, wasn't something you could do even if you were on 5G (which I still don't know a thing about).

I looked at my paws. The blue celestial flame from the flambeau now burst from each of them as I was channeling the power of heaven itself.

I extended my paws toward the Baobhan Sith. When I did, the entire world was unpaused. The creature collided with me, sinking her talons into my chest even as my celestially powered paws struck her.

The seven wolf spirits, the dark spirits, burst out of my body and tore at her flesh. The one wolf, the one I'd named "gratitude" ran in a circle forming what appeared to be a portal. The other wolves dragged her into it. Then, my wolf, "gratitude" returned to me. My magic faded, and I returned to human form in an instant.

Shifting back so quickly was disorienting, but I stumbled over to Rutherford. I took her in my arms.

"Cain... how did you?"

"Shh," I said. "I'm not sure I even know what happened myself. All I know is that the threat is over."

Rutherford snorted. "Good. Because you didn't wash off your plate last night. It's all caked with dried sauce and waiting for you next to the sink."

I chuckled, brushed a stray red curl out of Rutherford's face, and kissed her on the lips.

# CHAPTER TWENTY-TWO

WHEN I CALLED JESSIE'S phone back from Rutherford's phone (okay, Rutherford actually dialed her number, but I was the one who did the talking) she was quite surprised to hear me on the other side. She and the rest were even more shocked to hear that the Baobhan Sith had been dispatched back to the otherworld.

"It makes sense," Mercy said from the other end of the line. I guessed Jessie must've had her phone on speaker mode. "We felt the Morrigan depart just moments ago."

"I believe she may have played a role in what happened. Either way, it's done."

"And there's no more Baobhan Sith who might raise each year?" Hailey asked.

"I don't believe she'll be back. Not to our time, at least."

"I'm not even going to try and make sense of what that means," Mercy said. "Whenever the otherworld, Guinee, or whatever you call it, is involved, timelines and shit really screw with my head."

I chuckled. "You and me both, kid. Tell me, Mercy. What of the Scottish vampires?"

"I suppose they're back at Casa do Diabo."

I nodded. "We'd best get to work, then. Send them to the Vilokan Asylum extension tomorrow night for our group sessions. Before the next full moon, we'll have some issues to sort through. We might have prevented the rise of the Baobhan Sith and the spread of her progeny, but vampire-wolves could pose a fresh problem."

"What do you think someone would become if bitten by one?" Jessie asked.

"I don't know. It's hard to say."

"I'd rather not find out," Mercy added. "Though a single bite is often enough to turn one into a wolf. Turning a vampire is a more complicated process."

"That's true," I said. "But we don't know if vampirism might not go along with the werewolf curse if any of them bite someone. No matter the case, they will be priority number one, at least until the end of the next full moon. We'll need more than evening group sessions. I'd like to make appointments with each of them individually."

"I'll clear some space in your calendar," Jessie said.

"If Rutherford hasn't already beaten you to it!"

"If I haven't beaten her to what?" Rutherford asked.

I chuckled. "Jessie is going to clear some extra space on my calendar so we can schedule the vampire-wolves in for sessions."

Rutherford grinned. "Ah, fair enough. I think I'm done managing schedules, anyway. I'm more than happy to give that responsibility to her."

"Is everything okay?" Jessie asked.

"Just fine. Clear the space and make sure Mercy gets you into contact with each of them so you can get them penciled in. The sooner we can begin, the better."

"We might have enough time tonight," Mercy said. "We still have awhile before sunrise."

I sighed. "No. I think I'm going to spend tonight with the woman I love. We all need to take time to enjoy our blessings."

**Continued in *The Cowl Cain* (Keep reading...)**

# THE
# COWL OF
# CAIN

## THEOPHILUS MONROE

# CHAPTER ONE

THE SCOTTISH VAMPIRE-WOLVES WERE well-adjusted and returned home. Mostly, they were common vampires. Every full moon, things got a little wild, but Brendan learned over the first few shifts to lead his coven/pack through their issues and resentments in advance.

We still had regular group sessions with the rougarou and Abel's pack at the Vilokan Asylum extension site. Attendance was strong, but it had been months since we'd had anything remotely interesting to talk about. Small talk about the weather, or how well the Saints were playing, provided little fodder for constructive therapy.

Back in Vilokan proper, I still had a steady schedule of clients but nothing beyond the ordinary. New vampires abandoned by their sires taming their cravings. Hougans and mambos dealing with normal, human conditions and ailments. I had a witch or two who were suffering from the effects of a backfired vex. They were getting a little better every day. Not every hedge witch was as talented, or as lucky, as Hailey Bradbury. Most of them got in over their heads sooner rather than later and ended up in my care. Most of the time, a little therapy combined with a little intervention of the magical sort from the Voodoo queen was enough to handle it.

For the first time in years, I had spare time. I didn't have a television of my own. I read books. Psychology journals. The occasional novel. I rarely read history books. They usually frustrated me. I'd lived through actual history and it was infuriating how many important details were regularly missing from the narratives.

Then Rutherford introduced me to something they call "the Netflix." Now, I wasn't a complete caveman. It wasn't like I'd never watched television before. It just never struck my fancy until now. With the Netflix you weren't beholden to the schedules set by network programmers. You could watch when you wanted as often as you wanted.

Rutherford introduced me to a program called *Grey's Anatomy*. Talk about bait and switch. I'd read the book! I studied it! It's how I learned the intricacies of human anatomy. The detailed sketches were groundbreaking in the medical sciences. Sure, I was a psychologist, but that didn't mean I didn't have general medical interests. I expected educational programming. Little did I realize that the show was really about a character called Grey and everyone who got intimate with *her* anatomy.

I hate the show. I realized that long before I reached the tenth season, but I kept watching. I don't know why. Rutherford and I have a running bet on which character they'd kill off next. She has her money on Derrick. Preposterous! They'd never build up the romance between him and Meredith just to kill him off. I mean, the seeds of their epic love were planted in season one, episode one! Rutherford clearly knows nothing about clever plot development. They're killing off Richard next. All the signs are there. Just watch and wait. You'll see. Or maybe you already know I'm right. I think the show is still going. When I win the bet, Rutherford will be doing the dishes for a month straight.

I almost forgot to mention that Rutherford bought me a phone. I thought it was ironic that it was made by Apple, you know, considering that it was an apple that got my parents into trouble with the big guy. Could it really be a coincidence? I still didn't know how to do much with it. I could send a text. I could make a call. I could open up my Angry Birds game. I didn't venture off into the world wild web. Yes, I said wild. No, that wasn't a typo. That place is uncivilized. I was learning a little more every day. For some reason, the average time I spent each day on the toilet had also increased exponentially.

I regularly slept full nights. There was more time to study and meditate. I was caught up with my patients for the first time since I'd taken my position at the Vilokan Asylum of the Magically and Mentally Deranged. Could it be that the world of the supernatural was *calming down*? I hadn't even heard much from Mercy and the vampires. She and the council left New Orleans for a while to deal with some unruly Eastern European vamps who had a different vision for the future of vampirism that Mercy embraced. The only thing worse than vampire politics was human politics. I tried my best to stay out of both.

"Cain, dear, did you forget our class starts tonight?"

I pinched my chin as I kicked back into my recliner. "Class? What class?"

"We're taking salsa lessons."

I bit my lip. "Do we need lessons? It's pretty simple. Chip goes into salsa. Chip with salsa goes into mouth."

Rutherford walked into the room and stared at me blankly. "Don't play dumb."

I grinned. "I know. The joke is lame. Have you ever seen me try to dance? I think ducks have feet better suited for the dance floor than I do."

"Which is why there's a class for it, Cain. Look, think of it this way. Everyone in the class will be just as clueless about salsa as you."

"Except for you. You already know how to salsa dance."

"Which is why I want to take lessons. Look, dear. I love to dance. I'd love it more if you were my dance partner."

I put on my best pair of sneakers before we left. My white New Balance trainers were the most comfortable shoes I'd ever put on my feet. The rubber soles might not be the best for dancing, but I was more nervous about slipping and falling on my butt on the dance floor than my feet sticking a little on the wood.

The class was in what used to be an old church. Someone bought it and converted it into a coffee shop. The original stained glass gave the place a marvelous aura. The smell of roasted coffee beans replaced the usual musty smell associated with old churches. In what used to be a sanctuary, was an open dance floor. Tables and chairs, usually arranged on the floor, were now stacked by the wall.

The instructor explained the steps. How to count. I held Rutherford's hands and while I was supposed to "lead" found she was really directing me where to go. When she was supposed to step back, I was supposed to step forward. But there was a rhythm to it and I lost track. I stepped on her feet more times than I could count. To make matters worse, there were only three couples there for the class. More people were arriving. People dressed to the hilt.

"Is there another class after?" I asked.

Rutherford smiled. "The class is just to help you get ready for what comes after."

I stared at Rutherford blankly. "What are you talking about?"

The next thing I knew, couple after couple flooded onto the dance floor. One young fellow really got my goat. He was a skinny lad. Toothpicks for legs. His hips moved like he had gelatin for joints.

I think he made it his personal mission to dance with every female in the place.

Anywhere else, the little twerp would blend into the crowd. Here, though, he acted like he was some kind of god. The god of gyrating hips, if there ever was such a thing.

Javier. That was his name. At least, that's what he told everyone his name was. I didn't want to wait until he got around to asking Rutherford to dance.

"I think I'd like to leave."

"Oh, come on, Cain. I know you're still learning, but let's have fun."

I shook my head. "I know you would have more fun dancing with someone else. But if you dance with that Javier joker, I think I'll throw up a little in my mouth."

Rutherford chuckled and shook her head. "You realize Javier is probably young enough to be my son. You have nothing to worry about."

"I know. In the real world, I'm confident. Here, I feel inferior. It's not enjoyable."

Rutherford raised an eyebrow. "This isn't the real world?"

I shook my head. "Men can't move like that in the real world. If I tried that I'd throw my hip right out of its socket."

Rutherford grinned. "I get it, Cain. This isn't your thing. We can leave if you'd like. But you need to give me at least one more dance."

I sighed. "It's humiliating, Rutherford. Tripping all over the dance floor while *that* guy shakes his tush all around us. Who does he think he is, Patrick Swayze?"

Rutherford shrugged. "Maybe Ricky Martin."

I snorted. "Whatever. Asking me to go out and dance on the floor with him is like asking me to go out on a football field and try to play quarterback against Patrick Mahomes."

Rutherford laughed. "I'm surprised you even know who he is."

I raised an eyebrow. "I don't live under a rock. Besides, I enjoy sports."

Rutherford tilted her head. "Since when?"

"Since always. I just don't watch a lot on television. At least I didn't until recently. I always preferred to go to the games in person. I even competed in a few of the ancient Olympic games in Greece."

"Seriously? What was your sport?"

I grinned. "Pankration."

"What the hell is that?"

"It's like wrestling. Except, in pankration, you only win if your opponent submits or passes out."

"That sounds awful."

"I won my share of the laurels."

Rutherford raised an eyebrow. "First you mention football. Now you're going over your athletic credentials. It's almost like you're trying to show off your man card because you're intimidated by Javier."

"I don't have a man card. That's not a thing."

Rutherford stood up and grabbed my hand. "One dance, Cain. After that, if you still feel the need to defend your manliness, you can devote the rest of the night to making your case in private."

# CHAPTER TWO

FOR THE FIRST TIME in years, I took the weekend off. Jessie was both my junior nurse and interning as a therapist. She enrolled in a licensing program at a local university. While it wasn't my cup of tea as a psychotherapist, she'd gravitated to the cognitive-behavioral approach. It was a therapy model I used occasionally. It wasn't my specialty. She was still learning, but I was optimistic that she'd grow into a fine counselor. It was too soon in her program to log the requisite hours of supervised therapy sessions that she'd require for licensing, but it was never too late to get experience working with patients.

Given the issues we were dealing with at the asylum, I figured she could handle anything minor that might crop up. Worst-case scenario, she could call me up if anything got out of hand. Rutherford and I were only about ten minutes away. She'd just have to use the land-line that we'd had wired into the reception desk since we didn't have cellphone reception in Vilokan.

After our night dancing (stumbling around might be a more apt description of what I did) and a longer night of extracurricular excitement between Rutherford and myself, I slept in.

I woke up to the smell of bacon.

I thought I'd died and, finally, arrived in heaven. Abel told me they didn't have bacon in heaven. I didn't believe him. What kind of paradise would heaven be without bacon, anyway?

I rolled out of bed and stepped into my slippers. I grabbed my robe from the hook on the back of the bedroom door, tied it around my body, and stepped out into the hallway. The sizzle of the bacon in the pan only added to the allure already overwhelming on account of the smell.

I yawned as I stumbled into the kitchen. Rutherford was standing in front of the stove, flipping bacon in one pan and scrambling eggs in another. She was in sweats and an apron. Her hair was tied back. I sneaked up behind her and patted her on the behind.

Rutherford turned to me and grinned. "Well hey there, sleepyhead."

I yawned again. "You've never been more beautiful than you are right now."

Rutherford laughed. "Because I'm making you breakfast?"

"Exactly," I nodded. "The way to man's heart is through the stomach, you know."

"I know that. It's why I also have a cup of coffee ready for you."

"You really are stunning, you know."

"I know. You're a lucky man."

I chuckled. "Tell me about it."

I sat down at the table and took a sip of my coffee. A few minutes later, Rutherford set my plate in front of me and kissed me on the cheek.

"This is perfect," I said, taking a piece of bacon into my fingers. "Firm and crisp, but still soft in all the right places."

"Just how you like it! I presume you're still talking about bacon and not my body."

I laughed. "Well, the same principle applies. Though, I'd never dare compare you to strips of cooked pig. I might be a werewolf, but I'd rather not spend the night in the doghouse."

"Good boy. You're well trained. You'll always have a spot at the foot of the bed."

I took a bite of my first strip of bacon. "I appreciate you making the room. You realize, the way you spread out, I'm usually curled up on about a foot of bed on the edge while you take over the rest."

"And I'm always having to wrestle away the covers from you!"

"Epic battles over the bed. I don't know if any two people have ever shared a bed and didn't have the same struggles."

Rutherford made a plate for herself and sat down on the opposite side of the table. "So, what would you like to do today?"

I shrugged. "I don't know, honestly. It's been so long since I've had a day off that I've never really even considered what I might do if or when I ever had one!"

"We could go shopping. You need some new pants."

"What's wrong with my pants?"

"When's the last time you bought new pants? On one pair, the seam in the crotch is barely holding on by a thread. Another is missing the top button entirely."

I shrugged. "I tie them together with a shoestring."

Rutherford shook her head. "You could just sew on a new button or get a new pair of pants."

I snorted. "I don't sew. My fingers are too fat. Could you fix it for me?"

Rutherford nodded. "I could. But the same pair also has a stain on the back of the right leg. I've scrubbed it, but it won't come out."

"It just seems like a waste of a day off to go *shopping*, Rutherford. So long as my pants fit and are reasonably comfortable, I don't really care where they come from or what they look like."

"That's the thing, Cain. Pants are funny like that. Even if I know your size, every pair fits a little differently."

"We can grab some pants. I'm not trying on a thousand pairs. But after that, it's a nice day. I think I'd just enjoy taking a walk together through the French Quarter. Maybe we could grab some gumbo for lunch."

Rutherford grinned. "Sounds like a fine plan to me. Should we go pants shopping in the quarter, too?"

"Heavens, no. The shops around there are too expensive. Walmart pants are just as comfortable as any designer pair and they're a lot cheaper."

Rutherford chuckled. "Since when were you so price conscious?"

I shrugged. "I've always been frugal. It's not that I don't have money. I suppose, though, when you've ruined as many pants as I have during full-moon shifts, there's no sense in spending a lot."

"I thought you stripped before you shifted."

"When I have a chance, I do. But it's difficult to predict the exact moment when the full moon will take its force over my form. Even with my experience, every now and again I get taken off guard and shift earlier than expected. I suppose I'm also more cost conscious when it comes to pants because I can still remember the time when a pair of pants cost more than a month's worth of wages."

"By that standard, you should be able to justify all the designer pairs."

I shook my head. "Price psychology is a funny thing. You realize, the same factories that make Walmart's clothes produce pants with different labels and charge two or three times as much? People think the name makes it a better pair of pants. It doesn't. People buy expensive labels because they're insecure. They define themselves by brands invented and marketed by others. If my pants tell people I define myself by falling prices, then so be it."

Rutherford laughed. "Finish your breakfast. We'll go get your damn Walmart pants. Then we'll enjoy our day."

# CHAPTER THREE

"I HAVE A THIRTY-FOUR inch waist, Rutherford. I don't need to try them on."

"Just do it. And try these on, too." Rutherford handed me another pair.

"These are thirty-eight thirty-twos!"

Rutherford grinned. "Humor me, Cain."

I ducked into the Walmart dressing room and tried on my pants. I sighed. My thirty-fours were tight. Too tight. I could get them buttoned, but if I did, well, it was likely just a matter of time before it popped off. I sighed, removed my chosen pair of slacks, and tried on the thirty-eights. I hate it when she's right. I suppose that means I have a lot of hate in my life because, well, Rutherford is right more often than I'd care to admit. Though, the word "hate" is probably strong. It's probably better to say I found it annoying. Almost as annoying as the fact that I'd apparently gained weight.

I stepped out of the dressing room wearing the same stretch-pants I was wearing when we arrived at the store.

"We're buying the thirty-eights, aren't we?"

I snorted. "Grab a few more pairs. It's your fault, you know."

"What's my fault?"

"For feeding me so damn well!" I laughed.

"Well, I can stop cooking for you if you'd like."

I shook my head, still chuckling. "Your meals are worth the extra inches."

We left Walmart in my truck. We could have taken Rutherford's car. Although I had a lot more money than she did—I'd invested wisely through the years—her car was a lot nicer than my F-150 pickup. Still, when we went out together, I always drove. I realize it was probably one of those machismo things. You know, men feeling like they always have to drive in order to feel like men. Still, Rutherford didn't mind, and I didn't particularly like driving her car. She had one of those newfangled Teslas. Too many buttons to push and lights to interpret. If we were taking a trip or something, we'd drive the Tesla to save on gas. Otherwise, if I was driving, we took the truck.

Rutherford took me to a Cajun restaurant on Bourbon Street. I'd never been there. I rarely went to sit-down joints before I had someone to eat with. The place was loud and hopping. Despite all the ruckus, though, I quickly spotted two familiar faces seated in the corner.

Abel and Jessie. They were sharing a bucket of crawdads.

I cocked my head. "Rutherford, go ahead and order me a gumbo."

Rutherford nodded and approached the counter. I stepped over to the table where my brother and junior nurse were seated. "What are you two doing here?"

Abel looked at me, wincing. "We're getting lunch."

I glanced at Jessie. "Things under control at the asylum?"

Jessie nodded. "All is well. I'm on lunch."

"And why are you two here together?"

Jessie raised her eyebrows and turned away.

Abel sighed. "We're dating."

I snorted. I should have seen it coming. Abel had been flirting with Jessie intermittently ever since I introduced them. Until now, though,

I figured she wasn't interested. She hadn't exhibited any signals to suggest that the attraction was mutual. "When did this start?"

"A few months ago," Jessie said.

"A few months! Why am I hearing about it just now?"

"I'm sorry, brother. I wanted to tell you. We just weren't sure how you'd take it."

I sighed. "Mind if Rutherford and I join you?"

"Pull up a couple of chairs," Jessie said. "I'm fine with it."

I nodded. "You two are both adults. I will not judge either of you. I think it's fine. You should've told me. If I hadn't seen you two here, were you ever going to tell me?"

"We're not serious yet," Jessie said. "This is what, Abel, our third or fourth date?"

Abel chuckled. "That depends if you consider what we did last night a date."

"Wait, you're sleeping with each other?"

"It's none of your business," Abel said. "No offense."

I scratched my head and took a deep breath. "Like I said, you're adults. It's fine. I just wish you'd both trusted me enough to tell me what was going on."

Rutherford approached the table with a tray and a couple of bowls of gumbo. "Hey there, lovebirds."

I cocked my head. "You knew they were dating?"

Rutherford bit her lip. "Sorry. It wasn't my place to tell."

"Who else knows about you two?"

Abel shrugged. "Pretty much everyone. My whole pack knows. Cassidy and Ryan know we're seeing each other. I'm pretty sure Donald knows, too."

I shook my head. "Did you think I'd be angry or something?"

"It was my idea to wait until the right time to tell you," Jessie said. "I'm sorry, Cain. I just didn't want you to get the wrong idea."

Jessie had flirted with me pretty intensely shortly after Annabelle hired her. Rutherford didn't know about it. I didn't want it to color their working relationship. Still, I'd discerned from the incident the fact that Jessie had a complicated relationship with men. A lot of men had taken advantage of her. Abel wasn't in a position of authority. By appearance, they were of a similar age. Still, Abel was an amateur in matters of the heart. If I was concerned, it was more that I was worried that Jessie would inadvertently break his heart. This was the first girl he'd ever dated. While he was as ancient as I was, he was also as innocent as a teenager in love. From the way he was looking at her, I could tell already he was falling for her harder than I imagined she was for him.

A tingle spread across my brow.

Abel tilted his head. "Is that what I think it is?"

"You feel it?"

Abel nodded and gulped. "It feels like when the full moon rises."

"Or when Julie evokes the flambeau."

Abel shook his head. "It's not her. She's back at the asylum extension."

"We need to get out of here," I said. "There must be an infernal relic nearby. If it gets any closer to us, we will change. I'd rather not wolf-out in the middle of a restaurant if I can avoid it."

A loud howl echoed from somewhere outside.

"It sounds like someone else from the pack must also be nearby."

I shook my head. "We don't have a choice. Abel, we need to get out of here."

"We'll be right behind you," Jessie said as she and Rutherford stood up from the table.

"I'll get the food packaged up to go," Rutherford added.

"We don't know where the relic is," I said, glancing at Abel as we pushed our way through the crowd around the open door at the exit of the restaurant. "If we follow the wolf, it will get us closer. Whoever shifted, they must be closer to the relic than we are."

The werewolf in the distance howled again. Now, outside of the restaurant, I could get better bearings on the source.

"We need to move through the alleys and back roads. If we change, I'd prefer it not be in plain-view of a thousand tourists."

Abel nodded and followed me between two buildings. We had to move north toward the sound of the howl.

The tingle intensified. It was a good thing I wasn't wearing my new pants. My body expanded. So did Abel's. The transformation was fast. Infernal relics force the shift quicker, and more painfully, than full moons.

Abel howled.

The other wolf howled back.

We followed the sound again, bounding between buildings, until we reached Armstrong Park, just outside Mahalia Jackson Theater. The wolf was standing there, its head covered in a dark material.

It wasn't one of the rougarou. It wasn't a wolf who belonged to Abel's pack. I got a better look at the hood on the wolf's head.

I'd seen it before. I'd worn it before. The infernal cowl. I'd thought I'd destroyed the damned thing nearly three thousand years ago. The wolf wearing it turned toward me, roared, and took off in the opposite direction.

*Wait,* I said, speaking to Abel through the psychic connection we often used to communicate while shifted. *Let the wolf go. Whoever it is, they're here for me. I'm not inclined to give myself to them until I know who they are or what they want.*

# CHAPTER FOUR

IT WAS A FELICITOUS coincidence that we'd just been pants shopping. Rutherford pulled up with my truck, apparently having retrieved my keys from the pockets of my torn slacks after I shifted. So much for that pair. Abel and I were hiding behind a bush, completely naked, when she pulled up.

She and Jessie made a good team. Jessie followed us. Rutherford got the truck and delivered two of my new pairs to my brother and me where Jessie told her to go.

"These are awfully loose, Cain," Abel said. "I thought we wore the same size."

I sighed. "We used to."

"What the hell just happened?" Jessie asked.

I scratched my head. "I don't know who that was."

"Why didn't you go after that wolf?" Jessie asked. "It's not like you have to worry about anyone contracting the seven-fold curse anymore. You know, now that your mark is gone."

"It's not that."

Jessie cocked her head. "Or is it since you no longer have the mark, you fear that someone might try to kill you without consequences?"

I shook my head. "That's not it, either."

"What was that wolf wearing on its head?" Abel asked. "And where did that wolf come from? I haven't seen any werewolves outside of the rougarou or my pack in months."

"The wolf was wearing an infernal cowl. I thought I'd destroyed the damned thing three thousand years ago."

"Three thousand years?" Rutherford asked.

"We still need shirts. What do you say we get out of here? We can discuss it back at the asylum."

"Are you sure?" Jessie asked. "That other wolf couldn't have gotten far. I can use my elemental abilities. I can create a silver sword or something and get rid of it."

I shook my head. "I'm not sure that would be wise. Not until we know who it is we're dealing with."

Technically, riding in the bed of a truck down public roads is against the law. We managed to get out of town and all the way to the extension site with Abel and Jessie laying down in the bed.

I parked the truck and we went inside. We took seats around the tables we used for our group therapy sessions.

"I suppose I owe a bit more explanation to you all."

"I'd say so," Rutherford said.

"I wasn't the same man a century ago as I am today. I was an even worse man three thousand years ago. Dare I say, after my great sin against Abel, it took a long time before I really changed."

"We all understand that, Cain," Abel said. "As I've told you many times before, it doesn't matter who you used to be. It's who you are now that matters."

I nodded. "I appreciate you saying that. That's not the point I'm making now. I'm simply trying to provide the context to explain what happened."

"What happened, Cain?" Rutherford asked.

I rested my face in my hands. "Guilt is a funny thing. When you do something horrible, you have two choices. You can change your path and vow to do better or you can embrace the darkness."

"Are you saying you embraced the darkness?" Jessie asked.

"Yes, and no. I was trying to do the opposite. I was desperate and didn't know how to tame the wolf. So I sought a solution. I approached the Witch of Endor, an enchantress and necromancer who wielded infernal power."

"The same witch who fashioned Julie's flambeau?" Abel asked.

I nodded. "The same. I appealed to the witch. I didn't want to kill. If only I could prevent the wolf from emerging, I thought, I'd have a chance."

"Let me guess," Abel said. "That cowl was what she gave you?"

I scratched the back of my head. "She said it would be possible to keep my natural form during the full moon if I wore it."

"So you wore it, I presume?" Rutherford asked.

"I did. But she was crafty with her words. It was possible that I would not shift while wearing the cowl. What she didn't tell me was that the cowl turned me into a monster worse than the wolf. All my murderous rage, bottled up, was amplified a hundredfold under the cowl. I killed people. Dozens of people. If I stopped, the wolf would emerge. I was afraid if I became a wolf, with my mind already so warped by the cowl as it was, that the beast I'd become would be even more deadly. I wasn't wrong. What the Witch of Endor gave me was a literal answer to my appeal—a way to prevent the wolf from rising on the full moon. But she also turned me into more of a killer than I'd ever been before."

"If that's the cowl that this wolf was wearing," Rutherford asked, "then why did it appear as a wolf?"

I shook my head. "Because whoever is wearing it isn't a werewolf at all. If anyone who wasn't a wolf wore the thing, it would have the opposite effect."

Jessie tilted her head. "So it would make them super nice?"

"It would have the opposite physical effect. The mental impact would be the same. Whatever a person's vices or sins, while wearing the cowl, would be multiplied many times over."

"How did you free yourself from the cowl?" Rutherford asked.

I shook my head. "It wouldn't burn. I tried. The thing already coursed with infernal power so it was immune to flames. After so much killing, after the guilt welled up inside of me, I made what I thought was the right choice. I had to allow the wolf to return, but only after I calmed my mind. I couldn't do that with the cowl. So, I took it out on a ship into the middle of the Mediterranean, tied it to a large boulder, and sank it into the sea."

"So you didn't destroy it?" Abel asked.

"I thought I did. After this much time, I figured there was no way the thing still existed. All I can figure is that someone must've found it. Somehow, whoever has it also knows it's connected to me. I cannot think of any other reason they'd be here, in New Orleans. It's too great a coincidence."

"There aren't many people who know about the things you did three thousand years ago, Cain. How would anyone who found that cursed thing know it had anything to do with you?"

"I don't know, Rutherford. Perhaps when it turned them into a wolf, they did some digging and learned that I was alive, that I was the first werewolf. I suppose there's a chance they don't know that I once wore the cowl."

"The wolf didn't fight us," Abel said. "It was crying out to us. Do you think whoever it is might just be looking for your help? You said it yourself. After a while, that thing warped you so much that the guilt overwhelmed your compulsion to kill. Maybe the person wearing the cowl is a victim of its power as much as you were."

I sighed. "I wouldn't say I was a victim. If I wasn't already a killer, the cowl couldn't have made me one. It only exploits whatever desires, no matter how unsavory, we might harbor in the subconscious mind. Still, that doesn't mean whoever is wearing it now would do the things that he or she might do now under its influence."

"What do we do now?" Jessie asked.

I shook my head. "Until we know who is wearing the cowl, and how it might affect their mind, we can't do much. Ultimately, though, we need to figure out who this mysterious wolf might be. Whoever it is, so long as he or she is wearing the cowl, will remain a wolf. Except during the full moon."

"Except during the full moon?" Abel asked.

I nodded. "Again, whoever is wearing the cowl isn't naturally a wolf. The cowl inverts the cycle. The Witch of Endor enchanted the thing to manage the wolf. It must have the imprint of the werewolf's nature within the enchantment somehow. I believe the moon will make them human again. That will be our chance to discover this person's identity."

"And then what?" Rutherford asked.

"Then we have to figure out how to destroy the cowl once and for all. If we destroy it, separate it from whoever is wearing it, we might save them."

# Chapter Five

THE FIRST THING I did was call all the wolves back to the Vilokan Asylum. At the extension site, we could ensure that if our strange cowl-wearing visitor came near, that the infernal object wouldn't force them to shift in public. We'd be lucky if this lone wolf didn't make a scene alone. Whoever it was didn't appear to be acting especially aggressively. If the cowl worked the same way I remembered it affecting me, though, it was only a matter of time before things got out of hand.

We couldn't just hang out at the asylum and wait for something to happen. We needed to hunt the cowl wearer down.

Rutherford and Jessie tracked down all the wolves we knew in the area. The rougarou and Abel's pack. We had them at the asylum within an hour, which, I had to admit, impressed me. They weren't always the most timely bunch. Something about a rogue infernal object in the city that could force them to wolf-out in the middle of their daily lives proved to be a motivating factor.

Donald was the alpha of the rougarou. He was also a new father. It mildly surprised me when he was the first to show beyond the wolves who were in residence at the asylum extension—Cassidy, Ryan, and Julie.

It mildly disappointed me that Jessie and Rutherford didn't fully brief the wolves before they arrived. The entire world knew I was a murderer. It's in the Bible. Telling everyone that I was a homicidal maniac back in the 10th century, B.C., wasn't a conversation I was eager to have. Informing them that the damned object that made me that way had made an unwelcome appearance in New Orleans was even more disconcerting.

I finished explaining the situation and, when I stopped speaking, no one said a word for what felt like a solid minute.

Donald cleared his throat. "Well, then. It's pretty clear what we need to do."

"What's that?" I asked.

"We need to get our furry asses in gear and catch this lone wolf and destroy that cowl."

"Well, that's obvious," Cassidy said. "Did you say that the Witch of Endor made this thing?"

"I did."

"The same one who created my flambeau," Julie added.

"A necromancer," Cassidy said. "I know a few things about that."

I nodded. Cassidy was a necromancer of a sort. Technically, she was a mambo. A vodouisant who possessed the aspect of Baron Samedi. She also had a unique ability to raise the dead, not just as mindless corpses, but with their minds intact. "No disrespect to your abilities, Cassidy, but I've known a lot of powerful witches through the years. In all my centuries, I've never met a witch more powerful than the Witch of Endor. She wielded the power of hell itself."

Julie placed her hands on the table and grinned. "Well, now that my flambeau wields celestial magic, I'd say that gives us an advantage. We have access to the only power that can extinguish infernal power."

I took a deep breath. "That's true. However, the cowl infects the wearer with its power. If we use that against the wolf wearing it, we'll kill them."

"Is that the end of the world?" Jessie asked. "We're talking about someone who might go all Jack the Ripper in New Orleans if we don't stop them fast."

I rested my elbows on the table and steepled my fingers. "I refuse to kill. That's not who I am. That's not what we're about. Whoever is wearing the cowl is troubled. They need help. They could benefit from therapy."

Donald snorted. "And you're certain that whoever this person is, they've brought the cowl here looking for you?"

I nodded. "All the more reason we must keep this person alive. Until we know their reason, why they've sought me out, I refuse to harm them. My best guess is that somehow they know I wore the cowl before. They know I've moved past it. The cowl might lead someone to do the very worst that they could imagine, but it does nothing to assuage the guilt experienced by the conscious mind. That thing isn't just powered by hell, it puts whoever is wearing it through hell itself."

"No offense, brother, but how many people alive could know that you ever wore that damned thing?"

I shook my head. "I don't know. Not many. Someone must know something."

Jessie stood up from her seat. "If we can't kill this person, what do we do?"

"We convince him, or her, to remove the cowl. When it's off, the infernal power goes dormant."

Julie nodded. "Like my flambeau, when it's not materialized. The power is still there, within me, somewhere. But it isn't active."

Donald shook his head. "You really think this person will remove the cowl if we just ask nicely?"

I nodded. "If whoever is wearing it really wants my help, and since they ran rather than tried to kill me before, I have to believe they do, then yes. We ask nicely. But there's a catch."

"What's the catch?" Abel asked.

"We do it on a full moon. In a wolf form, especially for someone who isn't a werewolf naturally, you know, like we are, we need to do it when they are in human form."

Abel cocked his head. "How are we going to do that if we'll be wolves at the time?"

I turned to Jessie. "She needs to do the talking."

"Are you serious?"

I nodded. "I am. Thankfully, as you all know, we're only one night removed from the next full moon."

# CHAPTER SIX

THE PLAN HAD ONE major flaw. We had to prevent the lone wolf from killing anyone for a whole day before the full moon rose. We couldn't just force the cowl off of them. No one can remove the cowl except the wearer. That meant rallying the wolves. Plan A was to find the lone wolf and distract them as long as possible. Plan B was to intervene and stop them from hurting anyone.

We split into two packs. Julie was a member of both packs. The rougarou had always been with her. She was just a ghost at the time, but as the guardian of the flambeau back in Manchac Swamp, she'd led the rougarou before she became human again. Abel also bit her, making her the seventh who filled his pack when he was under the seven-fold curse.

This time, we decided it was best for Julie to go with Abel's pack. If they found the lone wolf first, their proximity to the cowl might force them to shift, they'd be more likely to lose control under the influence of an infernal object than a celestial one. Julie could evoke the flambeau and force them to shift before the cowl dictated the change.

If the same thing happened to the rougarou, aside from Cassidy and Ryan, they'd been wolves a lot longer. They were more accustomed to becoming wolves under the influence of the flambeau. In addition, since I was with them, I could also exert my influence to help keep them tame.

Rutherford was on standby, back at the original asylum in Vilokan. Whoever it was that had fallen under the influence of the cowl was going to need help. I wanted to make sure we had a room ready and everything was in place to give them the support they needed.

All things considered, I felt like we had as solid a plan as was possible. I'd covered virtually every contingency. We were ready. My stomach was turning in knots. I'd lived long enough since I wore that cowl that I rarely thought about it. It was a nightmare of an experience. The things I did under its influence were like a blur in my mind. Recalling exactly what happened was sort of like how people try to recall what happened after being drunk. That isn't a far off analogy in fact regarding how the cowl worked. It removed all inhibitions. More than that, though, it intensified one's vices; it amplified one's character defects and flaws. It brought the worst out of me. So far as I knew, until now, no one had worn the thing since I cast it into the Mediterranean. That didn't mean no one had. A part of me hoped I'd never know. Anything anyone did while wearing that thing fell on me. I was responsible. I thought sinking it into the sea was the only way to get rid of it. Clearly, my plan was insufficient.

I went with the rougarou to the French Quarter. Abel and his pack circled around the surrounding neighborhoods. We had to communicate by phone. I was still figuring mine out, but I had to admit, it was helpful in situations like this. I was checking mine constantly, just in case we received word from Abel.

So far, nothing. No tingle across the brow. No howls in the distance. It had to be odd, a group of our size walking almost in lock-step down one street and the next. I tried to play it off as naturally as possible. I tossed a dollar in a saxophone player's case as we walked by. He was talented. He deserved it. I gave another dollar to a man in gold shorts, his entire body painted to match, who stood as if he were a statue, not moving a muscle. Even his eyes didn't flinch as I walked past. I admired his dedication. For all he knew, I could have tossed a hundred-dollar bill in the little box in front of him. He stayed in character—if you can call playing a statue a character.

We walked past what used to be Marie's head shop. It was where I'd first met the Voodoo Queen, the original one who'd hired me. A lot had happened since then. Now, the head shop was under new ownership. Someone who had no clue about all the magical and mystical events that had originated in that place.

We turned and headed back toward Jackson Square. My phone rang. It wasn't Abel. It was an unknown number. I ignored the call. My phone immediately rang again.

I sighed.

"You should pick it up," Donald said.

I shrugged. "Probably a scammer. You wouldn't believe how much of that I get on this phone."

"If it is, you hang up."

I bit my lip. "Alright."

I tapped the little green button and put the phone to my ear. "Hello?"

"Well, how about that? He does answer his phone."

I knew the voice. "Annabelle?"

"Rutherford gave me your number. I thought you should know a body turned up in the lower ninth ward."

"A body? That's not altogether uncommon."

"But a body with its heart ripped from its chest certainly is."

I sighed. "A wolf attack."

"I suspect as much."

"Only one body?"

"So far."

"We're on it. Keep me posted if anything else turns up. If this is what we think it is, though, I might not be able to answer once we get close."

"Right. Rutherford said whatever this thing is might make you shift. I trust you'll exercise discretion, Cain. The last thing I need right now, while the authorities are investigating this strange homicide, is a report of a pack of werewolves bounding through the streets."

"Understood. We should be able to sense when we're getting close before we shift. We'll reassess our strategy then."

"It's still too risky, Cain. That many wolves, a whole pack moving at once, there's no way you'd be able to stay hidden in the lower ninth."

I sighed. "Fair enough. I'll go alone. If it's acceptable, I'd like the rest of the wolves to stay in Vilokan until we know what we're dealing with. The firmament there should be able to prevent the power of the infernal relic from forcing a shift if it gets too close."

"I was thinking the same thing. Tonight is a full moon, though, correct?"

"It is. I'll find out what I can. Until then, I'll call Abel and make sure he brings his pack into Vilokan as well. Just make sure they're out of there a good hour before sunset, so we have time to prepare."

"You can call back at this number at any time, Cain. Just let me know when you're ready."

I tilted my head. "You're on your office phone, correct?"

"Of course. Cell phones don't work in Vilokan."

"Stay close to the phone. If any more bodies start piling up, I may need help. If not from the wolves, from someone."

"I won't leave my office until I hear from you, Cain. Good luck."

# CHAPTER SEVEN

BETWEEN THE FRENCH QUARTER and the Lower Ninth Ward is the Upper Ninth Ward. It was roughly a five-mile trek. I opted against taking the truck. At a walking pace, I'd have a little warning once I felt the tingle before I got too close to the cowl to avoid shifting. If I was driving, moving much faster than I would on foot, there was a risk that I'd move too close to the cowl too quickly to turn back.

I knew if I was going to confront this person, now in wolf-form, I'd have to become a wolf, too. Could I exert influence as alpha? There was no way to know. This person wasn't turned into a werewolf by inheriting my curse—neither directly from me nor indirectly from another wolf's bite. They took a werewolf form because of the cowl's enchantment. It was an enchantment originally intended for me. The Witch of Endor deceived me and manipulated my desperation to quell the wolf. Then, the imprint of my other nature, my wolf, remained within the cowl. It was why a human wearing the cowl would become a wolf.

As I entered the Lower Ninth, I saw red and blue lights reflecting off the front of a boarded-up house at the end of the street. I followed the lights. So far, no tingle. Yellow tape connected between trees and a street sign suggested a crime scene. An ambulance was driving away. Its lights weren't on. That meant it left without a patient inside.

"Excuse me, sir. This is a crime scene. I'll have to ask you to leave."

I glanced at the cop's badge. "Apologies, officer. Has there been another killing?"

"You'd best get inside. We fear some kind of serial killer is at large."

"The victim's heart..."

The officer winced. "News travels fast, sir. The victim is in the same condition as the one found before. I'd encourage you to find someplace safe while the perp is still at large."

I saw another officer standing beside a woman near the closest house. I couldn't see the body. There were too many officers standing around it. One officer was speaking to the woman. Her eyes were wide with shock and filled with tears.

"Apologies, Officer. Is that the victim's spouse?"

The officer looked away for a second, took a deep breath, then looked back at me. "No, sir. She is the victim's mother."

The woman wasn't old. I'd guess she was nearly thirty. If the victim was her son or daughter, it must've been a child. I clenched my fist and shook my head.

"A child..."

The officer shook his head. "Please, sir. Again, I must ask you to leave the area."

I turned around and walked until out of view. Then, I ran. The wolf had to be close by. It wasn't close enough I could sense it yet, but wherever it was I had to find it soon. I couldn't allow another innocent person to die... especially not a child...

I wanted to scream. I can't say when I wore the cowl, I wouldn't have killed anyone who crossed my path. I was grateful, so far as I remembered, that none of my victims were young. I don't think even three thousand years of therapy could ever have assuaged that guilt.

I could only run so hard, so far. While in human form, I had en-hanced strength and endurance. There were a few crossover advantages to being a werewolf that persisted, regardless of my form. Even so, I had my limits. I didn't have any water. A cramp was nagging me on my left side. I had to stop to prevent myself from hyperventilating.

I sat on the curb to catch my breath. I felt a tingle, but it was too subtle to know if it was on account of the cowl or my exertion.

The tingle intensified.

It wasn't exertion.

I stood up. I looked up and down the streets. There was nothing out of the ordinary. Only a few cars moving through the streets. Still, the cowl and the lone wolf had to be nearby.

I didn't have a good place to hide. The tingle spread from my brow throughout my body. The shift was coming. The best I could do was hide in someone's backyard. Thankfully, whoever lived in the house in front of where I was sitting before didn't have a dog. I didn't see any evidence that anyone was home.

I removed my brand-new pants just in time to spare them. I don't know why I bothered. Chances were I wouldn't come back to retrieve them, but you know, why ruin a good pair of Walmart slacks when you don't have to?

My shirt didn't fare as well. The buttons tore and the back and arm holes ripped as my body expanded.

As a wolf, I sniffed the air. The other wolf had to be close. I howled. Then I waited.

The other wolf didn't howl back, but with my hearing more acute than before, I detected a whimper.

I bounded out of the backyard, over a chain-link fence, and into the next yard over.

I searched the yard before leaping into the next, then the next. Finally, I found it.

The lone wolf was curled in a ball, shaking, the cowl still firmly attached to its head. *Can you hear me?* I asked, using the psychic connection I used to speak to wolves in my pack before.

The wolf turned and stared at me, its snout quivering.

*Are you alright?*

*I... what I did...*

*You can't control your rage. I know how it feels. I've worn that thing before.*

*I know...*

*Why are you here? How do you know me?*

The wolf growled and turned its head away.

*Follow me to the swamps. If you don't want to hurt anyone else, you must get away from the city.*

*You don't understand...*

*You can remove the cowl.*

*I can't... I won't...*

*I don't know you. But you don't want to hurt these people.*

*You do know me. And you're right. I didn't come here to kill them. I came here to kill you!*

The wolf roared and leaped toward me, exposing its fangs.

I dove back at the wolf. I was bigger. I forced the wolf into the brick side of the house. The bricks crumbled.

The wolf snapped at me. I growled back, batting it in the face with one of my massive front paws.

When I hit the side of its head, I touched the cowl. It felt like electricity, repelling my touch. The jolt sent me flying back. I crashed into the yard.

The wolf returned to all fours and snarled.

No response. Too much rage. Too much anger. When the cowl had that much control, that much influence, the mind faded and primal instinct took over.

I snarled back. The wolf took a step back. Then it turned and took off in a blur, blasting through a wood fence and into the streets.

I'd shown my dominance, but this wolf wouldn't submit. Whoever it was knew me. It wanted me dead. Not enough so, though, that it dared try to attack me again.

At least now I had its scent. It would come after me again. When it thought it could take me by surprise. I had to track it. I had to stay on its trail.

Based on the position of the sun in the sky, it was only an hour or less before sunset. If I could keep the wolf in sight, if I could stay on its trail, I might be able to see the true face beneath the cowl. Until I knew who was trying to kill me, whoever harbored enough hatred or resentment toward me that the cowl led them here to do exactly that, I wouldn't know how to stop them. It would be my only chance to persuade them to remove the cowl.

I couldn't go back to get the other wolves. Perhaps they'd find me after they shifted. I couldn't let the wolf get too far away that I'd shift back. If I did that, I'd have to shift again almost right away. It would leave me weak. But that wasn't my biggest fear. If I let them get too far away, I'd lose the other wolf's scent. If that happened, I might lose my only chance to discover who was behind the cowl.

By following the lone wolf, I might have been walking into its trap. Then again, why would it tell me it intended to kill me at all unless it didn't? I could relate. The cowl drove this person to kill. Revealing the intention to kill me wasn't a threat. It was a warning. Whoever this was, someone who I apparently met before, had enough resentment against me that the cowl could turn it into murderous rage. At the same time, the person behind the cowl didn't want me dead. If they did, they wouldn't have told me. Despite what one might think from watching villains gloat in superhero movies, in the real world, if someone wants someone dead, they rarely broadcast their intentions to anyone—least of all their prospective victim.

I followed the werewolf through the Lower Ninth to the Sankofa Wetland Park. It included a short nature trail that, over recent years, had been adorned with hundreds of bald cypress and herbaceous trees. Short of making it to Manchac Swamp, where I frequently spent my full-moon nights, it was probably the best place we could go once the sun set to avoid being seen.

I caught up to the lone wolf just as the sun dipped beneath the horizon and the moon shone. Still held in my werewolf form by the cowl, I stayed the same.

The lone wolf's body changed. It was a female body. She turned away from me as she crouched down over her own frame, as she shed her form and returned to normal. The cowl was still on her head when she turned and looked at me.

I took two steps back.

How could this be possible?

I hadn't seen Merab in three thousand years. Not since before I took the cowl. We'd only been married for a year when she disappeared. It was after the first time she'd seen me shift into this form. I'd terrified her. The pain of that loss and rejection was among the reasons I sought the Witch of Endor to begin with. I'd hoped the cowl she made would allow me to win her back. If I weren't werewolf, if I didn't become a monster every full moon, perhaps she'd take me back.

How could this even be possible? How did she survive so long?

Merab stepped toward me, her long, curled black hair draping across her shoulders from under the cowl and accentuating her naked frame.

"I was afraid, Cain. Could you blame me? I never meant to lose you. But when I came back for you, you were gone."

I whimpered. I couldn't speak to her. Not like this.

"If I could only see your face again, just once, perhaps it would quell my anger."

Merab reached up and touched my face. Then she grabbed the cowl that still partially obscured her face, ripped it off, and threw it on me.

I roared. Then, I started to change. For the first time in nearly my entire existence, I was becoming human during a full moon.

When I'd shifted back, Merab wrapped her arms around me and wept. "I didn't want to kill you. Before, wearing that cowl, all I could think of was the anger I felt when I thought you'd left me."

"I didn't leave you, Merab. I was trying to win you back. I went to the Witch of Endor. I'd hoped she could stop the wolf from emerging, but this cowl, it changed me. I couldn't go back."

"I understand that now."

"How did you survive, dearest Merab? I don't understand."

Merab shook her head. "I did not. I lived a full life. I married. I died in old age."

"Then how is this possible? How are you here?"

Merab touched my face with her right hand. "The witch you sought has not failed you, Cain. She's brought me back to life. She's given us another chance."

My eyes widened in horror. "The Witch of Endor is alive?"

"Yes, my love. It was her hope that I might deliver this cowl to you."

I shook my head. I grabbed the edge of the cowl to remove it. Merab grabbed my hand. "You cannot remove it, Cain."

"I must, Merab. You don't understand what this thing did to me. As a wolf, I only look like a monster. When I wore this thing before, I truly became one."

"But you are strong, Cain. The witch assured me you could endure its influence. If I do not wear it, Cain, you must. If you do not, I will die again. My life is bound to the power within the cowl. If the cowl is unworn, if the magic within it wanes, I cannot survive."

# CHAPTER EIGHT

I DIDN'T BOTHER TEXTING anyone. The rougarou were werewolves by now, likely in Manchac Swamp with Abel and his pack for the night. Absent any word from me earlier, that was what they had to do. Annabelle was in her office. Rutherford was at the asylum in Vilokan. If I texted them, they wouldn't get the messages until they left Vilokan. All I could do was call Annabelle. She could help formulate a plan.

Bringing Merab to the asylum wasn't off the table. That was what I'd intended to do *before* I knew who she was and before I found myself wearing the cowl.

The first step was to find some clothes. I found the pants I'd removed in the yard back in the Lower Ninth. My phone was still in my pocket. We also found a sundress hanging from someone's clothes line in their backyard. I took it. Thievery isn't my style, but neither is public nudity. Sometimes, you have to do what you have to do. I'd leave some money in the person's mailbox later. Fully clothed, we had to check in with Annabelle. She said she'd be waiting by her phone. By now, it had been several hours. She surely was worried about what had happened.

Annabelle answered her phone after the first ring.

"Annabelle, I need your help."

"Cain? How in the world are you even speaking to me right now? The full moon..."

"I have the cowl, Annabelle."

"Wait. If you're not shifted right now, does that mean you're *wearing* it?"

I sighed. "That's exactly what it means. I have no choice."

"Cain! That's an infernal relic. It will warp your mind."

"I've endured the influence of infernal flames before. Not only when I wore the cowl, but when Julie's flambeau still coursed with hellfire. I believe I can withstand its influence for a time."

"What about the wolf who was wearing it before?"

"She is well. I don't know how to say this other than just to say it. She is my wife of three thousand years ago."

I heard nothing but static in response for nearly five seconds. "Necromancy?"

"The Witch of Endor, herself."

"Shit balls!" Annabelle exclaimed. "Seriously? Where is she?"

I shook my head. "I wish I knew, Annabelle. I know little more. It's not often I'm devoid of a plan, but I don't know what to do."

"I presume Rutherford doesn't know."

I snorted. "She doesn't. She's at the asylum. I don't know how I can tell her that my former wife is here."

Merab cocked her head and furrowed her brow. "Cain, are you married?"

I shook my head. "I'm not. But I am with someone."

Merab nodded. Annabelle sighed. "Is that her?"

"It is."

"There are already bodies piling up in the Lower Ninth. One of them was a child, Cain."

I took a deep breath. "I know."

"We can't leave her at large. I hate to say it, but you need to come in, too. Someone should watch you until morning when you can remove the cowl."

"I can't remove it, Annabelle. Not now. Not until we understand the enchantment. If we do, Merab will die."

"I see," Annabelle said, pausing a moment before she continued. "I still think you should come in. Perhaps we can figure something out. Maybe there's a way to remove the cowl and spare her, but I'll need to consult with the Ghede."

"After the full moon ends, I'll talk to Cassidy and see if she can help. She's the only necromancer I've met, aside from the Witch of Endor, who can restore a body with their soul intact like this. Julie might also be helpful since she's accustomed to working with infernal relics."

"I'll have them brought in as soon as possible," Annabelle said. "But we have to be careful. So long as that cowl is still active, we can't allow either Cassidy or Julie to get too close. I know they're tame wolves. At least, you've told me as much. Still, after the last few times it has happened and the body counts that resulted, the citizens of Vilokan won't tolerate any active werewolves in the city."

"Understandable. Should we meet you in your office?"

"I'll meet you just outside Vilokan in Pere Antoine Alley. I'm sure you can understand, Cain, that given the fact you're wearing the cowl and your former wife is also responsible for at least a couple of murders, I'll have to exercise some precautions."

I shook my head. "She isn't responsible for what happened. The cowl warped her mind."

Annabelle sighed. "And you're wearing it now. I'm not saying I don't believe you can't resist its influence, Cain. Maybe you can. But I have to consider the safety of Vilokan."

"You're considering not allowing us in?"

"Not what I'm saying, Cain. Until we know more about what's happening, though, I need to put the safety of my people first."

"I understand that. I'm sure you'll find when you meet us there that we're both of sound mind. At least we are for now."

"How soon can you meet me there?"

"We're five or six miles out and have to make the trek on foot. Give us an hour and a half."

# CHAPTER NINE

"Who is this woman?" Merab asked.

"She's a nurse. We live together."

Merab raised an eyebrow. "You live together, but she is not your wife?"

I sighed. "The world is a very different place than it was when we were married, Merab."

"I've noticed. These people have strange, armored chariots that move without the aid of ox or horse. They possess magic. They harness it through those trinkets, like the one you spoke into before. Some of them even shine light, as if their little squares could harness the power of the sun itself."

I smiled. "It's not magic, Merab. It's what people call technology."

"Technology?"

I showed Merab my phone. "I don't really know how to do very much with this thing. I'm not great with it. But this is not magic. It's an invention. Really, it's a collection of hundreds of different inventions that are all used together to create this device."

"I don't know if I could ever get used to this world."

I shrugged. "My brother did."

Merab raised an eyebrow. "Brother? Your brothers were all dead long before we met."

"Someone resurrected Abel through necromancy, Merab. He still has a lot to learn about the world, but he's adjusting well. I'm sure I could arrange a conversation with him if it would help to know someone who has been through this."

Merab coughed in her hand as we stood at a crosswalk waiting for the red hand to change into the little blue walking man. I had to grab her by the shoulders to prevent her from walking forward. "The red light means stop and wait. When it shows the image of a blue person walking, that's when we can cross the street."

"People are now blue and have red hands?"

I chuckled. "Not typically. They're just signs. Lights. They keep people out of the roads so we don't get hit by cars—those horseless chariots you mentioned before. There are other lights above the road that tell the cars when to stop and when it's safe to go forward."

The "walk" light illuminated and we crossed the street. Merab took my hand. "Are you well, Cain?"

I nodded. "So far, I sense little from the cowl. That's not surprising, though. The first time I wore it, the effects on my mind were so gradual I barely noticed the change. Not until my hands were covered in blood..."

Merab winced. "It was the same for me. After the Witch of Endor raised me and she gave me the cowl, I was fine. She told me where I could find you. She'd already made all the arrangements. We came here without incident."

"We? The Witch of Endor is here, in New Orleans?"

"I believe so," Merab said. "I cannot say where she went. She disappeared shortly after we arrived. I was lonely. Since the cowl kept me alive, but only as a wolf, I couldn't exactly ask for directions. The more

I panicked, the more I had to hide myself from view, the more rage I felt."

"You said you were going to kill me."

"I wanted to. Please forgive me, husband. It was not my true desire. It was out of the anger, fear, and pain I sensed after I discovered you were a werewolf. After you left..."

"That must have been terrifying for you."

Merab shook her head. "The wolf scared me, sure. But that was nothing compared to the terror I felt when I realized my husband was gone. Do you remember, Cain, how hard it was in those days for widows to survive? The king did not permit women to own property. Our lands were sold. It left me with little choice but to become a harlot or to beg for the affections of men who were of little note."

I scratched my head. "I'm sorry, Merab. I did not think clearly. I thought this cowl would put the wolf to rest. I hoped I could return to you. I should have, straight away, but I wanted to give it a couple of full moons to ensure that the cowl worked before I came home. But then, it was too late. The cowl had a hold on me. After the things I did under the cowl, after I became a wanted man... you realize, Merab, that many of the men who wanted me dead would have become wolves themselves if they ever found me and attempted to kill me?"

Merab stopped me on the sidewalk and took my hand. "You could have at least stopped by to explain, to say goodbye."

Tears welled up in my eyes. "You're right. I was afraid, Merab."

"What were you scared of, Cain?"

I sighed. "That you'd still see me as a monster. That you'd look at me again with those same eyes as when you first saw me become the wolf."

"I was shocked, Cain. Who wouldn't be? Yes, I was terrified, but I was more scared for you than I was for myself. I knew you'd never hurt me."

"Again, Merab, I am sorry. I am a different man than I used to be. I hope you can accept, however, that I have a life here. There's a woman I love."

"Could you not take more than one wife?"

I chuckled. "That's not legal. Not here."

"Then leave her so that we might be together."

"Merab, I love her."

"Don't you love me?"

"I did. You must understand, I've lived the equivalence of over thirty full lives since we were together. Could you truly expect me to still feel the same today that I did when we first met?"

"I married again. I lived a full life. My feelings for you never faded."

"Did you love your next husband?"

"He was a good man, Cain. Given my situation and desperation, that was all I could ask for. He cared for me and our children well."

"But did you love him?"

Merab nodded. "I loved him for who he was. Still, it was not the same."

"You don't suppose, had our roles been reversed, if you'd lived on for centuries and I was the one who lived but a single life, that you'd never find a love that rivaled what we once shared?"

Merab took a deep breath. "I don't know, Cain. I really don't. There's no way to anticipate what could have happened. I believe, though, that no matter what happened, a part of my heart would always long for you."

I bit my lip. Did I love Merab? I suppose I used to. Though, our marriage was young when it fell apart. We had passion. Our lusts when together were insatiable. Still, our relationship never matured. Our relationship turned from a spark to a blazing inferno of desire, but the flames never settled into a steady burn, the kind that sustains you and keeps you warm during the course of a long life. Long by the regular standards, at least. I'd had those marriages, the relationships that might not have burned as hot at first but lasted for decades.

Merab satisfied the desires of the flesh without question. She was as alluring as ever. At my age, though, I was now seeking something deeper, something more.

With Rutherford, our love was like a fine wine that got better with age. With Merab, while I cannot exclude the possibility our passions might not have settled into something more, it began like a shot of whiskey that burned on its way down, sent tingles across my body, and clouded my sensibilities.

The way Merab described her second marriage suggested that the love she and he shared was more like the love one has for a friend, or even a parent. Her husband took care of her. She was grateful. The relationship never moved her heart.

I could not blame Merab, I suppose, for thinking that what we had was the height of romance. She'd only lived a single life. It took me many lifetimes before I'd experienced the kind of slow-burn love that sustained me for decades at a time. Not everyone is so blessed to have loved in such a way, and I'd only known that kind of love a handful of times. That's what I was nurturing with Rutherford. I wouldn't dare throw it away for what I used to feel for Merab. I'd lived too long to find momentary and fleeting passions satisfying.

I didn't want Merab. At the same time, I couldn't take my eyes off of her. Was that me? I still had all the drives of the flesh common to other men. I rarely gave in to them. I certainly wouldn't, so long as I was with Rutherford. I couldn't remember, though, the last time my mind entertained the desires that now consumed my mind. It was as if the nights of passion Merab and I shared during our short-lived relationship were now front and center in my mind. It felt like it was just yesterday when she and I had married and gave ourselves to one another.

It was this damned cowl. It had to be. The first time I wore it, anger and rage provided the seeds that sprouted into murderous bramble. Now, the infernal relic was drawing on other basic desires and temptations that I usually suppressed. For now, I could resist. I still had my wits about me. If the cowl worked on me the way it had before, though, it was only a matter of time.

# CHAPTER TEN

ANNABELLE WAS WAITING FOR us, leaning against the wall where the mystical doorway that opened to Vilokan, in the side of the St. Louis Cathedral, was located.

Pauli stood beside her in his human-form. Technically, Pauli was born a human. After getting possessed by a nasty Loa who took over his body, they transferred his soul into a boa constrictor. Since he had the aspect of the Aida-Wedo, the Loa of Snakes and Rainbows, he could shape-shift and teleport. So, while he was now naturally a snake, he shifted as often as he could into a slightly trimmer, handsomer, version of his former human body.

He also served as something like Vilokan's city-wide bouncer. If Annabelle needed someone moved somewhere, she sent Pauli. He took his snake form—complete with luminescent, rainbow-colored scales—wrapped himself around whoever Annabelle intended to arrest, and relocated the prisoner or exile to the desired location.

Pauli was high-fashion, flamboyant, and as snarky as they came. He was an acquired taste. Mostly, I enjoyed his eccentric company. More than once, Annabelle had used him to deliver non-compliant patients to the Vilokan Asylum. His presence had me a bit off-put.

"Annabelle. Pauli."

"Hello, Cain."

"This is my former wife, Merab."

"A pleasure," Annabelle said. "Please do not mistake my precautions for rudeness. Given what has happened, I simply cannot risk either of you losing control and harming the citizens of Vilokan."

"What are you saying, Annabelle?"

Annabelle sighed. "Apologies, Cain. I'm sure you can understand why this is necessary."

With a flash of refracted light, Pauli took his serpent form, wrapped himself around Merab, and disappeared.

"Seriously, Annabelle?"

"Pauli is taking her to the asylum. Jessie and Rutherford will process her admittance."

"I need to be there. She's here for me, Annabelle. It's the power in this cowl that keeps her alive. I'm not sure if she can survive if not in proximity to me."

"You cannot remove it, Cain?"

I shook my head. "Not without killing her. If someone isn't wearing it, the power within it that also sustains her life will go dormant."

"Then, again, I must repeat my apologies, Cain. This is only a precaution."

"What are you talking about, Annabelle?"

The next thing I knew, I felt something constrict around my body. "Pauli, get off of me!"

"Sorry, bitch! It's off to the looney bin for you!"

"Pauli," Annabelle said. "That's unnecessary. I'll come to see you shortly, Cain."

"Annabelle, wait!"

No sooner did I say it, and rainbow colored energies flashed around me. The next thing I knew, I was standing in one of the padded rooms at the Vilokan Asylum.

"Pauli, let me go."

"Gladly," Pauli said, slithering off my body. "I just thought you could use a hug."

I snorted. "I will not hurt anyone. This cowl isn't affecting me the same way it did before."

"Bitch, please. Take it up with Annabelle. You are a werewolf and it's a full moon. You're also wearing an infernal object that Annabelle says turned you into a real ho the last time you wore it."

I snorted. "It made me a killer, not a ho, Pauli."

Pauli tilted his pointy snake head at me. "You know, if I were you, I'd embrace ho. It ain't good, but in your case, I'd call it a euphemism."

I sighed. "Thanks for the advice. Where's Merab?"

"In another one of your cells."

"These aren't cells, Pauli. I don't run a prison. It's a medical facility."

"Damn, because I have a lot more fantasies about prisons than hospitals. I was hoping to drop you off and go find myself a good time."

I shook my head. "Rutherford knows I'm here, right?"

"Bitch, I'm just the bouncer. A fabulous bouncer, no doubt. The best damn looking one you've ever seen. I don't know what Annabelle set up."

"But surely Rutherford realizes..."

"Get your panties out of a wad, Cain. Annabelle said this is just a precaution."

I clenched my fist as blood rushed to my head. The heat spread across my brow.

"Uh oh! That's my cue!"

In a flash, Pauli disappeared. I was alone in my room. That sensation, that rage, I didn't know I could feel so angry anymore. I hadn't felt that way in ages. It was the cowl. I was annoyed, no doubt. I understood why Annabelle had to do what she did. But all it took was a petty vexation for the cowl to take those seeds and grow them into murderous rage.

I sat on the edge of the bed. I didn't realize how thin these mattresses were. No wonder Pauli mistook the place for a prison. I kicked up my feet, laid down, and took a deep breath.

Meditation.

It was one of many tools I'd learned through the years to calm my mind. It was a part of what I'd taught the other wolves, so they'd be in the right frame of mind before a full moon. I had to let go of even the slightest frustration. I couldn't give the cowl a foothold. If I did, I wasn't sure that even this cell could contain me. I was a werewolf, after all. Even in my human form, I had the strength that, if fueled by rage, I imagined I could break the door right off its hinges.

I couldn't think about getting arrested. I couldn't even think about Merab. The second I did, a desire I didn't want to experience flooded my mind. So, instead, I thought about Rutherford. I envisioned myself sitting on our couch, my legs kicked up, and my dirty socks on the floor. I pictured her next to me, curled up, as we tried to squeeze both of our bodies into my oversized recliner. For the moment, it worked. The exercise quelled my rage. I could only hope that Annabelle would have an answer soon. She needed to speak with Julie and Cassidy. Between the two of them, along with Annabelle we had the expertise of someone accustomed to working with infernal objects and a necromancer. I liked our chances. Then again, none of them were half as powerful as the Witch of Endor. Breaking whatever enchantment she put on this cowl wasn't going to be easy—doing it in such a way that it wouldn't kill Merab would be even harder. I couldn't afford to allow myself to doubt our success. I had to remain optimistic. Positive thoughts. Happy thoughts. Anything else and there was no telling what kind of monster I might become.

# CHAPTER ELEVEN

SOMEONE KNOCKED ON THE door four times. Three knocks close together, the fourth just a millisecond later. It was the way Rutherford knocked on a door. I'd heard her do it hundreds of times before entering a patient's room.

"Come in," I said, raising my voice to ensure she could hear me.

I heard a key enter the lock and turn. Then the door swung open. Rutherford and Jessie stood there beside one another.

"Nice to see you two."

Rutherford took my hand. "How do you feel?"

"As well as one might expect when you're bound to an infernal relic that amplifies every unsavory inclination in the subconscious mind."

"And you're resisting those urges, correct?"

I nodded. "So far."

"I'm here to kick your ass if you don't," Jessie said, smirking.

I grinned. "I appreciate that. Have either of you spoken with Merab?"

"I have," Rutherford said. "She wasn't particularly kind."

I chuckled. "I suppose not. She's envious of you."

"I gathered as much. Tell me, Cain. Is it true what she said?"

"I suppose that depends on what she told you. That she was my wife?"

Rutherford nodded. "Yes. But that's not what I was referring to."

"Then I suppose you mean that the Witch of Endor is the one who brought her back?"

"And that she's here, in New Orleans?"

I shrugged. "I haven't seen her, Rutherford. But it must be true. Think about it. Who else could resurrect someone from *my* past, vest them with a relic she once made specifically for me, and send her here to find me? I don't know of anyone else who knew who I was, knew of the cowl, and has the power to do such a thing."

"Is it possible she modified the cowl?"

I bit my lip. "I hadn't thought of that. I suppose it is possible, if not likely. How she might have altered, though, would likely have to do with her purpose here. That remains a mystery I've yet to unravel."

Rutherford nodded. "This woman, Merab. Why do you suppose the Witch of Endor chose her."

"Probably to get to me. She needed someone with an emotional connection to me, something she could exploit through the cowl."

Rutherford huffed. "An emotional connection. Do you have feelings for her, Cain?"

"Rutherford, she was my wife once."

"So you do."

"Feelings, yes. I care for her as one I once thought I might love. But I don't love her. She is no threat to you, Rutherford."

Rutherford nodded. "She's very pretty, Cain. What feelings do you have for her? Do you desire her?"

I shook my head. "I do not. Not in my heart."

"Does the cowl care about whether your feelings come from your heart or your..." Rutherford glanced down toward my crotch.

"Rutherford... I would never..."

"But with the cowl, you might."

"Her desire for me runs deeper than my desire for her."

Rutherford snorted. "She loves you."

"She does. She also resents me. When she wore the cowl, it was her anger that prevailed. She wished me dead."

"Then why didn't she kill you?"

"Because the cowl amplifies any unsavory desires or emotions. It does not erase what is good. For now, her love for me was stronger than even the rage she felt, amplified by the cowl."

"Have you considered it was not merely her feelings for you that made her the Witch of Endor's choice to seek you?"

"What are you suggesting?"

"What feelings do you believe the cowl is trying to exploit within you? Have you had any inclination to kill?"

I shook my head. "None. I no longer harbor that rage. But you're right, Rutherford. I believe the cowl is trying to tempt me with lust. But as of now, that's not a worry. As much as her love for me prevented her from killing me, my love for you prevents me from acting on those urges."

"Maybe that's true, for now. Can you be certain that won't change?"

I shook my head. "The longer I wear the cowl, the greater its influence becomes. I need to speak with her now, while I can still resist. If there's anything she knows that can help us find the Witch of Endor, I'm the only one she'll tell."

Rutherford shook her head. "Being with her, Cain, will only give your... lusts... a chance to grow. It will speed up the influence of the cowl over your mind."

I sighed. "That's probably true. Still, I have to try. You can be there. You and Jessie, both. If I try anything... inappropriate... please intervene."

"Maybe in the morning. After Annabelle has consulted with Julie and Cassidy."

I shook my head. "The cowl gains influence over my mind by the minute. Even if the lusts aren't there, or the source of that lust isn't in front of me, the cowl continues to infect my mind with its infernal energies. By morning, it may be too late."

Rutherford and Jessie exchanged glances. Jessie grinned. "I say we do it."

"Are you serious?" Rutherford asked.

"Cain is right," Jessie said. "This might be the only chance we have while Cain has his wits about him to learn this witch's intentions."

Rutherford sighed. "Alright, but I'm not leaving his side."

"I won't either," Jessie said. "And like I said, Rutherford. If he steps out of line, I'll handle it."

I chuckled. "Right. You'll kick my ass."

"With permission, of course, Doctor Cain."

"If I misbehave in the slightest, Jessie, then yes. Permission granted to kick my ass."

# CHAPTER TWELVE

JESSIE HAD HER ETHEREAL club in hand. She held it in her right and patted it rhythmically in her left. If the cowl got the best of me, she'd use her earthen strength—courtesy of the aspect of the Loa of War—and knock my block off.

"You look like you're enjoying the prospect of beating me with that thing."

Jessie chuckled. "It's not every day that you have permission to beat the crap out of your boss. Do you know how many people out there wish they had that chance?"

I grinned. "Well, I like to think I'm a good supervisor."

Jessie snorted. "Sure. What do you want? A treat?"

Rutherford smirked. "No need for treats. A 'good doggy' and a scratch behind the ears usually does the trick."

I shook my head. "Ha. Ha. You and your werewolf jokes. As if I haven't been hearing those my entire life."

Jessie giggled. "Just don't mount and hump anyone and you'll be fine."

I rolled my eyes. "Thanks, Jessie."

Rutherford rested her hand on my lower back. "If it gets so far as humping, I'll roll up a newspaper and shove it where..."

"I get it. Alright. I'll behave. This cowl hasn't affected me so much. At least not so far as I can tell. Though, Rutherford, if that's how you discipline a dog, we might want to reconsider adopting one in the future."

"So you admit it? You're a dog, Cain?"

"No! That's not the point!" I sighed.

Rutherford chuckled, unlocked the door to Merab's room, and pressed it open.

"Cain!" Merab ran up to me and wrapped her arms around me as soon as she saw me. I gave her a half-hearted squeeze back.

Rutherford snorted.

"Merab, we must talk. We really must know more about the Witch of Endor."

Merab shook her head. "I can't tell you much. I don't know how she's survived for so long. I assume it has to do with her powers."

I sat down on the edge of Merab's bed and gestured next to me, inviting her to sit beside me. Rutherford and Jessie exchanged glances as if they half expected us to rip each other's clothes off any second. I maintained my focus. "Did the witch tell you anything about her plans? Did she say why she wanted you to find me?"

Merab shook her head. "She said that the only way for us to be together was to find you, to use the anger my cowl provides as fuel to track you down. Then, to give you the cowl before I acted on my anger."

I raised one eyebrow. "So she wanted you to give me the cowl?"

Merab placed one hand on my leg. "And she told me if I didn't, I'd lose myself. She assured me you could endure it and that it would help me win you over."

I avoided looking at Rutherford. I imagined her expression wasn't exactly pleasant as she listened to what Merab said.

Something like a tingle spread from her fingers to my leg as she slowly slid her hand higher. It wasn't a magical tingle. Not the same sensation that forced me to shift. It was the kind of sensation that accompanies desire. I grabbed her hand and removed it from my leg. "Please, Merab. I do not believe the witch's desire is merely to bring us together. She wanted me to wear the cowl."

Merab shook her head. "I don't know, Cain. I didn't question it. If you'd been dead for so long and suddenly came to life with the promise that you could be with the one you'd loved your whole life again, would you question it? Or would you be grateful?"

"I get it, Merab. The Witch of Endor is no Cupid."

"Who?" Merab tilted her head.

"Sorry, that myth wasn't a part of our culture. What I meant to say is that she isn't especially interested in love and romance. She seeks power. That's always been her drive. Her appearance is deceiving. She may look like an old woman, but the power she wields invigorates her."

Merab sighed. "She was weak. She often required rest. She was not with me every moment. She told me how to get here, to this land, and insisted I followed her instructions. At times she disappeared, engulfed in flames. Later, she'd return more vigorous, as if she'd just woken from a good night's sleep."

"Could others see her?"

"I don't know. I mean, I suppose so. How else would she secure a way for me to travel?"

I shook my head. "I don't know. It sounds like her hold on her material form is tenuous."

"I suppose that's right. It's like that fire took her some place that gave her strength. She went there to rest and recover."

I bit my lip. "You said she left you, engulfed in flames, after you arrived here in New Orleans. Do you believe she's still here?"

Merab nodded. "All I know is that's how she left me. I cannot say if she remains wherever she goes when the flames take her away or if she is elsewhere. She told me she would return to me once I completed my task and your true heart's desire was restored."

I scratched the back of my head. "My true heart's desire?"

Merab raised a hand to my cheek. "I think you know what I mean."

I grabbed Merab's wrist and clasped it with my hands. "Please don't do that, Merab. You've met Rutherford, I presume."

Merab glanced at Rutherford, who, given the situation, was doing a good job biting her tongue. "I've met the woman."

Rutherford snorted. "The woman?"

I raised my hand. "She means nothing disparaging by that, Rutherford. Remember, she comes from another time."

"I don't get it," Jessie said. "How do you even know how to speak English?"

Merab tilted her head. "A gift from the witch, I suppose."

I folded my right hand over my left. "Thank you, Merab. This has been helpful."

"Will you stay with me, Cain?"

"Merab, I cannot. This cowl, the influence it has over me only grows when we're together. Every word we speak, every time you touch me, fans the flames of the cowl's power. The Witch of Endor made this cowl for me. It impacts me differently than it does you or anyone else. I believe she's using us, Merab."

"Using us? Why would she do that?"

"As the cowl's power expands, it isn't just its influence over me that grows. The relic itself channels more infernal magic. I believe she's using me to charge this damned thing so she can use its power to resume her human form permanently."

Merab stepped back, shaking her head. "Give it back to me, then."

I tilted my head. "Merab, if I do that, I'll shift. We're in the middle of a full moon. You'll become a wolf again, too, once the sun rises. "

Rutherford cleared her throat. "Cain, if the Witch of Endor is using you as some kind of power source, this might be the only way to stop her."

I shook my head. "We don't even know what she's trying to do. She's not totally alive. At least not all the time, right?"

"That's right," Merab said. "She seems as real as you or me when she appears. But she spends her power and then has to disappear so she can recharge in hellfire."

"All I know is that whatever the Witch of Endor intends to do once she's fully revived, it won't be good."

"Then perhaps this was a mistake," Merab said. "Give the cowl back to me. Look, Cain. I never meant for you to suffer like this. If you love me, I'll love you in turn. But if you do not desire me, I don't want to force you to be with me by infecting your mind with the powers of hell."

"Merab, I don't want to put you through that. If one of the two of us has to wear the cowl for you to survive, and if you'll be a werewolf all the time except during a full moon while you wear it, that's not the kind of life you should want to have."

"You're right," Merab said. "But death is not so frightening. Allow me to wear the cowl tonight. I'll remain human until morning. Then, if we have no other choice, I'll remove the cowl. I'll die, but I never should have been raised."

I scratched my head. "No, Merab. I can't allow you to do that."

"Do you love me, Cain?"

"I care about you very much!"

"But do you love me?"

I sighed. "You know my heart belongs to her."

"Then give me one last night. You and I can be together one night, and then I'll die."

"Merab, I don't think…"

"I'm not asking you to sleep with me, Cain. You'll be a wolf, after all. I'm not that desperate. No offense. Perhaps you can take me into the forests. Let me feel the breeze in my face one last time."

"There might be another way, Merab. The Voodoo Queen is going to consult with a necromancer and an expert in infernal relics in the morning."

"Yes. The ones you call Cassidy and Julie. Take me with you into the forest. Find a place where you can restrain me come morning. I do not want to hurt anyone else. If your friends have an answer, so be it. If they do not, then I will remove the cowl."

"Are you sure you'll want to take it off when you're a wolf again?"

Merab shook her head. "Bind me for a month if you must. The next time I turn human, I will remove the cowl. I'll give it to you. If you will not wear it, perhaps you can figure out how to destroy it before the Witch of Endor can extract from it the power that it has absorbed."

I nodded. "If you're certain this is what you want."

Merab took a deep breath. "It's not what I want, Cain. You know what I want. But I also realize that you've moved on long ago. I cannot expect you to live in the past when you already have a future with her."

I nodded. "I promised Annabelle I wouldn't shift into wolf form in Vilokan. If we're going to do this, we need to get out of here."

Merab nodded. "I was about to suggest as much."

"I don't know," Rutherford said. "Annabelle insisted…"

"Annabelle doesn't know the entire story."

Jessie twirled her club in her hand. "We can go with them, Rutherford. Trust me, if it comes down to it, I can handle them. That's why Annabelle hired me. I know how to deal with werewolves. Whether they be shifted or not."

"But we're dealing with a witch and an infernal relic," Rutherford said. "I don't know if this is wise."

I turned to Rutherford. "I can feel the influence of the cowl growing by the second. Every moment we delay, every second I wear this thing, the more likely it is that it will accumulate enough power to resurrect the Witch of Endor for good."

Rutherford sighed, then turned and looked at Merab. "You're certain this will prevent the Witch of Endor's return?"

Merab shook her head. "I'm sure of nothing. What we know, though, is that the longer that Cain wears the cowl, the more likely her complete resurrection becomes."

# CHAPTER THIRTEEN

JESSIE AND RUTHERFORD TOOK the Tesla. Merab rode with me. She insisted. If this was going to be the last time she could speak to me, and was going to potentially give up her life, it was hard to forbid it. Rutherford didn't object. It was just a short drive, after all, from the French Quarter to Manchac Swamp. Once I removed the cowl, I'd become a wolf again. We'd also be near the other wolves who were running around through the marsh, playing werewolf games, or whatever it was they decided to do to keep themselves out of trouble.

"Would you at least hold my hand as we drive? I'm afraid, Cain. I know I've died before, but if I don't survive... it's hard to explain, but..."

"I get it," I sighed. "I suppose there's no harm in that."

I steered with my left hand as I extended my right. Merab placed her hand into mine and squeezed.

I felt that same tingle I experienced before. It was like a low-voltage current was coursing between her touch and the cowl that I still wore on my head. "Merab, I don't know if this is wise."

"I'm afraid, Cain. Please. It's not much to ask. I swear I won't take it any further."

I nodded and took a deep breath. I had to focus. There was something about her touch, even something so innocent as holding hands, that affected me on a carnal level. Her skin was soft. I couldn't help but imagine how her hands might feel on my chest... or elsewhere...

I had to clear my mind. This wasn't what I wanted. I don't know why my mind kept taking me there. It was the cowl, in part. But the cowl only awakens dormant desires and urges. Given the short-lived, but deeply passionate marriage that Merab and I shared, it was no wonder that my mind went there. In all my years, I'd never had better *physical* chemistry with anyone. That was where our intimacy began and ended. But it was profound. It was memorable. It was how she affected me, even now. All it took was a simple touch.

I tried to think about other things. Things that I don't find at all alluring or physically attractive. Random things. School buses. Tomatoes. Carburetors. The local weatherman.

None of those things were interesting enough to hold my attention for more than a second or two. All I knew was that I couldn't dwell on Merab's touch. I should have pulled my hand away. I couldn't. First, to admit that I was getting turned on by holding hands was mildly embarrassing. Sure, the cowl probably had something to do with the enhanced sensations I was experiencing. Still, come on. Holding hands? It wasn't like I was a teenager on his first date. I'd been around the block a few thousand times.

Second, I was a therapist above all else. I cared about Merab. I understood her anxiety over the situation. Holding her hand when she was still in love with me but couldn't be with me wasn't something I'd recommend to any of my patients if they were in such a situation. In this context, given that Merab wasn't long for this world, it seemed like a relatively harmless gesture. I wasn't trying to lead her on. She didn't expect that I was. She knew once she wore the cowl, then removed it after sunrise, that she'd die soon thereafter.

Third, I craved her touch. I knew it was wrong, that it was likely on account of the cowl's infernal influence, but it was a desire I couldn't deny. I didn't want things to go any further. Still, a part of me wondered if all the justifications I'd concocted to allow Merab to hold my hand were nothing but excuses to feel her flesh on mine—even if it was only a touch of hands.

"Remember the night we spent under the stars in my father's wheat field?"

I snorted. "I do."

"We were so nervous that someone would see us. To make love like that under moonlight..."

I sighed. "Merab, I don't know if it's wise to talk about memories like that. You know, given my situation..."

"We were married, Cain. There's nothing wrong with what we did. It was beautiful. How many times did we go? I think I must've finished four or five times..."

"Merab! Please, don't!"

I tried to pull my hand away, but she squeezed hard. I remembered that night well. Her nude frame, silhouetted in the moonlight. Her body on top of mine. Mine, on top of hers. The sweat that glistened off her skin.

"We could enjoy that again. Tonight. In the forests where you're taking me. While we're still in human form, the both of us. You want it, don't you, Cain?"

I shook my head. "I don't, Merab."

"By the look of the front of your trousers, I'd say you want it very much."

I bit my lip hard. I was trying to distract myself with pain. She was right. I desired her with nearly every part of me. Nearly. With everything, except my heart.

"I'm sorry, Merab, this was a mistake."

"What was?"

"Allowing you to hold my hand." I yanked my hand out of hers and placed it on the steering wheel.

Merab sighed. "I understand."

"You do?"

"I'm not long for this world. You love that nurse."

I nodded. "I really do. If I were not in love, perhaps it would be different. But we cannot continue discussing such things. The cowl burns hotter with hellfire every time I think about us."

"You love her. I don't doubt that. But how much could you possibly love her when you still have so much desire for me?"

I shook my head. "Love doesn't suppress one's carnal attractions. It only gives us the desire and strength to resist such urges."

"Forgive me, husband. In my case, my heart and flesh are united in their desire for you."

I nodded. "I'm sorry, Merab. I truly am. I know how difficult this must be for you."

Merab smirked, glancing again toward my lower mid-section. "Not so hard as it is for you."

I squeezed my thighs together. "Please, Merab. Were it not for the cowl, my body would not react this way."

Merab nodded. "I realize that. Again, my apologies, husband."

# CHAPTER FOURTEEN

I WAS GRATEFUL THAT it was dark outside. I could barely walk on account of my state of arousal. It was embarrassing for several reasons. With little more than moonlight to illuminate the path from my truck, on the edge of the gravel road where I parked, into the marsh, I was reasonably confident Rutherford wouldn't notice. I sure hoped she didn't. This wasn't me. This wasn't natural, even if it was carnal. It was a magically enhanced... situation.

Rutherford and Jessie parked behind the truck.

"Stay in view," Rutherford said. "We'll give you two the privacy to say your goodbyes before you remove the cowl."

I nodded. Rutherford and Jessie climbed into the back of my truck and sat on the edge as Merab and I followed a narrow path between the trees.

Howls from deep within the woods confirmed what I already knew—the rougarou and Abel's pack were in there, somewhere.

It had been a long night. When I removed the cowl, I'd become a wolf again. When Merab wore it, she'd remain human only until the full moon set and the sun rose.

"You need to go back to Rutherford and Jessie. After I remove the cowl. They'll take care of you and make sure that you don't hurt anyone after the sun rises and you become a wolf again."

Merab sighed. "I understand that. Tell me, Cain. Are you certain that what you feel while under the cowl isn't your deeper truth?"

"What do you mean? The cowl warps the mind. It only amplifies the darkest of our thoughts, the most unsavory of our desires."

"Are you suggesting that the intimacy we once shared was unsavory?"

I shook my head. "When we were together, it wasn't. Now, it most certainly is."

"But you're not married, Cain. Have you perhaps considered that the cowl only shows you the truth? There's something lacking in your relationship with Rutherford. You love her. But you are not as attracted to her as you are to me. Otherwise, your lusts would have been as intense for her under the cowl as they are for me."

I shook my head. "I don't believe that's true."

"You don't believe it because you don't want to believe it, Cain."

"Besides, Merab. If that were the case, if it revealed our truth, when you wore it you wanted me dead."

Merab wiped a tear from her cheek. "I suppose you're right."

"I must remove the cowl. There isn't much time left before morning."

Merab shook her head. "I don't think I'll be leaving with your nurses, Cain. There's no point."

"We may find answers soon, Merab. Tomorrow, after I've consulted with the others. There may be a way to save you. The cowl will keep you alive until then. If not, as we planned, we can remove it and destroy it later."

Merab shook her head. "Do you really think your people can handle me as a wolf? I don't know, Cain. What reason do I have to live? You do not love me."

I sighed. "You can find a new love, Merab. You can live a new life. All we have to do is figure out how to sustain your life apart from the cowl. One of my werewolves, one of them in the pack, is a necromancer. She might know a way to make it work. Another of the wolves might be able to redeem the cowl with celestial power, freeing you from its unsavory influence. There is reason to hope, Merab."

"Yes, there is reason to hope. We're so close, Cain."

I raised an eyebrow. "What do you mean? So close to what?"

"To finishing what I came here to do."

I bit my lip. "What are you saying, Merab?"

Merab grinned. She grabbed me by the scruff of my shirt and pulled me into herself. She pressed her lips to mine. The electricity spread through my body like a lightning bolt. She reached her hands under my shirt, pressing my torso against hers.

"Cain!" Rutherford shouted from a distance. Her voice was muted, as if she were yelling from a hundred yards away. She was a lot closer than that. Still, I couldn't deny the sensation, the desire, that overwhelmed me.

Merab broke the kiss before Rutherford and Jessie could make it to where we stood.

"Merab!" I shouted. "What did you do?"

Merab grinned. "Remove the cowl if you must."

I grabbed the cowl and ripped it off of my head.

A ring of hellfire formed around each of us, forming a wall between us and Jessie and Rutherford.

"You're truly pathetic," Merab said. "I meant what I said before. The cowl reveals the truth. I'm going to kill you."

"I thought you loved me..."

"I did, once. But you abandoned me, Cain. You left me to live a life with a man who treated me as little more than his property. His play-thing. To think that you harbored so much desire for me, you couldn't resist so much as a touch of our hands."

"Merab! What did you do?"

"She did as I told her to do," a high-pitched and raspy voice said.

An old woman appeared in the ring of fire alongside us. She wore only tattered rags and leaned on a crooked cane. She yanked the cowl out of my hands.

My body started to change. My skin hardened. My bones cracked. I was becoming a wolf.

The Witch of Endor cackled. "Behold, my dear Merab, your husband's cursed form."

"Can I kill him?" Merab asked.

The Witch of Endor grinned. "Not yet, my dear. You are still too weak."

"Then restore me, Zephaniah!"

I screamed. I hadn't heard that witch's name in thousands of years. Few people used it, even then. I could barely form words as the wolf took over.

"This was your plan all along!"

"Indeed, it was," Zephaniah said. "And my dear Merab, I will bless you beyond measure. Once my full power is restored."

My paws struck the ground. I howled as loud as I could. I could only hope that the wolves would hear. The fire surrounding me was too hot. I couldn't escape. The hellfire would consume my body.

Zephaniah, the Witch of Endor, placed the cowl on her own head. When she did, another column of hellfire blasted around her form.

"Yes! I can feel it! The eternal powers of hell itself!"

Merab buckled over, clutching at her chest.

I tried to dive at the witch. She raised a hand, blasting me back into the ground with hellfire.

Merab fell to the ground. The witch approached her. "As promised, dear child, you shall now become my greatest warrior."

The witch jammed her crooked staff through Merab's chest. Hellfire coursed from her staff into my former wife's body.

Merab gasped as she took another breath. The surrounding hellfire turned like a tornado. It focused on Merab's body and flooded into the wound the witch had made in her chest.

Merab's body expanded. She took the form of a wolf, but instead of fur, tongues of hellfire blazed across her body. She grew until she was nearly twice my size.

The witch cackled as she pulled her staff out of Merab's chest. "Thank you, the both of you, for your sacrifice."

In a swirl of flames, Zephaniah disappeared. Merab approached me, smoke pouring from her nostrils. I took two steps back.

Jessie ran up to her from behind, forming her ethereal weapon into a silver javelin. She struck Merab in the back.

Merab shrieked. Then she laughed. The silver turned red. Jessie released the javelin as it burned her hands.

With a swipe of her paw, Merab sent Jessie flying through the swamp. Jessie splashed in the waters.

I roared.

*What are you doing, Merab?* I asked, using the psychic connection I often employed to speak to other wolves.

*I'm here to destroy you, husband. Now, I can do it. You can't defeat me!*

I snarled. Jessie's silver javelin had no effect on Merab. She wasn't a werewolf. Not really. She only took a form, now, that mimicked my own. She was infernal power personified.

There was only one way to defeat her. I could only pray that the wolves were on their way. I was powerless against Merab. I could bite her. I could claw at her form. Would the hellfire burn me if I tried? If Jessie's javelin passed through her without effect, my teeth wouldn't do any better.

I howled again. The rougarou howled back.

I took off running in their direction.

Merab didn't chase me. Instead, she stopped and turned. She knew what I was trying to do. She was going for Rutherford.

I pivoted. The best I could hope for was to beat Merab there. Merab had a head start.

Merab roared. A torrent of hellfire shot out of her mouth toward my truck. Rutherford was inside. I dove into the flames just in time to shield Rutherford from Merab's attack.

I shrieked as the flames burned my fur from my body and charred my flesh. This wasn't just fire. It came from hell. I was resilient as a werewolf. Silver was usually required to kill me. Could I possibly withstand hellfire? All that power. It was within me before. When I wore the cowl, it raged within me. I resisted it then...

The difference between infernal and celestial power isn't as much as one might think. They are opposites, but they also come from the same source. I'd learned that in my encounter with angels and demons before. I had the power to change it, if only I could fight against it.

I extended my body as Merab's hellfire blasted into my chest. I was immediately filled with images of our time together thousands of years before. The same lust-ridden visions and memories I'd had when under the cowl. I resisted it before by thinking of Rutherford. Now, I wasn't just thinking about my love for her. I was sacrificing myself for her. If that's what it took to save her, if it meant my death, so be it.

The hellfire burned hot. Then, it didn't. Had it fried my nerves? They say when you're burning to death that eventually the pain wanes as the fires consume your flesh. I didn't know if that was what I was experiencing or if it was something else... there was another power within me welling up. I knew it well. All I had to do was to claim the infernal power as my own and bathe it in love, in sacrifice. This wasn't just some feeling in my heart. It was love in action.

A tingle spread throughout my body. It wasn't the same tingle I'd felt before. This time it was cool and pleasant. The red flames surrounding my body turned blue.

I fixed my eyes at Merab and exhaled, blasting celestial power back at her.

Our flames collided with a boom that shook the ground beneath me.

I didn't know how long I could keep this up. The only power I had was what I'd converted, what Merab already blasted into me.

Then another blue light struck her from behind. The rougarou were there. Julie held the flambeau between her jaws, channeling the heavenly power into Merab's form.

Merab turned to her. Julie's flambeau must've been more powerful than my blast. When Merab turned, my celestial power enveloped her frame.

Her flaming body, burning with rage, was reduced to a simmering wolf-shaped ember.

I barely noticed the sun rising as I channeled the last of the celestial power I had access to into Merab's form. I didn't shift. With Julie's flambeau still ablaze, it held all of us in wolf form. All of us except for Merab.

The charred embers of her form cracked and fell away, exposing her natural body.

Julie released the flambeau.

I returned to my human form. So did the rest of the wolves.

I approached Merab. Was she still alive? I touched her neck, searching for a pulse.

Merab's body collapsed in a pile of ash as soon as I made contact. She was gone.

# CHAPTER FIFTEEN

CASSIDY AND JULIE JOINED Rutherford, Jessie, and I as we made our way back to Vilokan. Annabelle was waiting for us in her office. I'd called ahead. I had to admit, cell phones were handier than I'd ever expected. No sooner did the elevator reach her office then she buzzed us right in.

Annabelle had a bible open on her desk. She wasn't just the Voodoo Queen. She was also a Catholic.

"Thank you for coming. This Witch of Endor is the same witch who appears here in the book of Samuel?"

"She is," I said. "Though that tale only tells a fraction of the truth."

"It's a remarkable story," Annabelle said. "Consulting with mediums is supposed to be forbidden in Jewish law, yet this king approached the witch and she actually evoked the spirit of a dead prophet."

"This is true."

"How could this be if she wields infernal power? Is it not reasonable to assume that this deceased prophet, Samuel, dwelled in celestial glory?"

I nodded. "I suppose it is. I was not there when that episode occurred."

"Still, if we presume that this incident truly occurred, it's quite remarkable. Cassidy, as a necromancer, is it possible to wield such power to call forth souls in either heaven or hell?"

Cassidy sighed. "Not with infernal power. All I can assume is that the Witch of Endor dealt with different magic, then. Something, I suppose, similar to my own."

I cleared my throat. "Julie, there was a time when the vampire witch, Mercy Brown, also was imbued with infernal power, correct?"

Julie nodded. "This is true. When she absorbed the infernal power that my flambeau used to wield, she could no longer use the magic that she'd used before as a witch."

Annabelle closed her bible and set it aside. "So this Witch of Endor may wield the power of hell, but because of that fact, she has given up what might be a far greater power."

"That is one way to look at it," Cassidy said. "If she wishes to recover her natural necromantic abilities, she'll have to divest herself of infernal magic."

I scratched my head. "We do not know which path she will choose. Still, we know she must choose one or the other."

Annabelle nodded. "That's what I'd call a positive development. Whatever this witch's intentions, they are unsavory."

"I believe that's accurate."

"We must be prepared for either contingency. Until we know what this Witch of Endor intends..."

"Zephaniah," I said. "That is her name."

"Very well. Until we know what Zephaniah intends, we'll have to be ready. From what I can tell, Merab was just a means toward an end."

I sighed. "Zephaniah used Merab to get to me. But I, too, was just a means toward an end. She knew that the cowl she'd made for me before was imbued with infernal magic. She knew she could use me to amplify that magic. I was an incubator. She used me to return to life."

Annebelle took a deep breath. "The witch literally brought hell to earth. I suspect she isn't done."

Jessie cracked her knuckles. "Well, when she starts whatever she's fixing to do, I say we kick her wrinkled resurrected ass."

Rutherford hadn't said more than two words to me since we arrived back at our apartment. I sat down on my recliner, kicked my feet back, and closed my eyes.

"That's all you're going to do? Sleep?"

I sighed. "I've shifted multiple times in the last twenty-four hours. I'm tired."

Rutherford shook her head. "Unbelievable."

I retracted the footrest and my chair and stood back up. "Rutherford, what's wrong? Talk to me."

Rutherford bit her lip. "Are you not attracted to me, Cain?"

I cocked my head. "Of course I am."

"Then why did that cowl draw you to your former wife? Why was she so easily able to manipulate your lusts like that?"

I shook my head. "She didn't."

"Please, Cain. I know what I saw."

"Rutherford, she knew what she was doing. She deceived me from the start. That cowl only amplifies unsavory desires."

"And you have no such... desires... for me?"

Rutherford sat on the couch and lowered her face into her hands. I sat next to her and rested my hand on her back. "Dearest Rutherford. There's nothing unsavory about my desire for you. My feelings for you, my desires, proceed not merely from carnal passion but from genuine love. The cowl wouldn't draw me to you like that because love, as I learned when I faced off against Merab's hellfire, is exactly the opposite of the kind of power the cowl uses."

Rutherford sniffed. "I love you, too. It was still hard to see how she affected you."

"It was just as difficult to experience, Rutherford. I'm merely human. Yes, I'm a werewolf, too. But I'm flawed. I hated the effect she had on me, the way she manipulated my animalistic urges."

Rutherford rubbed her eyes. "You said your love for me was what allowed you to change her magic? It's what allowed you to turn hellfire into celestial flames?"

I nodded. "Love is not of mere human origins. It is divine. It was out of love that my parents were first formed from the ground. My flesh may be broken and given to unsavory desires. Love, though, is a gift. I believe that's what it means to be made in the image of the Divine."

Rutherford stood up and extended her hand. I reached out and took her hand and stood up. "Then, in that case, let us go to bed. Can you find the energy to express that love for me for a few hours?"

I chuckled. "I'm not sure I'd last longer than five minutes."

Rutherford grinned. "You'd better. Though, if you do better than thirty seconds, I would be surprised."

I laughed. "I'm an old man. I can last longer than that."

"What are you even talking about, Cain? I'm tired. I was talking about sleeping together. Literally. You'd fall asleep in five seconds!"

My eyes widened. "Oh!"

Rutherford laughed. "Maybe, after we've both caught some shut eye, we can test your five-minute hypothesis."

I grinned. "I think I can do better than that."

"Good. Because we have another class tonight."

I raised an eyebrow. "Rutherford, salsa dancing isn't for me. I tried it. I didn't like it."

Rutherford laughed. "I wouldn't put you through that again. Tonight, I thought, we'd try ballroom dancing."

I bit the inside of my cheek. "You realize, with dancing of any sort, I'm still rather clumsy."

Rutherford laughed. "I'm just pulling your leg. I will not put you through that again. What would you like to do?"

I shrugged. "I honestly don't care, Rutherford. So long as we do it together, I'm game for anything. Yes, even if it means I have to try my two left feet at dancing."

"What do you say we go bowling?"

I couldn't suppress the wide smile that split my face. "Now that's something I can get behind. Let me warn you, though. Wolf strength gives me an advantage."

Rutherford chuckled, shaking her head. "You're such a man."

"What is that supposed to mean?"

"It's not always pure power or force that wins the game. Sometimes it's about finesse. Trust me, Cain. You haven't seen me bowl before. You've met your match."

I smiled and kissed Rutherford on the cheek. "Game on."

**Continued in Cain and the Cauldron**

# CAIN AND THE CAULDRON

### THEOPHILUS MONROE

# CHAPTER ONE

AN EAR-PIERCING SOUND STRUCK my ear as I approached the door to the Vilokan Asylum extension site. We'd been in the site for less than a year. Before that, it was the Mulledy Plantation. Annabelle, the Voodoo Queen, grew up there. Her family owned the place, going back to the antebellum period.

The sound that forced me to cup my hands around my ears came from a human voice. It wasn't a scream. It wasn't a screech. Not exactly. I tilted my head. Was that *music* behind all that wailing?

I opened the door and stepped inside. I followed the sound to what used to be a living room. Now, it was where we had most of our group therapy sessions. Abel was standing in front of the rest of the wolves in residence. He was holding a microphone. He was looking past me at the wall behind me. I turned to see a screen. Words were flashing across it.

Abel opened his mouth and belted out something about his mouth being alive and being hungry like the wolf. His tone was so off-putting I think I would have preferred if he'd been scratching his fingernails across a chalkboard.

Everyone else in the room—Cassidy, Ryan, and Julie, among others—joined in.

"Do do do do do do do do do doooo."

Abel raised one hand over head, waved it around, and shook his body just off-beat. Until this moment, I thought I was possibly the worst dancer alive.

I almost stopped them. We were supposed to meet for our evening session, after all. Then I noticed the wide smile on my brother's face. He was having *fun*. I couldn't recall a time when I'd seen him demonstrate such joy. I took a seat and enjoyed the show as cacophonous as it was. The music was terrible. The singing was worse. I couldn't help but laugh along with the rest.

The music ended, and Abel took a bow. I applauded. Sure, it was a slow clap. His performance wasn't laudable, but I appreciated what Abel and the other unshifted werewolves were doing.

Laughter spread across our small crowd.

"It looks like someone bought a karaoke machine!"

"I say you take a turn, Dr. Cain!" Cassidy piped up.

I chuckled and shook my head. "Trust me, you don't want to hear me..."

"Come on, brother! I have the singing voice of a rabid hyena, but I gave it a go."

I grinned. "I can't disagree with you. It's good when we recognize our weaknesses and focus on our strengths."

"That's great advice for choosing a career path. Not so much for letting loose and having fun." Jessie stepped into the room. I didn't even realize my junior nurse was there yet. She usually came for sessions. I suppose I shouldn't have been surprised that she'd been making the coffee. Jessie sat next to Abel and rested her hand on his leg. They were dating. I was a good thing for both of them.

I grinned. "Well, Jessie, you caught me. Truth be told, I have a horrid case of stage fright."

Abel snorted. "Let me get this straight. You can lead a group therapy session. You can present papers at conferences and you don't blink an eye. But you're nervous about getting up in front of your fellow wolves to sing a few notes?"

"That's different!" I insisted. "When I'm confident in my capabilities, I don't get nervous. When I know I suck, it turns my stomach a bit."

"Just picture all of us naked!" Jessie interjected. "I know you do it, anyway."

"I do not!" I laughed.

"You'd better not!" Abel added.

"Don't worry, Abel. I've never once thought about you naked."

Jessie giggled into her hand. "I think he meant you'd better not be thinking about *me* that way."

"Ah! That would make more sense! Rest assured. That's not the way I cope with my stage fright."

"How do you cope with it?" Cassidy asked.

"I don't get on stage. Certainly not for karaoke!"

"Don't we tell our patients that avoidance is an unhealthy way of meeting life's challenges?" Jessie smirked.

I sighed and scratched the back of my head. "Screw it. All right. I'll do it. Who has the list?"

"I have it," Abel said.

"Well, hand it over."

Abel pressed a laminated sheet against his chest. "I didn't get to pick my song. You don't get to pick yours."

I shook my head and grabbed the microphone. "If embarrassment is the goal, I suppose we should go all out. What's my song?"

A shit-eating grin split Abel's face. "I don't have any clue what this song is. I haven't been on earth long enough to know it. How about 'I'm too Sexy' by Right Said Fred?"

The room burst into cheers and laughs.

"I can't wait to see this!" Jessie said.

I nodded. "Can I claim I don't know the song well enough to sing it?"

"You can claim it," Jessie said. "But based on the look on your face, we all know you know the song."

I sighed. "Alright. You caught me. Here goes nothing. Hit it, Abel. It's time to do that little turn on the catwalk."

The music played. I know Abel chose the song because he thought the lyrics would embarrass me. In truth, it might be the one song I could sing with no singing talent at all. The singing part wasn't what made it awkward. It was knowing what to do with my body while I sang. I didn't dance. If I did, someone might call 9-11 thinking I was mid-seizure. Instead, I stood in front of the group like a board as I spoke the lyrics in a monotone. Was I holding the microphone too close to my mouth, not close enough? I moved it back and forth. I wasn't sure what to do.

I wasn't half-way done when Donald, Chris, Yvette and several of the wolves from Abel's pack shuffled into the room. I almost put the microphone down. It was therapy time, after all. The death stare Jessie and Abel were giving me made it clear that I had to finish the song.

It wasn't a problem. Given all the laughter, I doubted anyone could hear me anyway.

When I finished, I took a bow. I made eye contact with Donald. "It's karaoke night."

"Yup. I figured. Hey Abel, pass me the song list. I say the good doctor here gives us an encore."

I sighed and shook my head. "Oh, come on. You can't seriously want to hear me do another."

Donald scanned the sheet. "Here we go. I've go a perfect song for you."

I rolled my eyes. "What is it?"

Donald grinned. "I think, Dr. Cain, that it's time you admit the truth. You like big butts and you cannot lie."

"No!" I pressed my hands together as if praying. "Please, not that one."

Donald shrugged. "It's that or *Hips Don't Lie* by Shakira."

I rolled my eyes. "Very well."

"Let's hear it, Sir Mix A Lot!" Jessie piped up.

I sighed. "That's Doctor Mix A Lot to you, young lady."

# CHAPTER TWO

I'D SAY I WAS embarrassed. It was remarkably freeing to let loose in front of friends. Yes, they were patients. When you're a werewolf, though, and you've bonded to members of a pack, the connection runs deep. I wasn't just their doctor. They weren't just my patients. We were family.

I'd never claim under normal circumstances that I was too sexy for my shirt, nor would I admit I like big butts. I couldn't lie about that either, apparently. No matter, come to find out they set the whole karaoke thing up for therapeutic reasons. Jessie said she'd learned about the power of "ice breakers" in class. It was a bonding exercise, but more than that. It also helped the members of the group let down their guard. We were a pretty open bunch, I figured, all things considered. Still, after we'd taken turns embarrassing ourselves in front of one another, the wolves opened up about a lot of other deep-seated insecurities they'd been harboring. While I was hesitant to admit it at first, it ended up being quite the breakthrough for some of the wolves. This was especially true for the younger wolves.

Ryan admitted that despite his success as a student at LSU, he still struggled with homesickness. The pack is a supportive family, but it doesn't replace the bonds one has with his family of origin.

Cassidy admitted that she'd been thinking a lot about her brother. She missed him. Nico Freeman, later known as Niccolo the Damned, was a promising Hougan and her big brother when she was possessed by the spirit of another. When she was finally freed, he'd been sucked into the past and ended up becoming the world's first vampire. It wasn't surprising she'd have issues surrounding her brother. I was a little surprised she hadn't brought him up until now.

Everyone really opened up. Abel confessed he'd been dealing with hemorrhoids for the last month. He'd never heard of Preparation H. Thanks to our session, he now had a way to manage the bump in the rump.

Opening up in therapy really can save your ass.

If I hurried home, I'd still have a few hours to spend with Rutherford before I'd have to hit the sack and begin the next day's agenda of sessions back at the original asylum in Vilokan.

I was accustomed to late dinners. I didn't know what Rutherford had cooked. Whatever it was, it would be excellent. She was a fantastic chef. She always prepared two different meals. Rutherford also ate a plant-based diet which, I came to find out, was little more than a euphemism for being vegan. I couldn't go along with that. No matter what she made me, she almost always created some kind of plant-based alternative for herself that somehow managed to look almost the same. Don't get me wrong. I'd tried several of her iterations of the meals she prepared. She insisted they were delicious. I gagged every time. She thought it was because wolves are carnivores. Perhaps she was right. Or, maybe, I just didn't have a stomach for plant-based meal alternatives. Is it really that strange to find tofu and tempeh less appetizing than steak and bacon?

I grew up vegan. Sorry, "plant-based." Few people know that. You can read all about it in the book of Genesis. Think about it. My parents named all the animals. It wasn't until after the Great Flood when the

Divine gave mankind permission to kill and eat. Even then, it came with the qualification that thereafter animals would fear humanity. The connection between human beings as the stewards and caretakers of the earth and the creatures of the world would ever thereafter be broken.

I ate meat a long time before that. I was a wolf, after all. Before my wolf was tamed, I had a craving for hearts. Feral werewolves still behaved that way. They rarely turned humans into wolves. They killed. They ate. It was one such feral, in fact, that inadvertently turned Ryan shortly before we met him. He was in Missouri. He was in New Orleans on break for the next full moon. The only reason he survived the feral wolf's attack was because hunters were pursuing the same wolf who bit him. That we found him before a hunter did was a stroke of luck.

"Honey, I'm home!" The savory odor of what I guessed must've been a roast greeted me before Rutherford could.

A full plate was waiting for me at the table. Another plate of something that looked far less appetizing was set across from mine. Two lit candles were in the middle of the table.

Rutherford appeared around the corner. She was in a stunning dress, high heels, and was holding two glasses filled with red wine.

"Welcome, home."

I grinned. "This is certainly a surprise."

"Is it?" Rutherford handed me one of the two glasses.

I took a sip. It was sweet. Too sweet. "What is this?"

Rutherford shrugged. "Grape juice."

I furrowed my brow. "Why go to such lengths for a romantic meal and serve grape juice?"

"Why do you think, Cain?"

I pinched my chin. "Are we driving somewhere?"

Rutherford laughed. "You really don't know, do you?"

I shook my head. "I'm at a loss."

"We're having a baby, Cain."

I tilted my head and took another sip. "Come again?"

"I'm pregnant!"

"You're pregnant?"

"Yes, Cain!"

"Holy smokes. We're pregnant!"

Rutherford laughed. "That's what I said."

I bit my lip. "Why do I have to drink the grape juice then?"

Rutherford chuckled. "I made you your roast. When it comes to toasting the family we're about to become, we can share a bottle of sparkling grape juice."

# CHAPTER THREE

A FULL STOMACH MEANS a good night's sleep. Jessie, my junior nurse, had my whole day's worth of individual sessions scheduled to the minute. Most days, it would have been a grind. Working with several patients, shifting gears to address each of their concerns and counsel them through their issues is rewarding. It's also exhausting. Again, I said *most* days. This wasn't most days. Each step felt lighter than usual. It was as though I was prancing upon the clouds. I was going to be a father! Yes, I'd been a father many times before. Where there were a few pharaohs, kings, and emperors who'd born more children among their harems than I had over my six thousand years, I'd still known the privilege of becoming a father a hundred and thirty-five times. It didn't matter. The news was every bit as thrilling each time.

Jessie volunteered to handle my evening session with the wolves at the extension site. She was growing into a fine therapist. Eventually, well, perhaps she'd take over for me if I ever retired. Though, chances were, I'd stick with it another few centuries. I doubted she'd live that long. In the meantime, once she completed her program, of course, she'd be able to take over some patients and free me to focus on the most challenging cases.

On the agenda for the night? A trip to buybuy Baby. Rutherford already saw a doctor for confirmation. It was still early. The baby wouldn't come for nearly seven months. That didn't mean we couldn't start accumulating the necessary baby paraphernalia.

I picked Rutherford up in the truck. We went straight to the store. Walking through the front doors was like entering a baby wonderland. I couldn't believe how much *stuff* they sold to support the raising of an infant. For my first child, we had nothing at all except a small blanket. Through the years, they invented a few more items to aid in the task. I'd had a bassinet or two for some of my babies. It had been centuries since I last fathered a child. I knew we'd need a car seat, maybe a crib, and a lot of diapers. Now they had baby monitors. Not just small cameras with remote monitors. These were smart monitors. They interfaced with apps. So did dozens of other objects designed to aid in baby rearing. There was even a baby rocker that a parent could stream music to and adjust its speed from anywhere in the world, so long as they had an internet connection. The sales lady (she was nice enough) said that with a monitor and rocker both combined in one app, we could effectively manage the baby's sleep routine from across town while the babysitter sat in the next room.

I don't know why that was a selling point. If Rutherford and I are paying for a babysitter, I want to spend the evening together without thinking about it! Screwing with an app that allowed us to hear our baby cry wasn't exactly the way to enjoy a date night.

It wasn't the high-tech devices that confused me the most. I picked up a small box from a shelf. I showed it to Rutherford.

"What is a NoseFrida?"

Rutherford grinned. "Think of it like a straw. You stick the tube up the baby's nose and you suck up the snot."

I stared at Rutherford with wide eyes. "You *suck* up the baby's snot?"

"There's a filter in it. It's not like you'll get it in your mouth."

I shuddered. "Still, I cannot imagine. This will be your task."

Rutherford laughed. "So long as you handle all the poopie diapers."

"All of them?" I raised an eyebrow. "I work, you know. While counseling patients, I can't wipe my kid's butt."

"We're not bringing our child to work, Cain. That would be irresponsible given the population we work with."

"So we'll have to use daycare, then?"

Rutherford shrugged. "I was thinking of taking a few years off."

"Seriously? What will we do at the asylum while you're at home with the baby?"

"I'm sure you'll figure it out. Jessie should be more than capable of filling the void. It's either I take a break from working or we send our child to daycare. We don't need to both work. You have plenty of money. Unless you wanted to do it some days. We could split the work week."

I sighed. "I would. Jessie might be ready to fill your shoes in a few months. It'll be a year or two before she can carry my load."

"Why couldn't she work toward that now?"

I shook my head. "There are licensure requirements and standards of practice, Rutherford."

"I don't think any state licensing boards are involved with the Vilokan Asylum, Cain. You aren't beholden to their standards."

"Right, but if we're going to convince Jessie's program to allow her experience working with me to count against her hours, we have to at least keep up a front that we're a normal facility with the usual type of patients. That means playing by the rules. At least we have to at the extension site."

Rutherford shrugged. "We'll figure it out one way or another. Perhaps you should speak to Donald. His baby and ours will be less than a year apart."

"Not a bad idea," I nodded. "I'm sure he might have a few other ideas about modern parenting, too. Like, is a snot sucker really necessary?"

Rutherford grinned. "They also have bulb syringes. They work, too. Just not quite as well.

I scanned another shelf. "What in the world is the Peepee Teepee?"

Rutherford grinned. "That's only an issue if we have a boy."

"They pee in that thing? It's not big enough to hold much. How can you expect a baby to aim, anyway?"

Rutherford chuckled. "It's to shield you when changing them."

I snorted. "That's what a cloth, or a rag is for. This stuff is ridiculous."

Rutherford grabbed what looked like a small turtle with a screen on it. She tossed it in the cart.

"What in the world is that for?"

"It checks the temperature of the bath water."

I sighed. "You know, people have been having babies forever. We never needed a thermometer to check the temperature. We used our hands or maybe our elbows. Throughout history, there has never once been a pandemic of babies getting scalded by the bath."

"It's a lot easier, Cain. You can leave it floating in the water while doing other things. When the screen turns green, you know you're in range."

I rolled my eyes. "Fine. Whatever. I don't know how people ever survived without all this nonsense."

"It must've been a miracle," Rutherford chuckled.

My phone vibrated in my pocket. I pulled it out.

"Who is it?" Rutherford asked.

"It's Jessie. One second." I plugged my right ear with my index finger so I could hear and answered the phone. "Jessie. Is everything alright?"

"I'm not sure. How soon can you get back?"

"What's going on, Jessie?"

Jessie sighed. "It's the strangest thing. A bunch of new patients just showed up."

"Did Annabelle refer them?"

Jessie sighed. "No. They didn't show up like that. I mean, they literally just appeared out of nowhere. Maybe it was like the anti-rapture that some people believe in. God took a few people away, got to know them, then was like, whoops! These folks are annoying!"

I resisted the urge to chuckle. "How many patients are we talking about?"

"I don't know. I've counted a dozen new patients so far. There might be more. I have some of the other nurses canvasing the halls."

"Have you spoken to any of them?"

"They know nothing. Everyone is confused. They don't know me. Some of them are asking for you or Rutherford."

"Do you have any names?"

Jessie sighed. "No. One of them keeps taking off his clothes and running around asking other people to join him."

I scratched my head. "We had a patient who did that a while back. I mean, we've had a few streakers through the years. But one patient in particular who had a penchant for that."

"What happened to him?" Jessie asked.

"He died, Jessie. A loose werewolf in the asylum was responsible."

"Well, this guy isn't dead."

"Not anymore." I sighed. "This wouldn't be the first time we've had issues with necromancers as of late. With the Witch of Endor out there, somewhere, the only thing that's surprising about this is that she had tried nothing sooner."

"What do I do?" Jessie asked.

"Hold tight. I'm going to see if I can pick up Cassidy and bring her back to the asylum. As a necromancer herself, she might help sort out what's happened. The best thing you can do is to avoid them. Until we know more about why they're back or if the Witch of Endor really is the one who raised them, we need to exercise caution. Do not engage them unless you have to in order to protect yourself or other patients. Also, call Annabelle. Let her know what's going on."

"I already tried that," Jessie said. "No offense, but I called her first. She didn't answer."

"She might be out of her office. I'll stop by her office on the way in. Let me know, though, if things get out of hand. Worst-case scenario, you know the lock-down procedures."

# CHAPTER FOUR

I DROPPED OFF RUTHERFORD first. Now that she was pregnant, we couldn't be too careful. When magical things were afoot, we needed to make sure we knew what we were dealing with before we risked putting her in harm's way. I picked up Cassidy at the extension site and brought her with me to Vilokan. She and I entered the city through the mystical doorway on the side of St. Louis Cathedral in Père Antoine Alley.

We made the long trek down the narrow stairway that led into Vilokan. The Voodoo Academy, where Annabelle's office was located, was on the way to the asylum. The streets were more crowded than usual. A lot of vodouisants from all around the world often came to Vilokan at certain times of the year. I hadn't been told that any such festival or occasion was on the calendar. Usually, Annabelle prepared me for that sort of thing. By the looks on their faces, most of the people I saw on the streets were lost or confused. It wasn't a surprise. It was easy to get lost in Vilokan if you didn't know your way around.

"Something doesn't feel right about this," Cassidy said.

"What do you mean?"

"I grew up in Vilokan. Some of these faces I recognize... I haven't seen them in ages."

"Are you aware of any kind of Voodoo holiday or anything going on right now?"

Cassidy shook her head. "Nothing at all."

I pressed open one of the two double-doors entering the Voodoo Academy and stepped inside. An older gentleman I'd never met greeted me. Then he saw Cassidy and took a step back.

"What are you doing here?" Cassidy and the man both said in concert."

"We expelled you from this academy, young lady," the man said.

"And you're supposed to be dead, Asogwe Jim!"

I tilted my head. Asogwe Jim was one of the hougans who'd taught at the Voodoo Academy when Cassidy was a student. He signed the disciplinary report that recommended her dismissal from the program. He also died a few years back during the flood, when the firmament above Vilokan was shattered.

"This is definitely necromancy." Cassidy tugged at my arm. "We should go see Annabelle."

"Annabelle Mulledy?" Asogwe Jim asked. "She's likely in the first-year quarters."

I tilted my head. "She's the Voodoo Queen, Jim."

Asogwe Jim laughed. "Good one! She sure acts like it! I don't think Marie Laveau would ever give her title to such a young and presumptuous student as Annabelle Mulledy. Who are you anyway?"

"I'm Cain." I extended my hand. Jim grabbed mine. His fingers were ice cold.

"Ah, yes. You're the psychotherapist Queen Laveau hired."

I nodded. "That's right. If you'd excuse me, we're here to see the queen."

I moved toward the elevator that took us to Annabelle's office. Jim grabbed my arm.

"You won't find the queen there, Cain. That's Papa Legba's office."

Cassidy snorted. "Doesn't it make you wonder why there's an elevator here suddenly when it used to be an old staircase that led to Legba's office?"

Jim shrugged. "Things happen fast in Vilokan, young lady. Again, I must insist you leave. You are not welcome here."

I shook my head. "I'll vouch for Cassidy. She's with me."

"Ah, a patient. That makes sense. Very well. You are free to make an appeal to Papa Legba for her readmission to the academy, but I highly doubt he'll change his mind."

I smiled. There was no sense arguing with Jim. He thought it was several years ago. He believed Marie Laveau was still alive, and that Papa Legba was the school's headmaster.

I cleared my throat. Something didn't jive. When the flood happened, when Jim died, Erzulie was headmistress of the Voodoo Academy. Erzulie was the Loa of love. Legba had been compromised by Kalfu, a destructive Loa who'd remained bound to Legba for years. Annabelle ultimately defeated Kalfu. That's one reason Marie Laveau made her the new queen.

Whatever state of mind that Jim had recovered must've been some time before he actually died. Erzulie had been running the Voodoo Academy for a few months before the flood. Annabelle was still a first-year student. Since he knew who Annabelle was, but thought Legba was still the headmaster of the Voodoo Academy, his amnesia must've only blotted out the last few weeks or months of his life.

Cassidy and I made our way up the elevator to Annabelle's office. The elevator opened right into the office. She had to open it from the inside. Usually, she watched whoever was in the elevator through a camera that streamed to her desktop computer. She would speak through the intercom to let know whoever was coming to visit, whether they could come in or if they had to wait. There was always a chance, of course, she wouldn't be there. If that was the case, though, the elevator would have been disabled.

The elevator reached Annabelle's office. I looked up at the small camera. "Annabelle. Are you in there?"

No response.

"I don't think she's home," Cassidy said.

I shook my head. "She wouldn't leave the elevator on if she left. She must be in there. I'm just hoping she's well. Someone raised all these people from the dead."

Cassidy shook her head. "It makes little sense. That's a lot of dead people. I've never known a necromancer who could resurrect that many people at once. Even if they could, most mambos or hougans raise dead bodies devoid of souls, like zombies. Jim clearly had his mind intact."

"You've never seen what the Witch of Endor can do. You're right, though. Even in her time, I don't believe she had this kind of power."

"She wields hellfire, right?"

I nodded. "She did the last I knew. She also wouldn't be able to access her usual magic so long as she remained charged by infernal power."

"I don't know how infernal magic works," Cassidy said. "Is it possible that infernal power could raise this many people at once?"

I shook my head. "I really don't know. I find it hard to believe if that was the case that they'd all come back believing it was still several months before they really died."

Cassidy banged on the elevator door. "Still no response."

"Annabelle!" I shouted. "Are you in there?"

A bright green light from somewhere inside blasted around the cracks of the elevator door.

"Annabelle!" I shouted again.

A few seconds later, the doors parted with a ding. "Thank God. Someone who's actually looking for me and not Papa Legba."

"What's going on here, Annabelle?"

Annabelle sighed. "I just got back from Guinee. You know, the Garden of Eden."

Based on the green glow emanating from Annabelle's eyes, I discerned that Isabelle, her soul bound familiar, was with her. Usually Isabelle guarded the crossroads, a mystical place that governed which supernatural entities could or couldn't traverse between worlds. "Did you and Isabelle figure anything out?"

Annabelle nodded. "We flew on Beli across vast distances, to one of Guinee's distant kingdoms. According to Queen Rhiannon, someone entered their world and stole the Cauldron of Rebirth."

I scratched my head. "Mercy spoke about that once before. What is it, exactly? I presume it has something to do with the fact that dead people are swarming Vilokan."

Annabelle nodded. "The Cauldron of Rebirth has only been to earth on a handful of occasions. Most recently, a druid brought it to Missouri to fight off a demon named Vengeance. Shortly thereafter, the Morrigan brought it here to help Mercy defeat Moll."

"Who is Moll?" Cassidy asked.

I sighed. "She used to be Mercy's mentor in the craft. Back when Mercy was still human. She got involved in some real dark magic."

"How dark?" Cassidy asked.

"She summoned Lucifer," Annabelle said. "Dark enough for you?"

Cassidy's eyes went wide. "Yup. Hard to get much darker than the devil."

I cleared my throat. "She was also one of Hailey's ancestors. When Hailey first discovered her family's old grimoire, she'd cast a spell that was inserted into the book meant to raise Moll from the dead. She trained Hailey for years before she carried out her plan to use Mercy to channel the infernal magic she required in order to summon Lucifer."

"Alright," Cassidy said. "So this Cauldron of Rebirth is bad news?"

Annabelle shook her head. "Not at all. It's a blessed relic. It courses with a power that druids call Awen. It's the same kind of power that Isabelle can access. It's the power of life itself. In the wrong hands, though, there's no telling what someone might do with it."

I shook my head. "Do you suspect it was Zephaniah, the Witch of Endor?"

Annabelle nodded. "I can't prove it. It makes sense. No one heard a thing from this witch for thousands of years. I don't think she was alive all that time in hiding. I think thousands of years ago she must've broken into the otherworld, into Guinee, and only recently returned when she resurrected Merab and found the cowl that she used to enhance her power."

"And she used her infernal power to traverse the otherworld, where she stole the Cauldron of Rebirth?"

Annabelle nodded. "Like I said, it's just a theory. I spoke to many of the nymph in the otherworld and no one saw her or anyone else. That's not a guarantee she wasn't there. The timeline there isn't in sync with our own. The Witch of Endor could have gone there after I asked, or at some point so far in the distant past that no one remembered it happening."

I scratched my head. "This still makes little sense. The people we've seen who were raised aren't evil. They're common people. Citizen of Vilokan. Why would Zepheniah raise them? I don't think most of these folks would ever follow her or cooperate with the plans she has."

Annabelle nodded. "Perhaps the Witch of Endor is struggling to master the power of the cauldron. She intends to resurrect someone. The one thing I can say about the cauldron is that while most necromancers can only raise humans, the cauldron can raise supernaturals. Vampires. Witches. Werewolves. Anyone at all."

"Who would the Witch of Endor wish to raise and why?"

Annabelle sighed. "I was hoping you could tell me that, Cain. You have a lot more experience working with her than anyone else alive."

"I really don't know. I'm not even sure what her plans are now. I assumed she used me just to extract the infernal power from the cowl. I still don't know what she intended to do with that power."

"We know one thing," Annabelle said. "She used it to steal the Cauldron of Rebirth. Now, we have to figure out her end game. She's trying to resurrect someone."

"Maybe her usual necromantic abilities aren't working now that she has infernal power," Cassidy said. "Whatever she's planned, perhaps she needs to retain both her infernal power and the ability to resurrect people from the dead."

"People or other things," Annabelle said.

Cassidy nodded. "It's all possible. Still, while I don't know how this cauldron works, it's awfully strange that so many people who'd died in Vilokan are suddenly back. We saw Asogwe Jim in the lobby. He thinks you're still a first-year student."

Annabelle nodded. "I know. I'm as perplexed as either of you. Whatever she's doing, if we're right that it's the Witch of Endor doing this at all, it can't be good."

I heard a ding. "Is someone in the elevator?"

Annabelle nodded and looked at her computer screen. "Hailey, come in."

With another ding, the elevator doors parted and Hailey stepped inside, panting.

"What's wrong, Hailey?" I asked.

Hailey's red vampiric eyes were as wide as the sun. "It's Moll. Moll is back!"

I shook my head. "Speak of the Devil."

Annabelle nodded. "If Moll is back, you'd better believe the *devil* won't be far behind."

I sighed. "If that was who the Witch of Endor intended to raise, why all these people in Vilokan, also?"

Hailey shook her head. "Moll remembers nothing about how Mercy and I defeated her. She doesn't even know that we realize she was preparing to betray us."

"That could be a good thing," I said.

"I don't think so. The last time, Moll used Mercy as an incubator for infernal power so she could raise Lucifer. She probably hopes to do that again since she doesn't remember she already tried it and failed. If the Witch of Endor now has more infernal power than Mercy ever did, well, I suspect her plans might change. She may agree to work with this witch instead. In the end, though, we know what she planned to do before. With all that power, though, I'm not sure we'll be able to stop her like we did the first time."

"What did she do last time?" Cassidy asked.

"She used Lucifer to start the wild hunt. She chased Mercy and me all the way back to Rhode Island, accompanied by the spirits of other dead vampires who joined her hunt."

"Perhaps that's what she intends to do with those she's raised in Vilokan. I doubt it, though. These are vodouisants, not vampires. I suspect that if Moll and the Witch of Endor are working together, Zephaniah must've convinced Moll to pursue a different tactic."

"Where is Moll?" I asked. "She doesn't know we're onto her. We might use that to our advantage."

Hailey nodded. "Mercy is monitoring her. She'll text me if anything happens. I don't think that Moll is quite ready to reveal her true intentions just yet. So long as she thinks it's the past, that we don't already know what she's planning, the better."

"I can go with you to speak to her," Annabelle said.

Hailey shook her head. "So far as Moll knows, you and Mercy still hate each other. She doesn't know you two reconciled."

"I'll go. Moll won't think anything of it if I show up. Mercy was one of my patients, after all. Annabelle, could you check in on Jessie? Make sure she has things under control at the asylum. A lot of deceased patients also made a reappearance there."

Annabelle nodded. "I'll do that. You may need to call the phone at the asylum if you need me. I'll try to stay nearby the phone there or here so you can reach me if necessary."

# CHAPTER FIVE

IT WAS ONLY A few blocks from the exit of Vilokan in Jackson Square to Casa do Diabo. Only in New Orleans could an old mansion that had housed vampires for centuries remain standing in one of the busiest parts of the city without raising an eyebrow.

The front door was cracked open. Even at night, Mercy always kept the place locked tight. Hailey and I exchanged glances.

"Stay back," Hailey snapped her fingers. Her wand formed in her hand.

"Nice trick," Cassidy said.

Hailey grinned. "Sure beats trying to carry my wand in my back pocket. Watch your backs. Moll might look like an old woman, but she's crafty as hell."

I nodded. "As is Zephaniah. If she and the Witch of Endor are working together…"

"I might be strong enough with a little luck to get the better of Moll. When she died, I was only beginning to explore bloodwitchery. She doesn't know how much my power has grown. I'm confident I might stand a decent chance against her if she's alone…"

"But if Zephaniah is with her?" Cassidy asked.

Hailey shook her head. "I'd really need Julie's help. She has access to celestial magic. So far as I know, that's the only power that can defeat infernal magic."

"Julie's back at the asylum extension. I can try to send her a text."

Hailey nodded. "Fine. We need to find Mercy. Something happened here. She'd never leave the door open like that. Someone left here in a hurry."

"Is that you, Moll?" Mercy's muffled voice screamed, coming from somewhere else in the house. "Let me out of here or I'll drain you dry, you washed up old bitch!"

I chuckled. "Sounds like Mercy is fine."

Hailey shrugged. "She's herself, at least. This way."

Cassidy and I followed Hailey through a narrow door down a narrow corridor. Casa do Diabo didn't have a traditional underground basement. Basements weren't viable in New Orleans. The first floor, though, was raised over a small undercroft that was something *like* a basement. The ceilings were low. It was a place reserved mostly for storage. A few steps at the end of the corridor led down to the undercroft.

There were only a few lights in the place. It was enough that we could see what had happened. Mercy was sitting inside what looked like a circle of salt. A pattern, a veve of one of the voodoo Loa, was drawn in the middle of it in some kind of chalk.

"How the hell did this happen?" Hailey asked.

"It's the veve of Baron Samedi. Since we vampires have his aspect, it can be used to trap us inside."

"I know *how* it works," Hailey said. "I'm just wondering how you managed to let yourself get trapped here."

Mercy shook her head. "Fucking Moll, that's how."

I winced. I hated the F-word but when dealing with Mercy Brown tolerating her foul mouth was par for the course. "Surely you would have recognized what this veve signified. Why'd you go into it?"

Mercy glared at me. "I didn't see it, Cain. Moll was trying to retrieve her old grimoire. If Hailey didn't have it stored down here..."

Hailey huffed. "So it's my fault you let Moll trap you in a veve?"

Mercy scratched her head. "Look, I'm not taking responsibility. I'm not mature enough for that. I have to blame someone else."

I chuckled. "Can you get her out of there, Hailey?"

Hailey grinned. "Of course. The spell is pretty complex. This might take me a moment."

"Oh, shut up, Hailey. It's not that hard. Get me out of here! We have to find Moll. Now that she has her grimoire, there's no telling what she'll do next."

"Brace yourselves," Hailey said. "This is some pretty strong magic..."

Mercy rolled her eyes as Cassidy and I took a couple steps back. Then, Hailey extended her foot and broke the salt circled that surrounded the veve. "Ta-da!"

"That was it?" Cassidy asked.

Hailey grinned. "Casting a prison like this is a lot more difficult than breaking it. From the outside, at least."

Mercy got to her feet and stepped out of the circle, straightening her black dress and tucking her hair behind her ears. "I don't know what Moll is doing, but she seems to have no recollection at all of how we defeated her before."

I shook my head. "None of them do."

"Them?" Mercy raised an eyebrow.

"Someone stole the Cauldron of Rebirth from Guinee," Hailey said. "We think it's the Witch of Endor."

"There are dozens of dead people in Vilokan, hundreds maybe, who were also reborn from the cauldron's power." I scratched the back of my head. "Some of them died in the asylum. Most of those in the city died when Vilokan flooded a few years back."

Mercy nodded. "How the hell did she get the cauldron?"

"We don't know," Hailey said. "Annabelle went to investigate. She found a queen of Annwn who told her as much."

"From what we know, Zephaniah probably used it to resurrect Moll. She could use it to bring back anyone. Not just humans."

Hailey sighed. "I was hoping that Moll wouldn't figure out that we were working against her. Since Moll's memories go back to before she betrayed us last time, I thought we could use our knowledge of what she did before to anticipate her plans now."

"You thought she was preparing to call forth the wild hunt, again?" Mercy asked.

Hailey nodded. "That was my suspicious."

Mercy shook her head. "That was her plan before she had the Witch of Endor as an ally. We know what Moll was planning before. Whatever the Witch of Endor has told her must be alluring enough that Moll was willing to set aside her former plans. For now, at least."

"That can't be a bad thing," Cassidy said. "I wasn't around, then. But if Moll invoked Lucifer last time, I can't imagine what she's helping the Witch of Endor do could be much worse than that."

Mercy shook her head. "All I can figure is that the Witch of Endor must've warned her. Moll knows we stopped her before. Technically, we could do it again. She wanted her grimoire. That's why she came down here. She left here with more than that."

"What did she take?" Hailey asked.

Mercy shook her head. "Some of Nico's old things. He had it all packed in a box. He said it was stuff he'd used as a hougan. Before he became a vampire."

"Any idea what might have been in the box, Cassidy?" I asked.

Cassidy pressed her lips together. "If it's stuff from when he was still a student back at the Voodoo Academy, it's probably standard wares. Things he'd had as a part of College Samedi. I'm not sure why the Witch of Endor would need most of it. Evoking the Ghede usually involves drawing on the power of the deceased. She can already do that. With the Cauldron of Rebirth, I'd guess she can do a lot more than a first-year hougan's supplies might have allowed."

I pinched the stubble on the end of my chin. "But to draw on the power of the dead, a hougan or mambo must evoke one of the Ghede Loa, correct?"

"That's right," Cassidy nodded. "Baron Samedi. Baron La Croix. Maman Brigitte. Just to name a few."

"But could the supplies that Nico had be used to manipulate any other Loa apart from the Ghede?" Mercy asked.

Cassidy nodded. "I suppose so. Nico wouldn't have tried it. He had the aspect of the Baron."

"What could Moll do with something like that?" I asked. "Could she invoke a Loa?"

Cassidy shrugged. "That depends how proficient and knowledgeable she might be in voodoo. I'd think she'd need a caplata or someone powerful if she intended to manipulate one of the Loa."

I shook my head. "We know they used the cauldron to raise many vodouisants. There's no telling how many of them might be working with Zephaniah and Moll."

# CHAPTER SIX

"IS EVERYTHING UNDER CONTROL at the asylum?" I asked Annabelle through the phone.

"Jessie has everything handled. We're a little short on beds and the cafeteria will need to bring in some more food to take care of everyone."

"Nothing we can't handle. We may just have to double up the patients in their rooms and move some of the less serious cases to outpatient."

"What did you find out?" Annabelle asked.

"We think Moll and Zephaniah are working with a caplata."

"What makes you think that?"

"First, when we got here, Moll had Mercy trapped in some sort of veve."

Annabelle sighed. "Technically, a crude prison like that is something that any witch could do."

"Moll also took some of Nico's old things. Things that could be used to summon a Loa."

Annabelle sighed. "That could be a problem if a caplata is involved. I don't think a witch, even one as powerful as Moll or Zephaniah, would attempt it alone. When a proper mambo or hougan summons a Loa it is to bid the Loa for help. When a bokor or caplata does, they have a way of binding the Loa to their will. A caplata's thrall can manipulate even a good and noble Loa to do unspeakable things."

"That's what Cassidy was afraid of. Could they use the Cauldron of Rebirth toward that end?"

"I don't know, Cain. I really don't. This is uncharted territory. Technically, I suppose it could. Usually, any Loa who is summoned must pass through the crossroads. Isabelle could warn me if that happened. With the cauldron, though, they might bypass the crossroads entirely. They could call upon a Loa, bind it to their purpose, and we'd never know until it was too late. We need to find the cauldron. It may already be too late."

I sighed. "I can try to call the pack. Wolves are great at tracking other wolves. Without their scent, though, it will be difficult to find the witches."

"Switch the phone to speaker," Annabelle said. "I need to talk to Hailey."

I tapped the speaker button on my phone.

"Hey Annabelle. What's up?"

"Hailey, you've met the druids in the Ozarks before, right?"

Hailey nodded. "Elijah and Emilie. They're good people. Do you think they could help?"

"I do. The Cauldron of Rebirth courses with Awen. It's the power that druids wield."

"Can't Isabelle use that kind of power? When she possessed you, the magic, you wielded came from the Tree of Life."

"She can," Annabelle said. "She's the only one though who can lock down the crossroads. If she isn't guarding the crossroads, the witches could summon any Loa they wished even without the cauldron."

"Give the druids a call. They may already know that the cauldron has been stolen. I'd imagine they're looking for it as we speak. We might be able to work together to find it. When I was in Guinee, Rhiannon knew the cauldron was stolen. I believe her husband, the king of her domain, has a relationship with the druids. Now that we have a pretty good idea what's going on, we need to bring them in on this. They'll need our help and we'll need theirs."

"I worked with them before. When I teamed up with Nyx to stop the zombies in Kansas City. Elijah gave me his number. I'll give him a call."

"Let me know what's going on. In the meantime, I'm going to make sure the crossroads are secure."

I hung up my phone. Hailey retrieved hers and found the contact information for the druid. She called him and placed her phone on speaker.

"Hailey?" a male voice answered.

"Hey, Elijah. We might need your help."

"We're sort of in the middle of a crisis right now. What's going on?"

"Does the crisis have something to do with the Cauldron of Rebirth?"

"It does. How did you know?"

"We think an ancient witch stole it. You've probably heard of her. The Witch of Endor."

Elijah snorted. "I know the name from the Bible. My step-parents used to drag me to church. You're saying she's real and she's still alive?"

"She's come back from the dead. She's the one who took it. I'm not exactly sure where she is, but we know she's here in New Orleans. She's already used the cauldron to raise several hundred people here."

"Where are you now?" Elijah asked.

"It's a house in the French Quarter. Do you think you can come help?"

"I'll be there as soon as I can. Do you have an address?"

"I'll text it to you. Please hurry. We think she might use it to call on a Loa."

Elijah grunted. "See you soon. I just need the address."

Hailey hung up and texted the druid the address for Casa do Diabo.

"I hope he drives fast. By the time he gets here, it might be too late."

No sooner did I speak and a green tornado of energies appeared in the middle of the room. When the energies dissipated, a young man, probably in his mid-twenties, and a dark-haired girl of similar age appeared. The druid held a staff over his head. The girl with him held what looked like a small violin in her hands.

"Holy crap," Hailey said. "That was fast. I really need to learn that spell."

Elijah chuckled. "The power is within you. It's within all the living."

"Yeah, problem. I'm a vampire, you know."

Elijah smiled. "It doesn't matter. Perhaps I'll teach you in time."

"This is Cain and Cassidy. I believe you've met Mercy."

Elijah nodded at Mercy. "We met once before."

The druid held out his hand to me. I shook it. A tingle, like a small jolt of electricity, accompanied his touch. "I'm Cain."

"Pleased to meet you. This is my wife and my bard, Emilie."

I extended my hand to the girl. She shook my head. When she did, she gasped. "Holy smokes. You're actually Cain."

A closed-mouth smile spread across my face. "Last I checked."

"Elijah, he's the Cain from the Bible. I saw his tale in my mind the moment I touched his hand."

I furrowed my brow. "You can do that? You know someone's history with a touch?"

Emilie shrugged. "Not always. When there's a tale to tell that the Tree of Life believes I must know, it is revealed. I can see that your journey has been long. You're not the man they told us about in Sunday School."

I chuckled. "Not anymore."

"Were you raised by the cauldron?" Elijah asked.

I shook my head. "I was not."

"He never died, Elijah," Emilie said. "He's lived for thousands of years."

Elijah cocked his head. "That's remarkable."

"Can you help us find the cauldron?" Hailey asked. "We need to stop the witches who are using it. We don't know their plans. Not exactly. But we're pretty sure it's no good."

Elijah nodded. "I can. If these witches are as powerful as it sounds, I may need your help. The cauldron is incredibly powerful. The potion within it is how Awen was first brought to my ancestors many centuries ago. It's also a volatile substance. If the cauldron has already been used to raise several people from the dead, there's a chance the witch has corrupted it already. When we find it, I'll have to devote all of my energies to purifying it, or at least containing it. I won't be able to fight off the witches."

"Before we go," Emilie said. "It is essential that you all grasp the significance of what we're dealing with. There's a tale that must be told."

Hailey shook her head. "No offense, Emilie. I don't think we have the time to sit around and tell stories. Moll and the Witch of Endor might be using the cauldron as we speak."

A wide grin split Emilie's face as she raised her violin to her chin. "The tale will take but a moment in time to tell."

# CHAPTER SEVEN

THE YOUNG BARD PLAYED her violin. When she did, pink energies flowed out of the strings and swirled around the room.

"Behold," Emilie said. "The tale of Ceridwen and the Cauldron."

The magic continued to spin around us until it filled my vision and I saw nothing else. When the power faded, I stood in what looked to be an old grass hut. Hailey, Mercy, Cassidy, and the druids were standing along the perimeter of the room. At the center of the room was a boiling cauldron suspended over a fire. The flames ticked the sides of it. There was an old man reclined on one side of the room and a young boy tossing wood into the fire.

"The boy before us is the young Gwion Bach. Ceridwen charged the servant boy, along with the blind man, Morda, to tend the cauldron for a year and a day."

"They can't hear us, can they?" I asked.

Emilie shook her head. "We are not a part of this tale."

"Why a year and a day?" Hailey asked. "I've done many spells using cauldrons before. None of them required so much time to mature."

Elijah folded his hands in front of his waist. "The power of Awen is with all of us. It's also foreign to this world. Ever since the time of Ask and Embla's fall."

"Ask and Embla?" I asked.

Elijah nodded. "Your parents. Adam and Eve. The Nordic tales call them Ask and Embla. These tales found their way to my ancestors as well. You might call the recipe to this brew an answer to prayer."

"Ceridwen was a mother to two," Emilie explained. "Her daughter, Creiwry, was considered the fairest in the land. Her son Afagddu was born ugly."

"Well, that's not a very nice way to put it," Cassidy said.

Emilie smiled. "He had great deformities. They were so extensive that it is said that it turned the stomach of any who looked upon him."

"Damn," Mercy said. "That's some kind of ugly."

"It broke Ceridwen's heart. She concocted this potion that she might bless her son with a gift of immeasurable wisdom and eclipse the disadvantages of his appearance with a measure of poetic inspiration."

"A mother will go to great lengths for the sake of her children," I said.

Emilie nodded. "Only the first three drops of the potion would bestow this gift. The rest would be a fatal poison. Watch and see what unfolds."

"Add more wood to the flames," the blind Morda said. "We cannot risk spoiling the potion when we're so close to completing our task."

Gwion nodded. He stepped outside and returned with a bundle of sticks. He tossed the wood into the flames. When he did, the flames burst high over the sides of the cauldron.

"It burns too hot!" Gwion shouted. "We cannot risk it boiling over!"

"You must stir the potion," Morda said. "If so much as three drops boil over, it will spoil the lot."

Gwion grabbed a long wooden spoon and dipped it into the potion. He stirred. Some of the potion boiled up. Three drops struck the boy's hand.

"It burns!" Gwion shouted, raising his thumb to his mouth to tend to the burn. Then, he gasped.

"What did you do?" Morda asked.

"I... I don't know..."

The cauldron cracked. The potion spilled out all over the ground. A green energy spread through the soil.

"You must flee!" Morda struggled to his feet. "If Ceridwen learns what you've done..."

A woman burst into the room. "What is this? You have ruined the brew!"

"I'm sorry! I didn't mean..."

Ceridwen reached for the boy. He stepped out of the way and took off out of the hut.

"Get back here, boy!" Ceridwen shouted.

The boy's eyes glowed green. He had the same power I'd seen Annabelle wield when possessed by Isabelle. He changed his shape, become a small hare. We followed the boy and Ceridwen out of the hut.

Ceridwen clenched her fist. She turned into a greyhound and pursued the boy.

"Did she catch him?" I asked.

Emilie nodded. "Eventually. The boy later fled into a stream and became a fish. Ceridwen pursued him as an otter. He turned again into a bird, but Ceridwen changed into a hawk. Unable to avoid her pursuits, he changed himself into a single grain of corn and hid himself in a storehouse. Ceridwen turned herself into a hen. She ate every kernel, eventually swallowing him whole."

Mercy snorted. "Well, that's a corny way to go."

Everyone turned and stared at Mercy blankly.

"What?" Mercy shrugged.

Emilie cleared her throat. "That was not the end of Gwion's tale. When Ceridwen resumed human form, she found soon that she was with child. Young Gwion turned himself into a fetus in her womb. When the child was born, she cast him into the sea. Later, the child was rescued by a prince. He grew up to become the bard of bards, the legendary Taliesin."

"That's a fascinating story," I said. "How does that help us now?"

"Ceridwen's pursuit of Gwion is not why I showed you this tale. We must see what happened to the rest of the potion."

"The poison?" I asked.

Emilie nodded. "Let us watch as the poison spreads through the land."

We followed the green glow as it spread across the fields and reached a stream. The stream went aglow and flowed downstream to a field.

"These are the fields of Garanhir," Emilie said.

Dozens of horses were grazing in the field. The poison elixir spread from the river and across the field. One by one, each of the horses fell over dead.

"Damn," Mercy said. "Poor horses."

Elijah nodded. "The cauldron's power can give a splendid gift to some. It is a source of great power and wisdom. Once the brew within it has completed its purpose, it will kill."

I bit my lip. "Are you certain that the cauldron we're dealing with is the same one? The cauldron we saw in the hut cracked before the poison spilled out of it."

"Let us return to the hut and see what happens to the cauldron," Emilie said.

We followed the bard back to the hut. Several small winged creatures buzzed around it. "What are they?" I asked.

"Fairies," Elijah said.

The crack on the cauldron healed as the fairies buzzed around it. Then, a tornado of green energy like the one Elijah had used to teleport himself to Casa do Diabo formed around it and the cauldron disappeared.

"We believe that they returned the cauldron to Annwn," Elijah explained. "There, the cauldron was fed by the power of the Tree of Life. Pure Awen has brewed within it ever since. So long as it remains in the otherworld, in Annwn, it is a source of life. It is so powerful that it might bring to life those who have died."

"But the longer it remains on earth, the more the potion becomes like the brew that Gwion tended before. It will lose its power to give life and what remains will infect the land with death. Only this time, it will not be merely a few horses who fall to the poison. The cauldron now possesses power immeasurably greater than it did before. As much as it might bestow life and wisdom, what remains will kill with greater potency."

"It would kill any animals in the land?" I asked.

"Any who dwell on the lands it infects will die," Elijah said. "Not just animals. Humans. Vampires. Anything that has breath in the infected lands will die in an instant."

Pink energies again enveloped us and we found ourselves again at Casa do Diabo.

"Do you understand now why this is such a delicate matter?" Elijah asked. "My priority cannot be fighting the witches. They might be powerful. The power in the cauldron to give either life or death is greater than any spell they might throw at us."

"So we don't just have to get past Moll and Zephaniah," Hailey said. "We have to retrieve the cauldron."

Elijah nodded. "I must return it to Annwn before it is too late. Once the poison spills over and touches the land, there is nothing we'll be able to do to stop it."

"How far will the poison spread?" I asked.

Elijah shook his head. "Consider this. Only three drops in the tale we saw before could be used to grant the gift of wisdom and life. The rest was a potent poison. If what you say is true that the cauldron has already been used to bring dozens, if not hundreds, of people back to life, the poison that flows from the cauldron will infect the land at a strength in relative proportion."

"Three drops compared to a whole cauldron, before. A great dose of the potion now has been used to bring people back to life. How many hundreds or thousands of times more might the poison be?"

"It would be enough to wipe out all life on this continent. If it spreads further across the oceans, dare I say, it might extinguish all life on earth."

# CHAPTER EIGHT

WE STEPPED OUTSIDE OF Mercy's house. It was still relatively early in the night. The vision Emilie showed us seemed to take a few hours. Only a few minutes had passed. It was early enough that most of the folks traversing through the French Quarter were still walking in straight lines.

"Can you find the cauldron?" I asked.

Elijah nodded. "I can."

"Take us there," Mercy said. "We'll back you up."

"I can bring the wolves," I added. "One of us has access to celestial power. We can fend off the Witch of Endor's attacks."

Elijah grinned. "Do that. Emilie will show you the way."

"Why aren't you taking us?"

Elijah laughed. "Bring my clothes with you. I'll need them later."

"Excuse me?" I raised an eyebrow.

All at once, Elijah's body changed. No, he didn't become a wolf. He became an eagle. The druid left his clothes behind as he squeezed out of his shirt. He spread his wings and took off into the skies.

"Holy shit," Mercy chuckled. "I've known a few vampires who could become bats. I've never seen a human do *that*."

"Cool, right?" Emilie stood there with her hands on her hips as she watched her husband fly off into the skies. "Elijah can sense the power of Awen. Once he has the location, he'll send me a signal."

"What kind of signal?" I asked.

"A whisper through the trees."

I snorted. "He talks to trees?"

"Of course he does. The power of Awen is not the sole property of human beings."

"Right. But you're talking about *trees.*"

Emilie laughed. "I get it. This was all pretty crazy to me when I first learned of these things."

"Do trees make delightful conversationalists?" Mercy asked, a hit of cynicism in her voice.

"The trees don't speak in human words. Do any of you have a car?"

"I have a truck."

"And I drive a hearse," Mercy said.

Emilie smirked. "You drive a hearse."

Mercy shrugged. "I'm a vampire. I have a taste for the macabre."

"Not to mention," Hailey added. "We keep a coffin in the back. It's convenient if we ever find ourselves caught outside when the sun rises."

Emilie nodded. "I need to remain in the open air to hear Elijah's message through the trees. I'll ride in the back of the truck."

"We'll follow close behind," Mercy said. "Just give us a heads up to prepare. Hailey and I are strong on our own right. I don't think we can take these witches head-on. We need to take them by surprise."

"We'll rendezvous at the asylum extension site first," I said. "That way, I can gather the wolves. Including Julie."

Emilie raised her hand. "Wait."

"What is it?"

"Elijah has found something."

"The cauldron?" I asked.

Emilie shook her head. "Not exactly."

"The witches?" Hailey asked.

"No, they aren't there. Not anymore."

I cocked my head. "What did he find?"

"I'm not sure. Like I said, the messages he can send through the trees aren't in words. Think of the signals I'm receiving back and forth like yes and no answers. All I know is that he wishes us to come quickly."

"Hop into the truck," I said.

Emilie climbed in the truck's bed. Mercy and Hailey got in the hearse.

"Give me your number," Emilie said. "We'll communicate by phone. I can lie low in the truck and relay whatever signals I'm getting from Elijah."

I told Emilie my number. She called me as we pulled away from Casa do Diabo. I had to admit, I'd expected she'd be trying to shout through the rear window, which, given the wind when driving, would have made it a lot more difficult to communicate. To think until recently, I'd resisted getting one of these portable phones. I had to admit they were helpful in a pinch.

"Turn North!" Emilie shouted through the phone.

"I'm beholden to roads. I can't just turn north without a road going that direction. Not to mention, Lake Ponchartrain is directly north of here."

"When you can. Whatever Elijah wants us to see is directly north-ish of where we're at now."

I raised one eyebrow. "North-ish? I'm glad it's *directly* north-ish. That tells me exactly what I need to know."

"Here," Cassidy showed me a GPS map on her phone. It showed us where we were currently. "Just so you can get your bearings relative to what's directly north of here."

I bit my lip. "I know my cardinal directions. Thanks, though."

Cassidy chuckled. "Men and directions."

"It's not because I'm a man that I know where the north is. It's because I'm a werewolf. I always know the position of the moon relative to my location in the region."

"I'm a werewolf. I don't know my north from my left and right."

"The opposite of North is South."

"Right. I don't know the difference between what's north or south either. If I end up in the ocean... oops, that must've been south."

"It's more to the Northwest," Emilie said. "I think it's in the swamps."

"I thought you only got yes and no signals."

Emilie giggled. "The trees have a swampy accent."

"Trees have accents?" I bit the inside of my cheek, trying to suppress the tone of incredulity in my voice.

"Something like accents. It's the closest thing to what I sense I can describe. I'm pretty sure these are swamp trees. They're wild. Not like the city trees."

"City trees sound more sophisticated?"

"They're more hoarse. From breathing in the smog."

I shook my head. "I'll have to take your word for it."

"Wait. Slow down. I'm sensing danger."

"Say what? What kind of danger?"

"I don't know! Like I said..."

"Right, they don't speak in words. Why doesn't Elijah have a cell phone? That would make things easier."

Emilie didn't bother responding. Cassidy started giggling. "He can't use a phone as an eagle, Cain. No easier than we can as wolves."

I placed my free hand, the one I wasn't using to steer the truck, on my forehead to shield my embarrassment. "Yeah. Obviously. It was a dumb suggestion. If we're looking toward the northwest, though, that sounds like Manchac Swamp."

"*Our* swamp?" Cassidy asked. "Why would the witches take the cauldron to a place we frequent?"

I shrugged. "It's not a full moon. We're still a couple of weeks away from the next one. Perhaps they took it there for a while because they figured we weren't likely to go to a place we sometimes have to go when we didn't need to go there. Or, perhaps, it's just a coincidence."

"I don't think that's it," Emilie said. "The trees are in pain. The poison from the cauldron spreads faster through water than on land."

"That's bad. That's really bad."

"Why is that?" Cassidy asked.

"The swamp borders Lake Ponchartrain. Lake Ponchartrain is connected to Lake Borgne and the Gulf of Mexico."

"Do you think the witches are trying to spread the poison from the cauldron across the earth?"

I nodded. "That might explain why they raised so many people. You said before that the concentration of the poison the cauldron produces would be relative in proportion to the number of those raised."

"Why raise the people of Vilokan?" Emilie asked. "There are cemeteries all over, I suspect."

There are," I nodded. "The witches were trying to get our attention. They wanted us to find out what they were up to."

"Why would they do that?" Emilie asked.

I shook my head. "I don't know. I'm afraid we're about to find out."

"Stop at the edges of the swamps," Emilie said. "Elijah will meet us there. If there's a way to stop the spread of the poison, we might need Mercy's and Hailey's help.

# CHAPTER NINE

I COULDN'T BELIEVE MY eyes. My jaw was almost in the mud. The poison was moving through the swamp. Corpses of alligators, snakes, and other creatures floated through the poison like shadows.

Elijah, still in eagle form, flew over the swam and landed in front of me. He returned to human form. Cassidy's eyes went wide.

"Damn, Emilie. You're a lucky girl!"

Emilie giggled. "I know, right?"

Elijah sighed. "Clothes, please."

Emilie reached into the back of the truck and tossed Elijah his pants and sweatshirt.

"Is there anyway we can stop this?"

Elijah sighed. "I don't know. Theoretically, if we could funnel the poison back into Annwn the Tree of Life would purify it. I can't just form portals to the otherworld out of the blue. It's a complicated process."

I narrowed my eyes. "If we could create a portal to Annwn, would there be a way to guide the poison into it?"

Elijah nodded. "Sure. I can manipulate the currents in the water. I'm doing that already, in fact. It's slowing down the spread for now."

"Hailey, call Annabelle."

"That's fucking brilliant," Mercy said. "I thought she said that she couldn't use Isabelle right now. She needed her at the crossroads."

I shook my head. "We don't have a choice. We'll have to risk opening the crossroads."

"If the cauldron is already spilling poison," Elijah said, "they can't use it anymore. If I'm understanding how these crossroads work, if we pull Annabelle's familiar spirit out of the crossroads, a Loa might come through, right?'

I nodded. "That's exactly right."

"This might be a trap," Hailey said. "If Moll and Zephaniah know they've tapped out the cauldron, they might've figured the only way to open the crossroads is to force Annabelle to use Isabelle to cut a portal to the otherworld."

"Trap or not," Elijah said. "If Annabelle can do what you're suggesting, we don't have a choice. We don't know that this is a trap. We know for certain that if we can't stop the poison from spreading, the entire planet will become a mass grave in a matter of weeks, if not days. Once the poison hits the oceans, even with my power, there's no way I could direct enough current to keep the poison at bay."

Hailey already had Annabelle on the phone. Her message was clear. "Get your ass here now. Bring Isabelle. Screw the crossroads. If you don't bring her here fast, the whole world is fucked."

Hailey hung up the phone. "She's on the way."

I glared at Mercy. "You're a bad influence on her."

Mercy huffed. "Because she used the F-word? Come on, Cain. We're vampires. If a foul tongue is our biggest character defect, consider yourself lucky."

I raised an eyebrow. "Consider *myself* lucky?"

Mercy grinned. "If we gave in to our primal, vampiric urges... you'd probably have a lot more work on your hands at the Vilokan Asylum. Just saying..."

I grinned. "Point taken."

Elijah approached the water. The druid reached into his pocket and retrieved what looked like a twig, roughly a pencil's length. A little green magic flowed from his fingertips into the stick. It expanded into a long staff roughly six feet in length.

Elijah dipped the end of his staff into the water. "This will help me focus my power to hold the current. I'm not sure how long I can contain it."

"Long enough for Annabelle to get here?"

Elijah nodded. "Sure."

I tilted my head. "Sure?"

"I'm not a hundred percent confident."

"I can help." Hailey directed her wand at the water. "I have skills, too."

Elijah nodded. "Do what you can. I'm pulling the current to my staff."

"You're drawing the poison toward us?" I asked.

"It's the only way. Don't worry. The magic I draw from my staff comes directly from the Tree of Life. I can't totally dispel the poison, but my staff will prevent the poison from infecting us. So long as I can hold it."

"How can I help, exactly?" Hailey asked.

"Monitor the east side of the swamp. I'm reasonably certain I can draw ninety percent of the poison to my staff. If only ten percent gets to Lake Ponchartrain, and from there, to the ocean, well, it might not wipe out all life on earth, but it would still kill millions. Even if it only killed the world's sea life, the impact to the ecosystem would cascade in unthinkable ways across the planet."

Hailey pulled out her phone. Mine rang. It was Hailey.

I tilted my head and furrowed my brow.

Hailey stuck her phone under her bra in the front of her shirt. "Keep your phone on speaker, Cain. If I run into any problems, I'll let you know."

"Be careful, Hailey." I stuck my phone in the small pocket on the front of my button-up shirt. "We'll do the same."

# CHAPTER TEN

ANNABELLE PULLED UP IN her Camaro, skidding to a halt and spraying a little gravel into my shin. I winced.

"What do you need me to do?" Annabelle asked, jumping out of the car, her eyes green suggesting that Isabelle was with her.

"I'm told you can open a portal to Annwn," Elijah said. "Can you set it on the edge of the water?"

Annabelle nodded. "Sure. How large does it need to be?"

"I'm going to direct all the poison into it. Make it big enough so that when I pull the poison this way, there isn't any room on the edge of the shore for any to escape."

"I'd ask what happened here. You all can fill me in on the details later. This poison stuff. What could it do? Destroy the city?"

I shook my head. "It could kill all life on the entire planet."

Annabelle's eyes went wide. "Beli!"

The Voodoo Queen's soul blade formed in her hand. She approached the edge of the water and jabbed her blade into the air. When she did, gold sparks flew around the blade as she cut an oblong gash through this world's existence.

"As close to the Tree of Life as possible," Elijah said.

Annabelle nodded and continued cutting her gate. She dipped the blade under the water and pulled it through until she completed the gate. "Will that do?"

Elijah nodded. "That's perfect."

Green energies flowed from Elijah's hands as he drew the water toward his staff. He moved the staff back and forth, drawing the point out of the marsh and into Annabelle's portal.

Annabelle glanced at me and sighed. "I sure hope this was necessary. I fear the crossroads might be in jeopardy."

I nodded. "We don't have a choice. Has anyone attempted to draw a Loa through the crossroads yet?"

"Isabelle says no. But I received word a caplata who died a few years back was spotted near to here."

"Who was the caplata?" Cassidy asked.

"Her name is Odette. La Sirene killed her."

Emilie cocked her head. "You mean, Joni Campbell?"

Annabelle nodded. "The same. The last time Odette was alive, she had designs on destroying the world."

Mercy sighed. "Why do so many bad guys want to destroy the planet? It's stupid as hell. Rule the world? Alright. I can see the appeal. Destroy it, though? They don't really have a lot of hope for the future, do they?"

Annabelle's cheeks tightened, suppressing a grin. "I agree. In Odette's case, she intended to destroy the world so that she might re-make it. Odette was a slave. She believed the injustice that infected the world was incurable. She envisioned a new world, under her control and rule, that was more equitable."

I shrugged. "She had a legitimate grievance."

"Indeed," Annabelle said. "Murdering everyone on the planet, though, isn't exactly the way to bring about a more just version of human society."

"Let me get this straight." Mercy crossed her arms in front of her chest. "We already have Moll who once created a spell that allowed demons to possess vampires and also summoned Lucifer in her attempt to gain power over the world. Now we have a caplata raised from the dead who once had a similar stupid goal in mind?"

"Don't forget Zephaniah," I said. "The Witch of Endor has always had an insatiable craving for power."

"We've got a big problem here!" Hailey's muffled voice shouted through my phone speaker. "Someone's here. I can feel his power. I've sensed it before."

"Sensed it when?" I asked.

"Is Annabelle there yet?" Hailey asked.

"She is. What's going on, Hailey?"

Hailey didn't respond.

"Hailey? Are you there?"

Again, no response.

"Go!" Elijah shouted. "I've got this handled."

Emilie stayed with Elijah. Cassidy, Mercy, and Annabelle followed me as we ran as fast as we could around the perimeter of the marshlands.

My phone lost its connection as we ran. When we reached the east side, Pauli was standing there. Pauli was Annabelle's friend. His soul inhabited the body of a rainbow colored boa constrictor. Having the aspect of Aida-Wedo, he could shape shift. He usually took a human form that resembled the body that was stolen from him. Based on the way he was dressed, not in his usual fashionable get-up, but in a dark tuxedo and a top-hat, it didn't take long for me to connect the dots.

Annabelle gasped. "Kalfu."

Kalfu tipped his hat toward us. "Thank you for delivering my second. Hailey is much more powerful than before."

"What is he talking about?" I asked.

Mercy and Annabelle exchanged glances.

"What did you do with Hailey?" Mercy asked, baring her fangs.

"I've returned her to the crossroads. It's time to finish what I started before."

Annabelle gripped her soul blade. She charged Kalfu. Kalfu raised his hand forming a red energy barrier between himself and the Voodoo Queen.

"Fool me once. You'll never fool me twice."

"Hailey will never help you!" Annabelle screamed.

"She might. Do you know what these witches and this caplata who summoned me intend to do?"

"We have a pretty good idea," Mercy huffed.

"I think it might incline Hailey to agree to a bargain if it meant saving the world from what those witches plan to do."

Annabelle shook her head. "If a caplata summoned you, she controls you. You won't defy her intentions."

Kalfu laughed. "I don't have to. I just have to convince Hailey that I intend to *try* and stop the witches. She will agree to help me claim the crossroads if it means saving the world."

"She still won't help you!" Annabelle shouted.

Kalfu laughed. "I've been working on my wording for the bargain I'll propose to the young vampire. Tell me. What do you think about this. Help me claim control of the crossroads, Hailey, and I'll do everything in my power to stop the witches from killing anyone."

Annabelle shook her head. "Everything in your power is exactly nothing!"

Kalfu grinned. "Precisely. Oh, and don't even try to intervene. I've already levied my challenge to the crossroads. Until the challenge is complete, your power will not allow you access."

Kalfu snapped his fingers. In a flash of red energy, the Loa disappeared.

"Fuck!" Annabelle screamed.

I narrowed my eyes.

"Sorry," Annabelle glanced at me.

Mercy snickered.

"No," I said. "In this case, I think the F-word is more than justified."

Annabelle grabbed my hand. "There's something you need to know about Hailey."

"You never told him?" Mercy asked.

Annabelle shook her head. "It wasn't necessary."

"What is it, Annabelle?"

Annabelle sighed. "When Hailey was first turned into a vampire, it was all a setup. She was working with Kalfu."

I cocked my head. "Hailey was working *with* that Loa?"

Annabelle nodded. "To claim the crossroads requires a second. Isabelle controls the crossroads with Mikah. Another former classmate of mine. Hailey was already a powerful witch before she became a vampire. Kalfu chose her as his second to wrest control of the crossroads from Papa Legba."

"But Isabelle and Mikah took over instead?"

Annabelle nodded. "I got there before the challenge was issued. I was able to overcome Kalfu. I stabbed him with Beli and sent him into the void."

"But you didn't kill Hailey?"

Annabelle shook her head. "I was able to convince her that Kalfu was manipulating her. He was going to sacrifice her and appoint another second after he used her power to weaken me. She had a change of heart at the last moment. I never could have defeated Kalfu otherwise."

"So now that he's started the challenge over the crossroads, and Isabelle is here with you..."

"He'll only need to defeat Mikah to succeed. Isabelle won't be able to fight him. Not unless he takes over and we can go back and challenge him for control again."

"Why does he need Hailey?"

Annabelle rolled her eyes. "Kaful is a bit of perv. Maybe he has a thing for her. Or, perhaps, he feels he has something over her. Either way, he intends to make her his second. He can't take control without a second. Whatever the case, he's right. With her power combined with his, Mikah won't stand a chance."

"Could he defeat Mikah alone?"

Annabelle shook her head. "I don't know. He'd have a chance. If Hailey agrees to his bargain, though, his victory will be certain."

"Our best chance is to stop the witches," Mercy said. "If they aren't a threat anymore, maybe Hailey won't have any reason to agree to the bargain."

Annabelle shook her head. "That won't work. Hailey won't know if we've stopped the witches or not."

I pressed my lips together. "The caplata, Odette, is the one who controls Kalfu. What if we just stop her? If she's dead, suppose Hailey agrees to the bargain that Kalfu intends to propose. If the caplata can't control him, he will have to do everything within his power to stop the other witches."

Annabelle grinned. "That's exactly right. We might be able to end all of them if we only take out Odette."

Mercy shook her head. "That only works if Hailey agrees to the bargain."

I bit my lip. "You don't think she'll agree to it if she thinks it means saving the world?"

Annabelle sighed. "Hailey will try to kill Kalfu herself first."

I shrugged. "Would that be the end of the world? She could succeed."

"She might," Annabelle said. "But we'd still be left with the witches to deal with. The witches won't know if Kalfu has succeeded or not any more than Hailey will know if we've defeated them. My suspicion is that the witches intend to use Kalfu to bring other Loa through the crossroads so they can use their power to remake the world as they see fit. By the time they realize Hailey killed Kalfu, if she's able to pull it off, it will be too late."

I sighed. "The witches might already succeed in destroying the world."

"Lets hope Elijah has siphoned all the poison into my portal," Annabelle said.

"The cauldron isn't in the swamp," I said. "We don' t know that all the poison from within it was spilled here."

Annabelle took a deep breath. "I think it's reasonable to assume that it wasn't. The witches aren't done. This isn't the only place, I fear, they've spread the poison."

"We need to get back to Elijah. We have to stop Odette and need to find the cauldron. This whole thing might have been a diversion. Elijah said it before. If the poison reaches the ocean, it won't be so easy to stop."

Mercy cocked her head. "You think the witches are taking the rest of the cauldron straight to the ocean?"

"If your intention was to destroy the world, isn't that what you'd do?" I asked.

Mercy clenched her fist. "F-Bomb!"

I scratched the back of my head. "Thanks for censoring yourself."

Mercy snorted. "A bomb of fucks is infinitely worse than a single fuck. I didn't do it for your sake, Cain."

# CHAPTER ELEVEN

ELIJAH WAS JUST FINISHING up when we arrived.

"Mind closing this portal, Annabelle?"

Annabelle nodded and released her soul blade, When she did, the portal also vanished.

We explained everything that happened to Elijah and Emilie. The druid didn't waste any time. He quickly resumed eagle form and took off into the skies.

"Back to the truck?" I asked.

Emilie shrugged. "Might as well. If you're right and the witches took the cauldron closer to the ocean, we'd best head that direction. Though, if that's the case, I really don't know what we could do to stop it."

Annabelle tilted her head. "That might not be true. La Sirene is currently lecturing at the Voodoo Academy."

Emilie's eyes widened. "Do you think she and the Fomorian Wyrm-riders might be able to stop the poison?"

Annabelle shrugged. "The wyrms can create portals into the void. They might not be able to send the poison back to the Tree of Life, but the void would be just as well, wouldn't it? Plus, La Sirene and Agwe can manipulate the currents of the ocean."

I nodded. "I'm sure they'd at least like a warning. If the poison is heading out to sea, the Fomorian merkingdom will be wiped out."

"I'll talk to Joni," Mercy said. "Elijah might still need Annabelle's assistance here."

"That's right. You have a connection to La Sirene too, don't you?"

"What are you talking about?" I asked.

Mercy smirked. "I bit her once. When she is in human form, as she will be at the Voodoo Academy, she's a vampire."

I snorted. "Seriously?"

"I had to do it!" Mercy said. "At the time, Odette and another caplata had her enthralled. They were going to use La Sirene to spread a school of Zombie sharks all around the ocean and probably on shore if they could find someone to bite."

"Damn," I said. "How many times have you two saved the world now?"

Mercy started counting on her fingers. Then she shrugged. "I don't know. I'm not really keeping track. For what it's worth, I have a vested interest in protecting my food supply."

I chuckled. "You really have no interest in saving humanity because it's the right thing to do?"

Mercy smirked. "I'd never admit it if I did. I have a reputation to uphold."

Annabelle laughed. "Alright, Mercy. Go find Joni. Tell her everything. Have her assemble the wyrmriders straight away. If the poison has already hit the sea, we won't have much time to spare."

Mercy nodded. "Joni is also a siphon. If the poison is spreading into the ocean, she'll be able to sense it as soon as she hits the water."

Emilie scooped up Elijah's clothes and tossed them in the cab of my truck. Annabelle climbed into the back of my truck with Emilie. Cassidy rode shotgun. Emilie called me again so we could communicate as we drove away from the swamp.

We still didn't know where Zephaniah, Moll, or Odette were. Chances were better than not if Elijah found the cauldron, he'd find them as well.

"I'm going to head to the Vilokan Asylum extension site while we wait to hear from Elijah. If the witches haven't spilled the poison into the ocean yet, we may need the help of the wolves to stop them. Without Hailey or Mercy to help, we'll be at an even greater disadvantage in a confrontation with the witches than before."

"Good idea," Annabelle shouted through Emilie's phone. "We'll need all the help we can get."

"Plenty of trees near the asylum?" Emilie asked. "We'll need them to maintain contact with Elijah."

"Shouldn't be a problem. Hundreds of trees surround the grounds."

Cassidy pulled out her phone. "I'll text the other wolves and have them meet us there."

"All of them?" I asked. "That's a lot of texts."

Cassidy chuckled. "Haven't you ever heard of group texting?"

I shook my head. "Nope."

Cassidy grinned. "You know, considering that I was possessed for most of my teenage years, I have an excuse for not knowing how a lot of technology works."

"Considering the fact that I'm almost as old as dirt, literally, that's the only excuse I need. I won't say you can't teach an old dog new tricks. I learn new things. It just takes a while."

It was the middle of the night. It wasn't a tremendous surprise that we arrived at the extension site before any of the other wolves showed. Hell, I would have been shocked if they even got Cassidy's texts until morning. Who answers text messages while they're sleeping? Even if none of them showed, Cassidy could call them and they could meet up with us later. At the very least, Abel, Julie, and Ryan would be there. We'd have Julie's celestial flambeau at our disposal, which would help neutralize Zephaniah's infernal power. Hopefully, the rest of us could handle Moll and Annabelle could deal with the caplata. It wasn't the surest plan for victory I'd ever come up with, but it was the best we had given the situation. We didn't have to defeat them. We just needed to make sure they didn't dump the cauldron in the ocean.

The more I thought about it, if the task was just to best the witches in some kind of supernatural battle, we might stand a better chance than we did now. As much as it might sound simpler to steal the cauldron from them and send the thing back to Eden, it would also be a lot simpler for them to dump the thing straight in the ocean than it would for them to fight us off. There was a reason we hadn't seen the witches. They were avoiding us. They'd probably poisoned the swamp because they knew we'd discover it. It gave them a chance to do what they'd been planning all along. While we were busy cleaning up the swamp, they'd casually go about their plan to destroy the world.

Abel was waiting on the porch when I pulled up. Ryan and Julie must've heard me approaching. Werewolves have excellent hearing, even when in human form. They stepped out onto the porch only moments after I parked my truck.

So far, we had heard nothing from Elijah. Presumably, he was still flying around the region, looking for the cauldron or any evidence of spilled poison.

I was about to introduce Emilie to the crowd, but she took off toward the treeline behind the property.

"What's going on, Emilie?"

Emilie shook her head. "I haven't heard from Elijah yet. Something is wrong."

"Perhaps he's still looking."

Emilie sighed. "He still should have contacted us by now. I'm afraid he's either been hurt, or he's traced the magic too far from any trees to make contact."

"How far would that have to be?"

"A mile, give or take. There has to be a connection between trees, one message relayed to the next and so forth. It's sort of like playing the game of telephone except trees never misinterpret the signals and screw it up. I'm afraid if he's gone that far away from the trees, he might have already tracked the cauldron to somewhere out at sea. If that's the case, we're too late."

"He can teleport himself back here, right?"

Emilie nodded. "He doesn't know where *here* is. Still, he could teleport himself closer to a network of trees that covers this area and send a message."

"I'll head out with you to the treeline if you don't mind. Cassidy and Annabelle can bring the wolves up to speed."

Emilie smiled at me. "That would be fine."

When we reached the treeline, Emilie placed one hand against the trunk of what might have been the tallest tree on the entire property. I imagined it wasn't by accident she'd selected that tree. Perhaps tall trees are better at passing messages across greater distances. Sort of how radio or cell phone towers work. Emilie took and released several deep breaths as she focused on whatever messages she was or wasn't getting from the tree. She was either waiting for a response, or the tree she selected was a Chatty Cathy that wouldn't shut up. Either way, by the way Emilie squinted her closed eyes, pursed her lips, and furrowed her brow, she was clearly concentrating on something.

Emilie removed her hand and took a step back.

"Anything?"

"Nothing," Emilie pressed her lips together. "I'm going to try something else."

Emilie extended her hand. Her bardic violin appeared in her grasp.

"Well, that's a neat trick."

Emilie smirked. "You ain't seen nothin' yet. Just keep an open mind. The bardic insight isn't just about tales of old. It also has a way of showing you exactly what you need to find at the moment."

"How does it do that?"

"The human spirit is strong. So are the spirits of a place. A bard can discern those spirits."

"So if you play that thing, it will tell us where Elijah is?"

Emilie shrugged. "Maybe. It will show us something we need to know. It's not always straightforward. Half the time I'm shown some ancient tale with a lesson that I'm supposed to process and sort out. It's a pain in the butt when that happens. Whatever the case, it's usually something crucial."

I nodded. "Well, then. Play your song."

"We're in this together. This will be our song."

# CHAPTER TWELVE

EMILIE RAISED HER VIOLIN to her chin and played. As the time before, pink energies from her violin surrounded us.

We stood in the same hut we'd seen before. This time, the cauldron hung cracked and the fire beneath it had simmered down to but a few embers.

There was no more evidence of poison in the ground surrounding the cauldron. The blind Morda, the old man who'd supervised Gwion Bach before, sat erect. His eyes were shut. He breathed deeply.

"Is he meditating?"

"I believe he is," Emilie bent over and looked the old man in the face. As before, we weren't able to interact with the scenario. We were like spectators in some kind of virtual reality. This wasn't a digital world, however. Whatever we saw had happened or, in whatever plane of existence these visions occurred within, were happening and unfolding before our eyes.

Slow and deliberate footsteps from outside the hut stole my attention. I turned toward the grass-covered doorway as a woman, shrouded in black, stepped through the door.

"Lady Ceridwen, is that you?"

"I am not your mistress," the woman said, her voice smooth and high-pitched, but accompanied by an echo as if she were speaking from the back of a cavern despite the fact she stood in the middle of the room.

"Who are you?" Morda asked.

"I've come to bless the lady Ceridwen. I've heard her cries of agony on behalf of her son."

"She is not here. She has left in pursuit of the boy who mistakenly ruined her potion."

The shrouded woman nodded her head. "I am aware of where she has gone. You mustn't tell her of my arrival. Only show her the cauldron when she arrives."

Morda tilted his head as his open, blind eyes stared into nothingness beyond where the woman stood. "The cauldron cracked. It is useless."

"I will repair your lady's cauldron. I will also bless it with a seed that can produce unlimited quantities of Awen."

"A seed?" Morda asked. "Where does one find such a seed?"

"It cannot be found within this world."

"Tell me, lady. Are you divine? Who, other than a goddess, could accomplish such a thing? My mistress is the greatest witch in all the land and even she could not create Awen in any way other than through the potion she tasked me to tend to for a year and a day."

"It matters not who I am or from whence I've come. Know only that when your lady returns, she must use the potion quickly. In this world, the potion can only grant the blessing she seeks for a short while. After that, the cauldron will bubble up with unending quantities of a deathly elixir."

"Unending quantities?" Morda asked.

"The seed I am placing within the cauldron is taken from the source of all Awen. It will never run out."

"But if the batch will soon turn to poison, why should we desire such a thing?"

"The fairies will soon arrive to retrieve the cauldron and take it to a place where it's contents might remain pure. If your mistress still intends to bless her son, she must act quickly. Do you understand?"

"I do, m'lady."

The woman bent over and placed each of her hands on either side of the cauldron. A red energy, almost like fire, had heated the iron of the pot to the point of melting, coursed through it as the woman pressed the cauldron together healing the crack.

The woman stood straight, reached into her cloak, and grabbed what looked like a small acorn. The seed glowed with a dim, green, energy. She dropped the seed into the cauldron then, grabbing a wand from within her cloak, she shot a spell at it. The magic was red. Infernal power, perhaps, but I couldn't say for sure.

Another shrouded figure stepped into the room. "Come, we must leave. Ceridwen approaches!"

The woman who'd cast her spell on the cauldron turned and removed her hood.

I gasped. It was Zepheniah, the Witch of Endor. "Come, Moll," Zepheniah said. "We must leave quickly if we hope to return to the proper time."

"Yes, we must!" Moll stepped outside and Zephania followed her.

Moll turned and removed her own hood. I'd never seen Moll before. She was an old woman, at least as old by appearance as the Witch of Endor. Her hair was grey and long, her skin loose and wrinkled. " I must ask, and I do not mean to question your wisdom, if this was truly the proper course of action. Many might use the power of the cauldron in the future to defeat those who intend to accomplish deeds aligned with our own."

Zephaniah grinned. "Perhaps we've set the stage for others to fail where we might succeed. You've been quite patient, Moll, after I brought you back from the dead. You've watched as I completed my plans to acquire infernal power. Our enemies will believe I raised you from this very cauldron, but it matters not. When we return, we shall go again to Eden and retrieve the cauldron and bring it back with us to our proper time. Once we've used whatever power to bless remains in Annwn, the unending corruption that spills out will be beyond measure."

"Will it not kill us as well?"

Zephaniah grinned. "I will see to it we alone remain unharmed. Once the poison fades and the cauldron is destroyed, the world will once again be pristine and ready for our new creation."

"And you're certain the fairies of the otherworld will take the cauldron to where we might find it again?"

Zephaniah laughed. "You're an incredibly powerful witch, Moll. Tell me, when we both lingered in death, did you doubt me, then?"

"I did. I was wrong to do so."

"Did I not tell you that with our powers combined, we could escape the infernal hell and return to the world?"

"You did, Zephaniah."

"This time, do not permit your doubts to question your resolve. The fairies of Eden will not hesitate once they discern such large quantities of Awen present in the hands of a witch like Ceridwen. When we return to Eden, at the time in Eden's history where I intend to take us, the cauldron will be waiting and ready for us to use."

"How do we prevent the fairies from simply following us to earth and taking the cauldron back with them again?"

"Once the Awen within it is spent and all that remains is the poison that we intend to use, the fairies will be unable to locate the cauldron.

We will have to act fast. The sooner we can spend whatever quantity of pure Awen that remains in the cauldron, the better."

"We must also use the cauldron while it remains pure to bring forth our sister. We promised her we would and she might play a pivotal role in granting us access to the Loa."

Zephaniah laughed. "I might be an old woman, even older than you, but my mind remains sharp. I have not forgotten about Odette. You are correct. She is essential, even more essential than you, Moll."

"Do not undermine my contribution to our cause, Zephaniah. Were it not for me, you never would have known where to find Cain to begin with."

The Witch of Endor grinned. "For that, Moll, I am grateful. But do you imagine that in the realm of the dead, you were the only one who might have knowledge of the son of Adam's whereabouts?"

Moll narrowed her eyes. "Of course not. But I am the only one who both knew about Cain and would embrace your plan. Do not forget, I might still evoke Lucifer and carry out my intention from the start if your plan falters."

"You will not!" Zephaniah snapped. "The world is mine to inherit! I will not give it to the devil!"

"Ours to inherit..."

"Of course, Moll. Forgive me. I am tired. We have much yet to accomplish. We must return to the portal."

# CHAPTER THIRTEEN

EMILIE AND I STOOD again near the tree line behind the Vilokan Asylum extension.

"Fascinating," Emilie said.

I sighed. "And troubling. If the cauldron has an unending quantity of poison, and if there's no chance now that the fairies can find it, do you think Elijah will be able to locate it?"

Emilie shook her head. "I don't know. Elijah isn't a common druid. His mother was a dryad, a protector of the Tree of Life. Awen literally runs in his veins. He found the poison before. I have to believe he will again."

"There's also the matter that these two witches apparently concocted this entire scheme while both of then languished in hell. We still don't know how Zepheniah and Moll escaped. We also don't know how Zepheniah forged a portal into Eden."

Emilie shook her head. "That is perplexing. There are gatekeepers meant to prevent precisely this kind of thing from happening. Still more, to forge a portal that connected to the time of Ceridwen on earth, another one that sent them back to Annwn at a much later date, and finally to take a portal that took them here, today, is unlike anything I've ever seen. Not even Elijah can do something like that."

"There's no way to create a portal like that without a gatekeeper?"

Emilie shook her head. "Not unless you happen to have access to a pet dragon."

I snorted. "Excuse me?"

"Dragons were the first gatekeepers of Annwn. Annabelle's soul blade can create portals like she does precisely because it is the spirit of Beli, one of the most ancient of the dragons, who dwells within the blade she wields."

"So we might not only be fighting three witches and a nasty Loa while trying to stop a poison that could kill all life on the planet, but we might have a dragon to deal with, too?"

Emilie shrugged. "It's possible. Thankfully, Mercy went to get Joni. If she can bring the Fomorian Wyrmriders to help deal with any poison that might reach the ocean, they might also be able to deal with the dragon, if there's one at all. Joni has often flown one of the wyrms, Nammu, to Missouri to visit her son."

"Sea wyrms can fly?"

Emilie grinned. "Wyrms and dragons are each creatures of the void by nature. The wyrms prefer the sea. They can fly like common dragons as well."

I was about to ask another question when Emilie raised her hand. "Wait. The trees are telling me something."

I bit my tongue and pressed my lips together. I didn't want to risk opening my mouth and distracting Emilie as she tried to discern whatever message Elijah might have been sending her direction.

"Elijah is coming here to meet us. The trees will lead the way. Whatever he has to say is too difficult to explain through the trees."

"We should return to the others. When he arrives, it would be best if everyone was present to hear what he has to say. Time might be at a premium, especially now that we know the cauldron might spill unlimited quantities of poison."

I explained to Annabelle what we'd learned. She also agreed that a dragon was the most likely way that the witches traversed between the realms. How they acquired a dragon, though, was an enigma. Do dragons go to hell when they die? If some do, Annabelle guessed they might've recruited one as a part of their escape from the hot place. Whatever the case, they had the cauldron here, now. Stop the end of the world first. Figure out how the witches tried to pull it off later.

I heard a large shriek. We all turned and saw an eagle flying toward us. Emilie ran to my truck and grabbed Elijah's clothes. The eagle landed on the other side of the cloak. Thirty-seconds later, give or take ten, Elijah stepped out from behind the truck fully clothed.

"What did you find out?" I asked.

"It took a while. The poison hadn't spread out far enough at first for me to see it."

"Where is it?" Annabelle asked.

"They've sunk the cauldron in the middle of Lake Ponchartrain."

I sighed. "If the poison escapes the lake and reaches the sea, we're in trouble. Let's hope the Fomorian Wyrmriders can act fast enough to stop that from happening."

Elijah shook his head. "Even if they do, it seems like the amount of poison seeping out of that thing is far more than I could have expected."

"I was able to discern a vision," Emilie said. "An acorn stolen from the Tree of Life empowers the cauldron."

Elijah sighed. "If that's the case, it will release untold quantities of poison. Unless I can convince the sapling that dwells in the cauldron to stop."

I cocked my head. "You can do that?"

Elijah shrugged. "I can ask. It won't be easy to get through all the poison to do it. That stuff is like a barrier. My will can't penetrate it."

"Any sign of the witches?" I asked.

Elijah shook his head. "They may be nearby waiting for us to make a move. If they get close to even a single tree, though, I might learn of their location."

A truck turned through the gates to the asylum. I knew the truck. It was bigger than mine. It made me jealous. It was Donald.

"Once he arrives, I'll fill him in on the details. We'll lead the wolves around the perimeter of the lake. Hopefully, the Fomorian Wyrmriders are already en route.

"How many void portals can they open at once?" Emilie asked.

Annabelle sighed. "I have no clue. It's always a risk. Their wyrm holes, or portals, aren't like the worm holes on the Stargate shows."

I tilted my head. "I don't know what that means."

Elijah grinned. "In the Stargate universe, matter can only travel through a worm hole going one direction. You're saying that a void portal won't only suck the poison in, it could release something, too?"

Annabelle nodded. "It's possible. That's one reason they rarely create such portals if it's not an emergency and hardly ever outside of the ocean. Agwe and La Sirene can direct the currents of the water against the portal to prevent most anything from escaping the void. If they were to create a similar portal anywhere else, they wouldn't be able to do that."

"Couldn't they fly out of the ocean and create portals in Lake Ponchartrain?" I asked.

Elijah shook his head. "The poison in the lake is too extensive. It might kill them if they tried. Even if they could, unless we could be certain that they could draw the poison into the portals faster than the cauldron creates it, we'd never be able to catch up enough for me to reach the sapling in the cauldron to stop it."

"Not to mention, there are at least three witches and maybe a dragon who have a vested interest in preventing us from accomplishing that."

"That's right, Cain," Elijah said. "I'm not sure we could dispose of enough poison quickly enough to do this, anyway. To do it while trying to fend off powerful witches would be quite the tall order."

Annabelle scratched the back of her head. "I still think our best bet is to focus on eliminating the caplata. It would break the control she has over Kalfu. If Hailey has agreed to the bargain with him, he'll be oath-bound to help us stop it."

"Are you even sure that the Loa could stop the poison from spreading?" Elijah asked.

Annabelle shrugged. "He's a demigod. If he takes control of the crossroads, he could effectively send the entire lake into another dimension."

"Another dimension?" I asked.

"The crossroads connect to many destinations that one might follow in the afterlife. From there, the poison might be sent to the void. It could go to Samhuinn, or hell. It might even get delivered to the garden groves."

"Any of those options would work," Elijah said. "In the void nothing is alive and nothing is vulnerable to the poison. In the garden groves, it would be purified and restored into Awen instantly."

Annabelle sighed. "We'd still have the whole problem of Kalfu ruling the crossroads when all was said and done. And we don't know for sure if the terms of his oath would require that he stop the other witches."

"One thing at a time," I said. "Besides, we don't even know that Hailey would agree to the bargain. Mercy doesn't seem to think she would."

Annabelle shook her head. "What other choice do we have? We can't get to the crossroads to warn her. We have to try."

"Alright. Here's the plan, then. I'll lead the wolves around the perimeter of the lake. We'll try to track down the witches. If you hear anything from the trees, Elijah, let us know where they are. We'll hear you. Just shout as loud and speak as clearly as possible."

"All this will be for naught if the Fomorian Wyrmriders aren't there. I'll confirm they're involved. If not, I'll have to devote all my energies to trying to direct the currents away from the ocean. When I do that, though, the poison will eventually start spreading even faster through the lake. Once it reaches land, there's no telling where it will go or how fast it will spread."

"I'll go with Cain," Annabelle said. "Can I ride on your back?"

I sighed. "I suppose so. If La Sirene hasn't assembled the wyrmriders in time, though, Elijah might need you to create another portal. It won't stop the spread of the poison, but it might slow it down."

"Like I said, I'm going to prioritize eliminating Odette. I have to trust that the wyrmriders will be there. There's no way, given the threat, they'd ignore the problem."

Donald stepped out of the truck and approached. "What's the story?"

"I'll fill you in on the way. Julie, evoke the flambeau. It's time to go."

# CHAPTER FOURTEEN

"Woo hoo!" Annabelle shouted, clinging to my fur as I took off toward Lake Ponchartrain, the rest of the wolves running in formation behind me.

I chuckled a little. I couldn't talk to her. Not while I was shifted. Werewolf riding isn't a privilege given to many humans. I suppose if anyone deserved the chance, it was the Voodoo Queen of New Orleans. Most humans who saw werewolves were too busy running away, or peeing their pants, to think about riding one.

Lake Ponchartrain isn't especially deep compared to the ocean. So far, the poison hadn't spread to the shore. My first thought was that it was spreading through the depth of the waters before it expanded outward. As we continued running around the shore, I noticed the green glow moving in a single direction. It was heading toward the ocean.

*The wyrmriders are siphoning the poison toward a void portal.*

I slowed down a moment. It wasn't one of the wolves speaking to me through our usual psychic connection.

*Elijah?* I asked

*Druids can speak to animals.*

I would have laughed if it wasn't for the fact that as a wolf my laughs sound more like cackles. *Well, that's convenient.*

*It seems to be working for now. The void portal creates a current of its own, drawing the water through it. With it, the poison.*

*Any chance it will pull through the cauldron as well?*

*The current isn't strong enough. Still, if we have enough time, eventually they'll drain the lake. If we can get to the cauldron, Annabelle should be able to cut a portal and send the cauldron back to Annwn.*

*How long will that take?*

*I can't say for sure. It could take days.*

*We still have to find the witches. I hardly doubt they're going to just sit back and watch us foil their plans.*

*Stick to the plan. Eliminating Odette may still be necessary.*

I sighed. *You realize, if we eliminate her, we're still leaving Kalfu in charge of the crossroads. If Kalfu sends other Loa to earth, there's no telling what will happen.*

*Still, Kalfu would be bound to help stop the witches.*

*That might not be necessary anymore. Not if the wyrmriders can handle this. We need time. If we can get the cauldron back to Annwn, and I can reach Odette, she may not find that Kalfu's true plans align with hers and the other witches.*

*Fair enough. I'll leave that to you and Annabelle. I'm going to focus on protecting the wyrmriders. They currently represent the biggest threat to the witches.*

*In that case, I think we know where the witches will be going. We'll get as close as we can to sea.*

We ran all the way to the CSK Rigolets Pas Bridge. The bridge crossed the waterway that connected to Lake Ponchartrain to Lake Borgne. A lot of people are confused why Lake Borgne is called a lake at all. It used to be surrounded by land. Coastal erosion over the last century or two now made the former lake an arm of the Gulf of Mexico. The Fomorian Wyrmriders had formed a void portal just south of the bridge. The current carrying the poison into the void portal was slow but constant. I couldn't see the wyrms or the wyrmriders. They must've been beneath the surface.

The other wolves stopped behind me as I looked all around. Still no witches. Where on God's green earth were they?

A tornado of green and red energies swirling together appeared in the distance, about a hundred yards south of the void portal.

*Elijah, do you see what I'm seeing? It looks like the same kind of magic cone I've seen you cast to teleport.*

*It's not me. Be ready, Cain. Someone or something is about to come through.*

The tornado pulled some of the ocean up into it. Out of it blasted what might be the largest living thing I'd ever seen. I knew dragons were real. Every culture on earth had testified to their existence in their own myths and legends. Even though I'd lived during the entirety of human history, I'd never seen one myself. Not until now.

The dragon had reddish-brown scales. Its wings might have spanned half a football field. It focused its eyes on our position.

*Run!* I screamed to the other wolves. We took off across the bridge as a torrent of flames consumed the spot where we were standing before.

I turned and watched the dragon as I ran as fast as I could toward land. The beast flapped its wings and circled around us. We couldn't move fast enough.

The next thing I knew, three more beasts, the wyrms, jumped out of the water. They were adorned with black armor. Each of them was mounted by a wyrmrider. The long blond hair on one of them suggested it was Joni Campbell, aka La Sirene. I didn't know who the two men were riding the other wyrms, but they all charged the dragon.

I reached the other side of the bridge with the other wolves and looked back. The flames hadn't destroyed the bridge, but it was probably only a matter of time before the fire spread and compromised its structure. For now, the wyrmriders had the dragon distracted. The wolves were safe.

*We have another problem,* Elijah said.

*What is it?*

*The current flow has stopped. The poison is now spreading out from the cauldron closer to shore.*

I huffed. *Do you know how large of a portal Annabelle could make with her blade?*

*I can't say. Presumably as large as she could cut it.*

*I have an idea. Can you pass along a message to Annabelle? I can't talk to her, not like this.*

*I can't speak to her, either. Not in eagle form.*

*Resume human form. Get on my back. I think we can do this, but we'll have to act fast.*

"I think I need to help the wyrms," Annabelle said, oblivious to the conversations I'd been having with Elijah. Short of other options, I growled at her. She got the clue and gripped my fur again.

Elijah dive-bombed toward me. He landed on me, his sharp talons gripping my skin just behind where Annabelle sat.

"Hello," Annabelle said. "I'm not sure Emilie would approve."

Elijah snorted. "Sorry, no clothes. It's the only way I could tell you what Cain is thinking."

Annabelle snorted. "He's probably thinking he doesn't appreciate your junk on his back."

I growled again. *Tell Annabelle to summon her blade. We're going to form a portal to Eden around the entire lake.*

Elijah chuckled. "I like it, Cain. Annabelle, he wants you to cut a portal around the whole lake. Can you do that?"

"I think so. He's thinking we can send the cauldron and all the poison straight to the Tree of Life?

"I believe so."

"One problem. The horizon of the gate will appear at the height we're at. I'm not sure that will work."

"Let me handle that. I think I can create enough magical force to push your portal down, enveloping the entire area."

Annabelle chuckled. "Alright. Well, I suppose the Tree of Life is about to get a healthy watering."

Elijah chuckled. "It can take it. We have to move fast. I'm not sure if the wyrmriders can keep the dragon distracted for long. Once the beast figures out what we're doing, it will probably disengage from the wyrms and pursue us instead. Those witches must be controlling it."

"Let's do this," Annabelle said. "Beli!"

When the blade formed in her hand, I took off back across the bridge. We had to create the part of the portal there first. The dragon's flames were already consuming the bridge. If the bridge wasn't viable by the time, we made it back around, the entire plan would fail.

Annabelle extended her blade toward Lake Ponchartrain as I ran as fast as I could. The other wolves followed. If the dragon attacked us, there wouldn't be much they could do. Since we didn't know where the witches were, though, there was a good chance they'd attack us at some point once they realized what we were doing. Not to mention, I needed Julie and her celestial flambeau nearby to keep me in wolf form. Annabelle could keep cutting the gate even if I shifted back, but as a werewolf I could run a good ten times faster than a human and with enough endurance to keep up my speed until we completed the circle.

I ran as close to the lake's edge as possible. Thankfully, it was the middle of the night. The traffic on the highways surrounding Lake Ponchartrain was light. There was only a small section along Interstate 10 on the western side of the lake that ran over the water. We had to run alongside the highway. I hugged the shoulder as close as I could so Annabelle could run her blade past the guard rails. A few cars saw us.

Chances were, people would see the dragon and wyrms, too. Exposing our existence to the public was the least of my worries. If the poison spread, it wouldn't matter, anyway.

Once we got past the highways, a wildlife preserve bordered the northern side of the lake. It was easier running there. It wouldn't last for long. The areas on the eastern side of the lake were more populous. Still, being in the middle of the night, I didn't think anyone saw us. Until an old woman stepped out in front of us. She was probably only a few hundred feet in front of our position, but she was right in the path we had to take to complete the circle.

"It's Odette!" Annabelle shouted. "She's trying to stop us!"

"Keep running!" Elijah screamed. He extended his staff. When he did, tree roots blasted out of the ground and wrapped around Odette's body. I ran as fast as I could. Just as we were about to pass Odette, a torrent of flames burst out of her body burning away the tree roots. She retrieved a small voodoo doll from her knapsack. She fixed her eyes on me.

I clenched my jaw. This was going to hurt.

Odette gasped and fell to the ground. Mercy had her fangs sunk into Odette's neck. Damn, that vampire had good timing.

I kept running. We were almost there. A loud thud shook the ground beneath me as the dragon landed right at the spot where our circle had started. It reared back its head and inhaled.

One wyrm crashed into the dragon. Joni leapt off the wyrm and pointed a wand at the dragon. She wasn't casting anything at the best. She was siphoning power out of it.

Elijah jumped off my back and tumbled to the ground. "Finish this! Now!"

I ran the rest of the distance, and Annabelle's blade completed the portal. Annabelle jumped off my back. A blast of golden energies blasted in a column toward the sky.

Elijah extended his staff and with a blast of green power, he lowered the gate over the lake, sending the whole thing, including the cauldron, back to Eden.

Julie released the flambeau. Along with the other wolves, I returned to human form. At least now Elijah wasn't the only naked man standing there. I turned. Where the dragon was before now laid a woman.

"It's Moll," Annabelle said.

Mercy walked toward the witch who once taught her the art, who arranged to have her turned into a vampire, and later betrayed her. Mercy reared her head back as if hocking a loogie. She spit at Moll's body. Before Mercy's saliva hit her, Moll's body disappeared in a flash of light.

"What the hell!" Mercy grimaced.

"Did someone take her away?" I asked.

"I'm not sure," Annabelle said. "Perhaps that's what happens to a refashioned body like hers when she dies. I've never seen anything like that before."

"I hope you're right. Can we be certain she was dead?"

Joni stepped up, her legs wobbling. Apparently, since she usually had a mermaid tail in Fomoria, standing upright was still a bit disorienting for her. "Good to see you, Doctor Cain."

I nodded. "Apparently Moll was the dragon."

Joni nodded. "I don't know how she did it. But, yes. She'd mingled her form with that of a true dragon in order to control it."

"We still need Odette," Annabelle said. "She was controlling Kalfu. If we can convince her to compel the Loa to abandon his challenge for the crossroads..."

I sighed and gestured to Odette's collapsed body. "Unfortunately, she's dead. You didn't see that?"

Annabelle shook her head. "She didn't disappear like Moll?"

"She didn't."

"Damn," Annabelle said. "That makes me think Moll might not be dead, and now that Odette *is* dead we might not have a way to compel Kalfu. Who killed her?"

Mercy snorted. "I had no choice. She had a voodoo doll. She was going to break Cain's back if I didn't take her out."

Annabelle nodded. "Understandable. You did the right thing."

"What would happen if we brought her back to life?" Cassidy asked. "Would she regain control over Kalfu?"

"She would," Annabelle said. "So long as Kalfu remains in the same form he was when she summoned him before."

"Bring her body back to Vilokan Asylum," Cassidy said. "I might be able to revive her. If she was resurrected from the cauldron, though, it's a longshot that I'll be able to pull it off again without the cauldron's aid."

I sighed. "Moll might or might not be dead. Odette is dead, but we wish she wasn't. To add insult to injury, the most powerful witch of them all is still out there."

"The cauldron is gone," Elijah said. "That was the priority. It might not be an ideal resolution, but I'd call it a victory. If the Witch of Endor still intends to destroy the world, she'll need a new plan."

I sighed. "Knowing the Witch of Endor, I suspect she already has another plan in the works."

"And if Kalfu seizes the crossroads," Annabelle added, "there's no telling what he might do."

# CHAPTER FIFTEEN

JONI TUCKED HER WET hair behind her ears. "Kalfu is contesting the crossroads?"

Annabelle nodded. "He's taken Hailey with him as his second. We believe he's under Odette's control. Or, he was."

Joni narrowed her eyes. "I have Legba's aspect. He might not oversee the crossroads anymore. He can still get there. He's taken me there several times."

"I don't know if that's wise," Annabelle said. "Legba and Kalfu used to be joined in one body. Any spirit that has inhabited a body can still find a home in the same body again. If Legba entered the crossroads, Kalfu might leave his current body and rejoin himself in the body Legba inhabits. If that happened, Odette wouldn't be able to control him even if we raised her again."

"Is that a bad thing?" Mercy asked. "I know Doc Cain here thinks he can get through to Odette, but there's no guarantee it will work."

I sighed. "Hailey doesn't know we've contained the cauldron. Now that we have, our initial hope that she might agree to Kalfu's bargain is no longer a hope at all. Were she to agree to it, it would be without reason."

"That presumes she hasn't agreed to it already," Annabelle said.

"She hasn't," Joni said.

I cocked my head. "How do you know?"

Joni shrugged. "Legba told me. He and I are tight."

"Are you saying that Papa Legba retains some influence over the crossroads? He must if he is privy to what's going on."

Joni nodded. "That's correct, Dr. Cain."

Annabelle scratched her head. "Even so, if Kalfu intends to challenge for control of the crossroads, Isabelle isn't sure that Mikah can hold him off alone."

Joni extended a finger and placed her other hand to her head. "There is a reason one must have a second to challenge for control of the crossroads. The one who issues the challenge cannot strike the first blow against the crossroads' current guardians. Legba said it's a part of the design he implemented when he established the crossroads."

Annabelle's eyes widened. "You're saying that Papa Legba *created* the crossroads?"

Joni nodded. "He did. He did it long ago, before even Cain was born, in order to prevent certain Loa from coming to earth if they intended to do people harm."

I cocked my head. "Then how did Kalfu get her to begin with?"

"He already had a human host. The crossroads only govern the coming and going of those who have not yet mounted a human."

I scratched my head. "If Legba created the crossroads, why would he create protocol at all for challenging for control of the place?"

Annabelle sighed. "Because at the time, Kalfu was a part of him. A darker side of his own consciousness. Legba always feared that Kalfu's strength would grow to the point that he would either take Legba over entirely or, as has happened, become a powerful Loa separate from Legba entirely."

I sighed. "You're saying he basically wrote the challenge protocols into the fabric of the crossroads because he feared that someday someone might need to challenge him?"

"That's correct," Joni said. "You're both right. Let's hope that Hailey's resolve is strong. Kalfu can be incredibly persuasive."

Mercy shook her head. "She'd never join him to strike the first blow."

A bright light flashed at the center of the crater where the cauldron and Lake Ponchartrain were before. A figure appeared in the middle of it.

"Who is that?" I asked.

Mercy cocked her head. "It's Hailey!"

In a blur, using her vampiric speed, Hailey ran to our position. "I'm back!"

Annabelle embraced her. "Thank God! How'd you get out of there?"

"When the cauldron returned to Annwn, a surge of power swept through all the otherworld. I sensed it. I knew that Kalfu's proposal didn't have legs. He dismissed me as his second."

"That's great news," I grinned.

"Not as great as you'd think," Hailey said. "He had to appoint another second. Someone whose spirit was already probing the crossroads, transitioning to the beyond. He's already replaced me."

I sighed. "With Moll."

Hailey nodded. "I fear she won't have the same reluctance to strike the first blow that I did."

Joni sighed. "Mikah won't stand a chance against them both."

Annabelle bit her lip. "If I sent Isabelle back to the crossroads, she might give him a better shot."

Joni shook her head. "Legba says that won't work. Since the challenge has been issued, while she may return in a host, it cannot be one that currently possesses the aspect of another Loa."

Annabelle sighed. "And I also possess the aspect of Ogoun."

"As a Loa myself," Joni said, "I cannot volunteer to serve as Isabelle's host."

I shrugged. "I could do it."

"There's one problem with that," Joni said. "While Kalfu needs to defeat both current guardians to claim full control and take the crossroads out of contested status, he doesn't have to wait to defeat Mikah before you arrive. You might be facing him one-on-one."

Annabelle bit her lip. "Isabelle and Mikah are not just partners. They are in love. She wants to leave as soon as possible."

"How are we going to send them to the crossroads?" Elijah asked. "I can't create portals to go there."

"That's a part of the problem," Annabelle said. "To summon my blade, Isabelle and I must be joined. If Isabelle leaves me and joins Cain, the portal will dissipate."

"Is there anyway to keep the portal open?" Cassidy asked. "Don't mind me asking, but I've been learning a bit about what happened to Nico. You know, my brother. Wasn't it a Loa by the name of Aida-Wedo who held the portal open to the otherworld and closed it again when my brother was stranded there?"

Annabelle nodded and sighed. "It was. Pauli possesses the aspect of Aida-Wedo. If he cast a rainbow through a portal, it would interface with the sunlight on the other side. If we were creating a portal directly to the garden groves, it would work."

"The crossroads are not illuminated by any light that would correspond with that," Joni said. "Pauli might be able to send a rainbow into your portal, but it wouldn't hold. There wouldn't be enough light to refract on the other side to hold it open. So far as I know, there's only one way to get to the crossroads."

"What's that?" I asked.

"You must enter the void."

I bit my lip. "That sounds worse than death."

Joni nodded. "As my gran used to say about all sorts of things, better or worse ain't neither here nor there."

I raised an eyebrow. "That's a lot of negatives."

"Double or triple negatives don't cancel themselves out in the south, hun," Joni smirked. "We pile 'em up, one right on top of the other, like hens in a coup. When you're born in these parts, you aren't beholden to no queen's English."

I grinned. She'd double-negatived me again. This time, I didn't have to question the meaning. Joni didn't have a thick accent. The little I knew about her, she grew up on a plantation similar to the one Annabelle did—where we now had the Vilkoan Asylum extension site. The Campbell Plantation was somewhere around Baton Rouge. "I take it you can send me there through one of those void portals your wyrms used before?"

Joni nodded. "Sure can. Now, I've been to the void once or twice myself. Since you're still all flesh and bone, when you go there, it won't feel like a void. The place is non-existence. You put a little existence into non-existence things just don't jive. You'll experience the void as if you're in some kind of place. For me, it was a cave. Seems to manifest that way to most people who go to the void still in their bodies. I'll send Papa Legba after you to pull you out of there. When he does, you'll go straight to the crossroads."

"And Isabelle can wield her power through me?" I glanced at Annabelle.

"You just have to give her the reins."

I raised an eyebrow. "I'm a werewolf, not a horse. I don't exactly have reins."

"I mean control of your body," Annabelle said. "Now here's the thing, Cain. Isabelle will be able to read your mind. She'll know pretty much everything you know. So old as you are, no offense, that's a lot of information she'll have to process. She might be a bit disoriented for a short while. Use your time in the void to get to know her."

I tilted my head. "I thought I didn't have much time."

"Time is irrelevant in the void," Elijah said. "You could stay there a thousand years and only a second might take place here, or in Annwn, or even at the crossroads."

I narrowed my eyes. "You're basically saying that I might be there for a while."

"Shouldn't take too long," Joni said. "Papa Legba knows you're coming. He'll know when you're ready and show up when he thinks you and Isabelle have mastered your cooperative powers enough to give Kalfu a run for his money."

"So when this is over, will I be a steward of the crossroads, too?"

Annabelle shook her head. "You won't. That honor still belongs to Isabelle. You're just the vessel she's using to defend against Kalfu's challenge."

I pulled my phone out of my pocket. "Alright. I'm ready to do this. I need to send Rutherford a message. Just in case, you know, I don't come back. We're having a baby, you know."

"Wow! Congratulations!" Annabelle exclaimed. "Are you sure you want to do this?"

"Thanks! And, yes. I'll find my way back."

Donald cleared his throat. "One of us could do it for you, you know."

I shook my head. "You're a new father, too. We all have reasons not to go. The family I'm coming back to is why I have to succeed. Call it motivation."

I sent my message. I didn't give Rutherford a lot of details. If everything worked as I hoped, I'd be back in what would seem like seconds to the people here in the real world. I suspected I had a much longer journey ahead.

"Alright," Annabelle said. "This is going to be tricky. Hailey, I might need your help. Elijah, too. I need to transfer Isabelle into a fetish, or an object of some sort."

Joni grinned. "I can siphon and amplify Elijah's and Hailey's magic if necessary. That's sort of what I do. You know, aside from riding sea dragons, ruling an underwater mer-kingdom, and kicking my husband's butt."

I raised an eyebrow. "You kick your husband's butt?"

"When he's outta line, you betcha!" Joni giggled. "Every good man needs a strong woman to bust his behind from time to time. That's how a good man stays a good man."

"Metaphorically speaking, of course," I grinned.

"Well sure," Joni said. "If you prefer metaphors to the real thing."

"I've found that most men, and human beings in general, aren't that much unlike dogs. We tend to respond better to positive reinforcement than butt-busting."

Joni smirked. "Well, of course, I give my Agwe a treat from time to time. But that ain't none of your business!"

I grinned and turned to Annabelle. "Alright. I'm ready. I've never been possessed before. How, exactly, do we do this?"

# CHAPTER SIXTEEN

"I'M NOT COMPLETELY SURE this is possible," Annabelle said. "I have an idea we should try."

I cocked my head. "You don't even know if it's possible to move Isabelle into me?"

Annabelle sighed. "Theoretically, it's certainly possible. Isabelle isn't bound to me like she used to be. She can leave. The problem is binding her to you. I presume you've never had anyone inside of you before."

Mercy snickered. "No shame if you have, Cain. Everyone experiments a little when they're young."

I signed. For a vampire of nearly two hundred years, Mercy had an awfully juvenile sense of humor. I'd be lying, though, if Annabelle's choice of words hadn't struck me in the same way. I just didn't have the gumption to say anything about it. "I've had no one inside of me. Not in any sense."

"Not that he'd admit anyway," Mercy grinned. "It's okay, Cain. You're in the company of friends."

Annabelle rolled her eyes. "Isabelle is a human spirit. She's powerful, sure. She can draw on the Tree of Life like Elijah. Human spirits, though, aren't meant to possess any body other than their own. When she was first fused to me, it involves some powerful, dark, magic.

Nothing any of us can, or would be willing, to use. Even if we could, we don't want to fuse Isabelle's and Cain's souls."

I nodded. "What is your idea, Annabelle?"

Annabelle scratched her head. "Hailey, I know this is a lot to ask. You can control the power latent in blood, correct?"

Hailey grinned. "I think I see where you're going with this, Annabelle. The life, or soul, coheres within the blood."

"The Bible says as much," Annabelle added. "My theory is that if you can make Cain's blood identical to mine, Isabelle will be able to unite herself to him as if he were me."

I tilted my head. "Would I be able to summon Beli, your soul blade?"

Annabelle shook her head. "No. To do that, you'd need Ogoun's aspect. If you had that, well, you couldn't enter the crossroads for the same reason I can't just go there with Isabelle and handle this fight."

"Presuming that works, why do you need my power?" Elijah asked.

"I'm B-positive," Annabelle said. "What's your blood-type, Cain?"

"I'm type-AB."

"I think you can see where I'm going with this. Our blood types aren't compatible. I'm no doctor, but I suspect his body, including his organs, won't respond well to this process. Since Isabelle will be disoriented at first, we can't trust that she'll be able to heal him right away."

Hailey pulled out her wand. "I can change Cain's blood to resemble yours, but it won't last. Over several weeks, his blood will gradually replenish."

"Several weeks?" Elijah asked. "I can heal Cain from the initial shock. Once he's in the void, I won't be able to help him. Will Isabelle be able to heal him at that point?"

"Isabelle isn't sure," Annabelle said. "She thinks she can, but she isn't sure how much of her focus it will take to keep him healed from the effects of the blood."

"I'm still a werewolf," I said. "I don't think this will kill me. My curse should sustain my life as long as it takes for Isabelle to either heal me or for my body to replenish its own blood supply."

"Are you sure this will even work?" Joni asked. "If Cain's blood starts to replenish itself, will Isabelle be able to remain within him? If she gets separated from Cain in the void, retrieving her spirit could prove challenging. Papa Legba warns that he won't be able to draw Isabelle to the crossroads if she isn't completely contained within Cain."

"I think once she's within him, it won't' matter if his blood changes. She'll adapt and he'll become a vessel she can inhabit more easily in the future."

"You think?" I raised an eyebrow.

Annabelle nodded. "I'm about seventy percent certain. When a Loa mounts someone the first time, it's much more difficult and jarring than it is for subsequent mountings. Isabelle isn't a Loa, so I can't say I'm completely sure this will work. I'm going with a better-than-average chance that it will work."

"Good enough for me. If this doesn't work, well, I suppose I'll have eternity to find a way out of the void."

"Either way, we must hurry," Joni said. "Every second we waste talking about it risks the chance that Kalfu and Moll will succeed to eliminate Mikah before Cain and Isabelle get there."

"Agreed," I said. "I'm ready."

"Cast your spell on me, Hailey," Joni said. "I'll siphon and amplify it. It should speed up the process."

"You might want to lie down," Annabelle said. "You'll probably lose consciousness during the blending process. I'd hate for you to bump your noggin.'"

I sighed and sat down on the ground. Hailey aimed at Annabelle with her wand first. She muttered an incantation under her breath. A chain of red energies shout out of Hailey's wand and encircled

Annabelle like a lasso. Hailey nodded at Joni. Joni pointed her wand at Annabelle and inhaled, pulling the energy in. Then Joni turned to me and blasted me with the same red energy. This time, it struck me like the kind of photon charge the Starship Enterprise might use to take down a Klingon warship.

I screamed as an intense pain coursed through my body. Another blast, a green energy this time, enveloped me. It must've been Elijah's Awen. It soothed the pain. My vision faded to a blur. Annabelle removed her necklace. She clasped it in her hands. A green glow poured out of her hands into the necklace. Annabelle placed the necklace over my head. Another jolt. It wasn't painful, but it was strange. Not a tingle, either. It was more like I'd just drank a twelve-pack of energy drinks.

*Hello, Cain. I'm Isabelle. Close your eyes. Rest awhile. I have some work to do... but... wait... your mind... it's too much...*

# CHAPTER SEVENTEEN

I'VE NEVER HAD SURGERY. I'm told when you go under anaesthetic you awake with no sense at all of how much time passed. I wasn't a deep sleeper. It had been years since I'd rested so well.

I placed my hand on my face. I felt a long beard. My other hand was touching what felt like a cold, stone floor. I touched Annabelle's necklace. I didn't feel any power within it. Isabelle's spirit was now completely within me. Everything around me was black as night.

*Welcome back, Dr. Cain. It's done.*

"Isabelle?" I asked.

*That's right. It took longer than I expected. Six thousand years of memories combined with my mind was a lot to take in.*

I started to sit up. I was weak. I could barely move. "What's wrong with me?"

*Your muscles have atrophied. It will take some time to regain your strength. I can lend you a little to help you along.*

A surge of energy flowed into my body. It started with a tingle across my brow and spread down my neck, across my torso and through my arms and legs. I pressed myself up off the floor, found my feet beneath me and stood up. "How long was I out?"

*I'm not sure. It's difficult to count the days. I've been pretty busy living out your life, experiencing all your memories as if they were my own.*

"I've been asleep for six thousand years?"

*Not at all. I'm a quick study. Besides, you don't remember every minute of your life. There were many hours when you slept. There were times your mind was gone, especially during your first several hundred shifts into werewolf form. Then, there are experiences in your life you've just forgotten with the passing of time.*

"Cut to the chase. How long, approximately, have we been here? We are in the void, right?"

*We are. I'd guess you've been lying on that floor for a hundred years, give or take ten.*

I gasped. "I've been sleeping for a century?"

*It's no worry, Cain. To our friends, barely a second has passed.*

My head was heavier than I was used to. My hair had grown long. Really long. "I don't suppose the void has a good barbershop nearby, does it?"

Isabelle giggled. *You have a better sense of humor than I expected. While experiencing your memories, I've had many good laughs. I can say this much. It's been an entertaining century.*

"Everything worked? We're bound properly? My blood never kicked you out?"

*It was touch-and-go for a while. By the time your body had completely replaced Annabelle's blood with your own, I'd already lived out several decades of your memories. Thankfully, there were many gaps in your memory, so it didn't take as long as you would think. Nonetheless, I learned enough to bond with you. I was able to remain within you and have been here ever since.*

"What about Legba? Has he come to take us to the crossroads?"

*Not yet. It will be awhile. I know you fully. You do not yet know me. We must learn to work together if we're going to defeat Kalfu and Moll. When we're ready, I'm confident Legba will come.*

I nodded. "Alright. Where do we start?"

*It's dark here. Let's begin with a simple fire spell.*

"A *simple* fire spell?"

*We must begin small. Our partnership is not like it was for Annabelle and me. I cannot take the reins and work through you without your cooperation. Our souls are not fused, so I cannot take full control of your body. You're going to have to learn how to use my powers well enough to defeat Kalfu yourself.*

"I'm guessing he's had eternity to practice."

*Not exactly. Remember, it was only a few years ago when Kalfu became independent of Legba. As powerful as he might be, he's yet to reach his potential. I believe if we train long enough, we might eclipse him in strength.*

"You want to train here, in this... wherever we are... for years?"

*We have all the time in the world. You are an eternal being. Your body can endure it. You will not age, thanks to your curse. There is no time here at all, in fact.*

I cocked my head. "There has to be. I just woke up. I'm not awake now. You just said what you said to me and we haven't started training yet. All that sounds like time."

*Everything we experience here is a manifestation of your mind. As humans, as embodied creatures, our experience of the void occurs within time constructs of our own making. Technically, though, the void itself does not experience the passage of time.*

I sighed. "That's exactly why I had to be the one to do this, I suppose. Don't get me wrong, it's not that I'm not looking forward to working together..."

*I get it. It's already been a long time for me. From my perspective, we're in the home stretch. For you, I'm sure it seems like we still have a long way to go. Think of it this way: now you get all the time you want to get better acquainted with my sparkling personality!*

I laughed. "I suppose it's a blessing in disguise that Annabelle's familiar spirit has a pleasant personality. At least, if my first impressions are right, you sure seem to be a pleasure. Still, there are people I love. I miss Rutherford already. To think just a few hours ago we were shopping for baby supplies."

*That's why we're doing this, Cain. Yeah, yeah, I know saving the world is a big deal. What's the world worth saving, though, if not for the people we love who live in it?*

I nodded. "My thoughts, exactly."

*First things first. Let's get some light in here. We need to start with the basics before we start slaying dragons.*

"Dragons?" I raised one eyebrow.

*Dragons are born in this realm. There are plenty here we can fight. If Moll kept whatever ability she'd gained to become a dragon, we may need that experience once we enter the battle for the crossroads.*

"Right. So I might have to fight a dragon while also dealing with a nasty Loa at the same time."

*Mikah will be there to help. Remember, Cain. You aren't the only one who has left behind someone you love. For me, I've been apart from Mikah for much longer.*

I scratched the back of my head, again taken aback by how much hair I had. "I hadn't thought of that. I'm sorry."

*You have nothing to be sorry for, Cain. I'm grateful you were willing and able to do this. It may be the only chance either of us has to save both the world and the person we love.*

"Alright, well, not like we have time that can't be wasted. I'd like to get started. Besides, while I can normally see in the dark as a werewolf, I can't see a thing here."

*The Awen I can draw from the Tree of Life isn't only the power that invigorates human or animal life. It is a part of the force that Bondye used when he made the world.*

"Bondye?" I asked.

*Sorry, I've been hanging out with Annabelle in the voodoo world too much. It's the name they have for God. He is the creator. The one who made the world, even as attested to in the same book where your story was first told.*

"Alright. That's interesting. What can I do with that information?"

*My magic can interface with all the elements. There is a spirit, a living force, that coheres in all things. That includes fire. Awen is a pure source of power. We can adapt it to many forms. You just need to visualize it. I can help you do that. I can place the images in your mind. If you can focus on what I'm showing you, the power I'm channeling through us should materialize accordingly.*

"I just need to think about what I want it to do?"

*Yes. Awen will create the spirit that holds the pattern for whatever you wish to make. You certainly cannot create something out of nothing. You are not Bondye. But any force that ever existed, provided we have enough energy to do it, can manifest as you will it. Provided, of course, that what you ask of Awen is realistic.*

"What do you mean by 'realistic'?"

*Fire occurs naturally. To establish a flame is simple. It's realistic. No matter how many times you've watched Star Wars, though, you cannot create a light saber. Those devices are a fiction. Even real items, such as a piece of complex machinery, do not occur in nature even if the raw materials that are used to form such devices might be natural.*

"Right. So I can't just create a bazooka to blow a dragon out of the sky."

*Exactly. Also, the elements must be present to work. Here, while there are not any elements technically within the void, this place you've manifested operates with all the raw material you might expect in a cave. There's oxygen. You can create fire. There is water. What's here you can use. Make sense?*

I took a deep breath. "Sort of. Maybe it will make more sense as I get some practice working with your magic. I'm not a sorcerer. All of this is pretty new to me."

*Understandable.* Isabelle showed me an image of several flames dancing along the wall of a stony corridor. *Focus on that. Channel the energies the best you can. A staff or wand would be helpful, but we don't have anything like that here. Focus the energy through your hand. It should suffice.*

I extended my hand. "Open palm or closed fist?"

*Whatever feels most natural.*

I nodded. I clenched my fist, focused on the image Isabelle gave me, and punched the darkness. Several flames burst on the walls along the corridor ahead of where I stood.

*First try! You're a natural!*

I grinned. "Thanks! I didn't expect this place to look exactly like what you showed me."

Isabelle laughed. *I've been here for a while. This place is a manifestation of both our minds. I've managed to get a bit of a look around.*

"How'd you do that? You've been inside of me the whole time."

*It's called astral projection. I can extend my consciousness outside of your body.*

"How far can you go?"

*I don't know. With Annabelle, I could go a few miles out. With you, well, I've been limited to these caves. Still, I've seen enough to know there's more than enough space here for us to work with.*

"Alright. Lesson one complete. I give myself an A-plus."

Isabelle giggled. *There's another corridor up ahead branching to the left. We'll try the same thing. This time, I'll give you pure Awen. Use whatever light you have to work with from the last spell to create your own visual of how you'd like the fire to appear along the walls.*

I walked forward. My knees were stiff. My muscles were weak, but Isabelle was still invigorating my body with a dose of her power. In time, I hoped I'd regain my strength. In time... right...

There was just enough light from the first corridor that I could see about twenty feet down the next. Isabelle's energy created a tingle on my brow. I imagined another flame like the ones I'd cast before on the wall. I punched my fist forward, and the flame appeared.

*Good! Keep going until we have the whole place lit.*

"The whole place?"

*The cave is a manifestation of our minds. I'm not a complicated girl. Given your life, and your profession, your mind is a labyrinth. This might take a while. But you know, like I said before, time isn't a concern. Besides, it will give you a lot of practice.*

Isabelle wasn't kidding. I did not know how long I'd been at it. I still had my phone in my pocket. Based on what Isabelle said, the battery probably died a hundred years ago. I had no way to measure time other than my basic senses. Had I been at it a whole day? Darn near it. I was exhausted.

"How much more of this cave is there to light up?"

Isabelle laughed. *You've barely started.*

I sighed. "You have got to be kidding me. I need to take a nap."

*A century wasn't enough for you, sleeping beauty?*

I snorted. "I can say safely that in over six thousand years, you're the first person to ever call me that."

I curled up on the most comfortable rock I could find. It didn't take long before I fell asleep. I woke up whenever my body had decided I'd slept enough and did the same thing for another day. Then, another day after that. Isabelle was my only company. So far as company went, she wasn't bad. She was funny, smart, and knew me better than anyone ever had. I could have certainly been possessed by a less pleasant soul.

I woke up for the third or fourth time since I'd started. "Isn't this enough? From my experience so far, if we've seen one cavern or corridor, we've seen them all. Besides, I think I've got this fire thing mastered."

*To truly master this power, Cain, you need to explore the deepest and darkest recesses of your mind. In this case, the caverns that those parts of your mind manifested.*

"Are we getting close, at least?"

*I don't really know.*

"How don't you know? You said you've astral projected yourself through most of the place already."

*Most of what I could access while you were sleeping. When you woke, this place expanded. I only explored your memories, and those corridors formed by your subconscious mind before.*

I grinned. "You're talking my language."

*I know. Remember, I have your memories. I've studied with Freud, too.*

"So, I've explored the caverns that correspond with my subconscious mind now?"

*Not at all. You haven't yet been willing to go there.*

I snorted. "That makes no sense. I've been working on myself for years. I know my subconscious desires and flaws."

*It's one thing to explore that part of yourself in therapy. It's another thing to do it here, physically.*

"Then take me there. Let's get it over with."

*Can someone else show you the way through your subconscious mind in therapy, Cain?*

"Of course not. One must be honest and willing to face their darkness."

*Then, perhaps, it's time to step into the darkness. So far, you've been casting light into caverns while still standing in the light of your conscious mind.*

"Look, some of these caverns have low ceilings. There are deep pools of water and pits that fall deeper than I could imagine. It's risky to walk into the dark."

*Don't your patients also face a risk when they explore the darker parts of their souls?*

"Of course they do. They might not like what they discover. Until they come to grips with the truth, they can't really shed light on it."

*Exactly. You have an advantage, Cain. The work has been done. You've confronted your darkness before and you've emerged as a better man. Do the same thing here, and you'll emerge stronger and more powerful than before.*

# CHAPTER EIGHTEEN

"Don't you think I should learn to do a little more with your magic than lighting fires before facing whatever waits for me in the darkness?"

*The magic of the Tree of Life does not flow according to my will or even yours. It flows when there is need to those for whom it is given that it might be used for the sake of that need.*

"Why, then, did I have to practice lighting fires on the walls day after day?"

*That was the most pressing need we faced. Whatever your deepest fears might be, unless being afraid of the dark is one of them, the Awen that flows through us will give you the ability to meet whatever you need to overcome your fear.*

I chuckled. "I'm not afraid of the dark. At the moment, I'm more annoyed by it than anything else."

*When confronted with a threat, there are two responses one might take to cope.*

"Fight or flight?"

*Exactly. Entering the darkness might seem terrifying. You can either fight through the fear or run from it. If you flee, you might avoid the source of your fear...*

"But I will not overcome it. You're right. I wish I could know what I'd face once I enter the dark corridors and caverns."

*Whatever it is, it will be familiar. If not to your conscious mind, your subconscious mind.*

I grinned. "Well, at least I know I won't be facing these things alone."

*Usually, with your patients, you are the one who leads them through their darkness. Now, perhaps, I can do the same for you.*

"Well, here goes nothing."

I stepped into a dark corridor until I couldn't see a thing in front of me. I took each step cautiously and waved my hands in front of me. If I was going to walk into a wall it was better that my hands make first confrontation rather than my nose. I found a wall on the side of the cavern. I held one hand against the wall while using the other one to guard my face.

I spotted a dim light straight ahead. I couldn't tell how far from me it was. Walking through darkness can be disorienting.

*Keep moving. Whatever that light it, it must be a part of your mind that harbors your fear or trauma.*

I started walking again. As I did, I felt the wall I was touching move away from my path. Or, more precisely, my path forced me to move away from the wall.

When I approached the light, it expanded around me. I looked down. I was standing in a field of wheat.

"Is this your memory or mine?"

*It must be yours. Does this look familiar?*

I sighed. "I used to tend grain fields like this one. Back in the beginning..."

I heard a scream in the distance. I took off running over a hill and saw myself, a rock in my hand, stained in Abel's blood.

"No!" I screamed.

My other self didn't respond.

*This must be hard for you to see.*

I nodded. "Of course it is. But Abel and I have reconciled. This is no longer the trauma it once was."

I turned and walked back in the opposite direction. I found myself back in the darkness. A tingle spread across my brow. Flames emerged on the wall, illuminating the corridor.

"Did you do that?"

*I did not. You did.*

"How? I didn't cast these flames with your magic."

*You didn't have to. This was a part of your darkness you'd already illuminated and resolved well before we entered the void.*

"So my magic did this?"

*In a manner of speaking. Remember, this whole place is a projection of your mind and mine. You made this place. It can take whatever form your subconscious mind intends.*

"Fascinating. That doesn't help me figure out how to master your magic so that I can fight Kalfu and Moll."

*To defeat them, you'll need more than magic. Magic is a tool. Is it weapons that win wars or is it the bravery of men and women who risk their lives? What you need to help Mikah and me defend the crossroads isn't magic. It's courage. I cannot say if we are more powerful than Kalfu and Moll. What I can say is that we have more heart, a conviction rooted in something deeper than the resentment and quests for power that motivate our enemies.*

I grinned. "How'd you get so wise?"

Isabelle laughed. *You've heard the tale of Ceridwen, Gwion, and the cauldron. Awen grants wisdom above all else. That was why Ceridwen set the young boy to tend to her brew for a year and a day, that she might grant her disfigured son a measure of wisdom that would more than compensate for the disadvantage of his ungainly appearance.*

"So it's some kind of magically infused wisdom? How does that work?"

*Wisdom isn't something that can be zapped into your soul. Wisdom comes with perspective. Wielding Awen, the magic of the Tree of Life, is to embrace the power that connects all living things.*

"So, Awen doesn't give you wisdom directly. It gives you perspective?"

*Perspective is wisdom. Human sight is limited. Imagine an immeasurable veil. What humans can see by nature exists on one side of the veil. The grander truth of the universe, those things imperceptible to human beings, exists also on the opposite side of the veil. Imagine that one day a great god stuck his big toe through the veil. Many people were struck with awe by the discovery. They revered the toe. They bowed down to it and believed they'd finally discovered the meaning of life. Over time, different interpretations of what the toe represented developed. Some believed that the toe was divine. Others believed it was merely a gift of the divine. Some believed that the toe was not a toe at all, but a stubby thumb. Over centuries, this toe became the cause of great division. They fought wars over the significance of the toe. The disputes could never be resolved. No one knew what was beyond the toe. While some claimed to know the mystery of what the toe was connected to, and gave their lives to defend their view, the truth was always beyond their capacity to see. They lacked perspective.*

"That seems toe-tally understandable."

Isabelle remained silent for a moment. *I see you're well prepared to become a dad soon. Allow me to continue. Unbeknownst to many, the deity behind the veil pressed his foot further through the veil until each of his five toes was visible to mankind. When this occurred, many new theologies developed. New arguments emerged. How could one possibly be devoted to one toe while also revering another, or even all of them?*

*Those who revered the first toe demanded that many renounce their commitment to the other toes. These are false toes, they claimed.*

"But they all smell the same..."

Isabelle giggled. *And so some believed that these five toes were truly connected in a mystery beyond what anyone could possibly understand. Some believed that all toes should be worshipped, that each toe ultimately leads to a whole foot. It is the foot, these universalists claimed, that is the great mystery that can unite the people. One people, one foot. Still, some rejected this as an absurdity. The toes, while similar in some respects, were too different. They were seemingly vindicated when the deity extended five fingers through the veil as well.*

"I can see where this is going. Even the universalists, the footists if you will, lacked a complete understanding of what unified all things. They might have believed all toes led to the same foot, but they couldn't imagine that the fingers that were revealed led to the same body."

*This is how humanity often behaves regarding eternal truth. We believe we've found the truth. We recognize what we embrace as God, but we cannot see the connection or possibly comprehend the unity of what we revere versus what others worship.*

"Are you saying Awen allows you to peek behind the veil and see the genuine mystery, the body that unites everything that's revealed?"

*Not at all! We are still human beings. What I'm saying is that through Awen we grow content to revere and honor the mystery itself. We perceive the connection of all things without the pervasive need to prove it, or understand it completely. We recognize our place, our limitations, and thus embrace an unlimited mystery that is greater than what the mind might grasp. The greatest mysteries are meant to be adored, not investigated. When we attempt to investigate, when use limited knowledge to define what is behind the veil, then determine our conclusions must be correct, we are bound to become fools rather than sages.*

"I've lived long enough to recognize that's true."

*Still more, if you were to see a person's toe or foot, would you imagine for a second that you knew the person to whom the toe was attached in any meaningful way?*

I shook my head. "Even if I just saw a person's entire body, I wouldn't believe I really knew the person. To really get to know someone requires time, conversation, and trust."

*Indeed. Awen places us into contact with the voice of the great mystery. It does not solve the mystery. It does not show us all that is true, all that is beyond our comprehension, but the voice gives us an ability to converse with the principle that unifies us all. Whether you've seen nothing more than a toe, a finger, or even less than that, the ability to converse with Awen gives us a greater connection to the great mystery than any could possibly discover through investigation. It is one thing to know things about the great mysteries. It is another thing to know the mysteries.*

"I can relate to that. I've often encountered people who'd judged me based on a single story, the greatest mistake of my life, that they've leaned about from a holy book. As such, they never considered getting to know me. What was the point? They believed they knew the truth about me and they could not be dissuaded."

*I believe the same applies to all of us. I was born the daughter of slaves. I became a slave myself. There were some who saw me as little more than property. I could be nothing more than a maid or, perhaps, a woman one day that might breed more slaves. There was one man, however, who took the time to know me. He bought me from my first master for no other reason than that he might give me a better life. He raised me as his daughter. He treated me as an equal. While I died before I matured, what made the difference between this man and the man who owned me first was that one man did not judge my worth based on his assumptions about who I was. He took time to get to know me and cherished me, even though he didn't yet know who I might one day become.*

"So, tell me, what did you learn about me during all those years you spent probing my mind and memories?"

*Less than I've learned about you in the last few days since we've had the chance to speak. I know everything there is to know about you, including your past, your history, your likes and your dislikes. Only now am I beginning to know the real Cain.*

I chuckled. "Well, I hope you've grown to like me as much as I've come to appreciate you, Isabelle."

*I like you very much, Cain. And I believe it was no mistake that you were the one best prepared to become my partner as we defend the crossroads together.*

I nodded. "Well, we best move on to the next corridor. I'm sure we still have a long way to go before Papa Legba comes to take us to the crossroads."

*We are, perhaps, much closer than you realize. Still, I agree. We should continue to explore the darkness until all is brought into the light.*

# CHAPTER NINETEEN

WE EXPLORED SEVERAL CORRIDORS that detailed images of my past. We entered the memories I retained from when I wore the infernal cowl. The Witch of Endor had given me the cowl after I'd sought her out looking for a solution to my werewolf curse. When I wore the cowl, it brought out and amplified the darkest parts of my soul. I'd suppressed many of those memories. The cowl's influence had taken my rage and turned me into a murderer several times over. Seeing those memories again, which I'd hardly dared consider, was jarring. Yes, I was under the influence of the cowl. Still, I was the fool who sought Zephaniah's help to begin with. I couldn't hide behind the notion that the cowl made me do what I did. I had to take responsibility for my actions. That was the only way to shed light on these dark chapters from my life. Yes, I used to be a vile killer. Until I accepted that, I couldn't defeat the darkness.

Ever since the Witch of Endor returned, the truth of what I'd done stared me in the face in a way it hadn't for centuries. Could I use the cauldron and bring the people I'd killed back to life? Possibly. Would that really atone for my sin? It couldn't. The people I'd killed had families, they had lives.

There weren't many dark corridors left. Still, until I entered each of them and confronted what waited for me within, I couldn't leave. We couldn't go to the crossroads.

I found what looked like a narrow tunnel. "Where do you think this one leads?"

*I cannot say. It is worth considering why this tunnel is so small. I think we've walked past it a dozen times and I didn't notice it until now.*

I nodded. "I didn't realize it was here. It must've been. I'll have to crawl on my belly to get through."

*Remember, these caverns were manifested here in the void by your subconscious mind. Perhaps something we've done since arriving opened this tunnel to you.*

"I imagine it's so small because a part of me doesn't want to enter it."

*I agree. This might be something that you've never considered before. The size of the tunnel might be a part of your mind's resistance to it.*

"A defense mechanism?"

*Maybe. We cannot know for sure until we pass through the tunnel and see what waits for us.*

I sighed. I didn't care much for tight spaces. I suppose you could say I had a mild case of claustrophobia. It's not uncommon. Most people do, to some degree. It made sense if whatever was on the opposite side of the tunnel was something a part of me didn't want to face.

I couldn't bend over to get through. I had to crawl. As I moved through the dark tunnel, my knees ached. I did as I had before, using my hands to check what was ahead. The tunnel narrowed further. I had to drop to my belly and press myself through it. A green glow at the end of the tunnel told me that there was an opening on the opposite side. There was something there I had to confront.

When I finally reached the end of the tunnel, it opened to an enormous cavern, probably the largest I'd seen since arriving in the void.

The green glow emerged from something obscured by a rock formation, a column that reached from floor to ceiling.

I moved around the column to investigate the source of the glow. I gasped when I saw it. A large cauldron sat there, suspended over flames. The green potion within was the source of the glow that illuminated the cavern.

"Is this what I think it is?"

*It appears to be the Cauldron of Rebirth.*

"How is this possible? Annabelle's portal sent it to the garden groves of Eden."

*It was my portal, as well. The blade we used to cut the portal required both of us. We did not see where the portal led.*

"Did you know this was here the whole time?"

*I did not. Usually, when Annabelle and I cut a gate, it opens to the garden groves. Not always. Perhaps we sent it to the void. Or, maybe, someone else did after you came here. There's no way to know for sure.*

"Are we even sure it's the real thing? Maybe it's a manifestation of my fear. It was just minutes before we came here that the cauldron threatened to poison the earth."

*That is possible. I don't know. I wish I had answers.*

"What am I supposed to do? I don't understand."

A sober tone echoed through the chamber. It sounded like a violin. As the song got louder, pink energies swirled around the room.

"Is that Emilie?"

Before Isabelle could respond, Emilie and Elijah both appeared in the room. I cocked my head.

"How did you two get here?"

"Where are we?" Emilie asked.

"I'm in the void. This is supposed to be a cavern that hides some kind of darkness in my soul I'm meant to explore."

"How long have you been here?" Elijah asked. "Emilie started to play the moment you left. This is where her bardic instrument took the two of us."

"Isabelle says I've been here for more than a century."

"A century?" Elijah widened his eyes. "Incredible."

I sighed. "You're telling me. Where is everyone else? Didn't your song bring the others with you?"

Emilie shook her head. "Not this time. Perhaps it was our guidance you required. This is a tale that has yet to unfold."

I scratched my head. "Isabelle's magic is green, like Elijah's."

Elijah nodded. "We both draw our power from the Tree of Life."

"Why does your violin produce a different magic? Is it from a different source?"

Emilie shook her head. "My violin was hewn from the Tree of Life itself. Still, what my magic reveals is different. It is still Awen, but it's revelatory. It puts us into contact with a different aspect of the Divine."

I chuckled. "So it's not a big toe but a thumb."

Emilie tilted her head. "Excuse me?"

I grinned. "Never mind. Isabelle knows what I'm talking about."

*It's more than that,* Isabelle added. *If my Awen is like the mind of the Tree of Life, this power is its heart.*

I pressed my lips together. "No matter. I suspect you're about to tell me what to do?"

Emilie shrugged. "I cannot say. We must allow the tale to unfold. What you need to know will be revealed in the proper time."

While Emilie wasn't playing her violin, the song she'd played before she arrived continued to sound. I looked around. An old man reclined on the floor. I'd seen him before in the vision Emilie shared with me before.

"Morda?" I asked.

The old man looked up at me, his eyes looking beyond me. "Is that you, Gwion?"

I looked around. Emilie and Elijah were still there, only now their forms were translucent, as if they were specters.

*Tell him you are. I believe you're playing a role...*

I scratched my head. "I am Gwion Bach."

"Apologies, dear child. I did not recognize the tenor of your voice. Perhaps my hearing now fades to match the deficiency of my sight. The flames do not feel as warm as they must. A year and a day has nearly passed. We must not allow the flames to fail."

"Is there any wood nearby to tend the flame?"

"Yes, yes. Don't you know? You gathered the wood yourself. I cannot tell you where you put it."

I snorted. "Right. Of course."

I looked around. At some point, the cavern had changed and now I was standing in the hut from the tale before. I stepped out the door, found a bundle of sticks, and tossed it into the flames.

The flames burst around the cauldron just as they did in the tale.

"You must stir the pot, dear child. It must not boil over. The first three drops are most precious."

I could see where this was going. What choice did I have but to see it through? I grabbed a long spoon off a table. I dipped it into the cauldron and stirred. As expected, the boil bubbled up and the hot potion splashed to my thumb. I instinctively raised my thumb to my mouth.

In the tale before that was when the cauldron cracked. It was when Ceridwen stormed into the room and chased the young Gwion as the two shape shifted into a series of animals. This time, a hand reached up from within the cauldron and gripped its edge.

A person climbed out of the cauldron. Then another person followed. I took a few steps back. Did I know these people? They looked familiar. I couldn't place them.

A dozen people emerged from the cauldron. Each of them fixed their eyes on me. Their faces were full of rage.

"Who are you? What is the meaning of this?" I asked.

A man stepped out from the rest. "I was a new father. My first-born son had been born just weeks before you appeared and stole my life."

A woman stepped forward alongside the first man. "I'd done nothing to ever harm you. I did not even know who you were. Still, you burst into our home and choked me until I died. Why did you kill me?"

One by one, the others stepped up and made similar accusations.

"I am sorry. I do not remember. I was not in my right mind. The Witch of Endor..."

"You blame a witch for your actions?" the first man asked.

I shook my head. "No. I do not. I am responsible. If I could undo what I did, I would."

"You cannot change the past!" the man shouted. "You must pay!"

"Guilty!" the people all declared in unison. "Guilty! Guilty! Guilty!"

The people surrounded me. They grabbed me and lifted me from the ground. "Please! Forgive me!"

*Do not be afraid,* Isabelle said. *What is going to happen must occur.*

The people lowered me face-first into the cauldron. The potion scalded my skin. I held my breath as long as I could. Then I inhaled. The poison filled my lungs.

These people were not wrong. I deserved this. It was just. Still, what would happen to me? Was I dead? I saw nothing but darkness now. I no longer felt the pain from the poison in my lungs. Nothing burned my skin. I was floating in nothingness.

"Where am I?"

*You are where we were before. We are in the void.*

# CHAPTER TWENTY

EVERYTHING WAS BLACK. WE were literally floating through nothing. The prospect of that, I must admit, befuddled me. How could *something* float in *nothing* if nothing really was... well... nothing? Philosophical questions aside, I wasn't sure what to do. Could I do anything? Isabelle was still with me. This was my sentence. I suppose you could say I was doing my time for the murders I'd committed under the influence of the cowl thousands of years before. Then again, how could I possibly do time in a place where time was nonexistent, along with everything else?

*So, a druid, a vampire, and a mermaid walk into a bar...*

I snorted. "How does a mermaid walk?"

*Suspend disbelief! It's a joke. The point is irrelevant.*

"Why are you telling me a joke right now?"

*Why not? What else are we going to do?*

I shrugged. "Wallow in pity and self-loathing?"

Isabelle laughed. "That's a crappy way to spend what might be forever. I'd rather laugh may way through eternity rather than be miserable."

I took a deep breath wondering, even as I did, how I could breathe in the void. Perhaps I wasn't breathing. Maybe it was an illusion.

Whatever. "Fine, a druid, a vampire, and a mermaid walk into a bar. What happened next?"

*The bartender asked the three what they'd like to drink. The vampire ordered a glass of O-negative. The druid ordered a glass of mead. Before the mermaid could order, the bartender slid her a glass of water. The mermaid looked confused. 'What's this?' the mermaid asked. The bartender grinned. 'I just thought you could use a breath of fresh air!'*

Isabelle started giggling.

I cocked my head. "What's the punch line?"

*Fresh air! Mermaids breathe in water! Get it?*

"I understand that. I was just expecting the joke to be, you know, funny."

Isabelle made a sound in my mind that resembled blowing a raspberry. *Don't be such a party pooper.*

"There's no party to poop on! We're in the void, Isabelle. Why aren't you more worried about this? If we don't find a way out of here, Kalfu will kill your boyfriend and take over the crossroads."

Isabelle chuckled. *We're exactly where we need to be, Cain. Where's your faith?*

"I don't know what you're talking about."

*The cauldron was real, Cain. It wasn't an illusion.*

"How do you know that?"

*Don't you sense it?*

"Sense what?"

*The magic! The Awen!*

I shook my head. "It feels the same as when you were lending your magic before."

*I'm not channeling any magic to you, Cain.*

"What are you saying, Isabelle?"

*The magic you sense now is your own!*

I cocked my head. "The three drops from the cauldron..."

*Exactly!*

I took a deep breath. "That's surprising. What good will it do us now?"

*How should I put this? I have a friend here...*

"A friend? In the void?"

*Yup!*

"How does that happen?"

*Well, you realize that the soul-blade Annabelle and I can wield when together is actually the spirit of a dragon that only assumes the form of the blade on earth, right?*

"She's told me as much. I'm not sure what the significance of that is."

*When we summon Beli, we call his spirit out of the void. Remember, dragons are native to the void.*

"And you're telling me that Beli is here somewhere?"

*Somewhere... nowhere... what's the difference in the void?*

I chuckled. "See, that's a lot funnier than that mermaid walking into a bar joke."

*Oh, come on! Would you have preferred if there'd been a werewolf who walked into the bar?*

I shrugged. "Might have made the joke more relatable."

*Give me a minute. I need to think of something funny about werewolves. You know, so I can adapt the joke...*

"How about, 'eat your heart out!'?"

*I don't get it...*

"When the bartender is taking orders. The werewolf says 'I'll eat your heart out!'" I slapped my knee, laughing.

*Because werewolves eat people's hearts?*

"Yes! See, that's funny, Isabelle!"

*Not really.*

I sighed. "Whatever! Look, your dragon buddy is here somewhere. Can he get us out of here?"

*Of course he can.*

"Can he take us to the crossroads?"

*If Legba allows it.*

"Why wouldn't he?"

*It depends if he thinks you're ready. He has a vested interest in our success, you know. He knows you can spend an eternity here if that's what it takes to make you ready to face off with Kalfu and Moll.*

I shook my head. "I don't know how much more ready I could be. There isn't a lot to do here. In the cave, we could practice. Here, well, there is literally nothing to do."

*All these nothing jokes aren't really all that funny, either, you know.*

I shrugged. "I know. But what can I say? I've got *nothing*!"

Isabelle groaned. *Alright. Well, if we keep telling bad jokes, maybe Papa Legba will relent. He'll figure it's best to risk destroying the world than spend an eternity having to hear us make poor attempts at float-around comedy.*

"What is float-around comedy?"

Isabelle chuckled. *Well we can't exactly call it standup comedy. There's nothing to stand up on!*

I grinned. "So, how do we find this dragon?"

*We need to speak his name aloud. He should come. It works that way, anyway, when Annabelle and I summon him together.*

"But I'm not Annabelle. I'm not exactly summoning him."

*But you have Awen. Since it's your own Awen, and not what I'm borrowing, you can speak to the dragon through it.*

"Like how Elijah can communicate with animals?"

*Exactly!*

"And we couldn't do that if I borrowed your power?"

*It wouldn't work. My consciousness is confined to your mind. My words would not escape. Only with your own magic, your own Awen, can your words connect to other creatures.*

"And all I have to do is shout his name?"

*Bingo!*

I cocked my head. "I thought Beli was his name-o."

*It is! My goodness, Cain. There might be no one here, but if you keep trying to make jokes, somehow, someway, someone will show up here and throw a beer at you.*

"I'm not the only one telling bad jokes!"

*Mine are funny!*

I laughed. "Alright, well, I'm going to give it a shot."

*Shout it loud!*

"Beli!" I screamed into the void. A tingle spread through my brow when I said it. I was using Awen. Did it work? My words didn't echo. They just disappeared into the nothingness that surrounded us.

*Wait for it... wait for it... there! Look straight ahead!*

I narrowed my eyes. "I see nothing."

*Use your spirit-gaze.*

"My what?"

*Druids can enter another mode of engaging the world. It allows them to see the magic, the spirit, that coheres in all things.*

"How do I do that?"

*Close your eyes. Allow the Awen within you to be your sight.*

I bit my lip. I still wasn't sure *how* to do it. I figured it might respond the same way to how the magic worked when I visualized flames appearing on the cave walls. When I connected to my magic, when Awen enveloped my gaze, I discovered we were not alone. The void wasn't a void after all. Nothing can exist in nothingness. That would be a contradiction. This place was real. It was another plane of existence. It was a different mode of being. For someone material, like me, it was as if I was floating through nothing. For creatures of spirit, for those whose being consists of magic rather than matter, this place was very real. Dozens of dragons flew around us. One of them had its eyes fixed on me.

The others parted to either side as if Beli was Moses crossing the Red Sea. Someone was on Beli's back.

I felt someone touch my hand. I turned. "Isabelle? Is that you?"

Isabelle nodded. "It's me, Cain. I'm here with you. In the spirit gaze, we aren't confined to the limits of your body."

"You're an astral projection?"

Isabelle shrugged. "Maybe. If I am, so are you. Look, someone is on Beli's back."

I tilted my head. An old man, his skin wrinkled and dark, wearing overalls and a straw hat, was straddling the dragon's back.

"Hello, Doctor!" the man shouted.

"And you are?"

The man laughed. "Well, I'm Papa Legba!"

I snorted. "You're the Loa of the crossroads?"

Legba shrugged. "I've been called worse."

"Most of the Loa I've encountered have more of that... deathly look to them."

"Pfft. Don't get me wrong, Doctor. I'm every bit as alive and as dead as the rest. Something in between, I reckon. I'm more of a straight-to-the-point sort of Loa. I'm not big on the tuxedos and bravado."

"Or the rum?" I asked.

Legba retrieved a flask from his front overall pocket and took a swig. "Well, I wouldn't go that far. La Sirene, you call her Joni. She said you'd be coming. About damn time, I'd say."

"Time?" I asked.

Legba grinned. "It's always about damn time when time itself is just beyond your reach."

I smiled. "So, can you get us out of here? We have a contest to win."

Legba pulled a piece of straw from his hat and placed it between his lips. "Yup. I think you're ready."

"How do I defeat Kalfu?" I asked.

Legba shrugged. "You'll figure it out. You have everything you need."

I sighed. "I thought you were a straight-forward kind of Loa."

"Did I say that?" Legba waved his hand through the air as he stared down at me from the back of Beli. "You know what I meant. I don't talk in riddles. What I told you isn't a riddle. It's the honest truth. You have everything you need."

"You mean Awen? The power I received from the cauldron?"

"I mean what I said. Kalfu and the witch who serves as his second have great power. The witch even managed to merge herself with a dragon from here in the void. The key to your victory will be to use what you have that the others do not."

"I still don't think I get it. Can you be more specific?"

"You know what I'm talking about. You can ask your question in a thousand different ways, and I'll still have a single reply."

"To use what's already mine."

"See! I know you'd figure it out!"

I sighed. "Right. Of course."

I didn't have a clue what Legba was talking about. I hadn't endured this journey to end up with nothing. I had Awen. I had access to the Tree of Life. That must've been what he meant. I just had to figure out in the heat of a battle the best way to use it so that Isabelle and I could channel our magic together.

"Mind if we hitch a ride?" Isabelle asked.

Papa Legba placed his hand on Beli's side and whispered something in the dragon's ear. Then he hopped off Beli and floated around us. "He's all yours!"

I wasn't exactly sure how to move. I kicked my legs, almost like I was swimming. Isabelle laughed.

"Just visualize yourself moving, Cain. You don't have to kick your legs like a frog."

"Ya'll might want to get out of spirit gaze once you're aboard Beli's back. You can't go into the crossroads like this."

"Right. Isabelle is one of the stewards of the crossroads. To bring me with her, I have to serve as her host."

Papa Legba nodded. I managed to move my body over the dragon and lowered myself onto the dragon's body. I searched for a place to grip.

*Slide your hands under my scales.* Beli said, the dragon's voice deep and booming.

I almost jumped right out of my body. I probably would have if I was sure I was in my body at all in the spirit gaze. I dropped the spirit gaze. This time, Beli appeared in the void with me.

"Isabelle, you there?"

*I'm here! Let's go kick some butt!*

Beli grunted. The dragon spread its wings and flapped hard. It exhaled some kind of golden flame out of its mouth and formed what looked like a portal. We flew into the portal. I took a deep breath. Two gravel roads intersected beneath us. The roads extended as far as I could see in four directions. With its wings spread out wide, we circled around the crossroads, preparing to land.

A loud shriek caught my ear from behind where we flew. Another dragon. I recognized it. I'd seen the dragon before. "It's Moll!"

"Where's Mikah?" I asked.

*Look below us!*

I leaned over as far as I could without slipping off the dragon's back. A young, thin, man stood there with what looked like a spear in his hand. Kalfu blasted magic at him. Mikah deflected it.

*We made it in time.* Isabelle said.

I nodded. "Now all we have to do is figure out how to win."

No sooner did I speak and a barrage of flames surrounded us from behind. Beli roared. I lost my grip on the dragon and fell from its back. I crashed into the ground with a thud. I looked up, sensing the power within healing whatever injuries I incurred from the fall.

Kalfu cocked his head. "Well, how about this? The Son of Adam challenges me?"

"Isabelle is with me. We're here to defend the crossroads. You're the one who challenged us, Kalfu."

# CHAPTER
# TWENTY-ONE

I FOCUSED ON KALFU and visualized the power of Isabelle's Awen and mind combining to envelop the Loa in a column of flames. I punched my fist in Kalfu's direction. The flames blasted up from the ground to the skies.

"Isabelle?" Mikah asked.

"She's here," I glanced back at the young man who must've been Isabelle's boyfriend and co-guardian of the crossroads. "She's missed you."

"You need to run!" Mikah said.

I shrugged. "You really think he'll survive that?"

"Kalfu has absorbed every magical attack I've tried against him! It's almost like he's a siphon!"

"You mean like Joni? La Sirene, I mean?"

Mikah nodded. "Like I said, run!"

I took off following Mikah. I glanced up at the skies. Moll was dive-bombing toward our position. Still, in dragon form, smoke poured from her nostrils. Beli circled overhead, watching from afar.

"Beli!" I screamed.

*He cannot assist. It is against the rules. He is not one of the guardians here.*

I screamed as a blast of flames like the one I'd cast on Kalfu before now shot toward us out of Kalfu's cane. Mikah turned, grabbed me, and pulled me to the ground. He punched the ground and a sink-hole formed beneath us. We fell into it just as the fire shot past us.

"How in the world are we supposed to stop him?"

Mikah sighed. "I don't know. We were at something of a stalemate. It seems he can only attack us if we try to strike him first. I'm not sure why."

"What about Moll?"

"The dragon?"

"She's a witch. I don't know how she did it. She somehow mingled her essence with a dragon's in the void."

"She's a different story. I've been fighting her off the best I could."

"You have Ogoun's aspect, correct?"

Mikah nodded. "That's right."

"My junior nurse has the same ability. I assume you're strong, right? Isabelle said you could lift a few thousand pounds."

"Well, I don't mean to brag, but..."

I chuckled. "I get it. Can you throw a boulder at the dragon?"

Mikah sighed. "Tried that. I can knock the dragon out of the sky, but before I can get to the beast to crush its head, the damn thing just disappears. A few seconds later, it's right back in the skies."

"Moll is a witch. She has access to magic. I'm sure it's a spell of some kind."

*Cain, remember what Legba said...*

"I don't know what he meant, Isabelle!"

"What did Legba say to you?"

"You can hear her?"

"Of course I can. She's my girl."

I bit my lip. "I don't know how that works. Whatever. Legba said to use the one thing I had that they didn't. I thought it meant Awen. They have magic, but they don't have the same magic."

"There has to be a way," Mikah said. "Papa Legba wouldn't have sent you here if you couldn't help me defeat them."

I peeked over the edge of the sinkhole. "Damn it! That dragon is diving at us!"

Mikah nodded and thrust his fist into the ground again. This time, we sank deeper as another blast of fire blasted against the top of the sinkhole. Thankfully, the flames didn't penetrate.

A tingle spread across my brow.

*What was that? I felt it through you... It wasn't Awen...*

"It was my curse."

"You're Cain, right?" Mikah asked.

I nodded.

"I thought I recognized you. I used to be a student at the Voodoo Academy. You're a werewolf, right?"

"I am. All I can figure is that Moll must be carrying some kind of infernal relic. That must be how she maintains a dragon's form."

*That's it! That's what Legba was talking about! Fight them as a wolf, Cain!*

"Do you think that will allow me to defeat Kalfu, too?"

*It's worth a shot!*

"Mikah. Do you think you could throw me as far as you could throw a boulder?"

Mikah grinned. "Sure. You weigh less than most of the rocks I've tossed at the dragon so far."

"I need you to throw me at the dragon. When I get close enough to her, I'll shift. I'll try to mount her and take her out from the skies."

*You may only have one shot at this. If you don't kill her straight away, there's no way she'll let you get close to her again.*

I nodded. "One shot is all we need. Let's just hope my jaws are strong enough to pierce a dragon's hide."

*Use your magic if you need to. Awen can enhance your strength. Let it flow through your body.*

"Alright. I hope you have a good aim. I won't be able to redirect my flight path. Try to throw me when Moll circles around. If she sees me coming, she might get out of the way."

Mikah and I peeked over the top of the sinkhole. Moll was already circling around, likely preparing to come back at us again with another blast.

"This is our chance. We have to do it now!" I shouted.

Mikah heaved me up over his head, then with a force that I hadn't expected, threw me like a missile through the air. The breeze struck my face as I flew toward Moll. The tingle spread throughout my body as I drew near to her position. I shifted into werewolf form and caught the dragon by the neck.

Moll shook her body, but my grip was firm. I allowed my magic and Isabelle's to combine to enhance my strength and sank my teeth into her neck. Blood poured out from the wound. The dragon flailed through the air. I lost my grip with my paws and nearly fell off the side. I took another bite, just as I started to fall, and caught the dragon by the front of the neck.

The dragon screeched as its body went limp and together we went tumbling down to the ground. With a loud thud, our bodies smashed into the gavel at the center of the crossroads.

I used more Awen to heal whatever injuries I sustained, but the impact was jarring. My vision was blurred. The dragon shifted back into its human form. Moll was dead. My cowl, the one that the Witch of Endor has used to siphon infernal power from me before, was on her head.

I pressed myself up on all fours, fixed my eyes on Kalfu, and snarled.

The cowl on Moll's head exploded in a force I'd never before seen. Again, I used Awen to shield me. The healing power of its magic restoring me even as hellfire coursed over me. When the flames subsided, I returned to human form. The cowl was gone.

A boulder flew at the Loa. It bounced off of Kalfu's shield, but the force was enough to cause him to stumble.

"No! You can't make me do it!" Kalfu screamed.

I cocked my head. "Can't make you do what?"

"This is our only opportunity!" Kalfu shouted again.

His forehead red and his eyes aglow to match, Kalfu looked at me and then at Mikah. "I forfeit."

The Loa disappeared in a tornado of red energies.

"We did it!" Mikah shouted.

*Hell yeah!* Isabelle exclaimed.

"I don't understand," I said. "Why did he give up?"

A power left my body. Isabelle appeared in front of me. She looked as corporeal as any human. She looked at me and grinned. "I think our friends must've had something to do with that. It is done, Cain. The crossroads are secure."

A blast of green energies arrested my attention. In the middle of the crossroads, Papa Legba appeared, a wide grin splitting his face.

"I told you, Doctor Cain. You had what you needed."

"I don't understand. What happened to Kalfu?"

"He was under the compulsion of a caplata. Your friends resurrected her. I believe it was the one known as Cassidy who pulled it off. With Annabelle's and Hailey's help, they restored her with her will only partially intact. It was enough for them to manipulate her as any vodouisant might when restoring the undead."

"They used bokor magic to do it?"

Papa Legba grinned. "It's a fine line. I'd say what they did was proper to any noble vodouisant."

"And Cassidy was able to compel Kalfu to give up his challenge over the crossroads?"

"It appears that way," Papa Legba said. "I must warn you, however, these whom you defeated today were but puppets in another witch's schemes."

"The Witch of Endor?" I asked.

Papa Legba nodded. "I cannot tell you what she will do next. If I were you, I'd be on your guard. Thankfully, you have a few extra tools in your toolbox you can use to stop her."

I grinned. "You mean I get to keep my new magic?"

"You consumed three drops from the cauldron. Of course you do. That's how it works."

# CHAPTER
# TWENTY-TWO

WHO WOULD HAVE THOUGHT that leaving the crossroads was so simple? Getting there? That was another story. To leave, all you had to do was pick the road you wanted to follow and make the trek. Of course, I had to make sure I took the right road. One of them was a path to the afterlife, aka death. Another was literally a highway to hell. I doubted the song played when you walked down it, but I wasn't in any hurry to find out. I took the road that led back to my regular life. Some might think I would make another choice after six thousand years. There was a time when I very well would have. I was eager to get back to Rutherford. I was looking forward to the family we were building. At least for now, I was confident that the world was going to remain a habitable place.

I didn't know where the Witch of Endor was or why she never showed her face during this entire ordeal. Was she vulnerable in some way? Is that why she had to resurrect others who shared her goals, pulling their strings from a distance? That was my theory. Until we actually found her, we couldn't know for sure. Nor could we be certain what she'd do next.

I reappeared near Lake Ponchartrain. Elijah and Emilie were waiting for me. I looked around. The lake had already filled.

"Welcome back," Elijah said. "Since you're here, I presume it was a success?"

I nodded. "The crossroads are secure. I thought when I returned, only a few moments would pass."

"We had to change the plans," Emilie said. "After they threw you into the cauldron, the vision faded, but the cauldron itself remained. We weren't technically in the void. We were in the vision that my violin revealed. It's quite remarkable what happened."

I shrugged. "What happened?"

"The violin always shows us what we need to know. In this instance, it brought you into the same vision although you were on an entirely different plane of existence."

"Once we knew the cauldron was in the void, well, the wyrmriders entered the void to retrieve it. They brought it back here. Cassidy used her abilities, combined with Annabelle and a few mambos of the Ghede aspect, and they figured out how to resurrect Odette."

I nodded. "Papa Legba explained she was restored with her soul intact but her will bound to Annabelle's control."

Elijah shrugged. "I don't do voodoo. It's a little outside my wheelhouse. That's basically what happened."

"Still, why didn't I end up returning here the moment I left like we thought was going to happen?"

Elijah smiled. "Some mysteries are better adored than investigated."

"Isabelle said something a lot like that when we were in the void!"

"It's something my father used to say. I've repeated it a few times. I suppose it's no surprise that Isabelle picked it up somewhere along the way. She and I tap into the same source of power."

"It seems you do now as well," Emilie said.

I scratched the back of my head. "It's a work in progress. I tasted the three drops from the cauldron in the vision. I had a lot of practice casting fire in the cave with Isabelle. I healed myself a couple of times in the crossroads battle. I have a feeling there's still a lot to learn."

"I'd be happy to help however I can. Now, though, we really must return home. I have a son who is also a powerful druid. He has an important destiny ahead. However, if you ever are in our neck of the woods, you are free to stay with our order and learn as long as you might."

"Perhaps I shall take you up on your offer soon. Today, though, I remain responsible for many wolves and others who need my services at the Vilokan Asylum. The Witch of Endor remains at large. Is there nothing you can teach me, now?"

"The druid way is not what you think. We do not have prescribed spells or rituals that produce a definite result. Ours is more a communion with the spirits of the earth. Awen will show you your path."

"But surely there is more I can learn."

Elijah nodded. "You can. And you will. However, I had very little guidance when my connection to the Tree of Life was realized. My parents were powerful druids, but died when I was young. There were a few mishaps along the way..."

Emilie chuckled. "When we were seniors in High School, Elijah once sprouted a tree in the middle of the interstate during morning rush hour."

"That must have been quite the scene!"

"I think there are still a few photographs of the incident circulating on conspiracy theory websites." Elijah rested his hand on my back. "Eventually, I found my way. You will, too. Know only this. There are many paths. None are predetermined. You may choose your path even as your path has chosen you."

My phone battery was dead. That didn't really matter. When I shifted into wolf form in mid-air my clothes, along with my phone, fell more than a hundred feet. My screen protector failed.

Given the dim light rising in the east, it was early morning. I had to get back to work. Given what I'd been through, though, I figured Annabelle would understand if I took the day off. I'd probably regret it later. Work tended to pile up in my absence. Nonetheless, there was only one person I wanted to see.

"Honey, I'm home!"

"Another night saving the world?"

I grinned as I embraced Rutherford. "Of course. I know it's only been a single night for you. For me, it's been much longer."

"Longer? How is that?"

"It's a long story."

"Something looks different about you."

I chuckled. "Don't like the hair and beard?"

Rutherford shrugged. "I've never found Chia Pets attractive before, but you know, there's a first time for everything."

I rolled my eyes. "Hilarious. Just, hilarious."

"Really, though. What happened? A werewolf shift gone wrong?"

"Where I had to go, several days passed while less than a full night passed here."

"It happens," Rutherford shrugged.

"It *happens?*" I raised an eyebrow.

"Honey, when you've worked with supernaturals as long as I have, time-distortion isn't an entirely unfamiliar phenomenon." Rutherford narrowed her eyes and tilted her head. "There's something else that's changed about you, too. Something more than your hair. It's like there's a hint of green to your eyes."

"I absorbed some magic from the Cauldron of Rebirth."

"You were poisoned?" A look of concern flashed across Rutherford's face.

"No. I mean, I was. Sort of. I was blessed with the magic of the cauldron then thrown into the left-over poison part. Like I said, it's a long story. I'd be happy to tell you more about it once I have a little food in my stomach.

"Why don't you sit down? I'll make you some breakfast."

"Nothing extravagant. A bowl of oatmeal would be fine."

"Oatmeal?" Rutherford raised an eyebrow.

"I haven't eaten in days. I don't think I could stomach much more than that."

"Days? What are you talking about?"

I took a seat at the kitchen table. "I told you it's a long story."

Rutherford scooped some oats into a bowl, added water, and popped into the microwave. "You're late for work, you know."

I nodded. "Given what I've been through, I'm sure Annabelle will understand if I'm a little late."

Rutherford grinned. "From what I've heard, you entered the void. You defeated a caplata who was supposed to be dead. You overcame Moll. Also, dead. And you banished Kalfu from the crossroads."

I shook my head. "Mercy was the one who killed the caplata. The rest is accurate. Annabelle called you, I presume?"

"Of course she did!"

I laughed. "Until now, dealing with these necromancers, it was all people who'd haunted my past who came back. This time, it was several powerful witches who all had designs on destroying the world."

Rutherford shrugged. "And a nasty Loa."

"Right. It was like every bad guy... or gal... who ever had designs on destroying the world got together to make a second run at it."

"Some sequels never should be made."

I snorted. "Except in this case, the sequel rivaled the original."

Rutherford giggled. "*The Evil Empire Strikes Back*!"

I smiled. "I was thinking the *Injustice League*."

"Good one! How about *The League of Extraordinary Assholes*?"

I pinched my chin. "Not bad. I suppose it was a literal night of the living dead. Thankfully, a lot of the heroes who've saved the world before also came together at just the right time."

"They also had help, you know. The last time they defeated these villains, they didn't have Cain leading the way."

I grinned. "I suppose I helped a little."

"You're too modest," Rutherford said as the microwave beeped. She retrieved my bowl of oatmeal, added a scoop of brown sugar, and set it in front of me. "You did what no one else could."

I shrugged. "Modesty is the best policy."

Rutherford squinted. "I thought honesty was the best policy."

I took a bite of my oatmeal. I didn't bother to swallow before I blurted out my reply. "Yup. That too."

"Jessie already expects you to take the day off. Annabelle asked her to cover for you. Now that you've saved the world, how do you feel about joining me at my first midwife appointment?"

I grinned. "I'd like that. I didn't know you'd already chosen a midwife or doctor."

"It's not a done deal. There's a mambo in Vilokan who is also an experienced midwife. I've heard good things. I'd like to visit with her and hear about her process."

"Donald had a doctor that he and his wife recommend as well."

"We can see both. If we aren't comfortable with either of them, we can keep looking. I honestly never considered until recently that having a baby was a possibility. At my age, this might be our only chance."

I shrugged. "You're not that old."

"I'm in my forties, Cain. By normal human standards, that's on the upper-end of a woman's childbearing age. Whatever choice we make, I want to make sure it's the best choice for the baby. This might be our only chance at this."

"Certainly," I said. "We'll decide together, but I think it's most important that you're comfortable with the choice. I'll support whatever you decide."

Rutherford bit her lip. "I hope that applies to other decisions regarding the baby as well."

"I'd like to have input on the name." I scooped another spoonful of oatmeal into my mouth.

"Of course. I wasn't talking about the baby's name."

I tilted my head. "What do you mean?"

Rutherford's eyes shifted left and right. "If a few dozen boxes show up at our door over the next couple of days, don't be surprised."

"A *few* dozen?" I dropped my spoon into my bowl.

"I couldn't help myself! Once I started looking, I just couldn't stop buying things."

"Please, just tell me it's things we really need."

Rutherford snorted. She pulled out her phone, opened up our Amazon order history, and slid it across the table.

"A butt-wipe warmer? Seriously?"

"Would you want to use ice-cold wipes? Put an ice cube in your butt hole and see how much you like it."

I shook my head. "That's not at all equivalent to using room-temperature wipes. What about a crib? I don't see a crib in here."

"I wanted to look at those in person. It's not a rush. We'll find one. If we don't, we can always co-sleep."

I rubbed my forehead. "I really wish we wouldn't. Trust me, once you start that habit, you won't be able to break it until puberty."

"That's a bit of an exaggeration, Cain."

"I'm serious. I've done this before, remember? My fifth wife decided to co-sleep with our firstborn. We had to kick that boy out of our bed about the time he sprouted arm-pit hair."

Rutherford laughed. "We'll find a crib. Don't worry about it."

I continued scrolling through the list of items Rutherford ordered. "So, a crib isn't an immediate priority, but a smart-phone activated rocker was necessary? I don't even have a phone."

"What happened to your phone?"

I bit my lip. "I shifted into wolf form about a hundred feet over a gravel road. The phone fell to the ground with my clothes. It didn't survive."

"We can get you another one. It will be convenient to be able to adjust the rocker from the other room! Think about it, we can listen to the baby monitor. If the baby is fussing, we can adjust the rocker and get him, or her, back to sleep."

"Why did you order the Peepee Teepee? We don't even know if our baby is going to be a boy or a girl."

"Amazon has a generous return policy. We have to be prepared!"

## The End
## To Be Continued in Cain's Cobras

# ABOUT THE AUTHOR

**Theophilus Monroe** is a fantasy author with a knack for real-life characters whose supernatural experiences speak to the pangs of ordinary life. After earning his Ph.D. in Theology, he decided that academic treatises that no one will read (beyond other academics) was a dull way to spend his life. So, he began using his background in religious studies to create new worlds and forms of magic–informed by religious myths, ancient and modern–that would intrigue readers, inspire imaginations, and speak to real-world problems in fantastical ways.

When Theophilus isn't exploring one of his fantasy lands, he is probably playing with one of his three sons, or pumping iron in his home gym, which is currently located in a 40-foot shipping container.

He makes his online home at www.theophilusmonroe.com. He loves answering reader questions—feel free to e-mail him at theophilus@theophilusmonroe.com if the mood strikes you!

# ALSO BY THEOPHILUS MONROE

## Gates of Eden Universe

### The Druid Legacy
*Druid's Dance*
*Bard's Tale*
*Ovate's Call*
*Rise of the Morrigan*

### The Fomorian Wyrmriders
*Wyrmrider Ascending*
*Wyrmrider Vengeance*
*Wyrmrider Justice*
*Wyrmrider Academy (Exclusive to Omnibus Edition)*

### The Voodoo Legacy
*Voodoo Academy*
*Grim Tidings*
*Death Rites*
*Watery Graves*
*Voodoo Queen*

## The Legacy of a Vampire Witch
*Bloody Hell*
*Bloody Mad*
*Bloody Wicked*
*Bloody Devils*
*Bloody Gods*

## The Legend of Nyx
*Scared Shiftless*
*Bat Shift Crazy*
*No Shift, Sherlock*
*Shift for Brains*
*Shift Happens*
*Shift on a Shingle*

## The Vilokan Asylum of the Magically and Mentally Deranged
*The Curse of Cain*
*The Mark of Cain*
*Cain and the Cauldron*
*Cain's Cobras*
*Crazy Cain*
*The Wrath of Cain*

## The Blood Witch Saga
*Voodoo and Vampires*
*Witches and Wolves*
*Devils and Dragons*
*Ghouls and Grimoires*
*Faeries and Fangs*
*Monsters and Mambos*

*Wraiths and Warlocks*
*Shifters and Shenanigans*

**The Fury of a Vampire Witch**
*Bloody Queen*
*Bloody Underground*
*Bloody Retribution*
*Bloody Bastards*
*Bloody Brilliance*
*Bloody Merry*
*More to come!*

**The Druid Detective Agency**
*Merlin's Mantle*
*Roundtable Nights*
*Grail of Power*
*Midsummer Monsters*
*More to come!*

**Sebastian Winter**
Death to All Monsters
More to come!

# Other Theophilus Monroe Series

**Nanoverse**

**The Elven Prophecy**

**Chronicles of Zoey Grimm**

**The Daywalker Chronicles**

**Go Ask Your Mother**
**The Hedge Witch Diaries**

# AS T.R. MAGNUS

**Kataklysm**
*Blightmage*
*Ember*
*Radiant*
*Dreadlord*
*Deluge*

ND - #0302 - 090924 - C0 - 229/152/22 - PB - 9781804675830 - Matt Lamination